THE
OCEAN
DARK

THE
OCEAN
DARK

A NOVEL

JACK ROGAN

BALLANTINE BOOKS • NEW YORK

The Ocean Dark is a work of fiction. Names, characters, places, and incidents either are the product of the author's imagination or are used fictitiously. Any resemblance to actual persons, living or dead, events, or locales is entirely coincidental.

A Ballantine Books Mass Market Original

Published in the United States by Ballantine Books, an imprint of The Random House Publishing Group, a division of Random House, Inc., New York.

BALLANTINE and colophon are registered trademarks of Random House, Inc.

978-0-553-38518-2

Cover art: Carlos Beltran
Cover design: Jamie S. Warren

Printed in the United States of America

www.ballantinebooks.com

9 8 7 6 5 4 3 2 1

For my wife Nicole.
Every day.

ACKNOWLEDGMENTS

Thanks to editor extraordinaire Anne Groell for her patience, insight, and enthusiasm. Thanks are also due, of course, to David Pomerico and the entire team. For advice, assistance, and their expertise, enormous thanks to FBI Special Agent Dana Ridenour, Tufts University professors Susan Ernst and Anne Gardulski, and the helpful people at the Port of Miami.

-prologue--

The singing began at nightfall, and the dying soon after.

Braulio stood just inside the wheelhouse of the *Mariposa,* smoking a cigarette and listening to the creak of the fishing boat and the clang of the metal pulley against the winch out on deck. It sounded like a buoy dinging nearby, but there wasn't a buoy within half a day's sail of this place. They were off the map. Off the edge of the world.

The tip of his cigarette glowed orange in the gathering dusk. The breeze that swept through the wheelhouse carried the smoke away, but still the air felt stifling. Braulio had lived his whole life on the islands of Costa Rica or out on the open sea. At fifty-four, the fisherman was the oldest man on the boat, but even he had never been in these waters before. No one came out here, and there was no reason to do so unless you were lost, or you needed to conduct business in secret.

Illegal business.

Life had been easier for Braulio when it had just been about catching fish.

"Anything?" he asked.

Estevan sat in a chair bolted to the floor of the wheelhouse, leaning back with his eyes closed. In front of him, the radio whispered lonely static, soft and wordless. He opened his eyes into slits and looked at Braulio. "Do *you* hear anything?"

Braulio gave a shake of his head and turned away, walking out onto the deck. The ship swayed underfoot but his gait was steady. Sailor's legs. On land, he felt unsteady. Out here he knew who and what he was, or he had, until his age had caught up with him and work had grown scarcer, and need had turned him into a criminal.

Did he hear anything? Only the sounds of the old fishing

boat and the low muttering of the crew. Alberto and Javier played cards down in the cabin. Hector stood aft, fishing rod in his hands, letting his line drag with the current that swept toward the dark hump of the island in the distance. Cruz, the first mate, sat in the bow drinking expensive whiskey, though he was long past appreciating its quality. The captain, Ruiz, seemed happy to let Cruz raid his private stock, but the bastard never shared the good stuff with the rest of the crew.

Braulio took another drag on his cigarette, forcing his trembling fingers to be still. He cursed silently, exhaling a lungful of smoke. His hands had begun to shake several months ago—infrequently at first, but then more and more. He had told himself that his age was to blame, that he had damaged the muscles in his hands somehow while working the lines. But the tremors had grown worse. He ought to have seen a doctor, but by then he had decided that he did not want to know. Still, hiding the tremors from the crew had become more difficult. Just this morning Javier had noticed, and Braulio had spun him a lie about arthritis medicine.

Smoking helped, though. Focusing on the cigarette, holding it to his lips, somehow made the muscles in his hands relax. The whole process—the familiar comfort of a cigarette, the smell and the taste—had always eased his tension and anxiety. It might be filling his lungs with poison and probably would kill him in time, but right now Braulio needed to smoke, and not just to still the shaking of his hands.

Estevan sat in front of the radio. If there had been any contact at all, he would have heard and responded. He would have told Cruz immediately, and the first mate would have shared it with the rest of the crew. But there had been no contact—not from the buyers with whom they were set to rendezvous, or from Captain Ruiz.

That last one worried Braulio the most.

He leaned against the railing, facing away from the island. He didn't like looking at it, and did not want to think about why they had lost communication with the captain and three crew members who had gone ashore. The last glimmer of daylight burned on the western horizon and to the east the world had gone dark, but still no word from the island. That hadn't been the plan. The men who'd gone ashore should have been back by now.

The quiet troubled him. Troubled them all, though none of them wanted to show it. They were all holding their breath, wondering what the hell had happened. Not only had they lost contact with the captain, but the clients should have been in range by now for radio communication. Yet nothing.

Braulio watched the upper rim of the sun sinking into the water to the west, and shivered.

Fucking Ruiz had decided to get clever, and if there was one thing Braulio had learned over the course of his life, it was that trying to be clever nearly always led to disaster. The *Mariposa* had left port in Costa Rica with the guns on board, as planned. The job had been simple—rendezvous with the client, deliver the guns, pick up the cash, then catch a ton of fish before setting course for home. But Captain Ruiz just had to complicate things.

The island isn't on any of the charts, Ruiz had said that night in the bar, whispering low, his eyes glittering with whiskey and greed. He spread an old, yellowed map on the table and weighted the edges down with sweaty bottles of beer. *But it's here. This thing is old, maybe a hundred years. Still, what are those marks?*

To his credit, it had been a good question. Marks had been made on the map indicating . . . well, something. Ruiz had thought it an old pirate map, which Braulio considered ridiculous, though he did not dare say so out loud. And, after all, it could have been a pirate's map. Who was to say?

Ruiz had shifted the rendezvous to the open water not far from the island and the *Mariposa* had arrived a day early. The captain had wanted time to explore the island, to figure out what the marks on the map represented. The rest of the crew had been all for it. They were young enough to believe in buried treasure.

Braulio had not cared much either way, as long as he got paid. But then, a little more than six hours ago, after realizing that the coordinates on the map were slightly off, they had finally come in sight of the island. At his first glimpse of the place, Braulio had felt his skin begin to crawl.

The island was a cemetery. Not of human graves, but of sunken, derelict ships.

"What is this? What does it mean?" Hector had asked.

The captain, staring out at the wrecks arrayed along the coast, had not responded.

It had been Cruz, the first mate, who had laughed. "Are you a superstitious fool now? Haven't you heard the stories of the Sargasso Sea? The currents must cross here. Ships drift in and strike the rocks."

Some of the men nodded, satisfied with that story. Hector had glanced at Braulio as though looking for reassurance, but the old man had ignored him, focusing on the captain. Cruz always had an answer for everything and it made the whole crew want to throw him overboard at least once a day, but the explanation seemed sensible, if hard to believe.

That was when Ruiz had tried getting clever.

"Load the gun crates into the lifeboats."

Braulio had stared at him. *What the fuck?* But even as the question crossed his mind, he had known the answer. Ruiz intended to make the clients sweat, try to force them to come up with more money or something else in trade before he would turn the weapons over. And from the gleam in his eye, it seemed Ruiz had been planning this for a while.

That had started Braulio's hands shaking and he'd lit a trembling cigarette. He'd gone through an entire pack since.

With a sigh, he turned toward the railing, toward the island. The last of the daylight slipped over the edge of the world, leaving only the moon and stars to see by. The island loomed in the distance, the ruined ships dark shapes in the shallow coastal water, but he saw no sign of the lifeboats returning. And even if they tried, they might not be able to see the *Mariposa*. Estevan had a light on in the wheelhouse, but otherwise the fishing boat was dark.

"Estevan!" Braulio called. "Turn on the running lights in case they come back tonight."

He heard the little man moving in the wheelhouse, and then a voice from within. "Why?"

Braulio took a deep breath, then began to cough. Maybe

the cigarettes would kill him sooner than he thought. His hands began to tremble so badly that he had difficulty putting the butt to his lips.

Why? Estevan didn't think the captain would be back tonight, and nobody argued with him. Hector didn't even look up from his fishing pole. Alberto and Javier were silent belowdecks. Up on the bow, Cruz probably hadn't heard.

Braulio took a long puff on his cigarette, the tip flaring orange in the dark. He forced his hands to be steady as he turned toward the wheelhouse. He'd go in and turn the goddamn lights on himself, and then he would have a talk with Cruz, who would be boss if the captain didn't return.

Braulio strode away from the railing, already questioning his decision to get involved. It wasn't his job, after all. He was just an old fisherman. But if he wanted to get paid . . .

Three steps and he froze, a frown creasing his forehead.

"Hey," he said. "Do you hear that?"

It sounded like singing—a lone voice across the water, distant and quiet, but rising, like something he would have heard in church. There were no words, just that voice—not quite beautiful and yet soothing, aching.

Curious, he took a step back toward the railing.

Up at the bow, Cruz screamed. The sound, high and shrill, lasted only a second before being cut off.

Something fell over in the wheelhouse—maybe Estevan slipping off his chair—and Braulio swore, hurrying along the railing, wondering what the hell had happened. Had Cruz hurt himself? Fallen overboard? Now that he listened, Braulio thought he heard splashing from the water, and something slapping the hull, wet and slippery. *Drunk son of a bitch.*

He hadn't even reached the wheelhouse when another scream came from behind him. As he turned, he caught a glimpse of Hector's fishing pole clattering to the deck, then all he could do was stare at the big man, who was trying to beat at something on his back, to tear at a limb wrapped around his throat.

The cigarette fell from Braulio's lips.

Hector twisted around, struck the railing, and went over

the side. As he fell, the moonlight illuminated his attacker. Braulio's eyes widened, but he did not scream. *"Los diablos,"* he whispered, and began to weep.

They came over the railing then, two at a time, scraping wood and metal. In the wheelhouse, glass broke and Estevan started to shout. Gunshots echoed off the deck and out across the water, and Braulio fled, running toward the only shelter he could imagine—the cabin belowdecks. But to get there, he had to go through the wheelhouse.

Something grabbed him from behind, wrapping around his leg. He let out a cry and it fell on him, tearing at him, and he knew that God would not listen to the prayers of a criminal. In a breath, he told the Lord of his sorrow and regret.

More gunshots cracked the night air. Something splashed him, cold on his skin, though Braulio also felt the heat of his own blood running down his chest and soaking his pants. The grip on him loosened and he tore free and rose, staggering.

Only to see Estevan pointing the gun at him.

"Out of the way!" Estevan shouted.

But Braulio barely heard him. He careened for the wheelhouse door. As he passed Estevan, the man fired again, but Braulio did not bother to look back at what the bullets might have hit. He threw himself across the threshold of the wheelhouse, broken glass crunching beneath his shoes. A dark shadow twitched, half-dead, on the floor near the radio, but Braulio did not even slow down.

From the top of the stairs that led down into the cabin, where the crew had their quarters, he saw Javier and Alberto appear. The sickly yellow light gave them an ugly pallor, and glinted off the guns they must have fetched when they'd heard the shots from above.

"Stop!" Braulio cried, half-sliding down the steps. "Don't go up there!"

"What the hell—" Javier began.

"Look out the window!" the old man said, pointing toward one of the round portholes in the main cabin even as he moved away from the stairs.

Javier ran to the window, pushed his face up against it. The glass cracked. Something grabbed him, pulled, and blood sprayed.

Something broke inside of Braulio then. He ran, limping, into the short corridor where all their quarters were and saw the door to the head slightly ajar. Thinking only of shelter—of tiny vents and metal doors and no windows—he practically fell into the bathroom. Twisting the lock into place, his whole body trembling now instead of just his hands, he climbed on top of the toilet, hugging his knees to his chest.

Only then did the pain begin to truly blossom in his chest. Only then did he press his trembling hands against the wound, trying to keep his life from leaking out. Only then did he realize that he had not escaped death after all.

Braulio shook and bled and wept, and listened to the gunfire and the screams until there were no more of either.

Just after one o'clock in the afternoon on a pristine June day, Tori Austin stepped out onto the deck of the *Antoinette,* dying for a shower. The wind came up off the Caribbean, salty and warm, and pulled her clothes taut across her body. She breathed deeply as she walked to the railing, invigorated by the crisp, clean air. Then the wind shifted slightly and she caught the scent of rust that always lingered on board the freighter, and her nose wrinkled in distaste.

Back on land, some people drove BMWs and some drove run-down pickup trucks. Out on the ocean, the *Antoinette* was the equivalent of a long-haul trucker, with a cab full of fast-food wrappers and empty beer cans, and a trailer full of anonymous cargo. The broad expanse of the *Antoinette*'s deck carried one hundred and eighty-eight massive metal containers, each one the size of a big rig's trailer, but the principle was the same. This had been Tori's first voyage aboard the *Antoinette*—hell, aboard anything larger than the sightseeing ships that ran tours on Biscayne Bay—but in her time working for the vessel's owner, Viscaya Shipping, she'd learned all sorts of things about the cargo business and the ships in Viscaya's fleet.

To her left, the view might as well have been of some harbor dockyard. Containers were stacked six high, some of them covered in rust and graffiti, others gleaming and new. On the ship's bow, a crane of dull gray steel towered over them. Tori went to the right, walking back to the aft railing. The accommodations block—a white tower of crew cabins, showers, and common rooms topped by the captain's bridge—was just as modular in appearance as the containers. It looked like a Fort Lauderdale beachfront apartment building had been dropped down onto the deck, right at the stern.

Some container ships had the accommodations block more toward the center, but Tori appreciated its placement on the *Antoinette*. Standing at the back railing, she could take in the breathless, vivid blue of the Caribbean without having to look at the cargo. She'd enjoyed the voyage so far, and surprised herself with how much she liked the work. But the sameness of those stacks of metal blocks had begun to get to her.

The wind kicked up again—no rust this time—and she relished it. She really did need to get inside and shower. Her skin felt coated with grease from the two hours she'd spent in the galley. Josh always prepared something simple at lunch—today it had been blackened chicken sandwiches— but every couple of days he added a special on the side. This afternoon, the twenty-four members of the crew had been treated to scallops wrapped in bacon.

Tori wondered if Viscaya Shipping, the owners of the *Antoinette,* knew how well the crew was being fed. She'd seen the ship's ledger, and either the captain was hiding the cost or he was paying for the extras out of his own pocket. It was the sort of thing Tori ought to be looking out for. Technically she'd been sent along on this trip for quality control—to evaluate efficiency and expenditures, to look over the manifests, and to help out in any way she could.

The Rio brothers—Gabe, the captain, and Miguel, the first mate—weren't happy about it, but since nobody else acted like she had the plague, she presumed they had kept it from the crew. Which was fine with Tori. She hadn't asked for the assignment. All she'd wanted was to crew one of the Viscaya container ships, just once. She would have swabbed the deck or polished the railings if they'd asked.

As a girl, she had loved to read classic stories of adventure— Jack London and Jules Verne foremost among them—the sort of books that caused her teachers to mutter in disapproval and attempt to interest her in the Brontë sisters, or even Nancy Drew. The teachers at St. Catherine's had rigid opinions about which books were and were not proper for girls. But reading offered her an escape from the poisoned air of her home, and dreams of someday having her own adventures.

By her sophomore year of high school, she had ceased to believe in escapes or in dreams, and had stopped reading almost entirely. Yet she'd never forgotten those stories. They'd had a deep impact upon her, and filled her mind with powerful presumptions—not the least of which was that rough men could be honorable creatures. Her father's cruelty, far from disabusing her of that notion, had only reinforced it. If men like him existed—brutal bastards who took pleasure from the pain of others—then the world must also contain his opposite: a rugged hero who would be better with his hands than his words, kind to friends and lovers, but fearsome and merciless to those who crossed him.

Rough men didn't have to be bad men. Books had taught her that. But all too often, life had given her a different lesson.

For Tori, this voyage marked the completion of one journey, as well as the beginning of a new one. She'd sailed thousands of miles and seen the beauty and the industry of five Central and South American ports. She had found her adventure. Now she could pause, take a breath, and make a new beginning at last. Until then, she would enjoy the time she had left on the open ocean.

It wasn't complicated work. A container ship, like any cargo freighter, was loaded at one end of the journey and unloaded at the other, and during the voyage the work was about keeping the vessel clean, staying on course, and making sure the crew got fed. People paid to have their lives packed up in one of those big metal sheds and shipped overseas, and corporations paid to load their products the same way, but they didn't pay to keep the big boxes shiny. As long as the inside stayed dry and nobody damaged Mr. Hodgson's Georgian chairs—or his new Mercedes, or the 175,000 superhero action figures being shipped to coincide with the release of a late summer blockbuster—nobody cared.

So Tori didn't have to shine railings or wash the deck, but she had vowed to help out in any way she could. On the very first day at sea, she'd volunteered to assist in the galley. Granted, that had been partly due to Josh—a sexy mess of a man with several days' stubble, sky blue eyes, and raggedly cut light brown hair. Since then she'd been Josh's right hand for every meal, and had been surprised to find that she enjoyed the work.

As for the quality control assignment, she paid attention to the *Antoinette*'s heading and looked out for anything that seemed an obvious waste of Viscaya Shipping's money. But when it came to the copious drinking, the occasional fistfight, and the long hours some of the crew spent lazing around, she turned a blind eye. As long as everyone did their jobs—a potential issue with five new hires this go-round—that sort of thing wasn't doing any harm.

Still, the Rio brothers had been edgy around her throughout the trip. When she'd been working in the Viscaya offices and they would come to pick up their checks or the manifests for an upcoming voyage, she had always gotten on well with them. Both brothers had flirted with her, brought her coffee. But when Viscaya assigned her to the *Antoinette,* even though it was only for one trip, that had changed. They didn't trust her anymore, and though she couldn't really blame them, she hated it.

It wasn't as though they had anything to hide. Tori knew more about Viscaya's illegal operations than the Rio brothers ever would. And though half the crew of the *Antoinette* pretended blissful ignorance when it came to unscheduled ocean rendezvous with fishing boats or small Central American cargo ships, even the thickest among them had to know something shady was going on. The company chose its employees carefully. Most of the men who crewed the ship had their own secrets—little stints in jail, court-ordered alimony they wanted to avoid by being paid under the table—and they returned Viscaya's loyalty with their own silence.

The other half of the crew took a more active role when it came to Viscaya's side business. Viscaya Shipping frequently carried cargo into and out of the United States that would have landed dozens of people in prison. Drugs, guns, stolen goods, sometimes even banned animals. But they drew the line at chemicals, powders, and radioactive materials, and they damn sure weren't going to bring in people. Frank Esper and Bobby Jewell ran illegal enterprises alongside their legitimate business, but they were Americans. Anything that had even a hint of terrorist connections, they stayed far, far away from.

The guys from Viscaya had their own code, and Tori respected that.

For herself, she had long since surrendered any thoughts of an ordinary life. Tori had spent her life in the orbit of dangerous men, trapped by their gravity. The worst of them had been Ted—an uptown guy with a taste for cocaine and hookers who had played at being an old school thug for so long that he'd become one. Of course she'd married him. It had taken courage and the hand of fate to free her, and now Ted lingered only in her nightmares.

Tori had escaped with her life, and for a long time she had waited for fate to catch up with her. New York had given way to Miami, where she'd promised herself a new start. In the three years since she had said good-bye to Ted in Penn Station, she felt sure she had learned to steer clear of truly bad men.

The people who ran Viscaya Shipping weren't good guys by any stretch of the imagination, but they had rules. They might smuggle drugs, and even sample the product from time to time, but Frank and the others weren't addicts. They might bring guns into America under cover of the night, but they made sure they knew who their customers were.

The management at Viscaya liked Tori, and they trusted her. In the time since they had first taken her into their confidence, she had adopted their approach. Business was business. As an office manager, she'd handled their legitimate and illegitimate endeavors with equal professionalism.

So the chill she'd been getting off the Rio brothers throughout this voyage—all the way from Miami to Brazil, and now more than halfway back again—both insulted and irritated her. And disappointed her on a personal level, because she genuinely liked them.

When she turned and started for the stairs that crisscrossed the outside of the accommodations block and saw Gabe Rio leaning on the railing one level above her, she decided that the time for a confrontation had come. He was staring out at the Caribbean with a cigarette in his hand, and glanced at her as she approached, taking a drag off his cigarette. He had an air of authority about him, of sheer confidence, that had nothing to do with him being captain of the ship.

Tori mustered a confidence she didn't feel as she started up the stairs, the breeze whipping at her hair, tugging a dark strand loose from the ponytail she always wore in the galley.

"Hello, Captain," she said when she reached the first level. "They won't even let you smoke on your own bridge now, huh?"

Gabe Rio blinked, as though she'd woken him from a trance, and his sad, contemplative expression took on a sardonic edge.

"Wouldn't want you to report me, Tori."

She ought to have seen it coming, yet still she flinched.

"Come on, Gabe. Has it really been that terrible having me along? I don't hear you complaining at mealtime."

He gazed at her, his eyes flat, defensive shields up. With a flick of his finger he knocked the ash off the end of his cigarette and the wind took it, just as it did the smoke he exhaled.

"We've had this conversation. I just don't like being spied on," he said, in the light accent that came from his Mexican parents.

Tori sighed. "Gabe—"

"Out here it's 'Captain.' "

"Fine. Captain. It can't be spying if you know I'm here. Look it up in the dictionary. I'm not trying to get anyone into trouble. I begged Frank to let me come along on this trip because I was sick of sitting in an office. I practically blackmailed him into it. It's what I've wanted since the day he first asked me to work at Viscaya—to be on a ship, just once."

Gabe puffed on his cigarette, then he turned to look at her, studying her as though seeing her for the first time. He had deep brown eyes, a long nose, and a perpetually sad face, but the gray in his neatly groomed goatee added a certain charm, and at least the illusion of wisdom. For a woman who'd grown up with a little girl's romantic fantasies, the brooding and mysterious Gabe Rio cut an intriguing figure. The circumstances of his employment at Viscaya only added to that allure.

According to the whispers—which Frank Esper had more or less confirmed when Tori had asked him—Gabe had quit Viscaya when he'd first learned of their illegal operations. Loyalty had brought him back, but not loyalty to the company. Miguel Rio had a temper and a history of letting it, and his fists, get him in trouble. He had spent seven months in prison for aggravated assault. If Viscaya fired him, he would have a hell of a time finding a company that would bring him on, especially as an officer. He'd have been lucky to get work as a deckhand. But Frank had been left with little choice when Miguel had gotten into a bloody fistfight with Gabe's predecessor. Gabe had gone to Frank and asked him to give Miguel another chance, and Frank had agreed on the condition that Gabe come back to Viscaya and take over as captain of the *Antoinette*. If Gabe would hold the leash, Miguel could keep his job.

Which was how Gabe Rio became a smuggler.

"I don't get it," the captain said, studying Tori's eyes. "Why not just take a cruise? Have people wait on you? Who the hell wants this job?"

A ripple of anger went through her. "*You* do. You love it. Maybe you don't love Viscaya, but you love the job. And maybe you're so used to seeing me behind a desk that you never really paid much attention, but do I seem like the kind of woman who wants to go lay in the sun with the shiny, happy people on a cruise ship?"

The captain chuckled softly, a grin appearing. "Now that you mention it, no. But that doesn't mean I wouldn't want to see you in one of those teeny bikinis the American girls wear out here in the islands, where their parents won't see."

Tori smiled. They were three-quarters of the way through a round-trip intercontinental voyage, and the ice had finally broken.

"Maya would cut your eyes out if you looked at me too long," Tori said.

Gabe's smile vanished, defensive shields clanging into place again. "Once, maybe. Not anymore."

The awkward moment stretched. Tori had no idea what to say. Maya Rio seemed perpetually pissed with her husband, but that didn't mean she wanted him sleeping around. Whatever was going on with them, it was none of Tori's business. Yet she felt a wave of understanding and relief wash over her. If Gabe's marriage had fallen apart, his cold, distant behavior took on new dimensions.

"Sorry. I didn't mean—"

"Forget it," Gabe said, waving at the air with his cigarette.

The tension between them grew. Tori still felt as though she had a layer of grease on her clothes and skin, and the Caribbean sun would fry her if she stayed out here too long. She squinted and peered out across the ocean, comforted by the absence of any land at all. The ship cut the water with a constant shushing that normally combined with the thrum of the engines to set her at ease. But at the moment, a lullaby wouldn't have soothed her.

"It's about trust," Gabe said.

Tori turned to him. "I've never given you any reason not to trust me. I told you the first day, I'm here to learn, maybe make some suggestions about the business when I get back, not to talk about who drinks too much or who's fucking whom."

Standing up straight, he flicked his cigarette out across the undulating water.

"Not everything's about you, Tori."

"Captain, listen—"

"I worked for Viscaya for five years before I quit, and seven years since. Farzan might be the shipping manager now, but when I started at the company there was no such job title. I got my orders from Frank Esper directly—no bullshit, no middlemen, and for sure no 'quality control manager.' Okay, I had my issues with them, which is why I left, but in the time since I've been back I figured I'd earned their trust. Makes this hard to swallow, that's all."

Tori glanced around to be sure they were alone. Then she

reached out and put a hand on Gabe's arm. He gave her a surprised look, squinting against the sun.

"Captain," she said, voice low, "they know I'm loyal. And maybe I dropped out after a year of college, but they also know I'm smart. They trust me. That's a hard choice for people in this kind of business to make, but they trust me. Now they're just trying to figure out how they can use me down the line. They want me to learn how it's all done."

He stared at her, unmoved.

"And they trust you, Gabe. Don't be a dumbass. You know they do."

He threw up his hands. "How do I know? I've got a fucking babysitter now."

When Tori looked at the captain this time, she kept her gaze as grim and unflinching as his own. "If they didn't trust you, you'd be dead by now."

He flinched, staring at her, but she saw in his eyes that he knew the truth. Gabe let out a breath, a little grunt of air.

"Damn, girl, when did you get so hard?"

"In another life, before I came to Miami. But I'm not a hard woman. I've just got a little perspective, that's all. If you spend enough time lying to yourself, then one day all you ever want from anyone is the truth, and it doesn't matter anymore how ugly it is."

-2--

The *Mariposa* rocked gently on the open sea, adrift and silent. Braulio flitted at the edge of consciousness, cradled and swayed by the boat as though in his mother's arms. His eyes fluttered open and for the first few seconds he felt pleasantly numb. Then the pain blossomed anew—a wave of gut-deep agony that nearly drove him down into the blackness again.

He cried out—half in pain, and half to force himself to stay conscious. With the pain, and that cry, memory returned in full. Limbs slow and leaden, he turned slightly. Fresh pains stabbed at his abdomen and leg, seared his face and chest, and blood began to seep from wounds he feared had already killed him.

Angelique.

He squeezed his eyes closed and wept once more, hating the weakness of his tears. Images of his granddaughter's face filled his mind. Six-year-old Angelique had been a gift, her birth bringing his son, Marvin, back into his life. The boy had been the result of a single night's fumbling with a waitress past her prime—a woman who had taken an interest in Braulio when he had been young and handsome, or at least young. He'd had very little contact with Marvin over the years, but that had changed with Angelique's birth. Abandoned by the baby's mother, and his own having passed on years before, Marvin had needed help. Braulio had little enough money, but he did what he could. His time, though, he lavished upon the girl.

Angelique was worth living for. Worth fighting for.

Sunlight shone through the small vent in the outer wall of the head. How long had he been out? Was this morning or afternoon? A wave of nausea rippled through him as he wondered how many hours remained before night would come again. Would the devils return? Was it even safe to assume they came only at night?

He steadied his breathing, stopped his tears, gritted his teeth against the pain, and listened. The creak of the ship. The clank of cables and pulley against the winch. Nothing else. Not so much as a gull's caw to indicate he might have drifted toward land.

He thought of the captain, of the guns they'd brought to the island.

Of the radio.

Did he hear the soft crackle of static, even down here? He thought he did.

Mustering what little strength remained to him, he forced

himself to stand. Waves of pain tore through him and he grunted, too weak even to cry out, and he pressed his hands more tightly to the seeping wound in his gut. Fresh beads of sweat popped out on his forehead and back and began to trickle down his skin. Blackness swam around the edges of his vision and he fell against the door, began to slide to the floor, unconsciousness claiming him yet again.

But Braulio fought it. Breathing through his teeth, lips peeled back, he forced his eyes to open. He adjusted one hand to clamp tightly on his wound and with the other he scrabbled at the lock and the handle, fingers slick with his own blood.

The radio.

The door had buckled in the middle, dented by the pounding of the devils. It stuck in its frame, but Braulio kept the image of his granddaughter firmly in his mind—that smile with the missing tooth in front. He pulled, heard a pop, and as the door opened something tore deep inside him and a fresh gush of blood squirted through the fingers he held clamped over his abdomen.

He wouldn't allow himself to think of it. If the devils were still on the boat, would they smell it? Surely they would hear him. It didn't matter. If he couldn't radio for help, he would die.

But his instincts had been correct. As he slid himself along the wall and into the main cabin, nothing moved. The sun shone through the windows and he caught glimpses of blue sky. Sorrow engulfed him as he thought about Angelique. He needed to see her, to touch her face, to smell her hair. Braulio knew he had sinned in his life, and knew there would be hell to pay someday. Then Angelique had come into his life and, for an instant, he had changed his mind. How bad could his crimes have been if heaven could bring such a light into his life?

But no; now his payment had come.

He staggered up the steps into the wheelhouse. His vision blurred and he held tightly to the handrail. If he fell unconscious here and did not wake before nightfall . . . He had to use the radio and then get back to the head, lock himself in again.

Then it would be up to God who found him first—men, or devils.

In the wheelhouse he paused, listening. Where was the hiss of static? The radio had gone silent. Steadying himself, blinking to focus, he stared at the radio, thinking it had died.

Then a voice, clear and crisp, came from the radio.

"Mickey, this is Donald. Come in, Mickey."

-3--

Tori watched as Gabe's face clouded over, and it seemed like he went somewhere inside himself for a second. And whatever he found there, it wasn't pleasant.

"Captain?"

He forced a smile. "You got a lot of thoughts rolling around in that head."

Tori shrugged. "What you see is what you get. I'm out on the edge of the world, surviving, just like you. I tried 'normal.' Tried the housewife thing. It almost killed me."

For almost a minute they stood together at the railing, enjoying the breeze and the peaceful ocean. This conversation had been a long time coming and Tori had imagined it becoming much uglier, so she felt a measure of relief.

"Thank you," she said.

"For what?"

"For talking it out with me. For trusting me."

Gabe grunted again, then stood and started patting the pockets of his loose cotton pants and the patterned, cream-colored shirt he wore untucked. He located his cigarettes and a lighter, and fired up a fresh one.

After he'd taken the first real drag and made sure the butt had ignited, he glanced at her.

"You know my little brother's still going to be a prick, right? He hates anyone second-guessing him. He's pissed at the boss, and you're getting the spill-off from that."

Tori turned up her hands. "I can't control what Miguel thinks. He'll get over it, or he won't."

Gabe nodded, took a drag off his cigarette. As he exhaled, he seemed about to say something more, but they were interrupted by a shout and running feet.

They looked up to see red-haired Tom Dwyer rushing up to the railing on the stairwell landing above them. The Irish kid, maybe twenty-one or two, was one of the five new members of the crew, but he'd adapted fast, worked his way into Miguel's good graces, and landed himself the gig as third mate, working the bridge with the Rio brothers.

"Captain!" the kid said, practically hanging over the railing above them.

"What's up, Mr. Dwyer?"

"Mr. Rio needs you on the bridge. He said to tell you 'Ortega's house is coming down.'"

"Fuck!" the captain snarled, running to the stairs.

He didn't even toss his cigarette, just let it fall from his hand to the deck, where the wind spun it around and danced it overboard.

Tori looked up at Dwyer. "What the hell is that about?"

The redhead studied her a second, then shook his head. "Sorry. You'll have to ask them."

As Gabe passed him, Dwyer fell into the captain's wake, the two of them clanging up the metal stairs toward the bridge at the top, leaving Tori to wonder. She was curious, and even a bit alarmed, but not frightened. Whatever it was, the Rio brothers would take care of it. They were capable men. Rough men. Some might even say bad men, but Tori would have argued the difference.

You always knew where you stood with men like the Rios. If things got too rough, you could always walk away. With truly bad men, there was never any walking away. Not without pain. Not without blood. Bad men didn't let go as long as you were alive.

That was Tori's secret, and her strength.

As far as anyone from her old life knew, she'd been dead for years.

THREE YEARS AGO . . .

She didn't go by Tori, then. That wasn't her name. But it didn't really matter what her mother named her, because her husband mostly just called her *bitch*. As in, "What are you lookin' at, bitch?" "Get me a beer, bitch." And "What the fuck you do around here all day, bitch?"

There were other pet names. Sweet nothings. Sometimes Ted called her *whore* just to change it up. Sometimes worse. It rarely bothered her, him not using her name. Even when she'd been a little girl and her father had actually called her by the name she'd been given at birth, it had always come out sounding like *bitch*. The tone was key. The disdain. The dismissal.

On a rainy Sunday morning the week before Halloween, she sat in the backseat of a taxi as it slid through the streets of Manhattan. Just why there were so few cars on the street, she couldn't have said. People didn't go to church anymore, did they? Most offices were closed, and the number of trucks rolling through the labyrinth of the city fell almost to nothing. A lot of people were out walking. No, strolling.

The word *peaceful* came to mind, and she almost laughed. What did it even mean?

Ted shifted on the seat next to her and she glanced at him, then quickly away, dropping her eyes in deference. She didn't need more than a glimpse to see that he could change his mind at any moment. The usual mix of poisons swirled behind his eyes. Anger, suspicion, paranoia . . . and cocaine. Most people had pancakes or bacon and eggs on Sunday morning. Ted enjoyed the breakfast of champions—fried Spam sandwiches, his childhood favorite, and half a dozen lines of high-grade blow—after which he'd demand she go down on him. When she was done, he'd hit her, slap her, sometimes kick her—either in fury because he hadn't been able to get off, or in disgust at what a slut she was if he had.

And so she drank. Once she tried to get medication for depression—she'd seen one of those ads on TV—but it had gone badly when Ted found out. Said all she needed was a better attitude, maybe to take a little more pride in their Upper East Side apartment, in her appearance, in her goddamn husband.

She hadn't had a drink this morning. Strangely enough, her hands were not shaking. In the back of the taxi, she glanced down at them and found herself astonished to see how still they were. Her hands felt detached, as if they belonged to someone else.

"Here you go, folks. Penn Station," the cabbie said.

He pulled up at the curb and flicked off the meter. When he announced the total, Ted shot her a look: *See what you're costing me, bitch?* She didn't speak, didn't challenge, only waited for him to pay and get out of the cab, and then she followed. On the sidewalk, she stood one step behind him while the driver took her suitcase from the trunk and set it by Ted's feet.

"Thank you, sir," the bearded, dark-skinned man said in an accent she didn't recognize.

Ted ignored him and picked up the suitcase. As the taxi driver climbed back behind the wheel and started to pull away, Ted looked at her.

"Well?"

He waited. Terror lanced through her. She had known the moment would be coming, and here it was. He would change his mind now, refuse to let her go. With the wave of a hand he would summon another cab and force her into the back with nothing more than the silent promise of what would happen if she defied him. Back to the apartment with the gleaming wood floors and the twelve-foot ceilings and the sixty-thousand-dollar kitchen where she cooked elaborate meals only to escape.

"What the fuck are you waiting for?"

"Nothing." She shook her head. "I just . . . did you want to get a coffee or something?"

Her soft smile felt carved into her face. At some point she'd forgotten to breathe, remembering only when she'd had to speak. Now her heart beat so hard it hurt her chest.

Ted scowled, the message obvious. Why would he want to have coffee with her? Bitch was leaving him to fend for himself for three days, get his own meals, endure his own company, muster his own orgasms.

"Don't want to miss your train," he said, his tone just a half-note away from schoolyard mocking. Then he sniffed and wiped at his nostril, as though imaginary crumbs of coke hung there, irritating him.

She started walking and he fell into step behind her, close enough that she could feel his shadow on her like it was her leash. They descended into Penn Station, underneath Madison Square Garden, and passed by the flower vendors and the restaurants and shops that reminded her of some dingy airport.

People jammed the waiting area. It was Sunday morning, and everyone who'd come up for the weekend was heading back to DC or Philly or wherever. Mothers with strollers, twentysomethings kissing their boyfriends good-bye, business suits. She saw an actor she recognized from a cable TV show. He played a cop, but not the star. Nobody else seemed to recognize him, or they were too polite to bother him. New Yorkers tended to mind their own business. How else to explain why no one had ever asked her about the bruises she so often hid under makeup or sunglasses?

Ted pulled her along in his wake to the departures board. Her train to Philadelphia left in less than thirty minutes. They waited in silence, her skin prickling with his presence, her heart in her throat, her voice silent. She wished she could just vanish, but the best she could manage was to say nothing, to keep still, afraid that any word or motion might be enough to trigger him.

The train was late. The suitcase sat by her feet. At the scheduled departure time, Ted gave a low huff.

"Fuck." He turned to look at her. "Your mother better really be dying this time. It's the last fucking time you go down there."

The words cut deep. She let him see how much they hurt because she had learned that was what he wanted. If she'd smiled, tried to brush it off, soothe him, he would know something was off.

"Honey, she's my mother. And it's only the second time."

Ted reached out gently, like other husbands might caress their wives. Instead he pinched her forearm fiercely between thumb and forefinger, digging in. With a sharp gasp, she fought tears, but she said nothing. If she drew attention, she'd pay for it.

"It's the last time," he said.

"Okay. I know. The last time."

And it was. The first time had been a test, to see if he'd let her go, and to see if she'd have the courage.

They called her train. Fighting the elation that fluttered in her chest, she picked up her suitcase.

"Hey," he said, that tone in his voice. Sweetness. The *c'mon baby* voice. "Say good-bye."

This time, the smile felt real. It made her stomach turn, but she kissed him. Ted stood in close, his chest against hers, taking his time with the kiss.

"Who loves you?" he asked.

"You do."

"And who loves me?"

"I do."

If there'd been fewer people around, if others weren't already pushing past them, he'd probably have grabbed her ass in one hand and ground himself against her to make sure she felt him. Instead he stepped back, reached out and cupped the side of her face, stroked her cheek roughly with a thumb.

"Three days. Don't make me come after you." He smiled like it was a joke.

She smiled, too.

Then she got in line, wanting to scream at the shuffling passengers in front of her to hurry, to get out of her way. Forcing herself to breathe in tiny sips, her heartbeat thrumming through her body, she managed to keep from shoving anyone.

A heavyset Hispanic woman checked her ticket, let her pass. A sign on the wall said TICKETED PASSENGERS ONLY BEYOND THIS POINT. A warm flush ran up the back of her neck, maybe the heat of Ted's eyes upon her, maybe just exultation. She probably should have turned to wave, just to make sure he didn't suspect. If he did, he might buy a ticket, try to come after her before the train pulled away. That would ruin everything. But she couldn't turn.

He'd still be watching, though. She knew that much. Right now he'd be watching her go, the anger and resentment already building up inside of him. When she got back, he'd make her regret having gone, just like he had the first time. When she got back . . .

Halfway down the stairs into the underground platform area, she finally let the smile bloom. It terrified her, that smile. Too soon, she knew. Her whole body trembled and where she'd been warm before, she now felt a terrible chill. God, she needed a drink. Screwdriver—vodka and orange juice—an old-fashioned drink, totally uncool, but God, they tasted good. And if you got the mix right, they were deadly.

She needed to drink.

But she wouldn't. Not until she reached her destination. Maybe, if she had the strength—and she was beginning to think she might—not even then.

"Don't get ahead of yourself," she whispered. "Don't be stupid, bitch."

She winced, sickened by the word, by the knowledge that he'd trained her so well, taught her who she was and what she was good for. Hating Ted and herself and unsure which of them she hated more.

The train idled, engines rumbling, wanting to go, a race-horse ready for the starter's pistol. She turned right, stepped on board, and moved herself in among the other passengers, looking for a seat. Passing one by. A perfectly good seat, plenty of space. And then another.

She kept her eyes front, knowing he couldn't see her but terrified that he could, that somehow he'd realized and come down after her and even now walked along the outside of the train peering in windows, watching her. Her stomach roiled and bile rose up in the back of her throat. Her eyes burned and she bit her lip to keep from crying. A part of her mind—the part that kept silent while he beat her, the part who'd gotten halfway to believing she deserved it—screamed at her to stop, to get off, to run upstairs and confess and apologize and take her punishment and never do it again, because what he would do when he found her would be so much worse.

It got so bad she had to stop and take a breath.

"Are you all right?" a woman asked—dark hair, kind eyes, well-dressed. A stranger, really wanting to know.

She could only nod and move on.

Into the next car, picking up momentum now. The train hissed and she knew she had to hurry. Suitcase in her hand knocking into people, muttering apologies, not waiting to see if they were accepted. Bells dinged inside the train and it would be soon.

Into the next car, far, far out of sight of the stairs.

Turn right again, out the door, onto the platform, into the shadows.

Heart so loud, pulsing, she could feel it in her face and hands and she closed her eyes, a tear sliding down her cheek, still clutching the heavy suitcase. A conductor looked at her oddly from the window.

"If you're coming, honey, you better get on. Doors are closing," he called, over the growl of the train.

She took a deep breath. And shook her head.

The conductor shrugged and turned his attention back to the passengers on board. Electronic voices crackled inside the train, then the doors closed, and there could be no turning back now. The voice deep inside screamed that she had done it now, that Ted would never let her forget it.

She licked her lips, throat parched, wishing for orange juice and vodka, and watched the train judder, hitch, then pull out of the station. Would Ted still be upstairs? Would he be trying to peer down the steps, get a glimpse of her departure, or would he already be back on the street, headed downtown, into the swirl of drugs and hookers and brutality that was his life's work?

The train vanished into the tunnel car by car until only the rear lights were visible.

She would wait, fifteen minutes at least. Maybe thirty, just to be sure Ted would be gone. What if he went for coffee without her, now that he thought she had left? Better make it an hour.

Resigned to waiting, she set down her suitcase. Her hands still shook, but she took a breath and her heartbeat began, at last, to slow.

The force of the explosion blew her off her feet.

-5--

Captain Rio double-timed it up the metal steps to the wheelhouse. The bridge, people called it. If you were in the Navy or watched too much *Star Trek,* that was fine. But Gabe and Miguel had been raised by a fisherman, so it would always be the wheelhouse to them.

Metal clanged underfoot as he reached the landing, whipped the door open, and stepped in. The windows looked out on what seemed like acres of brown and gray steel containers. Beyond them lay the wide ocean, bright aqua all the way to the horizon, where it met the powder blue of the sky. The sun shone down on the Caribbean. Most people, seeing that view, would have thought it looked like paradise, but Gabe had seen men die at sea. He'd known people who had drowned because they were too far away from the help they'd needed to survive. He'd been through storms that seemed like the end of the world. He loved the sea, but had no romantic illusions about it. The open ocean was no different from desert badlands—anything could happen out here.

The second mate, Suarez, had the wheel. That was all right. The old Cuban knew more about ships than Gabe would ever learn. Miguel, the *Antoinette*'s chief mate, was shouting into the radio handset, and the fire and frustration in his eyes set Gabe off immediately.

Ortega's house is coming down. That had been the message he sent with Dwyer. Nobody else would know what the hell it meant, just part of the secret language of brothers, the lexicon of shared childhood in a small town on the Gulf Coast of Mexico, when they'd walked up the street in the aftermath of a hurricane and watched as a neighbor's house, still mostly standing, collapsed under the weight of its own ruin. Ortega and his pretty daughter, Miranda, had died in there. Maybe had been dying while the Rio brothers watched their home slide down on top of them.

It meant disaster. Some people would have said Code Red, but this was more than that. *Ortega's house is coming down* meant Code Fucked.

"Miguel!" Gabe snapped, striding across the wheelhouse.

His brother spun around, his eyes alight with fire and frustration.

"Shut up!" Miguel shouted into the radio. "Just be quiet and listen to me!"

"—God has turned from me! They are all damned now, but you can save me! Now, before it gets dark again—"

"Fuck," Miguel growled, then thumbed the toggle on the radio again. "Slow down, idiot. What happened? Are the guns safe?"

The second the word was out of his mouth, Miguel gritted his teeth, cursing himself, knowing what he'd done.

Gabe strode across the wheelhouse and snatched the radio from his brother's hand. The man on the other end—someone

on board the ship they were supposed to rendezvous with—
had started screaming about God again. Terror or madness
had given him religion; either one was bad news.

"Mickey, this is Donald," Captain Rio said. "Go to radio
silence, right now. Use your tracer signal. Radio silence,
goddammit!"

He took his thumb off the toggle and for a second he
thought his words had been heeded. But then he heard the
breathing, quick sharp breaths, almost whimpering. Through
the radio, they heard the man on the other end begin to whisper the Hail Mary in Spanish.

With a click, the signal died, followed by static.

"Jesus," Miguel said. "What the hell was that?"

Gabe stared out at the ocean.

"Radio silence."

-6--

"Another triumph for you, sir," Tori said, in a fake English
accent.

Josh stood in front of the stove in the galley kitchen, stir-
ring a huge pot with a ladle. "Damn well better be. It took me
since lunch to make that dinner."

"I know. A labor of love, you said. Which is why I'm definitely not going to tell you how many of them are already
asking what's for breakfast tomorrow."

"What's for—?" He turned to look at her, then rolled his
eyes. "My art is lost on these savages."

"Okay, diva," Tori said.

Josh laughed, though she knew he was only half-joking
about his "art." This morning he'd woken up before five
o'clock, taken a shower, and hit the galley. And other than a
few hours after breakfast, he had been there ever since. Lunch
had been quick and simple, though as tasty as ever, but today's

dinner had been something he called Louisiana Chicken and Dumplings—a spicy stew that had taken hours to prepare. The crew had come to dinner in two shifts—the second was still out in the mess eating—but nearly everyone had commented on the dish. The only ones who hadn't mentioned how delicious it tasted were those too busy enjoying it to speak.

"They'll be having cereal for breakfast if they don't show a little more appreciation," Josh said.

Tori knew better. Josh loved his work, and he had told her a dozen times over the past few weeks, since they shipped out from Miami, that the empty plates and bowls that came back from the mess were all the appreciation he needed. His diva-chef performance was meant to amuse her, and it worked.

And yet, easygoing as he seemed, he had a rough-around-the-edges quality and his mischievous eyes sometimes took on a hard glint. A rough man, but not a bad man. Maybe even a good man—though, much as she'd been trying to change her ways, that might be too much to hope for.

Still, whatever might happen with Josh, galley duty had turned out to be much more interesting than she'd thought.

"You know, all joking aside, you really should give yourself a break," she said. "Isn't there something you could give them tomorrow morning that would be fast and easy? Tater tots or something? For that matter, what's wrong with making them eat cereal for once?"

Josh stirred the pot again, then set the ladle aside. Now that everyone else had eaten, it was their turn, and he had put the remainder of the stew back on the burner. Tori had tasted a spoonful earlier and couldn't wait to eat. Her stomach had been growling for hours, ever since the smells of the stew had started to fill the galley.

"Well," he said, turning to face her again. "Remember those breakfast burritos I made, when was it, Sunday? I made a double batch that day and froze the rest. I could thaw them out for tomorrow."

"Great. You deserve it."

He gave her a small shrug. "Yeah. Though there was this one recipe I've been meaning to try."

Tori laughed. "My God, you're a cookaholic."

"You say that like it's a bad thing," he replied, one corner of his mouth lifted in a lopsided grin, his blue eyes gleaming with their usual mischief. "By the way, that was the worst English accent I've ever heard."

Tori grabbed a dishcloth, twisted it up, and snapped it at him. Josh tried to dodge, backed up, and promptly swore, hissing through his teeth, as he burned his arm on the edge of the stewpot.

"Oh, shit, I'm so sorry," Tori said, rushing up to him.

Holding up his arm to inspect the burn, Josh gave her a rueful look which broke into a smile. "You're a dangerous woman."

She reached for his arm, wanting a better look, and he winced a little but did not pull away. Just the feel of his skin under her fingers sent an electric ripple through her. This close, she could smell the aromas of the kitchen and the spices he'd used today, combined with his shampoo and just a hint of his own, almost earthy scent, and it quickened her pulse. Why some men stank and others smelled so damn good to her, she'd never know, but Tori liked Josh's scent, as weird as that sounded.

"Do you want me to get some ice for that?" she heard herself say.

He gazed at her with those sky blue eyes, and when he smiled again it was as though snapping himself from a trance. "It wouldn't hurt my feelings."

Tori's throat went dry. She didn't want to move away from him, but she forced herself to back up a step.

"Don't let the stew burn," she said. "We've earned it."

He nodded and turned to stir it again, holding his burnt arm against his body, letting the cotton of his shirt soothe it. She had burned herself twice in the time she had been helping in the galley, so she knew he had a tub of salve somewhere that would take the sting out, but first he would want to ice the bright red scorch mark, to numb the skin.

You could find other ways to distract him from the pain, she thought, and felt herself flush slightly. Maybe it was time for her to get out of the galley for a while.

When she had first met him, she had been convinced that

Josh wasn't her type. Oh, he pushed her buttons, all right. Quietly confident, mischievous grin, amazing cook, bedroom eyes, scruffy in all the right ways. The man was sex on a stick. But that first day, he had seemed almost too nice, too safe, without the rough edges that she always seemed to find so attractive.

Then they'd started cooking together, and she'd seen his passion for the work, watched his temper flare, and begun this ongoing, breathless flirtation that seemed to exist in every word they spoke to each other, even though it hardly ever became overt.

When he argued with Captain Rio about the supplies he wanted to get when they made port, she loved to watch his eyes flare. They had fallen into a pattern of teasing each other, but for Tori it had built to a point where it had gone past teasing. Now, as he grabbed a couple of bowls and ladled stew for the two of them, she watched him, studied the way his muscles moved under his shirt and the little sheen of sweat on his neck from the steamy kitchen, and desire drained all the strength from her body.

Jesus, shake it off, girl.

She smiled, laughing at herself, as she got a bunch of ice and wrapped it in a dishcloth. It wasn't the first time she had felt this way. The trip from Miami to Fortaleza, Brazil—with stops along the way—had taken nineteen days. The sexual attraction had been immediate, but at first nothing more than she had felt toward many men before. As the weeks went by, though, and they spent so much time together in the galley, her interest had turned into a desire so strong it sometimes made her feel shaky. Embarrassed by the strength of her reaction to him, she had worked to keep things cool, but the undercurrent remained.

She found it hard to believe Josh didn't feel it, too, but he hadn't acted on it, and so she had to wonder. Maybe she was the only one thinking about sex pretty much every time they were together.

"Thanks," he said as she handed him the ice.

Tori picked up the bowl of stew he'd prepared for her and raised it as though in a toast.

"No, thank *you*." She spooned a bite up to her mouth and her eyelids fluttered with pleasure at the flavor. "This is so good."

But Josh was watching her eat, that familiar mischief in his eyes, and since it didn't seem likely he would break the tension between them with a kiss, she needed to do something herself.

"You know what? I'm going to get this all over my shirt if I don't sit down. I'm gonna head out into the mess, grab a table. Are you coming?"

Josh pulled the ice from his arm, glanced at the burn, then pressed it down again. "You go ahead. I'll be out in a minute."

Tori left, both relieved and disappointed. It might have been all the cayenne pepper in the stew making her face flush with heat, but she didn't think so.

-7--

Angie Tyree had scrubbed her hands with industrial cleanser—the slimy shit that could get off just about anything—then used gritty powdered soap with water. She went through the same process two or three times a day, but could never seem to get all of the grease and oil stains off her skin. As long as they were at sea, her caramel-brown skin would be streaked with black. It would take days away from the engine room, from the pipes and valves she spent every trip maintaining and repairing, before they would fade.

She didn't really mind. As long as her hands were as clean as she could make them, she viewed the stains like a badge of honor. Angie had grown up poor in Honduras, in a neighborhood where only the men involved in the drug trade had any money. But her father had put food on the table at every meal. Sometimes they didn't have much to eat, but they never went hungry. He had taught her the value of hard work, and of keeping your head down and knowing when to look the other way.

"I'm tellin' you, Sal, I don't know," Dwyer said, pleasant as anything.

He sat next to Angie, their knees touching under the table. Most of the crew were Neanderthals, so whenever the company added someone new to the crew, Angie scoped them out. This time out, they had five new bodies on board. The cook, Josh, kept himself fit and the man was damn pretty, but Angie didn't like them too pretty. On top of that, it had been obvious from the second Josh spotted Tori Austin that the two of them would hook up eventually. And aside from Josh, the pickings had been slim—except for the skinny Irish guy. But Dwyer had the benefit of youth and enthusiasm. His techno-geek qualities—apparently he had a magic touch with navigation and communications equipment—had gotten him the job as third mate, but it had been pure luck and a slanted grin that had landed him in Angie's bed.

Now she playfully brushed his hand away.

Across from them, Sal Pucillo rolled his eyes. Also a new guy, Pucillo had to be in his early fifties, with a weathered face and gray hair, but he kept fit, and his body was lean and powerful. He had something about him that said ex-military, but when Angie had asked, it turned out he'd just been born with a stick up his ass. Once a dock foreman in Baltimore, he'd gotten divorced and decided on a change of scenery. That was all Angie knew about him. Pucillo didn't care to say any more, and she sure as hell didn't care enough to ask.

"Come on, Dwyer," Pucillo said. "You're on the bridge half the day. The captain and his brother have been acting squirrelly all morning. Something's wrong, and we've got a right to know, don't we?"

Angie kept her focus on her tray. Josh, the magician of the galley, had come up with a stew that was unlike anything she'd ever eaten, with chicken and Cajun spices and soft dumplings and tons of vegetables. Usually when she shipped out with the Rio brothers, the food was barely edible, so she spent most of her time working. As third assistant engineer, and the ship's best mechanic, she spent a lot of time sweating in the belly of the *Antoinette*. But with Josh and Tori cooking, Angie thought she might actually gain weight this trip.

"Why do you think something's wrong?" Dwyer asked, his Irish accent slipping through.

Pucillo sighed. "Are you even listening?"

Dwyer threw his hands up. He tried for exasperated, but with his red hair and freckles, he couldn't quite pull it off. Angie thought he looked adorable when he was exasperated, and she knew what she wanted to do right after dinner.

"What are you asking me for, Sal?" Dwyer said. "You think something's wrong, ask the captain or the chief mate. You don't want to talk to them, ask Suarez. He never leaves the bloody bridge, does he? I don't know that he ever takes a piss. But I don't know shit, all right? Besides, what do you care if the boss gets upset? It doesn't involve you."

Pucillo laughed softly, his expression dark. They called him the cargo manager, but really he was still a dock foreman. While at sea, he was just another hand—though damned old to be considered an able-bodied seaman—but in port he oversaw the loading of the metal containers at one end, and the off-loading at the other. He had to have heard that there were some things that went on aboard Viscaya ships that the crew were better off not knowing, but Pucillo had a habit of asking questions he shouldn't. Obviously he wasn't comfortable with Viscaya's secrets, but if he didn't start minding his own business, he was going to be out of a job by the time they made port back in Miami.

Of course, Dwyer asked his share of questions, too, but Angie understood that. The kid had scored a nice gig, and if he wanted to keep it, he had to educate himself, so that he could make himself useful to the Rios if the time ever came when they needed help.

"If the captain's got trouble, that could be trouble for all of us," Pucillo said.

Dwyer started to reply, but Angie beat him to it. She dropped her spoon and looked up at Pucillo. "Sal, we're trying to eat here. Maybe you should man up and say what you've got to say to the person you want to say it to."

She picked up a piece of bread, tore off a chunk, and

popped it in her mouth. Pucillo glared at her, trying to decide how to reply. If he took it seriously, he'd have to tell her off, and the ripples of such a conflict would affect the whole crew.

He looked at her hands, at the oil stains there, and she could see the revulsion on his face. Pucillo had a neat-freak thing going on. The guy was meticulous. He'd probably have starved before he would have eaten with dirty hands. Angie wanted to tell Pucillo that nobody had clean hands, that sometimes it just looked that way, but he wouldn't have understood.

"You can make jokes all you want, but this affects us all," he said. "And you're not funny, Angie."

She grinned through a mouthful of bread.

Pucillo sneered in disgust and got up, stalking away.

Dwyer slid a hand onto her thigh under the table and whispered into her ear, "You're sexy when you're a bitch."

"So I'm sexy all the time."

"Pretty much."

They started nuzzling closer, about to kiss, but then Angie glanced past Dwyer and hesitated. She forced a smile.

"Save your energy for later," she said.

Dwyer didn't ask; he didn't have to. On the *Antoinette*, there were only a handful of things that could've made her hold back from kissing her guy. The freighter wasn't on fire, and there was no sign of a tidal wave about to swamp them. That just left Hank Boggs.

Maybe forty-three, the chief engineer stood six foot four and was built like a pro football player who'd started going to seed—still plenty of muscle but too much beer to go with it. He kept his head shaved down to about a quarter inch of stubble and only took a razor to his face when it grew longer than that. Sal Pucillo annoyed her, but she liked him all right, since he was pretty much harmless. But that wasn't a word she'd apply to Hank Boggs.

As he walked to the counter where Josh and Tori had set out the stew, bread, salad, and the rest of the evening's meal, Hank took several furtive glances at Angie. Whenever his gaze strayed toward Dwyer, the big man got a hateful glint in his eyes, a mixture of jealousy and confusion. The son of a bitch just couldn't figure out why the skinny little Irishman got to share Angie's bed, when she'd barely give him the time of day.

"Your boss loves me," Dwyer whispered to her.

Angie smiled, unable to help herself. Dwyer touched her under the table, fingers dancing along the insides of her thighs, where she was ticklish—and sensitive in other ways as well. She rolled her eyes at him, gave him that coquettish "quit it" look, then caught Hank staring again.

"One of these days, he's going to start something," she said, voice low.

Dwyer's smile slipped. "Why? It's not like you two ever . . . wait, you didn't, right?"

She shrank him with a look. "You better be joking."

"If I wasn't, I am now."

Angie poked him under the table. "I'm serious. Be careful." She glanced over, saw Hank slopping stew into a bowl. "He thinks I'm his territory or something. Creeps me the fuck out. If the captain hadn't told him to back off . . ."

She left the thought unfinished, playing with what little food remained on her plate. As the ship's chief engineer, Hank was Angie's boss, but since she'd spoken to Captain Rio about the way Boggs treated her, she didn't really have to answer to him. Provided she did her job and kept things running, she didn't answer to anyone except the captain. It drove Hank a little crazy, mostly because of how badly he wanted to get into her pants. You couldn't be a woman doing Angie's job without having to deal with assholes with caveman mentalities, but Hank Boggs fairly simmered with repressed violence and sexual tension. Ever since they'd first started working together, he'd made his interest plain in ways implicit and explicit, but Gabe Rio had told him to cool it.

For a while, it had worked.

But then she'd started sleeping with Dwyer, and it blew Hank's mind. If she was screwing somebody else, he couldn't just pretend she was a lesbian or an ice queen. That meant she just didn't want *him*. Angie could've eased the tension a little, put on a work shirt instead of the tight tank tops she favored, but it got damn hot down in the bowels of the ship. And if the guy got off on sweaty, oil-stained girls in sagging blue jeans, what was she supposed to do about it? Change who she was because Hank had the social skills of a brain-damaged sociopath?

Sometimes she let him take a good long look. Angie hated him enough to enjoy tormenting the guy, but she was pretty careful not to get into too many public displays of affection with Dwyer when Hank was around. Waving too much red in a bull's face was never a good idea.

The engineer sat a couple of tables away, but there were a total of five tables in the room, so that was close enough.

"Hey," Dwyer whispered in her ear. "You want to get out of here?"

Before she could reply, there came the clatter of a tray on their table. Angie looked up to see Tori sliding into a chair across from them.

"Hey. Do you guys mind if I join you?"

Angie just looked at her. The *Antoinette* was a freighter, not some little dinghy, but there wasn't a lot of space for the crew to get away from each other, aside from their own cabins and the two rec rooms, so they put up with the proximity. Sharing a table in the mess hall with other people came with the job. You didn't ask; you just took the available seats.

But Tori asked, quiet and polite, because even after a nineteen-day jaunt down to Fortaleza and halfway back again, she didn't know the protocol. It was her first time out. Maybe that was why she made such an effort to be nice. She was like the new girl in school trying to make friends in the cafeteria.

The right thing to do would have been to give her a few minutes, make her feel comfortable. But Angie had spent years on ships with men who didn't think she belonged there, so when thoughts about *the right thing* entered her mind, she pushed them away. This wasn't high school. It was her job. And right now, she was off duty.

Angie stood up, grabbed her tray. "We were just finishing up. No offense."

Tori's face fell.

"We really were about to leave," Dwyer said quickly. "Sorry to abandon you."

Now Tori smiled and Angie saw, not for the first time, that skinny as she might be, and lost in her own thoughts half the time, the woman was very pretty. She didn't like Dwyer being so friendly.

"It's no problem. Next time," Tori said.

"For sure," Dwyer told her. "The stew was great, by the way."

Angie almost jumped in with something about how Josh made the damn stew and all the office girl did was chop vegetables and fill pots, but Tori beat her to it.

"Nothing to do with me," the woman said, shrugging. "Wish I could take the credit, but Josh is the master. I'd like to take him home with me."

Angie raised an eyebrow. "Oh, would you? Things getting hot in the kitchen?"

Tori actually blushed. "Only on the stove."

"Kinky," Angie said with a laugh. "But don't worry. Only a matter of time for you two."

She took Dwyer's hand and led him to the door, leaving Tori with a weird look on her face, like she wasn't sure if Angie had been making fun of her.

They stepped out onto the deck and started under the steps that reminded her so much of a fire escape, going up the outside of the accommodations block. Dwyer paused at the next landing and they turned to look at the moonlight glinting off the water. The engines thrummed loudly. He slid his arms around her.

"What is it about her?" he asked.

"What do you mean?"

"Tori gets under your skin for some reason. I mean, yeah, Hank Boggs I get. Toss the fucker overboard and have done with him. But what's she done to you?"

"I've got nothing against her," Angie said, surprising herself with honesty. "But she acts like we oughta be girlfriends, right? For no reason except that she's the only other woman on the ship—like that's enough. But I've never been the sleepover, cry-on-my-shoulder, paint-each-other's-nails kind of girl. Plus, you can't tell me you don't feel the chill Gabe and Miguel give off when they're around her—"

"The captain seemed fine with her today," Dwyer interrupted.

"Maybe. But you heard what Pucillo was saying about him and Miguel acting strange, and you didn't deny it. I'm not in a hurry to make friends with a woman the Rios don't trust."

Dwyer nodded, brow furrowed in thought. "I've gotta wonder why they don't trust her. It can't be just because she's new. This is my first time on the *Antoinette,* too, and there are a few others."

Angie reached up, touched his face, grabbed his ear, and tugged it, none too gently.

"Ow!"

She grinned, stepped in close, ran her hands over his chest. "I have a question for you." She looked up into his eyes. "Why are we standing out here on the deck talking about Tori Austin, when we could be up in my quarters, naked?"

Dwyer kissed her, fingers twining in her hair before his hands slid down her back, over the dirt-streaked cotton of her tank top.

"That," he said breathlessly, "is one hell of a good question."

-8--

Rachael Voss sat in a deck chair on the prow of a boat that had once belonged to a Colombian drug smuggler named Alvaro Rojas, before the FBI took it away. She thought it unfortunate that a guy stupid enough to get caught his first time making a run north wouldn't ever understand the irony of his boat being used in the fight against the smuggling of drugs and guns. It would've been nice to rub it in.

But how the Bureau had justified holding on to the impounded boat, she'd never know. Christian DelRosso, the special agent in charge of the field division operating out of St. Croix, had a reputation for getting creative when it came to getting the job done. Maybe he'd filed reports suggesting they might be able to use the boat to lure some of Rojas's buddies, the guys he kicked back to. Or maybe the SAC had just not bothered to make his report about Rojas yet.

Voss didn't care much about the how. All she knew was that Rojas's boat might be just the tool she needed to keep her partner alive if the shit hit the fan out on the water. Whatever SAC DelRosso put in his reports, that was fine by her.

Not that DelRosso had been doing any of this to help her out. He was just pissed at the way the Counter-Terrorism squad had been trying to get into the Viscaya Shipping case. None of the evidence they'd turned up so far—calls, e-mails, witnesses—had even suggested Viscaya had any connections to terrorism. But that's how Counter-Terrorism got their glory. When they were bored and had nothing else to do, they looked around for a good case where there was serious money involved, slapped the Terrorism label on it, and claimed it as their own. Thanks to the Patriot Act, they could step on just about anybody's toes.

The worst part for DelRosso was that Ed Turcotte— supervisory special agent in charge of the Counter-Terrorism squad—stood two rungs lower on the ladder, but had connections and influence that went way over DelRosso's head. Voss's squad, out of St. Croix, reported to DelRosso. They were his people, and Viscaya Shipping was their case. But the reality of it was that Turcotte had pull DelRosso couldn't match, and if the SAC complained, someone somewhere would start accusing him of disloyalty. He'd be put out to pasture like the federal attorneys who didn't want to play ball with the post-9/11 interpretation of the Constitution. The Patriot Act had split the Bureau into two camps, and now they were involved in the ultimate pissing match, with Viscaya Shipping as the current target.

Special Agent Rachael Voss had no love for DelRosso. The guy barely communicated with the field agents, especially the undercovers, preferring to communicate through his assistants. Half the time, he didn't even give the supervisory special agents—the people who actually ran the squads—a pat on the head when a job had been well done.

But she didn't want Counter-Terrorism getting involved in her case, especially with her partner undercover on board the *Antoinette*. If they came in now, they'd only make a huge mess of things. So right now, Voss liked DelRosso just fine. They had a shared interest in getting the Viscaya case wrapped up quickly.

Another day or two would be all they needed.

One way or another, it would be over after that. They had Coast Guard and ICE units on standby, but none of those boats were going into the water until she got word from her partner that the *Antoinette*'s rendezvous was imminent. Immigrations and Customs Enforcement was gung ho these days, but they weren't any more eager than the Coast Guard to have a bunch of people sitting idle for twenty-four, maybe forty-eight hours, waiting for a go-signal that might never come.

Voss smiled. Nope, it was just her squad that got to float around drinking mai tais, waiting for the shooting to start.

As if anyone drank frigging mai tais anymore.

Bob Marley sang "One Love" on her cell phone. She shifted in her chair, took her feet down off the rail, and pulled out the phone. When she flipped it open she was careful not to drop it, knowing with her luck it would end up going right over the side. She'd dropped her keys in the water a couple of years back and never heard the end of it.

"Voss."

"The clock is ticking, Rachael."

"I left my watch in my other shorts."

"What about this is funny to you?"

She settled back into the chair, gazing out across the Caribbean, the night wind still warm and sweet with the scents of the tropics. Maybe it was her imagination. St. Croix was thirty miles away or more; it wasn't like she could smell the flowers. But out here under the moon, the boat gently rocking, quiet except for occasional laughter from inside, life was good. Or it would have been, if she could just have worked the tension out of her neck and shoulders.

Which was not going to happen until they busted the entire crew of the *Antoinette,* without anyone catching a bullet or a knife in the gut.

"I don't know if 'funny' is the word," Voss said into the phone. "But the fact that I'm out here sipping a strawberry daiquiri and you're probably still at your desk sucking back those nasty energy drinks is at least amusing, don't you think?"

The sigh on the other end of the line was crystal clear. "You don't drink."

"How do you know I haven't started?"

"If you did, you wouldn't drink something as girly as a strawberry daiquiri."

"Shit. I was going to say mai tais."

The grunt on the line could almost have been a laugh. "Nobody drinks mai tais anymore."

"Which is why I didn't say it. What's on your mind, Chauncey?"

"Time, as I've already said."

Voss had worked under him for nearly two years, but she still hadn't quite gotten used to her supervisor. SSA Chauncey Alfred Bosworth III seemed like some kind of gag. People didn't name their children things like that anymore, and even when they did, they didn't raise them to become FBI agents. The guy's family was probably ashamed that he wasn't a senator. Even worse, he was always trying to get people to call him "Chuck," or at least "Agent Bosworth." He'd even once suggested that Voss call him "sir."

But she loved calling him Chauncey. At first he'd get irritated, but eventually he'd seemed to realize that it had created some kind of bond between them, that Voss actually liked him in spite of his quirks, so he didn't bother her about it anymore. He might stiffen up when she used the name, but he no longer corrected her.

Chauncey had a mannequin's sense of humor and he was a stickler for the rules, but at forty-six he counted as old school FBI. These days, the Bureau recruited new agents for their education in languages or their cyber skills. Chauncey had come up in an era when they had wanted lawyers and accountants. He'd been the former. That was something he and Voss had in common, though she was eleven years younger.

"So, what's the bad word?" she asked.

"Turcotte, of course."

Voss stared out at the ocean, thought about jumping in for a swim. "DelRosso was running interference."

"Only so much the SAC can do when Counter-Terrorism starts pulling in favors. In January, one of the guys linked to Viscaya sold a shipment to a major dealer in Aubergine, South Carolina."

"So?"

"Remember the flight school the Bureau tagged for training half a dozen of the guys from the cell that got broken up in Baltimore?"

Voss remembered. Four Saudis and two Jordanian nationals, none of them with proper identification, all but one of them shipped to Guantanamo, and that guy only got a free pass because he was a cousin of the Saudi royal family.

"Let me guess. Aubergine, South Carolina?"

Chauncey grunted that maybe-laugh again. "Not even. Another town, almost fifty miles away. But Counter-Terrorism is using that to support their argument that they should get the Viscaya case."

Voss wanted to argue, but there would be no point. Once DelRosso got a push from above, it was out of his hands, and sure as hell out of hers.

"How long?"

"The handoff's in DelRosso's office at ten o'clock tomorrow morning. You'll need to be there."

Which meant she had to be back on the island of St. Croix by nine.

"My partner is out there right now, Chauncey. On the hook."

"You think I don't know that?"

Voss pressed her eyes tightly shut and massaged her left temple. A headache had started spiking deep.

"What if it happens tonight? What if we get the go-signal?"

Chauncey paused, but only for a second. She loved him for that.

"Well, then I doubt you'll make it to the meeting."

He hung up without saying good-bye. Voss nodded, breathing evenly, as she flicked her phone shut and slipped it into her pocket.

She narrowed her eyes, looking out at the darkness, wondering where the *Antoinette* might be at that moment, how far from their rendezvous.

Hurry up, you bastards. It's not polite to keep a girl waiting.

-9--

Gabe Rio stood on the metal landing just outside the door of the *Antoinette*'s wheelhouse, smoking a cigarette and staring out across the water. Suarez had the wheel, and Miguel sat in the chair beside him, surveying the instrument panel, hands down but ready to react, like a man about to try defusing a bomb.

The analogy wasn't lost on Gabe. The whole situation was a bomb, about to explode in their laps. They could wait maybe a day, two at most, and then they'd have to sail on to Miami. More than eight hours had passed since the raving they'd heard on the radio. He had no idea what had happened to the rendezvous ship—pirates or mutiny or violent betrayal—but it had sounded totally fucked, and pretty final. He'd wanted the idiot on the other ship to go to radio silence, but there'd been nothing since. No beacon. No contact.

Miguel opened the door to the wheelhouse.

"We're here."

Gabe frowned. He'd felt and heard the engines slowing, but thought they might just be correcting their course. His cigarette dangled from his fingers and he took another drag, blew out smoke with his words.

"You sure?"

His brother cocked his head in irritation.

Gabe nodded. "All right. Don't get an attitude. Front office said the rendezvous was six or seven miles off the shore of an island, but I don't see any lights."

"Me, either. No lights. No boat. Nothing on radar."

"How long do you think we wait?"

"You're the captain, *hermano*."

Gabe smiled. "Why is it you only remind me of that when there's trouble? When things are going good, you've got more opinions than anyone I ever met. Except maybe Maya."

Miguel didn't smile. "Wouldn't have hurt you to listen to her opinions once in a while."

A chill settled between them. The burning tip of Gabe's cigarette trembled in his hand and he brought it to his lips, took a long drag, then blew it out slow. He shot a glance at his little brother, saw Miguel trying to stand his ground, and looked away again.

"You telling me things would've worked out if I'd just listened to her more?" the captain asked. "Maybe if I brought her flowers? Smiled more? Agreed with her when she wanted me to get a job on land so I could be home more?"

"I'm not saying—"

Gabe shot him a look that silenced him. Neither of them needed reminding that if Gabe quit working for Viscaya, Miguel's days with the company would be numbered.

"I'm not the easiest guy to live with, Miguel," Gabe added. "But Maya didn't end things because I didn't listen enough. She ended it because she started fucking somebody else."

"You don't know—"

"The hell I don't," Gabe snapped, voice low. He turned his back on his brother. "A man knows."

The cigarette had burned down almost to the filter, but Gabe held it between his thumb and forefinger for one last drag. Behind him, he heard Miguel open the door and go back into the wheelhouse, and only then did he flick the butt overboard. His brother had tried talking to him about Maya a hundred times, and Gabe always bristled. What did he know about having a wife? He'd had plenty of girlfriends but never married, never had to deal with the crushing weight of a woman's expectations. Maya had known he wasn't a talker when she married him. She had known that the sea meant everything to him, and that what he did for a living was sometimes illegal, but she'd smiled and said she didn't need the details as long as he wasn't hurting anyone. Gabe had lied to her about that part, but the look in her eyes had told him that she *wanted* to be lied to.

And it had been a small lie, hadn't it? He wasn't some kind of bonebreaker. The only people he'd ever hurt with his own hands had been in brawls that had nothing to do with the work he did for Viscaya. He was captain of a ship—the only thing he'd wanted to be since the age of five. Gabe believed that ought to have meant something to her. Yet Maya had wanted him to give it up, to stay home with her. Even if he'd agreed, they'd never have lasted long after that. One of them would have ended up full of resentment, either way.

He told himself it was easier like this. Now he didn't have a home to return to. The *Antoinette* would be his home from now on.

The door to the wheelhouse opened and Suarez stepped out, his eyes narrowed and grim.

"Captain. Mr. Rio needs you."

Suarez ducked back inside.

Gabe followed, not bothering to close the door. As he entered the wheelhouse he saw Miguel tapping keys, checking charts on the navigational computer's screen. The captain was about to ask what had happened when he heard the noise.

ping

"Is that—"

Miguel turned, nodded hurriedly. "The beacon from Mickey, yeah. Either someone just turned it on, or it's *been* on, and we're just coming in range of its signal."

Gabe glanced over to see Suarez waiting at the wheel, then hurried to his brother's side. "Where is she?"

"Due west. Way off the original coordinates. Thirteen, fourteen miles."

Gabe peered out from the wheelhouse, looking west.

"You have your course, Mr. Suarez. Full ahead."

-10--

Sometimes Tori wished she would never have to set foot on land again. Out on the ocean, the expectations of the modern world burnt off like morning mist. You took people at face value and judged them by the work they put in. What they might do on their own time—especially back on solid ground—didn't matter a damn.

The crew of the *Antoinette* didn't talk much about their lives, and that suited her just fine. Sailors were rough creatures with quick-draw emotions, but they seemed to share her desire to forget the world they'd left behind. Oh, they might have families back home, wives to make love to and children to feed, but in Tori's experience they were all running from something. Escaping the past, and a world that didn't love them enough.

There might be exceptions to the rule, but Tori wasn't one of them. Like the rest, she had joined the crew of the *Antoinette* in search of simplicity. Out here, it didn't matter who she'd been before, and nobody would even wonder. Without that freedom, the ability to be someone new, she doubted she would ever have been able to make the connection with Josh that she had. She liked being at sea, apart from the world.

Now they were headed home, with just a couple of stops along the way. Three years earlier she had adopted a new identity and a new name, but inside she had been the same woman, trapped in the same thought patterns. Leaving Ted had been the beginning of a change, not its completion. Trying to bury the past, to shed the skin of the woman she'd been—to whom names like *bitch* and *whore* had been the closest thing to terms of endearment—and to start over, she had gone through many phases, many cycles of hope and dejection. But with the culmination of this voyage, she believed she would finally have achieved that change. Once they were back in Miami, Tori really would be starting over. And as kind as the guys at Viscaya had been to her, and as much as she owed them, she knew that sometime soon she would have to begin one last time, in a job and a life where no one carried a gun or made their living outside the law.

That night, Tori lay on her bunk with a book propped on her chest, pillow and blanket behind her head, and her legs tangled in the bedsheet. It could get chilly in the middle of the night in the accommodations block, but the remaining heat of the day lingered so that—despite the bed itself being a sort of torture device—Tori was quite comfortable. On land she sometimes had trouble sleeping, but throughout this voyage she had slept like a baby, lulled by the hum of the ship and the rocking of the sea.

Warm and comfortable, she felt sleep coming to claim her. Several times the book began to dip in her hands, but she struggled to keep reading. Only when a knock came at the door did she realize she had nodded off. The book had slipped from her hands, closing, and she'd lost her page.

"Who is it?"

"Hey. It's Josh."

Tori nearly fell off the bunk extricating herself from the sheet. She dropped the book on the mattress and grabbed the shorts she'd shucked off earlier. Thongs had never been on her shopping list—too uncomfortable—but the high-cut underwear she had on didn't leave much more to the imagination.

"Hang on!"

Her hair had been damp from the shower when she lay down and had dried wild. She picked up the worn-out black scrunchy she used to keep her hair off her face when she was washing up and pulled it all back into a ponytail.

As she flung open the door she realized she wasn't wearing a bra—that it hung from the back of the worn and scratched ladder-back chair next to the bed—but it was too late to do anything except blush.

Josh stood in the gangway carrying a covered plate and a small carafe of purplish-pink liquid. He had showered and changed since the last time she'd seen him, rinsing off the day's grime, and now he wore blue jeans and a loose blue cotton shirt. His sneakers had seen better days.

"Oh, crap," he said, a sheepish look on his face, "I woke you up. I'm sorry, I didn't think you'd be—"

"I wasn't," Tori said. "I was just doing some reading, actually."

She gestured into her cabin, intending to draw his attention to the book on the bunk but likely only succeeding in pointing out the boring beige bra hanging from the chair. To his credit, Josh didn't immediately glance at her chest to examine the aesthetic effect of her braless state. It took him an entire five seconds. He was fairly subtle about it, too.

"Oh. Cool." He paused, shifted uncomfortably, blue eyes showing second thoughts. "Look, maybe I shouldn't have—"

"No, it's fine," Tori told him. Which was when he checked out her breasts. She had a T-shirt on, but still felt curiously exposed. Most men couldn't help a glance now and then. Women learned to put up with it or ignore it. But Tori found herself glad he was looking, and wondered how badly she was blushing.

"So, what did you want?" she asked.

Josh gave her that lopsided grin and she felt a delicious warmth spreading through her belly.

"I made something I wanted you to taste, if you don't mind being my test subject."

Tori stepped back to let him pass. "If it's something you're cooking, I'm always happy to play guinea pig."

She debated leaving the door open, then closed it. The cabin created an immediate intimacy that couldn't be avoided and, once again, the space between them seemed to crackle with electricity.

"I can't believe you were cooking this late, after the day you already put in," she said, leaning against the door as she studied him, trying to work out what, exactly, he had in mind.

Josh smiled. "I spend too much time thinking about ways to make the meals interesting. Anyone who knows how to cook and doesn't mind a little hard work could do this job, but I want it to be fun. I want people to be surprised."

Well, I'm *surprised,* she thought.

"You could cook in some swanky restaurant, Josh. The crew on this ship is probably used to eating stuff they wouldn't serve in school cafeterias. Trust me, you've been surprising them since day one."

"Sit," he said, pointing to the chair.

Tori obeyed, glad to block his view of her bra.

"The problem is, we're running out of surprises," he said. "I picked up some fun spices and things when we resupplied in Brazil, but pretty much all of the stuff I brought on board is gone. Now I'm just improvising with the things that are left."

He set the carafe of juice on the floor so he had one free hand, then took the metal cover off the plate and put it on her bed. A little steam rose from what appeared to be an omelet with chopped peppers mixed into the egg.

"I'll have breakfast potatoes with this in the morning, a little cumin mixed in, but nothing special. Try this, though."

"What happened to the frozen breakfast burritos?" she asked, arching an eyebrow.

"They're a last resort, for a day I really need to sleep in, or if I'm sick and you need to make something easy," he explained.

"What, you automatically assume I'm not any good in the kitchen?"

It was Josh's turn to raise an eyebrow, but if his thoughts were reading any innuendo into her words, he didn't let on.

"Eat," he commanded.

"You're the boss."

He'd had a fork on the plate, so she picked it up, split the omelet down the middle, and cut off a small bite. She saw cheese of some kind, bits of asparagus, and what she thought was ham. Taking the plate from Josh, she held it on her lap as she brought the fork to her mouth.

She tasted eggs and peppers, but as she chewed, other flavors asserted themselves: sharp provolone cheese, asparagus, and sweet prosciutto. The prosciutto had its own wonderful flavor and texture, but instead of overwhelming any of the others, it seemed to enhance them.

Tori swallowed. "That's really good."

Encouraged, Josh raised the carafe. "I didn't have enough hands to bring a glass but have a sip of this."

Balancing the plate on her knees, she raised the carafe, careful not to let it spill. Just a sip, and then another, and a third small swallow.

"Strawberry and something," she said. "It's good. Did you add sugar?"

"Not really. It's pomegranate juice and actual strawberries, but of course I didn't have fresh so I had to use the frozen kind and they're in that syrup. I drained most of it off, but the flavor is still there."

Tori handed him back the carafe and had another forkful of the omelet. She wouldn't have thought she was hungry, but it was really good.

"So I take it that's a thumbs-up?" he asked.

She obliged with both thumbs. "Oh, yes. I wish you could cook for me every morning."

His eyes sparkled with mischief. "There are an infinite number of replies to that comment, most of them suggestive and some downright crude."

The tiny cabin felt very close again. Josh was perched on the edge of her bunk, his knee only inches from hers. Tori felt her ugly past crushing in around her, but she'd had years now to work at overcoming it, and she forced such thoughts away. For three years, she'd felt dogged by the shadow of a fate she had averted, convinced it would catch up with her eventually. But her voyage on the *Antoinette* had started her thinking that perhaps she had a different fate in store after all.

"I'll bet half of them involve breakfast in bed," she whispered.

When he leaned over to kiss her, she held her breath. The situation should have felt ridiculous, her with a plate of eggs on her lap and him still holding that carafe of juice, but nothing about it felt silly. His lips brushed hers gently, and then he kissed her more deeply, his free hand coming up to touch her cheek and neck, and she shivered.

Tori had wondered about this moment, thought that when

it came the electrical charge between them would vanish. But the effect was quite the opposite. Josh cupped the back of her neck with one hand, fingers tangling in her hair, and deepened the kiss, their tongues lightly dancing.

He slid the plate from her lap and set it on the floor, then rose slightly, almost bent over her as he kissed her eyes, the line of her jaw, brushed his lips over her throat. She felt his breath hot and intimate on her neck. Tori opened her eyes wide and looked up at Josh. The lopsided grin had vanished, replaced by a look of pure desire. She had seen men hungry before, but never like this. The way he stood above her, so utterly in control, made her slide down in the chair in surrender.

But Josh had other ideas. Slowly, tracing his fingers along the bare flesh of her arms, he knelt on the floor in front of her chair. Looking up at her now, their situation reversed, he reached out and gently stroked her body through the thin cotton of her shirt. The backs of his fingers brushed across her nipples and she uttered a tiny gasp of pleasure, arching her back, as little shocks spread out from her core. With one thumb he traced circles around the nubs that were so prominent now, straining against the cotton, and with the other he reached up to caress her face.

It seemed strange not to be kissing him—not to be pressed together, eyes closed, lost in herself the way she had often been with men. It felt so open, so intensely wanton, that she was torn between wishing he would tease her like this forever and craving the finish, the gratification of his flesh.

Keeping her gaze locked with his, she reached for his belt, but Josh pushed her hand away. Now the lopsided grin returned and, for an instant, she stopped breathing entirely. He pulled her down to kiss him, and as he did, he hooked his fingers into her shorts and panties. She rose just enough for him to slide them down, and he removed them with unhurried tenderness.

When he touched the insides of her thighs, her legs fell open of their own accord and he settled on his knees between them, hands opening her farther, kissing her there, tracing every line with his tongue. And all the while he never took his eyes off hers, gazing at her, not letting her look away, even when her body began to quiver and then to tremble and then to buck against his ministrations.

"Oh, my God," she whispered, pushing her fingers through his hair, still staring into his eyes as the first wave subsided.

Josh reached up again, but this time he pulled her down onto the floor, onto him. Tori helped him undress but made no attempt to move them to the bed. If he wanted her on the floor, that was where he would have her. The metal was cold and she felt the sway of the ship against her back, but her skin was hot and flushed. Josh stroked her hair and kissed her deeply, trembling now himself with each breath. When he slid inside her, she thrust upward to meet him halfway and wrapped her legs around him. As he moved within her, his hands on her body, his lips upon hers, Tori felt another orgasm building. And suddenly it was as if they were no longer on board the *Antoinette*—as though nothing remained of the world but the places where their flesh came into contact.

With her legs around him still, Josh sat back, pulling her up onto his lap, and they made love in that undulating embrace until his breath began to hitch and she saw a warning in his eyes. With a whisper, she assured him he had no need to hesitate, and then she held him as he bucked inside her.

"Wow," she said softly, as their bodies rested against each other and she felt his heartbeat against her chest, slowing in time with her own.

"Yeah," he whispered, brushing the hair from her face and kissing her softly.

They grinned at each other, then laughed a little, and she tensed with tremors of pleasure because he remained inside her.

"It's about time you got the hint," Tori said.

"Are you kidding?" Josh asked. "I've been struggling to keep my hands off you for weeks."

She stared at him. "Why would you do that? Vow of chastity?"

Josh gave her a tiny shrug, causing another wonderful tremor. "You said you had a thing for bad men. I didn't want you to think I was one of them."

"I *used* to have a thing for bad men," she said. "It's something I've been working on."

Josh arched an eyebrow. "I wish you'd been clearer about that."

She ran her fingers across his chest, smiling up at him. "Me, too," she said, and then she grew serious. "So, you're a good guy, are you?"

He kissed her again, then studied her, unsmiling. "I've done my share of bad things. But I try."

Barely realizing it, she had begun to slowly rotate her hips on his lap, and though he had nearly slipped out of her, she felt him stir once more.

"Good enough," she whispered.

Tori stood and led him to her bed. The first time had been slow and powerfully sensual, her arousal completely intoxicating. Now their rhythm changed and they tore into each other with hunger and abandon, hard and fast, and in the end she screamed, and didn't care who heard.

In the aftermath, she lay in his arms, the two of them tangled together in her sheets. *It's been too long,* she thought. And then chided herself—for, in truth, it had never been like this before. It wasn't love—Tori didn't think she believed in love—but it was glorious.

"Do you feel that?" Josh asked, his voice sounding very far away.

Tori would have answered in the affirmative, thinking he had been referring to the intensity of what had just happened between them, but then she opened her eyes and saw his troubled expression, and knew he wasn't talking about sex.

"We're changing course," she said.

But not just changing course. Usually a change in heading was so gradual it was hardly noticeable. They were turning.

"And speeding up," Josh said. He looked in the general direction of the bridge, as though he wished he could see through all that metal. "What are they up to, in the middle of the night?"

Tori wondered as well. Was this the sort of thing she ought to be looking into as part of her job doing quality control? Under normal circumstances, she would think so. But just today Captain Rio had seemed to lose some of his irritation with her, and she hesitated to piss him off. And right now, naked and drained, she really didn't feel like getting up.

"Maybe we'd just gotten off course somehow."

Josh shrugged. "Maybe. Weird, though."

"Yeah." She thought about it a moment, then sighed. "Damn it. I should probably go up and check it out."

"Are you sure?" he asked.

The temptation to stay and see if he had it in him to go a third round was powerful, but she knew what her bosses would expect of her. They had given her the gift of this work, this voyage, and the adventure she'd always hoped for. She owed it to them to do the job.

"Unfortunately. Anyway, you've gotta be in the galley before dawn, so your bed is calling. But this isn't over."

Josh kissed her. "Not even close."

They dressed quickly and she made him take the plate with him. He set the juice next to her bed. "I'll leave this in case you want some later, but don't let it sit too long. Once it warms up, it won't taste very good."

She thought of several filthy retorts, but decided to save them for another night. She opened the door for him.

"I'll see you in the morning."

"Bright and early," Josh agreed.

As she ushered him out, preparing to lock the door behind her, they heard someone else coming down the corridor and turned to see Dwyer heading for his quarters. The deckhands and Hank Boggs's engine room minions all had to bunk up two to a room. But the mates, like Dwyer and Suarez, got their own space, as did Josh and Tori.

"Hey. What's going on? Why are we in such a hurry all of a sudden?" Dwyer asked. He looked squirrelly, like a kid who'd been interrupted looking at porn on the Net.

"I should be asking you that," Tori replied.

"I'm not on duty right now."

"I'm headed to the bridge, if you're curious," she told him.

Dwyer hesitated, then gestured for her to continue. "I'll be up in a minute. Just need to stop off at my quarters first."

He went on, sliding past them in the narrow corridor.

Something about the way he said it made Tori watch him as he went, and frown.

"What is it?" Josh asked.

She shrugged. "Nothing."

Maybe Dwyer and Angie had had a fight. Whatever it was, something had him on edge.

Josh reached out, linked his fingers with hers for a second. "See you in the morning."

Tori looked at him. The last thing she had expected when she had signed on for this voyage was that she might meet a cute, soft-spoken guy who would wake a passion inside her unlike anything she'd ever felt. Her legs were still weak. Up until now, they'd only been friends, working side by side, getting to know each other. What would happen next, she had no idea, but she found, for the first time in forever, that the unknown excited her. He did have an edge, a roughness that appealed to her. But whatever he might have done in his past, she knew Josh wasn't a bad guy. She'd had her share, and no black-hearted man could make love like that.

She gave his fingers a squeeze. "It's not breakfast in bed, but I'll take it."

-11--

Drug runners really knew how to live. Special Agent Rachael Voss lay on the bed in the master suite of the impounded yacht and felt like she was reclining in the hand of God. Either that or a cloud made of money. The thick spread and memory-foam mattress embraced her, and the fluffy pillows reminded her of all of the Cinderella-princess fantasies she'd had as a little girl—until the age of five, when a boy had pushed her down for the first time. She'd gotten up and pushed back, and that had changed things.

Too many people never learned to push back.

Voss still liked pretty things, even something fancy and frilly once in a while, but the luxury that had gone into decorating Rojas's master suite bordered on the absurd. Drugs made you stupid, and drug money let you finance your stupidity.

While his usual mules raced go-fast boats through the Caribbean, drawing the attention of every agency interested in breaking up their business, the real lords of the Colombian drug trade had sent Rojas straight up the middle, looking like nothing more than another rich asshole. If not for a total fuckup paranoiac informant they had on the inside, he might have gotten away with it.

Instead, the arrogant, bloated sack of shit got concrete and steel bars, and Voss got to sleep in Rojas's bed.

Which might've meant more if she could actually have fallen asleep.

They were anchored in the shallows off a small island she hadn't even bothered to find out the name of, not far from St. Croix. Chauncey wasn't going to let her get far when she had to be back early in the morning to brief Turcotte on Viscaya Shipping—as if the bastard hadn't already read everything in the file a hundred times. Voss's partner was out there on the *Antoinette,* but Turcotte didn't give a damn about that. Counter-Terrorism had an almost religious zealotry. Turcotte wouldn't want to abandon an FBI undercover agent in the field, but he'd let the undercover gig ride as long as he had to in order to get what he wanted—some kind of connection to al Qaeda, or whatever terrorist organization had been making his bosses froth at the mouth this month.

Voss wanted this thing wrapped up now.

"Fuck it," she said, under her breath.

Climbing out of heaven, she clipped her weapon to the waistband of her shorts, grabbed her cell phone, and headed for the door. She didn't drink, but somewhere on the boat someone would have coffee. There was always coffee. And it would give her hands and her mouth something to do, calm her and hype her all at the same time. It didn't look like she'd be getting any sleep tonight anyway, so what difference did it make?

Voss left the suite barefoot. She'd barely taken three steps when a figure blocked out the moonlight and Pavarotti descended into the cabin. Special Agent Joe Plausky didn't look a damn thing like the dead Italian tenor; he was thinner, clean-shaven, and very much alive. But he sang opera in the shower, and the squad had bestowed the nickname on him. Voss hadn't even been around when Plausky was in the shower, but the nickname stuck.

"Oh, hey. I was just coming to get you," Pavarotti said, fairly buzzing with energy.

Voss cocked her head. "Please tell me we're a go."

"Call just came through on the sat-phone. The *Antoinette* just made a sudden course change and they're running flat out."

She swore through her teeth and pushed her blond hair away from her face with both hands.

"No confirmation that they've made contact with the sellers?"

Pavarotti threw up his hands. "Come on, Rachael. You knew it wasn't going to be perfect when we set this mission up. We could wait, but then we risk the deal going down before we get there and we've got jack shit. This was a roll of the dice from day one."

Voss laced her fingers behind her head and blew out a long breath. "We go. Tell Nadeau to get under way, top speed to the sat-phone's coordinates, and we'll wait there for the beacon."

Dark eyes intense, he turned and started topside.

"Hey, Pavarotti?"

Pausing, he glanced back.

"It's Special Agent Voss. Agent Voss if you're feeling casual. Even just Voss, if I'm not in the middle of giving you an order. My mother, my boss, and the guy I'm currently sleeping with get to call me Rachael, and even from them I don't like it much."

Pavarotti did not smile. That was good.

"I'll make a note of it."

Then he was gone, scrambling topside, and Voss climbed up after him. While he talked to Agent Nadeau—who was at the wheel of the impounded drug boat—and then started

spreading the word among the rest of the squad, Voss walked
aft. The chair she'd been sitting in earlier still sat by the railing, empty, but she was too wired to sit down now.

Voss flipped open her phone, auto-dialed her supervisor.

"You coming in?" was how he answered.

He didn't sound sleepy; in fact, he sounded like he'd been
waiting for her call. Too many of those nasty-tasting energy
drinks. Voss tried to tell him they were the same kinds of
things snake oil salesmen had purveyed as miracle tonics in
another era, but he loved the disgusting things.

"Going out, actually. We got the call."

Chauncey hesitated before going on. "You're sure about
that? I don't want Turcotte getting in the middle of this, either,
but trying to jump-start this thing could end up blowing the
whole—"

"Shut up, Chauncey."

"Now hold on—"

"You think I'd risk my partner's cover, never mind his life,
just so I could stop Turcotte from taking away our case? I
told you, we got the goddamn call."

Again, he hesitated. But this time when he spoke, his tone
had changed. "I'm sorry, Rachael. I wasn't thinking."

"Get on the line to Coast Guard and ICE. We need everybody in the water, ready to go."

"Done."

"And, Chauncey . . ."

"I know. Don't call you Rachael."

"Yeah. And don't forget to cancel our morning meeting.
Give Turcotte my regrets."

By the time she closed the phone, they were picking up
speed, white foam curling away from the hull. Voss started
up toward the prow of the boat. She still wanted that coffee.

A warm Caribbean breeze followed Tori into the wheel-house. The Rio brothers stopped talking mid-sentence and glared. Her presence was unwelcome, but she didn't care.

"Evening, Captain," she said, like nothing at all out of the ordinary had transpired.

"What do you want?" Miguel asked. As chief mate, he had every right to challenge her presence on the bridge, but Tori ignored him, focusing on his brother.

"We're running at speed, burning fuel, and have changed our heading," she said. "Either we were off course to begin with, or we're about to do the business Viscaya doesn't tell its shareholders about."

As always, Suarez was at the wheel. He didn't blink. The illegal transactions that the Rio brothers handled for Viscaya didn't interest him. The old Cuban sailor did his job, kept his mouth shut, and collected his pay.

A low, rhythmic beep came from the radar screen. Gabe studied the screen and looked out the window at the night-dark sea, eyes seeking something.

"Why don't you go back to your cabin?" Miguel asked. Shorter and slimmer than the captain, he had hypnotic eyes and a dark, brooding appeal. In many ways, Gabe Rio seemed like the prototype for his handsome younger brother, but Gabe left no doubt who was in charge.

"Don't be an ass," he said, barely looking up. "Tori's here because Frank wanted her here."

Miguel narrowed his eyes, displeased. *Too bad,* Tori thought. She had liked him so much better when his greatest ambition seemed to be getting a look down her blouse. But she wasn't sitting behind a desk anymore.

The captain shot a look back toward the wheel. "Reduce speed, Mr. Suarez. We're almost on top of her."

"So what's going on? Some of the crew might be sleeping, but anyone who's awake is going to know something's happened."

"Half of them know exactly what we're doing—" Miguel began.

Tori shrugged. "And the other half don't want to know. I get it. They get paid to look the other way while we make unscheduled stops and pick up strange cargo. I've been doing *both* sets of books for Viscaya for nearly a year, guys. I know how much every person on this ship earned last month, over *and* under the table. Like it or not, I'm Viscaya's eyes and ears on this trip, and I'm asking. I'll help if I can, and stay out of the way if I can't. So fill me in."

The brothers exchanged another look, and Gabe gave a curt nod before returning his attention to the instrument panel.

Miguel sighed. Despite whatever resistance he'd had to her, they all worked for the same employer. His body relaxed and he even gave a slight smile. Tori stopped hating him, for now.

"We had contact from the sellers earlier today. One of them, anyway. When he wasn't blaming God or screaming, he gave us the idea some of his crew were dead."

Tori blinked, mouth opening in a little O. Dangerous men doing illegal business was one thing; murder was something else entirely.

"What happened?"

"No idea," Miguel said. "The guy signed off. If I have to guess, I'd say someone hit them for their cargo, some kind of setup. Or maybe just pirates."

A ripple of fear went through her, the skin prickling at the back of her neck. "So where are we headed now? If you lost contact—"

"We've got one ship on radar," Captain Rio said, peering out at the dark. His grim features were reflected in the glass. "It's either the sellers, or whoever took them down."

Tori looked from Gabe to Miguel to Suarez and then back

to the captain again. "And if it's pirates, then what? You're delivering our legitimate cargo into their hands."

Gabe fixed a withering glance on her. "The ship we're coming up on is too small to pose a threat. How would they get on deck? You've got your answers, Tori. If Frank Esper calls you into his office and asks for a report, you can make one. But we don't have time to hold your hand."

She blinked, stung. "I don't need—"

"Reverse engines, Mr. Suarez," the captain said, ignoring her. "Full stop."

As Suarez complied, the door swung inward. Josh stepped onto the bridge wearing an expression altogether different from any Tori had seen on his face before. Normally his face was open and friendly, but now his eyes were dark and cold.

"What are you doing here, Mr. Ford?" Gabe asked.

"Offering my help."

Gabe glared at him. "We've got all the help we need, thanks."

Josh smiled. "Viscaya didn't hire me just for my cooking, Captain. I had a reference from a guy who used to be on your crew. Jorge Guarino?"

Miguel Rio gave a soft laugh. "How do you know Jorge?"

"Cellmates in Gainesville Correctional."

"You were in prison?" Tori asked. Her voice sounded small and far away to her. She'd been around criminals for most of her life, some of them bad men and others just guys who didn't think the rules applied to them. Addicts and dealers and smugglers and thieves. Josh had said he had done bad things, but she hadn't pegged him as an ex-con.

Her body still throbbed from their encounter. She could still taste him on her lips, feel him on her skin, but now she felt unclean. It wasn't fair to Josh, and she knew that. After all, she had never really probed too deeply into his background, so he had never lied to her about it. Still, she felt deceived, not to mention disappointed. He had seemed rough on the outside, just the way she liked them, but solid and decent and kind on the inside. Tori had thought that maybe, finally, she had found a good guy who could give her the rush that she usually only felt with hard, dangerous men.

Josh must have heard something in her voice—surprise or

disappointment—and he gave her that lopsided grin. "Where do you think I learned to cook?" He turned back to the captain and raised his hands in mock surrender. "You don't want me involved, no problem. I was headed back to my quarters, but then thought I should at least offer. Now I've offered. I'm here if you need me, no questions asked. I knew the rules when I signed on."

The *Antoinette* moaned as it slowed, reversed engines bringing it to a halt. Suarez behaved as though they were all ghosts, like he was alone on the bridge.

Noise out on the metal landing drew their attention and everyone turned to see the redheaded silhouette of Tom Dwyer. Looking pale and worried, he opened the door and stepped onto the bridge.

"Where the hell have you been?" Miguel snapped at him.

Dwyer flinched like the first mate had spat at him. "Nowhere. I was just . . . I came as fast as I could."

Miguel snickered. Even Suarez smiled.

"I'm sure Angie appreciated that," the captain said.

Dwyer might have been a skinny young man, but violence glittered in his eyes. He didn't like being teased about Angela Tyree, that much was clear. What Tori didn't understand was what had taken him so long. She'd gone ahead while both Dwyer and Josh had rushed back to their rooms, but Josh had beaten him here.

"Had to use the head," Dwyer said, voice low.

"You ready to work now?" Captain Rio asked.

Dwyer nodded.

The captain examined each man intently, then turned to his brother. "Take Mr. Dwyer and Mr. Ford for a little boat ride. If there's anyone left alive for us to pay, radio it in. Otherwise, just bring the shipment back with you."

Miguel frowned. "There are half a dozen guys we could—"

"Just get it done, *hermano*. Fast and quiet. I want to know what happened to that boat."

Tori's pulse quickened. "I should go along."

The Rio brothers looked at her in that dismissive way men had, their faces telling her that to them, even the suggestion was absurd. Josh wore a different expression now—one that said she'd surprised him, that she was a puzzle he hadn't quite figured out yet. As of tonight, the feeling was mutual.

Tori sniffed, focusing on Gabe. She hoped that he could read her expression as well as she could read his, that he saw the message in her eyes—*I've survived worse than bullets, and I don't scare easily.*

But they had a situation on their hands and confronting their assumptions about women would have to wait for a day when their jobs, and possibly their lives, weren't on the line.

"I guess that's a no," she said.

Gabe nodded toward his brother. "Get going."

Dwyer held the door open for Miguel, then stepped through, forcing Josh to grab it before it shut. He glanced back at Tori, eyes full of promises—that they'd have a long conversation when he got back. Dangerous men had always been her curse.

One of these days, it would get her killed.

-13--

THREE YEARS AGO . . .

Her ears were still ringing as she walked north to Times Square, hugging close to buildings, averting her face from the street, while New Yorkers frantically responded to the explosion underground. She had intended to take the subway, but every train in the city had been halted the moment the news spread.

She trembled as she walked, terrified that Ted might have hung around. If he saw her, it would all be over. He would know she hadn't gotten on the train.

The train.

Oh, my God.

Her face felt tight and she wondered if the heat from the explosion had been enough to burn her. Police and transit workers had been first down the stairs onto the platform after the blast had knocked her off her feet, but ordinary citizens had come down after them, wanting to help. If she'd been a man, the cops might have looked at her more closely, but when a stylishly coiffed black man in an expensive suit and a dreadlocked white guy who'd been playing guitar in the station near the ticket booth helped her up the stairs, nobody paid any attention. They were focused on the crisis.

When EMTs and firefighters started coming down into the station and the transit workers forced people to move back, it was a simple thing for her to slip away.

The dreadlocked guitarist had carried her suitcase up for her. It banged against her leg now as she walked hurriedly north. A giddy amazement ran through her like an electric charge.

Wherever Ted was, he didn't know where *she* was.

For the moment, she was free. Now she had to stay that way.

When she reached Times Square, she realized that she had done it. Left Ted behind. She tried not to let her elation show. People were talking about some kind of bombing downtown, maybe a terrorist attack, and it felt like a somber time. She didn't want anyone to think she was laughing about the train.

As she walked, the sky above Manhattan had started to clear. It all seemed too perfect, like she was in a movie and at any moment the music would begin to swell. It felt like a dream, but the blue breaks in the gray sky were real. The sidewalk under her feet was real. The weight of the suitcase in her hand.

But the weight of dread that had sat on her shoulders for years had vanished.

Sirens wailed as emergency vehicles sped southward. A city bus idled in the crux of the intersection of Broadway and Seventh Avenue, waiting while the fire trucks and police cars flew by. The blat of the fire trucks' horns hurt her ears, just as it always had when she'd sat and watched the Christmas parade pass by as a little girl.

Between waves of emergency response, she crossed the street. The Millennium Broadway Hotel sat on the corner of

Forty-fourth Street, a monolith of glass and steel and marble, and it was a thing of beauty. The doorman and a cab driver were talking grimly about what might be happening, wondering aloud if this was some follow-up to 9/11. They didn't even look up as she walked by, and she opened the door for herself, went straight to the elevator and rode up to the seventh floor. Afraid to write anything down, she'd committed the room number to memory and for days had feared she would forget when the time came.

But she didn't forget. 719.

She knocked so softly she couldn't imagine anyone inside would hear it.

He answered in seconds, and when he opened the door she had a moment of disappointment. George had lied to her. The photograph he'd e-mailed must have been at least five years out of date. The man in room 719 had thinning hair and weighed a good twenty pounds more than the one in the photo.

But then he smiled, his eyes alight with such elation that she forgave him instantly. As lies went, it was a small one, and perhaps as much a lie to himself as to her.

"Is it really you?" he asked, for he'd never seen a photo of her. Everything he knew about her she had told him in the long, rambling conversations they had online when Ted had let her go to the library.

"It really is."

George laughed and stepped out into the hall, crushing her into an embrace. She stiffened, unused to being touched by anyone but Ted. Unused to being touched out of love.

"Sorry, I'm sorry," he mumbled, stepping back, eyes full of horror at his own presumption and the idea that he might have upset her.

"No," she said quickly, shaking her head, reaching for him. "Please."

She stepped into the room, dropping her suitcase by the door, and pulled his arms around her, weeping with years of pent-up sorrow, newborn relief, and astonishment that anyone would want to hold her.

George reached out and swung the door closed without letting go of her. Then he just held her, speaking comfort to her in low, gentle tones. Three quarters of an hour passed and they had barely moved.

At last, he asked her a question that required an answer.

"Who are you going to be now? You get to choose. A new place. A new name. Everything. Have you decided on a name?"

She took a deep breath, smiling against his chest, and nodded.

"Victoria," she said, stepping back and beaming up at him. "Tori."

George's eyes lit up. "Hello, Tori."

"Hi, George." She stood on her toes and kissed the big man's cheek. "You saved me."

He actually blushed and looked shyly away. "You saved you. You were brave enough to make the jump."

They'd talked about this many times. Tori squeezed his hands in hers. "Only because you gave me the faith that you'd be here to catch me."

For hours, they talked, but they never left the room. Tori knew it was irrational, but she feared that Ted would find her, out on the street. Less irrational was the thought that she might see someone she knew, someone who knew *him*. And then he would know.

They ordered room service, and afterward Tori wanted to take a shower. It had been so long since she had felt clean.

When she came out in the fluffy white cotton hotel bathrobe, George was perched on the end of one of the two beds, watching CNN. His mouth hung slightly agape and she wondered how long he had been sitting like that, staring.

"Did you see—" he started to say.

Then something clicked in his mind. Maybe earlier he hadn't taken note of the scrape on her elbow or the ruddiness of her cheeks or the dirt on her clothes. Now it hit him. George had a heart as big as the world, full of love and faith in the basic decency of people, which sprang from his own basic decency and his need to believe that others were like him. But he was also an intelligent man. Only his joy at seeing her had blinded him.

"You were there when it happened. Oh, my God—"

He started to say her old name, the one she'd left behind in Penn Station, then corrected himself.

"Are you all right?"

She nodded quickly. "Don't I look all right?"

"If you'd gotten on the train—"

"I'd be dead. If I believed in God, I'd say maybe you weren't the only one looking out for me today."

Her voice shook as she said this last, and her hands trembled as well. But she bit her lip and she smiled to show him it was only nerves. And then she told him every detail of her day. Afterward, he held her again for a while, the two of them sitting on the bed together, and Tori waited for George to kiss her or slide his hands up over her breasts. Not that she wanted this, but she expected it. The choices she'd made had put her in the role of damsel-in-distress, but she knew that Prince Charming existed only in the pages of fairy tales.

Yet George only held her. She knew he wanted her—he'd made that plain in the conversations they'd had online—but he didn't try anything.

"If you're just joining us, at least seventy-three people are dead and dozens more injured in a train explosion beneath Manhattan today," the CNN anchorwoman was saying. "Authorities so far refuse to speculate publicly on whether the explosion was the result of a terrorist bombing, but other theories have also been put forward, with some suggesting a massive gas leak might be responsible. Meanwhile, rescue and recovery efforts are still under way. Many passengers were treated for minor injuries and have already been released, but other victims of this tragedy remain hospitalized, some in critical condition.

"We're now hearing from several different sources that many of those who died in today's explosion were so badly burned that identifying their remains may be impossible, creating a nightmare for their families that is only just beginning."

The redheaded newscaster kept going, the tragedy in an endless loop of information and grim footage of rescue vehicles and people weeping. But Tori could only stare past George as laughter built softly in her chest and then came out in a giddy, hysterical babble. It lasted only a few seconds and then she realized how manic she must seem, and how morbid. People were dead, burned beyond recognition, and she was laughing.

"I'm sorry," she said, pulling back and looking up at him. "I'm not . . . it's just . . ."

George looked at her, face tinged with horror. Then realization crept over his features.

"You're dead. I mean, as far as Ted knows . . ."

Tori took a shuddery, emotional breath and nodded. "He would've come after me once he figured out I wasn't on the train. But now he'll never know. No one will."

-14--

Out on the dark water, the night took on an indigo hue and the moon lit every roll of the waves. Warm as it had been that day, the breeze that came off the water made Josh shiver. He let it happen once, then braced himself against the chill, not wanting to reveal any weakness in front of Miguel and Dwyer. Thoughts of Tori flooded his mind—the intensity in her eyes while they'd made love on the floor of her cabin, the way her body arched and shuddered at his touch, and the disappointment written on her face when he had told the captain about his time in prison.

You're an asshole, he thought to himself. Though he'd implied otherwise, Tori had told him that she had been trying to break a lifelong habit of getting involved with bad men. They were in the galley together for hours every day and their conversations were practically stream of consciousness. The woman had secrets, but even in the things she didn't say, he had understood that she was looking for some kind of redemption in her life.

He should have stayed away instead of complicating things

for her further. But with all that time together, he had found himself wanting her more every day, loving her laugh and her sometimes sharp tongue, and even the sadness that often crept into her eyes when she thought he wasn't looking. It had felt like a circuit connected them, carrying an electrical current back and forth between them.

When he'd made that omelet and mixed the juice and brought them to her quarters, he had told himself that he just wanted a taste-tester, that Tori could tell him if the concoctions were any good. But Josh had never needed a taste-tester before. He knew whether what he'd cooked was or was not a success. He'd lied to himself, just to have an excuse to go to her, and he'd let her see him the way she wanted to see him, so that nothing would stop them from closing the circuit, from breaking the tension.

Now his mind felt fogged with images from the time they'd spent in her quarters and guilt weighed heavily on him as well, because he knew that he was not what Tori wanted, and far from what she needed.

Josh was drunk with her, distracted, and he knew he had to shake her off, get his act together. Something fucked-up was going on, and distraction could be dangerous.

Miguel had rounded up a handful of the *Antoinette*'s crew and had them lower a lifeboat into the water. The thing wasn't much bigger than the twelve-foot Boston Whaler in which Josh's father had often taken him fishing, but its engine had a hell of a growl. It was Lifeguard Orange, boxy and utilitarian, but it charged across the water as if the waves bowed down before it.

Josh had taken note of the guys Miguel had called on to put them in the water, and there hadn't been any surprises. Tupper, Jimenez, Anton, and the hardcase engineer, Hank Boggs. But he'd spotted Sal Pucillo watching from the accommodations block catwalk, two levels up, and wondered what the hell the guy was looking at. And when Pucillo realized he'd been spotted, he had pulled back into the shadows, like he didn't want to be caught. Pucillo was a skulker—the kind of guy who whispered when other people's backs were turned and stuck his nose in where it didn't belong. It was mostly harmless, unless the Rio brothers started thinking maybe Pucillo was paying too much attention to their operation. Then it could be bad news indeed for Pucillo.

It wouldn't be the captain, Josh thought. *But Miguel*—he stared at the back of the younger Rio brother's head as the lifeboat skipped over the waves—*Miguel would be dangerous. He'd fuck up Pucillo big-time.*

Dwyer steered the lifeboat while Miguel stood in the stern, staring straight out at the darkness. Aside from the moonlight, the only illumination out on the water came from the *Antoinette.* The container ship loomed behind them now, a dark, hulking metal beast. Gabe Rio would be watching from the wheelhouse, grim and expectant, wondering what the hell had gone wrong.

Josh wondered the same thing. Whatever their plan for tonight's rendezvous might have been, this wasn't it.

The silhouette of the fishing boat grew larger as they approached. Next to the *Antoinette,* the sixty-footer might as well have been a dinghy, but it was no pleasure craft. Whatever fishermen caught off a boat that size, they had plenty of room to store it.

The lifeboat was maybe twenty yards out from the fishing boat when Miguel pulled up a seat cushion and opened a compartment beneath it. Reaching in, he withdrew a shotgun, its black barrel gleaming, and called to Dwyer, who turned to accept it with a nod, keeping one hand on the wheel. Next from the magic box was a Heckler & Koch submachine gun, smooth and stylish and looking more like a *Star Wars* toy than a killing weapon. Miguel kept that for himself, checking the magazine and then reinserting it before setting the H&K beside him.

He turned to look at Josh and said something in what sounded like Portuguese, loud enough to be heard over the wind. Josh shook his head. He spoke four languages, but Portuguese wasn't one of them.

Miguel gave him an angry look, then reached back into the hidden cache and pulled out a handgun. He held it out for Josh.

"Sig Sauer. Nice," Josh said as he took the gun. "Santa put one of these in my stocking a few years ago."

"Then you know how to use it," Miguel replied, eyes slitted and dark.

He checked the safety and slid the gun into his rear waistband. "I know which end goes boom, if that's what you mean."

Miguel didn't laugh, and that troubled Josh. Not that he thought himself especially funny, but the line hadn't gotten so much as a polite chuckle. Something had unsettled Miguel, and Josh thought the dark, silent, drifting fishing boat was only a part of it.

-15--

Papi. Wake up, Papi. I want to play.

Braulio hears the tiny voice, the precious giggle, and his eyes flutter open. Angelique is there before him, hands on her hips. She arches an eyebrow, far too grown-up for a girl of six. So smart, his granddaughter. The future holds great things for her, he knows.

Car engines rumble outside. Tires screech and he listens for the whump of collision, the crunch of metal.

Papi, come on. Get up!

All right, angel. All right, darling.

Angelique takes his hand and half drags him out of bed. Braulio expects the usual aches, the pop of old bones, but as he stands he feels nothing at all. His knees don't hurt and he doesn't feel the gravity of age that usually pulls on him. A good night's rest, maybe, but it must have been the greatest night's rest he'd ever had.

He smiles, and Angelique smiles back.

On the beach. She's up to her knees in the surf, hands still demandingly on hips, urging him to come into the water with her.

Papi, come on. You need exercise. You're getting a big belly.

He laughs at this. The girl spends too much time around

adults and listens very well. Too well. And she knows that he will indulge her.

All right, my angel. I'm coming. Just give me a second.

The sand shifts beneath his feet as he steps into the water. Tiny waves burble around his ankles. Another step, and another, and soon he is up to his knees as well. He doesn't like the soft bottom, the way the sand under the water gives way, causing him to stumble a bit, to shift his weight.

He glances up and sees that Angelique has kept pace with him, so that now she is up to her waist in the water.

Braulio frowns. There is no one else in the ocean. He glances around. No one else on the beach. The only sounds come from a distant buoy, a clank of metal, the dinging of a bell. But something is wrong. They are alone, but not alone.

Not alone at all.

Beyond Angelique, something moves underwater.

She grins. Dark shapes dart beneath the waves, long and sinuous. Braulio knows they are not sharks.

No! She's not for you, devils. I'm the one!

Braulio rushes toward her in the water, arms out, reaching for his granddaughter. Angelique laughs as if he is playing a game. She doesn't try to run or swim away, but still he cannot reach her, still she seems farther and farther away, and those dark shapes are sliding around her in the water.

He screams her name—his angel, his blessing.

The soft ocean bottom gives way beneath his feet and he slides under. He cannot breathe. Cannot see. Underwater. With them.

Braulio opened his eyes, his breath coming in shallow gasps. His body was contorted uncomfortably, his hands pressed to his open wound—glued there by tacky drying blood. He felt broken. Understanding dawned slowly, but when his fading mind cleared for a moment and he realized where he was, he managed a slight smile. Angelique was far from here. She was safe.

Numbness, nothingness, embraced him again, and he began to drift.

There came a thump somewhere on the boat's hull, stoking

the spark of terror within him. Wood creaked with the weight of movement up on the deck. The devils had returned after all.

"Angelique," he whispered.

But that was all. Even fear could not keep the nothingness at bay. The old fisherman surrendered, drifting once more, hoping he would dream of Angelique, and that she would hold his hand in the dark, as he had so often held hers.

-16--

As Dwyer maneuvered the lifeboat alongside the fishing boat, Josh saw the writing on the stern that identified her as the *Mariposa* out of Costa Rica. Dwyer cut the engine and let the transport drift over to bump against the side. In the sudden quiet, Josh caught a sound on the breeze—a lone voice singing high and ethereal. He strained to hear more but it was gone as quickly as it had come, snatched away by the shifting wind, and he wondered if he'd imagined it.

"Did you hear that?" he whispered.

Miguel cocked his head, listening, the H&K slung over one shoulder. "What?"

"Music," Josh said, feeling foolish.

"Maybe a radio on board," Dwyer muttered. In the moonlight, his white skin gave him a ghostly countenance.

Miguel grabbed hold of the ladder and kept them in place while Josh and Dwyer tossed a couple of bumpers over the side to keep the boats from smashing together, then tied up to the *Mariposa*.

Dwyer stepped back and raised the shotgun's barrel, swung it in an arc, but no one appeared on the deck of the fishing boat. Pulleys clanked against metal posts as the waves rocked both vessels, but nothing moved on board the ship.

With the barrel of his H&K, Miguel gestured for Josh to climb the ladder. He didn't like the idea much, but couldn't argue. He'd volunteered to help, after all—practically insisted on coming along. If he tried to balk now, Miguel would not be happy. And given the weapon in his hands, Josh wanted to keep the chief mate in a good mood.

He went up the ladder in about three seconds, stayed low as he came onto the deck, and snatched the Sig Sauer from his belt. Standing, he clicked off the safety, making an arc with the gun, checking the shadowy places. The moon showed details in black and white, bathed in gold. There had been a fire on the port side, though it had been put out before any real damage had been done. Equipment had been bent and broken. All but one of the wheelhouse windows had been shattered. Some serious shit had gone down out here, but the *Mariposa* was still afloat.

Josh beckoned Miguel and Dwyer to follow and started toward the wheelhouse. His heel slipped in something but he managed to maintain his balance. In the moonlight, the damp, jellied mess on the deck looked like the innards of some fish. There wasn't much of it; a handful, really. But a trail went across the deck toward the far railing, just a hint of something viscous that had been smeared there and then dried.

What the fuck am I doing here? Josh thought.

Taking a breath, he kept on. Miguel and Dwyer came aboard as quietly as they could, but in the near silence they were far from stealthy. Still no noise came from within the fishing boat. If anyone remained on board, they hadn't heard or had heard and not responded. This last thought troubled him. Certainly there existed the possibility that someone lay injured below and couldn't come up to investigate the noises they were making, couldn't call out. That didn't worry Josh. His concern was whether or not there might be someone on board who had *chosen* not to respond, who didn't want the intruders to know they were not alone.

With a glance back, he confirmed that Dwyer and Miguel were in motion. They moved quickly across the stern—the sticky deck where the fishermen would have hauled much of their catch out of the water. Josh had already confirmed for himself that that section of the boat was clear, but he didn't blame Miguel for not relying on him. Then they started moving up the port side, past the burnt section, until they were parallel with Josh on the starboard. With a signal from Miguel, all three of them continued forward, weapons at the ready as they reached the wheelhouse.

Josh and Miguel moved in sync, stopping to peer through the shattered glass of the wheelhouse windows, weapons trained on the darkness within. They sidestepped, searching for movement, but saw nothing as they continued making their way around the ruined box of a room. The instrument panel looked as though someone had taken a sledgehammer to it, the radio and radar destroyed.

At the front of the wheelhouse, they paused. Miguel gestured silently to Josh to stay put and Josh nodded, pistol trained on the wheelhouse as Dwyer and the first mate searched the bow. The *Mariposa* was large for a fishing boat, but there weren't very many places to hide on the deck. They were back within moments.

The three of them moved together to the stairs that led below. This time Miguel went first, the barrel of his H&K preceding them all into the dark. Dwyer flipped a light switch to no effect; the darkness remained. Josh descended last, one hand on the thin wooden rail. His fingers passed over a deep groove, and then another, and he investigated further, feeling scars in the wood.

In the common area of the cabin, they all paused while their eyes adjusted to the diminished light available from the four small portholes in the room. The broken pieces of a wooden chair were piled in a corner near a small card table and another, unmarred chair. The benches seemed untouched, but a rack of DVDs and CDs had been spilled onto the floor. A TV sat unharmed on a shelving unit set into the wall beside the stairs.

Miguel started forward, moving along the short, narrow corridor toward the three smaller cabins. One would have belonged to the captain of the fishing boat, with the crew splitting up to bunk in the other two.

"Josh," Dwyer whispered, his pale face seeming to float in the dark. He pointed to one of the portholes, which had been shattered.

With a glance back up the steps and then down the dark corridor, where Miguel was now only a shadow, Josh went over to see what had drawn the Irishman's attention. Dwyer nodded toward the porthole.

"What do you make of that?"

Only a few jagged shards of thick glass remained in the frame, but around its edges the metal had been smeared with something that in the moonlight looked like paint or tar. It had run in streaks down the wall beneath the shattered porthole.

Dwyer reached out to touch it.

"Blood," Josh said.

Hesitating, Dwyer sniffed the air. His lip curled and his hand came back to close around the shotgun as if the weapon was his most precious possession.

A thump came from the corridor.

Josh spun, Sig Sauer coming up in a two-handed grip. Dwyer fumbled with the shotgun and they were all lucky he didn't accidentally pull the trigger.

Miguel stood at one end of the corridor, outlined in the open door of one of the crew cabins, the assault rifle lodged against his shoulder. The three men aimed guns at one another for several heartbeats before twitching the barrels aside.

Completely still, they listened, rocking with the gentle sway of the boat, but the only sound was the distant clang of pulleys and winches back on deck. Then Miguel waved them closer, swinging the H&K toward a closed door. He'd been nearer to it, and seemed pretty certain now about where the sound had originated.

Josh padded down the short corridor with Dwyer at his back. He nearly tripped over a single black boot that lay in his path. The oddity of it registered, but he didn't have time to focus on it.

The thump had come from the head. The room would be tiny—as small as an airplane restroom, with a mini-sink and toilet jammed into a space the size of a closet. Something might have fallen over, but Josh's pulse quickened, pounding in his ears, and his skin prickled. Someone was on board with them. He'd had the sense that they weren't alone from the moment they had come down into the cabin, but hadn't wanted to say anything. He could've been wrong. Now he was sure he wasn't.

He narrowed his eyes, nodded toward Miguel, gestured to the other two cabin doors. Both hung open. No way the chief mate had searched those rooms well. The thump from the head had distracted him from that job. In the gloom, Miguel's eyes narrowed. Reluctantly, he nodded and turned in the corridor, put his back against the wall and held the H&K ready so that if anyone tried to come at them from one of those two cabins, he could strafe the doorways with bullets.

Josh looked at Dwyer, held up a hand to make him pause, to get him ready. The Irishman might be young, but he'd clearly held a gun before. He seemed unfazed by the tension in the air. Dwyer leveled the shotgun at the door to the head.

With his free hand, Josh tried the door and found it locked. Nothing had fallen over. They weren't alone.

He glanced at Miguel, then Dwyer, a simple warning, then stepped back at an angle and put a bullet through the lock, blowing a hole in the door. The report echoed in the closed space and he flinched before he reached for the ruined door and yanked it open.

Dwyer aimed the shotgun into the cramped space. No one came out of the cabins. Josh had expected a scream, some kind of reaction. But no sound rose from within.

A man sat on the toilet in torn, bloody clothes, pressed into the corner of that tiny room with his legs drawn up under him as though he had tried to make himself smaller, forcing his body into a ball. His legs were covered in horrible gashes, blood crusting over, and what they could see of his body through the torn clothes showed dark welts in strange patterns all across the flesh. His face was turned toward them, eyes wide and glassy, lips pulled back in a rictus of terror and frozen in place. Were it not for the tremulous hitching of each breath, Josh would have been certain he was dead.

But the skinny little man still lived, for the moment.

"Jaysus," Dwyer whispered, his accent flaring up. "What the fuck happened to you?"

The man began to shake and to weep, and he spilled into the narrow corridor like a house of cards coming down, revealing a seeping hole in his stomach. He'd been holding a hand over it, had bunched himself up in that corner to try to keep his insides from poking out.

Now he covered the hole with both hands again, pressed down, curled in upon himself, shuddering. Death had come to the *Mariposa,* and this man had survived its visit. But not for long.

-17--

On the bridge of the *Antoinette,* Tori waited in silence. Captain Rio spoke to the ship's engineer, Hank Boggs, out on the metal landing, leaving her alone with Suarez. For the most part, the second mate didn't acknowledge her, though once she muttered something about the adventure of working with the Rios, and he smiled thinly to himself, exposing nicotine-yellowed teeth and a merriment in his eyes that surprised her. Suarez didn't say much, but he loved his job. Tori envied him that pure devotion.

Her own life was a work in progress. When she'd escaped her husband, she'd intended to leave the world of drugs and violence behind. But without a usable social security number, there weren't a lot of places she could have worked. Hello, my name's Tori, can you pay me under the table? It was like wearing a sign around her neck identifying herself as a fugitive. Most people would think her a criminal herself, maybe hiding from a parole officer or an arrest warrant.

George had helped. Her guardian angel, coming through again. He'd e-mailed her information about a shelter for battered women, and one of the volunteers there had helped her get her first job in Miami, waiting tables in a little Italian restaurant tucked away in a hotel in Bal Harbour. Another week and she'd have been dancing in a strip club, so the job at Castaways had come along in the nick of time.

Bal Harbour had a huge population of retirees, but the Royal Floridian skewed younger, and a great deal of business got done in the bar and restaurant—not all of it legal. The concierge, Paolo, could get hotel clientele anything they desired, with drugs and girls at the top of that list. Tori thought he was kind of sweet for such a shady character. Paolo never tried to sell her drugs and never tried to get her to sell herself to any of his clients—though he did tell her several had asked.

Tori steered customers his way, took messages for him, even hung out sometimes with Paolo and his friends after work. They'd flirted with her, of course, but they'd treated her with respect. The one time she'd slept with Paolo, she'd been the one to initiate it, and he hadn't expected anything afterward.

Paolo had introduced her to Frank Esper, explaining that she needed to stay off the books, that anonymity kept her safe from bad men. Those were his words. Bad men. She'd laughed at the time, wondering what Paolo would have said if she'd asked him to define the phrase. But Frank had understood, and a couple of days later, he'd offered her a job at Viscaya, under the table, no reporting to the IRS.

She couldn't help feeling a little guilty now that she planned to leave Viscaya behind, but Frank couldn't have expected she would stay there forever.

The radio squawked, shaking her from her reverie. She glanced at Suarez, who seemed about to tell her to answer, but obviously he thought better of it.

"Fetch the captain, please," he said.

Tori nodded, heading for the door. The bridge smelled of industrial cleaners and mildew, like whoever washed it down every few nights just kept mopping with the same filthy water. When she pulled the door open, she got a refreshing blast of sweet Caribbean air, but on her second breath it was tainted with the other scents of their journey—the oil of the engines and the acrid odor of rusting metal.

Gabe and Hank Boggs halted their conversation the second the door opened, looking at her curiously. The engineer's lips were a thin line of annoyance.

"The radio," she said without being asked.

The captain nodded and turned to Hank. "Whatever they come back with, I want only my people there when they come aboard."

"I'll make sure," the engineer replied, and then he started down the metal steps.

Tori held the door for Captain Rio as he hustled onto the bridge and over to the radio. Miguel's voice crackled on the speakers. "Come in, Donald, this is Mickey."

"Mickey, this is Donald. Over," Gabe replied.

"We've got one, Donald. I repeat, one, and the clock is ticking."

From the look on Captain Rio's face, Tori didn't need to ask, "One what?" One survivor, wounded somehow and failing fast.

"Shit," Gabe snapped. He blew out a breath and visibly steeled himself.

"What about the cargo, Mickey?"

"No sign, but we're searching."

"Every inch, Mickey. Radio with an update ASAP."

"Will do. And, Donald?"

There'd been a pause and now Miguel Rio's tone had shifted. Tori frowned, glanced over at the captain. Gabe had noticed it, too, and a look of concern revealed lines on his face.

"What is it?"

On the radio, Miguel launched into a flood of unfamiliar language, inflection rising and falling, rapid-fire words to which Tori listened closely. Some she thought she understood. It was like listening to a song she was sure she knew but being unable to remember its name or how the chorus went. She assumed it was some variant Romance language— Catalan or Portuguese. In the gloomy artificial light on the bridge, she watched Gabe's expression twist and darken with anger.

He signed off, then turned to cast a baleful look at Suarez. The old sailor must have understood, for he nodded slowly.

"What language was that?" Tori ventured. "You guys are from Mexico, aren't you?"

"Yes," Gabe said as he turned grim eyes upon her. He seemed to be weighing her, trying to decide how much he trusted her, how much he needed her—there was a lot of that going on.

"I have a job for you, Tori."

His expression was so contorted with anger that she only nodded. Captain Rio took a key ring out of his pocket, chose a long key and removed it from the ring, and then handed it over to her.

"This will open all of the crew cabins. Go down and search Josh's quarters, now, before they get back. Then come see me."

Her stomach tightened, giving a sour twist. She could taste rust on her lips, the scent of it still in her mouth from being outside, even briefly.

Her pulse raced.

"What am I looking for?" she asked, wondering if Gabe saw the regret in her face.

His eyes were hard. "Anything he shouldn't have. Weapons. Radios. A fucking badge."

"A badge?" She stared at him, mouth agape, then shook her head. "No way. Not Josh. Where the hell are you getting this?"

Gabe scowled. "Turns out our cook isn't who he says he is. And he couldn't wait to go with Miguel, get a firsthand look at what's going down out there. I thought he was a little too eager, but I didn't figure him for a Fed."

"How do you *know*?" Tori demanded, refusing to believe it.

"That story about him sharing a cell with Jorge Guarino? It's bullshit. People who lie about prison usually do it to hide the fact they served time. The only people who lie about doing time they never did are cops working undercover."

Tori blanched, and a rush of anger replaced the last traces of the pleasure Josh had given her earlier. She wondered if she would survive prison.

Wondered if it could cure her of her love for men with secrets.

"You're really sure?" she asked.

"Ninety-nine percent. And that's why you need to hustle your ass down to his quarters before they come back."

She swore as she rushed from the bridge. The people at Viscaya had put their trust in her, put their secrets in her hands. With the exception of Ted and his sleazy friends, bad men had always been honest with her. It turned out that the good guys were the liars.

And Tori hated being lied to.

-18--

Josh stared at the fisherman who lay dying on the floor of the *Mariposa*'s cabin. His breathing was a shallow, ragged wheeze, and wet with the sound of something torn and leaking deep inside him. Where his hands were pressed over the wound in his abdomen, less and less blood seeped around his fingers, his body winding down, heart slowly ticking away the last of his life.

"Open your eyes, asshole. Stay with me!" Miguel shouted, slapping the man's cheeks.

"Come on, man," Josh said.

Miguel whipped his head around and glared. "Come on, what? You wanted to help, right? Help by shutting your mouth."

"Leave the guy alone. He's almost gone, for Christ's sake."

Miguel pressed his eyes tightly closed, like he was trying to shut Josh's words out, then opened them again and stared down at the fisherman.

"Where is everyone?" he shouted, spittle flying from his lips.

Josh gritted his teeth. At least Miguel hadn't hit the man again. If he tried, Josh might have to step in, and that would only get ugly. A fight was not what they needed right now and when Dwyer came back up from searching the hold, there would be no doubt whose side he would be on. The Irishman took orders, and he'd already shown how comfortable he was with a gun in his hand.

"Open your eyes!" Miguel shouted, and he reached out and pressed down on the man's hands, putting new pressure on the hole in his abdomen.

Josh started forward, but the fisherman's eyes snapped open and he drew in a wet, shuddery breath.

"Where did they all go?" Miguel demanded.

The man's eyes did not seem to focus, instead drifting around the darkness of the cabin. Sorrow and fear filled his features, and Josh wondered if they were his reaction to waking to find himself still alive, still suffering.

"Waiting for you," the man began, a few syllables spilling out in one breath. "We find . . . *el cementerio.*"

The fisherman's eyelids fluttered closed again. Miguel sat back on his haunches, looking confused. The H&K hung from a strap across his back, but he seemed to have forgotten it entirely.

"He's not making any sense."

Josh threw up his hands. "No shit. Maybe because his whole body's shutting down?"

Miguel shifted forward. "What cemetery? Where is everyone?"

The fisherman began to cough and choke, and then a line of thick, dark blood dribbled from the corner of his mouth. Josh thought that would be it, that he wouldn't speak any more, but the man opened his eyes and let his head loll to one side, still gazing at nothing.

"We never come to the island . . . before. No one knows."

Josh took a step nearer, crouched down and tried to get the man to meet his gaze. Miguel didn't even seem to notice his approach.

"What island?" Josh asked.

Miguel ignored him. "Your captain told *us* about the island. He wanted to use it as a landmark, but we couldn't find it on our map. He must have been there—"

"No. He never been. He found a map, very old. He say . . . maybe it's a pirate map. He loves pirates."

Josh tried to process that. It sounded absurd, but he supposed it wasn't as ridiculous as it seemed. Pirates had roamed these waters for years, in massive numbers.

He looked at Miguel. "This island you're talking about, you couldn't find it on your charts?"

Miguel nodded, mulling it over. "There are so many little dots on the water, you'd be surprised what's not on charts, especially out here. We're way off the usual shipping lanes, not on the way to anywhere."

"So a secret place—"

The fisherman started coughing again, flecks of red spittle flying from his mouth. The effort caused a fresh flow of blood to seep from his wound, up between his fingers.

"Shit," Miguel snapped, leaning in toward the man. "Tell me about the cemetery. Is it on the island?"

The man wheezed, a wet burbling coming from his throat. "Ships."

Josh frowned, trying to puzzle it out, but it seemed to just piss Miguel off. He raised his hand, looked like he was about to slap the fisherman again, and Josh started toward him.

Which was when Dwyer came tromping back down the steps into the cabin. One look at his face ought to have been enough to tell the tale, but Miguel still asked.

"What did you find?"

"Fuck all," the Irishman said, looking like he might throw up. "Got three guns, carried 'em up on deck. All of 'em loaded, so either they weren't part of the cargo or these guys were borrowing them. But no crates. No cargo. No guns. No explosives."

Miguel let loose with a string of Spanish expletives, turned, and slapped the fisherman with the back of his hand, knuckles cracking loudly against the man's cheekbone. He struck before Josh could have stopped him, and it was enough to snap the man's eyes wide again.

"Where are they, God damn you!"

"Miguel . . ." Josh began, reaching for him.

"Back the fuck off!" Miguel roared, slapping his hand away. "Dwyer, if the cook gets one step closer, shoot him."

Dwyer blinked like he wasn't sure if Miguel was serious. Josh thought maybe he was, so he took a step back, pistol heavy in his hand. Familiar. Cold.

"The devils came . . ." the fisherman whispered.

Miguel pushed his face in close. "Where are my guns?"

The man laughed, coughing again. Miguel flinched away as blood spattered his face. He tried to wipe it off but only succeeded in smearing it in streaks.

"Ruiz take them . . . to the island." A fresh rivulet of blood came from the corner of his mouth and dribbled down his jaw.

Miguel shook his head. "Why would he do that?"

The man shuddered, not listening, lost in his own pain. *"Los diablos—"*

"I know, I know," Miguel said, rising. "The devils. So you said. What you didn't say is who the fuck they are, or what you're talking about!"

While Miguel ranted, Josh stared at the fisherman. The man couldn't have been very old, but thin as he was, drawn and pale and rigid, he looked ancient. As Miguel railed at him, the man shuddered and began to gasp silently, unable to draw air. His neck arched a few times, as though perhaps he could breathe if only he reached just a bit farther. His body trembled. A thin line of blood ran from his right nostril.

And he died.

Dwyer saw it happen, too. "Boss?"

Miguel turned, eyes frantic, obviously trying to figure out how he was going to deal with such a colossal fuckup. Josh thought he would scream, but instead, Miguel deflated, lowering his head. After a moment, he took a deep breath, ran his hands through his hair, and sighed. He looked up at Josh, then at Dwyer.

"What the fuck is going on here?"

His eyes were haunted, and Josh felt a chill go through him that had nothing to do with the breeze off the sea. When he had signed on as the *Antoinette*'s cook, he had thought himself prepared for anything. But tonight, it felt like they had sailed off the edge of the world.

Dwyer shrugged. "Pirates."

Miguel arched an eyebrow. "Come *on*."

"Why not?" the Irishman asked. "You hear things all the time about ships getting hit, people killed and robbed. Some cruise ship's crew fought 'em off with guns a few years back."

"They'd have to be pretty desperate pirates to hit a fishing boat."

"So they knew what they were looking for. The wrong people found out about Ruiz's cargo and they came and took it, killed everyone, dumped 'em overboard."

From the look in his eyes it was obvious Miguel wanted this to be the truth. Josh turned it all over in his head, trying to see it from different angles, but no matter how he approached it, none of those theories made sense to him.

"You guys are unbelievable," he said.

Miguel narrowed his eyes, staring at him through the slits. "Something you want to say?"

There was open contempt in the man's voice, but beneath that, Josh sensed something else. Blame. Suspicion. Miguel had an edge to him, arrogant and self-righteous, but this went beyond attitude, and Josh didn't like it at all. Still, he couldn't just keep quiet.

"You heard the guy, saw the marks on his skin, never mind the damn porthole and the damage to the boat, and you're seriously going to go back to your brother with that story?"

Miguel cocked his head, a kind of horrid amusement in his eyes, and then he swept the H&K around, not quite aiming it at Josh.

"You got a better explanation, *cook*?"

Dwyer looked back and forth between them, brows knitted. He didn't move, waiting to see what would happen next.

"All I know is, it wasn't just a rip-off. This guy might've been nuts, but I'm betting he didn't start out that way. Throw in blood loss, fine, he was raving, but something scared him so badly he was talking about devils. And someone murdered the rest of the crew—"

"You don't know that," Dwyer said.

Josh frowned, staring at him. "What?"

Dwyer shrugged, looking at Josh like he was stupid. "Like

you said, the fellah was raving. But some of that didn't sound crazy. He said Ruiz went to the island. Could be there's some of them still alive."

"Fine," Josh replied. "I'm just saying that whatever happened on this boat, it wasn't about stealing guns."

Miguel turned his back on them, walked over and looked out at the darkness through the gore-encrusted broken porthole. The *Mariposa* swayed gently on the water, cradled in the arms of the ocean, but Josh didn't feel soothed. He'd been in even more remote places in his life, but had never felt farther from home. Thoughts of ghost ships lingered in his mind, of vanishing crews and drifting mysteries.

"I know where our cargo is," Miguel said. "That's all that matters to me, and it's all that will matter to Gabe." He turned to face them. "Dwyer, gather up the guns you found and load them onto the transport. Josh, go down into the hold and knock some holes in the hull.

"Sink the bitch."

-19--

Tori stood on the metal walkway outside Josh's room. The accommodations block creaked along with the rest of the ship. The metal underfoot no longer held any of the heat from the day, and this far out at sea, this late at night, the Caribbean breeze had lost much of its warmth. At least she told herself that was why she shivered, standing there with the captain's key in her hand.

She pressed her eyes shut tightly, trying to force away images of Josh gazing up at her, memories of his hands on her, and the sick feeling twisting now in the soft, tender place inside her that he had reached. She had trusted him, and it looked like she might be about to pay dearly for that.

Gabe had said she was looking for anything that shouldn't

be there. But he'd given examples, too, and they'd made his suspicions clear. Her stomach hurt. She was all twisted up inside, but that was good. With her guts fisted with anxiety, she wouldn't throw up.

If you used me, asshole . . . she thought, but stopped herself right there.

All men lied. She'd come to that conclusion a long time ago. But the kind of men she'd always been with were expected to lie. Only a fool would presume anything else, and though she had been a fool once upon a time, she'd thought herself cured of that condition. Good men, though . . . they were dangerous. They were the kind of men a woman could put her hope in, and their lies cut so much deeper because of it.

Shit.

With a sigh she put the key into the lock, turned the handle, and let herself in. The door swung inward, nudged by the wind, and she drew the key out and slipped it into her pocket. For a long moment she stood on the threshold.

The ship rolled so gently on the sea that, rather than rocking, it seemed to breathe, as though it were a living thing. The metal sighed, and then she heard a creak, and footsteps.

Sal Pucillo came around the corner of the tower, tipping a beer can back to get the last dregs. As he lowered the can, he caught sight of her and a smile played at the corners of his lips. He glanced through the open door into the darkness of Josh's room, and pointed a finger at her.

"I knew it," he said, listing to one side. Sal was not entirely sober.

"Knew what?"

He gave a dramatic roll of his eyes. "You and Josh. Knew you had something going on. You two played it pretty cool, but I'm not stupid." He tapped a finger beneath his left eye. "I've seen the way you look at each other. Anyone paying attention coulda figured it out."

Tori spread her hands, smiling. "You caught me."

Sal frowned, craning his neck to look into the room again. "Doesn't look like he's around, though."

For a moment, she wracked her brain for some explanation, then she realized there was no point. Pucillo was a nosy bastard, but Gabe was the captain, and Viscaya the owners, and Pucillo didn't have any business sticking his nose into the job that the captain had sent her to do.

Tori showed him the key the captain had given her. "He's working up tomorrow's menu, and I'm planning to surprise him."

She put a finger to her lips and shushed him. Pucillo arched his eyebrow even higher, a suggestive grin on his face, and imitated the shushing. Then he mimed locking his lips and throwing the key away.

"Not a word. I'm off to bed anyhow."

He put the empty beer can on the metal walk and crushed it under his boot, instantly forgetting about it. Tori hesitated. If the man was that drunk, wandering the metal walkways that terraced the sides of the accommodations block was seriously dangerous. Pucillo could go right over the railing and crash down onto the deck below.

"Sal . . ." she started.

Pucillo paused and looked at her.

"Be careful, okay? Watch your step. And good night."

He wagged his eyebrows with a lighthearted laugh, an entirely different man than he was when sober. "You, too, Tori. Josh is a lucky guy."

"Thanks."

Pucillo walked on, chuckling to himself. Tori backed into the room and clicked the door shut, locked it, then hit the light switch. Turning around, she scanned the room. Josh kept it neat enough—military neat—but that fit with what she knew of him. He liked the galley spotless and completely organized, and his cabin reflected the same sensibility, with a pair of boots and two pairs of sneakers arranged together under his rack, but otherwise everything was put away. An iPod sat in its dock on the small table near the bed.

Tori hesitated. She was torn between the fear that she'd find something that would take them both to ugly places, and the fear that she'd find nothing and Josh would learn that she had violated his trust, instead of the other way around.

Then she remembered the look in Gabe Rio's eyes—regret and anger in equal measure—and she knew she had to search.

"Sorry, Josh," she whispered to the room, to whatever of himself he had invested inside those walls.

His neatness made searching easy. Suspicion told her it came from a military or police background, but he'd said he had spent time in prison, and the Spartan arrangement of his things could easily be explained by time behind bars or even spent at sea. In the small closet, his jackets and shirts were hung. In the bureau, she found underwear and socks and T-shirts and several pairs of pants, along with an envelope with his passport and a sheaf of cash inside.

On a shelf above the bed were maybe a dozen books, westerns and mysteries, dog-eared paperbacks that looked as if they'd been read many times. No porn. No drugs. No gun. No badge. He had some cookbooks that he kept down in the galley, and she found two battered hardcovers under the bed.

And deeper, behind the boots and sneakers, a backpack.

"Damn it," she whispered.

On her knees, she reached underneath the rack and dragged the backpack out. It had been zipped up tightly and she blew out a breath before running the zipper open. When she looked inside, she frowned, trying to decipher what exactly she was looking at. A brightly colored towel. A plastic bag full of sunscreen and sunburn ointment, just in case the sunscreen didn't do the job. Two pair of sunglasses. A ratty sweatshirt. A pair of flip-flops.

Rocking backward, Tori laughed and shook her head. She very much wanted to kiss Josh at the moment. He'd put together a quick shore-leave kit, everything he'd need to go to the beach if they happened to get a day in port somewhere. The fact that he apparently burned easily only endeared him to her more.

Whatever Gabe had thought she would find, this wasn't it. Tori picked up the backpack, zipped it, ready to slide it back under the bed. But when she dropped it to the floor, it made a heavy thunk. She frowned at the sound, running the bag's inventory through her head, trying to figure out what could have made it.

Tori let herself deny the obvious for a few seconds longer,

and then ice trickled down her back, bringing a numb sort of dread that she wished wasn't so familiar.

Josh was a liar after all, and his lies were about to put her in a bad spot. She could feel it, even as she unzipped the backpack again and dumped its contents onto the floor. There were a couple of paperback books in there that she hadn't seen, stashed under the sweatshirt, but the last thing to tumble out was in a black nylon bag. It could've been a flashlight or an electric razor, but seemed too big to be either.

Tori loosened the string around the mouth of the bag, reached inside, and drew out a bulky black plastic thing that looked like a combination walkie-talkie and telephone receiver. She'd seen enough movies to know what a satellite phone looked like.

"Son of a bitch."

This time, she didn't whisper.

Whoever Josh really worked for, it sure as hell wasn't Viscaya Shipping. The ice inside her started to melt, replaced by a streak of fear that made her skin flush. Jesus, she couldn't go to prison. How much did Josh know? Was his name even Josh? Had the whole thing with her—the flirtation, the sex— been an act, or had he just fucked her because he could, knowing all along that when the voyage was over she would be in prison and he'd be moving on to another case?

Tori had been totally falling for him and now she wanted to scream, but there was nowhere to hide on board the *Antoinette*. Nowhere she wouldn't be found.

Her heart raced. Breathing through her nose, trying to fight the nausea rising in her, she stuffed his things back into the backpack and jammed it under the bed. Her hands fluttered as she stood, looking for something to do, as if fixing her hair or tucking in her shirt might somehow make her feel better.

It wasn't supposed to be like this, she thought. *This isn't how my story goes.*

Alena Boudreau loved the silence under water, the only sound around her the steady rhythm of her own pulse inside her head. She could think down here in the gloomy depths, and so she took her time exiting the Donika Cave, swimming languorously, her gear weightless in the water. The antidote to gravity, her own buoyancy tried to force her up, and reluctantly she began to rise, swimming toward the surface, thinking about the extraordinary things she had seen in that cave.

White, eyeless spiders without webs chased their prey with deadly speed. Leeches ate worms through mouths they were not supposed to have. Water scorpions darted in the murk, bearing poison deadly to the tiny blind toads with which they shared the stagnant pools, both so white that observers could see the blood running through them. The level of carbon dioxide in the cave reached ten times the norm, so the team inside the cave had to keep their O_2 tanks on while working.

Remarkable.

Alena had spent most of her life pursuing the remarkable, and had seen things that people with ordinary lives simply would not have believed. Yet the wonder of it all never completely vanished, and the amazing never became mundane. Radioactive crystal formations in Utah caverns and giant rats in Indonesia; ancient toxins trapped in Antarctic ice and warring species of poisonous frogs; lost worlds and cryptozoology; arcane artifacts and genetic anomalies. They were all her job, and had been for more than forty-five years.

Turning toward the rock face, she angled toward the surface and came up only a dozen feet from the metal platform that the joint EU bio-science team had bolted into place. Officially, the people in charge of unlocking and studying the secrets of the Donika Cave were part of an independent organization called Alliance Européenne pour l'Exploration Scientifique, but in reality they answered to the current president of the European Union. Upon her arrival in the nearby town of Rovinj, it had been obvious that the Croatians resented what they naturally considered interference by the EU, but with Croatia still awaiting approval to join the European Union, they had to play ball.

The resentment of the Croatian biologists and geologists worked significantly in Alena's favor. She was the lone American on the scene, there as an official observer and representative of the U.S. government, and the Alliance Européenne pour l'Exploration Scientifique hated her with a fiery passion. It was adorable, really, the snits they got in whenever she showed up at a dig or discovery. But since both the Croatian government and the leaders of the EU had issued an invitation—under pressure from the U.S. State Department—they really had no choice.

Alena didn't mind. She'd transcended any need to be loved decades ago. That wasn't to say she couldn't enjoy fondness and affection, but she never troubled herself searching for them.

Reaching up, she grabbed hold of the ladder and emerged from the Adriatic Sea, water sluicing off her skinsuit as she climbed to the platform. Half a dozen techs and assistants were camped there, monitoring transmissions from the cave. The team medic, an attractive Austrian man, watched Alena as she pulled off her goggles and slid them onto her arm. She pulled off her gloves, tucked them into the belt on her suit, then tugged back the headpiece and shook out her shoulder-length silver hair.

From the corner of her eye she caught the medic watching the show and it made her smile. She figured the guy for mid-forties, handsome and fit. Alena's daughter, Marie, had turned forty-seven in February—she herself had celebrated her seventieth birthday only a week ago—and the Austrian studied her with an appreciation that might embarrass him if he knew her age.

Alena pushed her fingers through her hair and shook it out

again, then bent to remove her flippers. She carried them, hooked on her fingers, over to the metal walkway that led to the top of the cliff. As she passed the medic, she tipped him a smile and a wink and he grinned happily, knowing he'd been caught.

"Fresh air and red wine. The secret of eternal youth," she said.

"I must drink more wine," he replied, his accent thick.

His eyes were alight with mischief—a come-on. Sex with older women had come into vogue in recent years—*thank you, Helen Mirren*—but still men often seemed astonished to learn her age. Even Alena herself was a bit astonished. *Seventy, my God.*

She considered flirting further, even suggesting some wine later on, but she had been traveling too much lately and knew she would not have the patience for a dalliance during this trip. It would be a brief visit. For all of their arrogance, the EU team was doing a perfectly competent job of cataloging the new species discovered in the cave. There were other things that interested her about the microcosmic ecosystem there that had nothing to do with bugs and worms.

As she walked up the metal stairs that made up the last dozen steps to the top, Alena didn't bother looking back to see if the Austrian might still be watching her. If she caught him studying her ass, she might be tempted to go back. A bottle of red wine would go well with dinner tonight.

Then she saw Martin Jungling hurrying toward her from the hastily arranged camp headquarters—a series of box trailers arranged in rows to provide lab space and sleeping quarters for the EU team and their Croatian counterparts.

"Ah, Dr. Boudreau. I feared you might never return," Jungling said, with a faux-pleasant smile. Tall and painfully thin, the Belgian had an aspect of the reaper about him, with sunken cheeks and humorless eyes.

"Feared, or hoped?" Alena asked, arching an eyebrow.

"You wound me," Jungling replied. He had perfected the face of diplomacy, the one that said, *I'm just being polite and I don't care if you know it.*

Alena smiled. "You'll be happy to know that I expect to

return to the States tomorrow. If you'll keep me apprised of any new developments, my superiors and I will be grateful, but otherwise I suspect I've got what I need to make my report."

Jungling's face twitched. "We'll be sorry to see you go."

They fell into step side by side, walking back toward the camp's central lab.

"It's quite a remarkable thing, isn't it?" he said.

"It is. Over the years I have been called in to examine or investigate dozens of claims of supposed 'lost world' discoveries, but this is among the most unique. Do you really think the five-million-year estimate is accurate?"

To her surprise, the question did not seem to offend him. Jungling must have been even happier at the prospect of her departure than she had expected.

"There is room for error, of course," Jungling admitted, "but if we're off a few hundred thousand years in either direction, what difference does it make? An ecosystem closed off from the rest of the world, evolving on its own over the course of millions of years. There's never been anything like it."

Alena cocked her head. "Surely that's not true. There must be others. Now that this one has been discovered, we must allow for the probability that there could be an untold number of such caverns that remain undetected in the planet's womb, each with its own unique properties."

Jungling nodded in contemplation. "Of course."

Silence followed for half a dozen steps as they both considered the implications. The walls of the cave were covered by gray-white mats of fungi, which in turn were home to a unique bacteria that processed water, carbon dioxide, and hydrogen sulfide to produce food for many of the cave's troglobite species. Granted, the venom of the water scorpion—a deadly poison that had cost two members of the initial Croatian exploratory team their lives—could be of interest to her employers, but Alena felt the cave's bacteria presented far more avenues for inquiry. Crossbred to exist elsewhere, what else might be engineered to survive on the sustenance provided by that bacteria?

She wondered if her employers would want the secrets of

the cave explored, or destroyed. Fortunately, the latter was not often a part of her job.

"I'm afraid we must part ways here," Jungling said, though he did not seem at all regretful. "I have a meeting."

"Of course," she said, holding out a hand. "Until next time."

One corner of Jungling's mouth rose in the ghost of a smile as he shook her hand, but he did not release his grip.

"Dr. Boudreau . . . Alena . . . who do you really work for?"

She squeezed his hand a little, gave it a shake. "Is your memory failing, Martin? The National Science Foundation—"

Jungling released her hand. "I have friends at the NSF. They've all heard of you, but none of them have ever met you."

"I'm not in the office much. Anyway, you've seen my credentials."

"American government credentials—"

"And the NSF is part of the government."

"Yes. It's just that I'm not sure it is the part you work for."

Alena gave a light shake of her head. "You're a strange man. *Au revoir*, Martin."

She strode away, following the path that would take her to the main lab. There were files she wanted copies of before she could return home. As she walked, she knew that Jungling watched her go, his attention entirely different from that of the Austrian medic. The Austrian had been intrigued by her, and the Belgian intimidated.

Alena could not decide which reaction pleased her more.

-21--

Angie stood on the embarkation deck, one hand on the curved arm of a small crane to keep herself from falling as she bent to look down into the water. The lifeboat rocked and bobbed on the waves. She watched the chief mate and the cook grab hold of the cables and get them hooked up, ready to haul the lifeboat back on board. In the moonlight, Dwyer's red hair looked like rust with hints of gold. While they'd been gone, Angie had had the unsettling realization that she had grown quite attached to Dwyer. It pissed her off.

"You bend over any farther, I'll consider it an invitation," Hank Boggs murmured, much too close to her ear. His breath felt warm.

"Back off before I chuck you overboard."

Boggs's chuffing laughter made her want to puke. There were four other guys on the embarkation deck—two assistant engineers and a pair of able-bodied seamen. They were more loyal to the Rio brothers than to the chief engineer, but one of the engineers, an eternal sidekick named Tupper, smirked knowingly every time Boggs made a piggish comment or tried brushing against her tits while they were working. They were cut from the same cloth, those two, except that Tupper didn't have the balls to make a move on her.

"Maybe we should just leave Dwyer down there, huh?" Boggs murmured, still in close. She caught a whiff of whiskey on his breath before the Caribbean breeze swirled it away. "Drag him behind the ship, a kiddie ride for your little boy."

Angie sighed, closing her eyes.

Boggs misinterpreted. "You know you're gonna give it up eventually."

It was the laugh that pushed her over the edge, a soft, suggestive chuckle, like they were already lovers. Like he *knew* her.

Angie turned, right hand already whipping up. She backhanded him across the face, knuckles slapping his flesh with a satisfying whack. Boggs jerked back, face screwing up in fury, bald pate flushing, but Angie wasn't done. She followed through, matching his step back with her own forward motion, and jabbed his throat with her outstretched fingers.

His eyes went wide and he staggered back.

"Hey!" Tupper shouted, starting for her.

Angie spun on him, pointed a finger. "Just try. Go on."

Tupper hesitated, glancing around at the other three guys but getting no support. The two deckhands weren't going to even pretend they were interested, and the other engineer—Valente—just gave Tupper a disgusted look.

"He had it coming," Angie said.

Boggs had both hands on his throat. His eyes were full of rage but he kept a wary distance. "You fucking bitch. I'll have you off this boat."

"Answer to my prayers," Angie said. "But we'll see who goes first."

Then the chief mate started shouting from below. They were all set to come aboard. Boggs gave her a last, dangerous glance, then gestured to Tupper and Valente, who checked the cables that ran down the side of the ship from the twin cranes. The lines clear, Valente toggled the control and the cranes started to whine as the cables were reeled in, lifting the lifeboat out of the water.

"Captain on deck!" one of the hands snapped.

Angie turned to see Captain Rio striding toward them out of the darker shadows of the accommodations block. They were at the rearmost lifeboat on the starboard side, but other members of the crew could easily have seen them working if they happened to be out on the metal walkways on the starboard side of the tower. This late at night, the only people still up and around were likely to be the men on watch, one of whom would be up in the wheelhouse, and the other of whom was one of the deckhands down here with them.

Not that it really mattered. Nobody on this tub really believed they had clean hands. They might not know what the special cargo would be, but nearly every journey included at least one unscheduled stop. Most of the crew knew better than to ask questions. If they didn't ask, they wouldn't have to get answers they really didn't want to hear.

"How's it coming, Chief?" the captain asked.

Angie caught something in his tone, an edge that she didn't like. Anger simmered there, and though his brown eyes were kind, she understood that if pushed, the captain might turn out to be a dangerous man.

"All's well, Captain."

Gabe gave Boggs a curious look. "Just the three of them?"

"Yes, sir."

The captain nodded, then stood by quietly as the cranes whined and the cables retracted and the lifeboat rose. As the deckhands stepped forward to help guide the lifeboat onto the deck by hand, Captain Rio took up a position just beside Boggs, nearly out of Angie's earshot.

He spoke softly, so that she barely heard.

"Angie's liable to hurt you pretty badly if you keep pushing her, Hank," the captain said, dark eyes stormy. "And I wouldn't blame her."

Boggs turned angrily toward the captain as though he might argue, but then he remembered his place, took a deep breath, and only glowered like a petulant child. When the captain looked over at Angie, his expression remained grim, but he nodded once, to let her know he understood, and the conflict was over. For now.

Tupper helped Miguel out of the lifeboat, the chief mate slinging a heavy canvas bag over one shoulder. Angie didn't have to guess what was in that bag. She'd seen it before, and seen what came out of it. Guns.

Josh, the cook, stumbled out of the lifeboat on his own, glancing around as though expecting someone to be there to greet him. Angie stepped up to give Dwyer a hand. He smiled at her, let his fingers caress her wrist and arm, but didn't kiss her or take her into his arms. Out here on deck, they were part of the *Antoinette*'s crew. What happened back in their quarters was another story. That was their time.

As the Rio brothers met on the deck, whispering to each other, backs to the others gathered there, motion from the accommodations block caught Angie's attention. She glanced up to see a flash of white, then Tori emerged from the shadows of the stairs. In the moonlight, the woman looked pale, her dark hair pulled back in a ponytail. Her sweatshirt hid the curves of her body.

Angie studied her as she approached, assuming Tori had come down to meet Josh, but then she noticed the chill Tori gave off, and saw that she was purposely ignoring the cook. It seemed weird, given the intimacy Angie had witnessed between them earlier.

Tori went straight to Captain Rio and pulled him aside.

Gabe bent to let her whisper to him, nodding. He gripped Tori's upper arm in thanks or comfort, Angie couldn't decide which, and the two of them gazed at each other for a moment.

What the hell? Angie thought. *Is she making a play for him?*

Gabe lowered his head, shoulders bunched, and sighed. Angie had spent enough time with the Rio brothers to recognize the danger of that pose, that sigh. It was a moment of hesitation the brothers shared, a moment while they tried to muster their calm, to contain their anger.

"Captain?" Dwyer asked worriedly. This might be his first journey aboard the *Antoinette,* but he knew that pose as well.

Miguel looked alarmed. The other crewmen had stepped back, waiting for orders. Josh glanced around, vaguely mystified.

Gabe Rio moved with a swift assurance that belied his size. In three strides he crossed the space that separated him from Josh, gathering up the front of the cook's shirt, his right fist driving forward. Josh tried to twist away, to fall back from the blow, but the captain had an iron grip.

The first blow took Josh in the temple, staggering him. The second hammered his nose, blood squirting from both nostrils.

"Holy shit," someone said. Angie wasn't sure who.

The third time Gabe's fist swung, he hit Josh so hard he couldn't keep his grip on the cook's shirt, and finally Josh fell backward, sprawling onto the deck, arms and legs splayed. He managed to get himself up on his elbows, but couldn't rise any farther.

"Mr. Boggs, take this man to the rec room on level three, lock him in, and set a watch on both doors," Captain Rio said.

"Yes, sir," Boggs replied.

"The rest of you return to your duty or your quarters," Gabe continued, before turning to his brother and Dwyer. "We need to talk."

Angie watched all of this with astonishment, mouth slightly open. While the captain had been beating the shit out of Josh, Tori had stood by and watched, eyes dark with grim acceptance, perhaps even approval.

Now, as Angie walked away, she glanced over her shoulder. The captain had dismissed everyone except for Dwyer and Miguel, but Tori hadn't left. She stood with the three men, talking low, hands gesturing. She looked worried. If it had just been her, Angie wouldn't have been troubled, but all four of them wore anxious expressions.

If the Rio brothers were worried, Angie figured they were all pretty much screwed.

-22--

Tori had her arms crossed, tight to her body, afraid if she let go she might fall apart. Skin flushed, heart racing, she felt wired in a way she had only ever experienced once before—down in the bowels of Penn Station, picking herself up off the ground after the train exploded. Gooseflesh rose on her arms, not from the night wind, but from the anticipation of the unknown.

Staring at the three men on the deck with her—the tempestuous Rio brothers and the eager Tom Dwyer—she saw something she did not expect. Their eyes were just as wide as hers, their faces equally haunted.

"Why aren't any of you talking?" she asked. "What are you going to do?"

The wind took the words, but not before she realized what she'd said. Not *what are* we *going to do,* but what were *they* going to do. For better or worse, she'd always relied on the judgment of men, and now she was doing it again. Joining the crew of the *Antoinette* had been the first major step she'd made in her entire life that had been of her own devising, and now it appeared to have been a mistake. Just as falling for Josh had been.

Miguel's dark eyes flashed with anger. So damn handsome. Usually the air of danger that came off him was alluring, but tonight he only seemed lost, even childish.

"We're thinking," he said.

Gabe ignored them all. The dynamic between the Rio brothers sometimes seemed more like father and son, with Miguel the more impetuous and Gabe carrying the grim wisdom of command. The effect had never been more pronounced than at that moment.

"Captain?" Dwyer ventured. The trust he placed in the Rio brothers shone in his eyes. He was worried, but he would follow whatever course they set for him without question.

Once that would've been me, Tori thought. *Blindly following.* She had always given her faith too easily.

Gabe turned to Tori. He'd been mulling things over, but obviously he'd heard her question. She had no idea which way he'd go with this. Gabe Rio wasn't a criminal by nature. He'd gotten on the wrong side of the law solely because he had wanted to look out for his brother. But he had to have known that tying his fate to Miguel's could lead to ugly places.

The ship swayed beneath them, and the silence of the sea engulfed them. Though Gabe's eyes were full of determination, to Tori he looked trapped, and she realized that was exactly how she felt. How they could be trapped in the middle of the sea, a hundred miles from anywhere, was hard to imagine. But it was the truth, nevertheless.

"We're going to get the guns back," Gabe said.

Miguel stuffed his hands in his pockets, looking like a sullen teenager. "What about the FBI?"

Tori froze. "You think Josh is FBI?"

"Gotta be," Gabe replied, looking around surreptitiously. They all gathered close to hear him. "Nobody else is gonna come out this far. Ocean interdiction . . . if it's guns or drugs . . . that's got to be FBI."

"We'll find out soon enough, I guess," Miguel said.

Tori didn't like the way the men looked at one another then. She had already figured out what the next step with Josh would be, but hearing the weight in Miguel's words, the truth of it struck home. Only hours ago, she'd made love to the man who had betrayed them all, who was their prisoner.

FBI. Shit.

Two instincts were at war within her—one terrified to go to

prison and the other unwilling to stand by while they beat Josh, or even killed him. He had deceived her, but that had been his job. And now that she had pondered it a while, she couldn't believe that the passion in his eyes, the urgency, had been a charade. She played the last few weeks over in her head and understood now why he had waited so long to make a move on her, no matter how obvious she allowed her attraction to him to become. He had wanted to avoid the complication, but the sexual tension had become too much for both of them.

Damn it.

If she let this happen—if she let them kill him—she wouldn't be able to live with herself.

"I'm coming with you," she said. "I want to be there."

Dwyer scoffed, but averted his eyes when she glared at him. The Rio brothers shared a wary glance before Gabe shook his head.

"Not gonna happen, Tori. You're here to be the eyes and ears of Viscaya Shipping, and there are some things our employers don't need to know. Some things they don't want to know. It's how they protect themselves."

"Gabe—"

The captain shook his head. "No. Your part in this is done." He turned to his brother. "Miguel, you and Dwyer get up to the wheelhouse. Set a course for that island, and pick a landing party. I want those guns."

The two mates started immediately for the stairs. In the moonlight, Gabe turned back to Tori.

"We'll go ashore at first light. If you want to come along for that, you're welcome. But for now, go to bed. It's better you sleep through this."

He hesitated, but when she didn't respond to his dismissal, Gabe turned his back on her and followed Miguel and Dwyer. Tori watched him go and then looked out to the sea again. Moonlight glinted white off the black tips of the waves.

Sleep. How could she possibly sleep with the memory of Josh's kiss still on her lips?

-23--

FBI Special Agent Joshua Hart sat in a chair in the level-three rec room, waiting for the captain to arrive and wishing for an ice pack for his face. Gabe Rio had only hit him three or four times, but the man could throw a punch. The left side of Josh's face throbbed, and if he made any kind of expression at all, it ached like hell. His nose had to be broken, but right now it just felt swollen. Adrenaline wasn't helping. His heartbeat sped along, pumping blood, making the throbbing in his cheek and mouth that much worse.

"Fuck," he whispered to himself. He used his tongue to probe his teeth, making sure they were all intact. He didn't find any loose or broken, so he had that going for him.

The thought made him laugh, softly, and that sent a fresh shot of pain through his face.

Then he thought of Tori, and the pain worsened. What must she be thinking now? The moment they had met, he had felt the powerful connection between them, and the more he learned about her, the more he admired her. Secretive as she was, still he had gleaned some bits of an ugly past. But Tori had put that past behind her, whittling away the bits of her that had allowed her to be a victim until all that was left was the strength at her core.

From the outset, there had been a sexual frisson between them. Josh had reminded himself a thousand times what the rules were, and what Voss would say. He had flirted and joked but kept a wall between himself and Tori, until at last he had stopped caring about the rules and the vast amounts of shit he'd end up taking from his partner.

But he'd also stopped thinking about what it would mean for Tori, and that made him feel like an utter prick. If there was anything he could do to make it up to her, he would.

First, though, he had to make sure the Rio brothers didn't kill his ass and throw him overboard.

At least the chair was comfortable. He'd been sitting in it ever since Boggs had hustled him into the room with a slap on the back of the head and a promise to return with the captain. Josh wasn't looking forward to that. Boggs had already hated him, even before tonight, just for the connection he had made with Tori. Not that the gorilla had any particular interest in her—his focus was Angie Tyree—but Boggs was that kind of guy. Suspicious of men who didn't treat women like shit, jealous and hateful toward men around whom women were comfortable.

The guy had kinks galore. He'd been itching to hand out a beating to someone ever since the day they set sail. Now he would get the chance.

Tupper and Valente had accompanied Boggs and Josh up to the rec room, and they were probably the ones guarding the doors right now. Josh knew he ought to have at least made an attempt at escaping, but really, there would be no point. Hand to hand, he could probably have taken the loutish Tupper, and Valente seemed a decent enough guy that he'd probably hesitate, giving Josh an opportunity to take him down, too. But Boggs would be out there, and though the room had two doors, there would be no telling which exit Boggs might be covering. And even if he picked the right one, managed to get past one man, the captain would be along shortly, and no one on the crew would let Josh pass. Not even Tori.

No. Better to wait for a time when they weren't paying so much attention. Let them ruminate a bit, realize that they were out at sea and he had nowhere to run, no way to escape. When they let their guard down, he could get a signal out.

He just had to hold on. Keep calm. Stay in control.

And get some ice for his face.

Glancing around, he saw the soda machine on the wall beyond the Ping-Pong table and got up, hoping that someone had bothered to refill the machine. The machine had been bypassed so it didn't cost anything to get a soda out of it, and they kept it stocked from the *Antoinette*'s supplies. Already anticipating the feeling of an icy Coke can held against his swollen face, he made his way around the Ping-Pong table.

That's where he was standing when the starboard side door swung open and the captain stepped in, with Hank Boggs lumbering behind him.

Gabe Rio froze, staring at him.

"What the fuck you think you're doing?" Boggs asked.

Josh didn't bother to shrug. "Getting a Coke." He tapped the button, the mechanism inside groaned, and the familiar red can clanked down into the machine's dispensary tray.

As he picked up the Coke, Boggs stormed across the room and slapped it out of his hand. Josh gritted his teeth, desperately wanting to throw a punch, crush his larynx, but reminded himself he had nowhere to go. He had to bide his time.

Still, it was hard to remember that when Boggs grabbed the back of his neck and propelled him across the room, then practically slammed him back into the chair.

"You wanted a Coke, huh?" Boggs asked. "You're a fucking comedian."

Now Josh did shrug. "I like Coke."

Boggs reached down and grabbed him by the neck, starting to choke him. All Josh could see was the big man's sweat and grease-stained shirt and his greasy face and his flaring nostrils. Then he heard the captain's voice.

"Chief. Back off. That's not what we want."

The chief engineer's eyes filled with deep, almost childlike regret, but he let go of Josh's throat and took a step back. Then another. He retreated to the door and stood there, arms crossed, his stare making silent promises of pain yet to come.

Gabe strode over to the Coke machine, tapped the button, and brought Josh a fresh can. Maybe the guy was actually trying to behave rationally, but Josh thought these two were just a natural good cop/bad cop team. He and his partner, Rachael Voss, had played the game a thousand times. With Boggs and Gabe, though, it wasn't a game; it was who they were.

"Who are you?" the captain asked.

Josh opened the Coke, took a sip, happy to have it. He held the can up to his swollen face, not worried about letting them see his pain. Pretending to be a tough guy wouldn't get him anywhere, and the cold metal soothed him.

"FBI."

Gabe took a deep breath, then nodded. He seemed troubled, and Josh knew he wasn't the only source of the captain's problems.

"I figured as much," Gabe said.

"Can I ask you a question, Captain?"

"Go ahead."

"How did you know?"

"You said you had a reference from Jorge Guarino," the captain said. "That you served time with him, shared a cell. I guess that worked when you applied for the job with Viscaya, but the higher-ups don't pay much attention to who hires on in the lower ranks. Apparently they didn't know Jorge didn't speak a damn word of English."

Josh took a breath as that sank in. "I'm guessing Jorge spoke Portuguese?"

Gabe Rio nodded. The picture became clear. Miguel had suspected something, and had tried speaking Portuguese to him while they were out checking on the *Mariposa*. When Josh didn't understand, he knew the Jorge Guarino connection had been a deception.

"You done with your questions now?" Gabe asked.

"I do have one more."

"Get it over with."

At the door, Hank Boggs curled his lip and rolled his eyes. If Gabe Rio had seen him make that face, Josh had a feeling Boggs would've regretted it.

"It's just that I've been thinking," Josh went on, holding the cold Coke can against his face again, trying to numb the swollen flesh. "Whoever hit the *Mariposa*—"

"Devils, according to the man you found on the boat."

Josh stared at the captain. "You don't believe that."

Gabe sat down in the chair across from him, settled in, comfortably in command of the room and the situation. "No. I don't."

"So someone stormed that boat in force, killed the crew. But if they had time to stash the guns on that island, they knew they were being followed, knew an attack was coming. Why give them that kind of advance warning? Nothing about this makes sense."

Gabe's eyes were dark, blank. "Was there a question in there?"

"Just wondering if you have any idea who else is out here after those guns."

"You really think I'm going to have that conversation with you?" the captain replied. It didn't matter. Josh could see the answer in the way he narrowed his eyes, in the set of his shoulders. And it had been clear, out on the *Mariposa* with Miguel and Dwyer, that none of them had a clue what was going on.

"Guess not," Josh said, taking a sip of his Coke. The metal wasn't as cool now, but it hadn't done much to numb his face anyway. "So what now? You think they're still there? 'Cause I'm figuring whoever killed your friends on that fishing boat is probably long gone with the guns by now."

Gabe leaned forward, hands clasped between his knees. "Let's talk about you, Agent . . . ?"

"Just Josh is fine."

The captain nodded, smiling bitterly. "Right. Undercover. How could I forget? So, Josh, you've got people waiting, boats, but so far they're not on our radar. I'll keep looking, and I'm sure they'll float into view sooner or later. What I'm wondering is which it will be. What's the status of your backup?"

"On their way," Josh said, keeping his eyes hard, trying to match the cold, cruel gaze of Gabriel Rio.

"Bullshit. They wouldn't move until they were sure we had the guns. Until you called them on your satellite phone to tell them. You haven't done that yet because we don't have the guns. And from what I know, leaving an agent out here alone isn't the way you people operate, so I'm guessing you've got something other than the sat-phone for them to track us by. Some kind of homing signal. So where is it?"

"You give the FBI too much credit," Josh said.

Gabe smiled. "I don't think so."

The captain stood, turned to Boggs, and bowed his head, gesturing toward Josh with a courtly flourish of his hand.

"Chief Boggs, you may proceed."

Josh shot out of the chair, charging at the chief engineer. He whipped the Coke can at Boggs's face, brown liquid arcing across the room, splashing the man's T-shirt as he raised his hands to defend himself. Gabe cursed in Spanish, something about his mother, but Josh's focus wasn't on the captain. Boggs was the one standing between him and the door.

The engineer darted his head to one side and the Coke can sailed past his face, grazing his ear. And then, finally, Boggs started switching from defense to offense. He shifted his body, pivoted his hips, and got ready to swing a fist. But Josh had bought himself the moment he needed. He lowered his head and drove a shoulder into Boggs's chest, pistoning his legs, putting all of his weight behind the hit. Boggs slammed against the door with a grunt and a loud thump that had to be his skull bouncing off metal.

As Boggs tried to get a grip on his head or throat, Josh drove one knee up, crushing his balls. The little scream that came out of Boggs's mouth gave him no pleasure; it was just the mark of a job well done. He kept his shoulder down, kept his face buried, hidden from Boggs's hands as the engineer tried to grasp him, then attempted to shove him away. He ought to have been pummeling Josh by now, but Boggs's entire body needed time to reset after the knee between his legs. Josh had counted on that.

Boggs tried pushing away from the door, wanting to get Josh away from him, to give himself space to fight. Josh dug in, drove himself forward again, and this time when Boggs hit the door, Josh started throwing punches to his gut, rapid-fire, half a dozen blows to the solar plexus.

Unable to breathe, the big man went down. Josh moved aside to let him fall, heard Boggs starting to retch, knew the smell of vomit would follow in a moment, and reached out to grab the door handle.

Seven seconds, maybe eight. Too long.

Metal glinted in his peripheral vision. Josh barely registered it before he felt the gun barrel strike his skull. He staggered sideways into the wall, knocking down an old framed movie poster: Martin Scorsese's *Taxi Driver*. His vision blurred and he felt all the strength go out of him as he slid to the floor. He tasted blood on his lips a second before feeling the warmth of it trickling down his face from where Gabe had hit him with the gun.

Josh blinked, his vision clearing.

Gabe Rio had a world-weary wisdom and a relaxed air that made him an easy man to work for, and to respect—or would have, if he hadn't been a smuggler of guns and drugs. Tonight all of that amiable nature had been stripped away.

The captain aimed the pistol from five feet away, smart enough to know that a pistol was a ranged weapon, that if he got too close it could be used against him. The dark hole in the barrel seemed to wink at Josh, as though imminent death were some kind of joke.

On the floor by the door, Hank Boggs moaned, wiped the back of his hand across his mouth. The puddle of vomit in front of him had already begun to reek. His eyes were closed and he breathed through his clenched teeth.

"That was stupid," Gabe said.

Josh leaned his head against the wall, still disoriented, and wondered how badly he was bleeding. "I had two choices. Try to avoid a beating, or just sit and take it. I've never been good with sitting and taking it."

Gabe sighed, raised the barrel of the gun a few inches, steadied his aim. "You ever study the Spanish Inquisition?"

Frowning painfully at the weird segue, Josh gave a small shrug. "Not in depth."

"The Inquisitors would get it into their heads that someone was a witch and they would torture them for a confession. If they confessed, they were executed as witches. Only if they died without confessing did the Inquisitors believe they were not witches, and by then it didn't matter anymore."

With the knock to the head he'd just gotten, the pain in his face, and the blood dribbling down his cheek, Josh didn't feel like being a smart-ass anymore. Still, he almost thanked the captain for the history lesson. He wanted to pretend he didn't know where Gabe was headed with this line of thought, but that would have been a lie.

"You're going to tell us where the beacon is," the captain

went on. "You don't want to tell us, we hurt you. If you keep pretending there isn't some kind of tracking device on board my ship, we hurt you. Deny it exists, and the only way I'm going to believe you is if you die without telling me where it is. By which point, you being here won't be an issue anymore."

The gun barrel did not waver. Nor did Gabe Rio's furious gaze. Josh had some doubts that the man would actually kill an FBI agent aboard his ship, knowing that capture might be imminent. But he didn't want to test those doubts.

Boggs started to climb wretchedly to his feet. His chest rose and fell as he continued to catch his breath, and he focused watery, raging eyes on Josh.

Gabe Rio might not kill him, but Hank Boggs would do it just for fun. Death ranked number one on his list of Things to Avoid, followed closely by torture.

Josh opened his hands in surrender. "It's attached to the back of the stove down in the galley."

Gabe didn't smile. "Was that so hard?"

A dozen retorts crossed Josh's mind and he rejected them all. His mouth had gotten him in trouble in the past, but those lessons had been valuable. He might piss people off with a sharp tongue, but he wasn't about to taunt the man with the gun in his hand.

"You don't want to mess with it, though," Josh said. "If you try to shut it down or detach it from the back of the stove, you'll automatically send a distress signal, and the cavalry will come running."

"Bullshit," Boggs sniffed.

But the captain didn't look so sure. "You're lying."

Josh shrugged. "Better for me if you don't believe me."

"Captain," Boggs began.

Gabe turned to the chief and nodded. "I want to check it out. Make sure he's telling the truth. If you want to have a little payback while I'm gone, I wouldn't blame you. But try not to break him, Hank. I may need him later."

Boggs didn't even look up at the captain. Instead he stared at Josh with bloodshot eyes and nodded slowly.

"Yes, sir. He can bleed, though?"

"Oh, hell yeah. Make him bleed."

The captain slid the pistol into the rear waistband of his pants and went out the door. Someone moved outside, one of the men guarding the room. Then the door closed, and the pain began.

It couldn't have been called an interrogation. Boggs never asked any questions.

-24--

Rachael Voss had been against her partner going under-cover on a Viscaya ship from the outset. The case had been simmering for a long time and it killed her to think Turcotte would move in with his Counter-Terrorism group and snatch the thing out of her squad's hands, but she'd warned Josh again and again that it was too dangerous.

In private. They'd whispered a lot before and after meetings and spent a lot of time alone together—so much that Chauncey had gotten up the guts to ask if they were sleeping together. Against the rules and all that. Voss shouldn't have been sur-prised. She was single and Josh's marriage had fallen apart the way so many agents' relationships did. If they had ended up in bed together, no one would have blamed them. No one but Chauncey, who was such a stickler for the rules.

But as close as Voss had gotten to Josh Hart in the time they'd been partners, and as much as they sometimes bick-ered, their intimacy had never extended to the bedroom. Still, Josh meant more to her than any of her boyfriends ever had.

The drug lord's impounded yacht couldn't go fast enough to suit her.

Voss couldn't stay below, but she didn't want to be in the wheelhouse, either. She'd been out on the foredeck for a while, but even with her sweatshirt on, the wind had snaked chill fingers down her spine, and she'd grown frustrated with staring out across the dark water in search of some sign of the

Antoinette. The weight of expectation she felt was irrational; they were still a long way from the point of origin of Josh's satellite phone call, and even when they reached those coordinates, the *Antoinette* wouldn't be there, unless it was just sitting around in the water waiting for them to arrive.

No. They were waiting for the beacon.

And Voss hated to wait.

Now she sat on the aft deck in a white simulated-leather bucket chair that was one of a quartet attached directly to the deck. They were meant for fishing, complete with belts to strap herself down in case she got a bite from a swordfish or whatever. Voss didn't fish, and she doubted Rojas, the drug lord who'd owned this boat before the FBI took it away from him, had done much fishing, either. The chairs were glorified bar stools. Voss obliged by drinking a piña colada that Pavarotti had whipped up in the tiny galley, albeit without the rum. She felt fourteen again, but deprived of sleep and wired with adrenaline. Neither alcohol nor coffee would help her do her job tonight.

The cold drink made her shiver even more than the wind off the sea, but the flavors of pineapple and coconut were wonderful, and kept her body distracted. Though too tense to eat, she could manage the piña colada just fine.

"You should get some sleep."

Voss jumped a little, then turned to see Pavarotti standing beside her. With the wind blowing, she hadn't heard him approach, and now she was embarrassed. She forced herself not to let it show.

"You're stealthy for such a big bastard."

Pavarotti smiled to let her know he didn't mind the teasing. Voss made sure her expression told him she didn't care if he minded or not.

"Seriously. I know you're worried about Josh—"

"Special Agent Hart," she corrected.

Pavarotti actually laughed. "He'd choke on his coffee if I called him that, and you know it. I get it, you hate being called Rachael. This is your squad, Agent Voss, and that's fine by me. But Josh isn't going to drink with anyone who calls him Special Agent Hart."

Voss wanted to argue, but she forced herself to exhale. Uncoil.

"You're right. I'm a little tightly wound right now."

"I don't blame you. But none of us is going to be any good when this goes down if we don't get at least a little sleep, and that includes you. The doctor prescribes rest."

"How am I supposed to rest down there with all of you guys playing cards and watching movies?" Voss asked.

Pavarotti put a hand on the back of her chair. "Nadeau and Mac are in the wheelhouse, keeping us on course and waiting for the signal, dealing with incoming communications. I'm on watch. Everyone else is asleep. It's nearly three a.m."

Shit, Voss thought. She hadn't realized she had been out here so long.

"Incoming communications?" she asked.

The agent glanced toward the wheelhouse. "Nothing except what we expect. Immigration and Customs has a couple of boats in the water, and we've got three Coast Guard ships on course to rendezvous with us at those same coordinates. We'll be there just after sunrise, but they're a few hours behind us. And then we wait."

"I'm so sick of waiting."

"Me, too," Pavarotti said. "We're sure this beacon is gonna work, right? We can track it wherever they go?"

Voss had been over that very subject dozens of times with Chauncey and with Josh. The satellite phone would only be good if Josh could call them on it, and keep up the call. They had needed something that could act as a continuous tracking signal. The FBI's own tech guys had shrugged off the query, claiming they didn't have anything that could be easily hidden on the *Antoinette,* somewhere Josh would be able to get to it. What they offered was a tracking device the size of a land mine.

Then Voss had talked to a friend who worked as an outfitter in Alaska and spent most of his time in isolated, inhospitable areas with no cell phone signal, and he'd told her about the personal locator beacon, which operated like a reverse-GPS, sending an emergency signal that could be picked up and followed, whether in the outback or on the ocean. The idea that the FBI's techs would be ignorant about the existence of PLBs made her nuts. The things were available to the general public, but the FBI didn't know about them? It made her wonder what else they didn't know about that might save her life someday.

"It'll work," she told Pavarotti.

She didn't see any reason to go into the one thing that really scared her about the PLB. Once Josh turned it on, there was the distinct possibility that the signal would interfere with the *Antoinette*'s instruments, which could lead them to seek out the competing signal on board.

Once the beacon went off, they'd be in a race to reach the container ship before the Rio brothers figured out they had an agent on board. If Josh's cover was blown, then even when the ICE and Coast Guard and FBI moved in, things were likely to get very ugly. Josh could end up a hostage, or dead.

Voss took a sip of her piña colada. "You go ahead," she said. "I'll take watch."

Pavarotti stood his ground. "Not going to happen. I've already had a few hours' rack time anyway. It's your turn. I'll wake you at dawn. You're not doing Josh any favors if you're—"

"All right," she said. "I get it. Will it shut you up if I go down and pretend to sleep?"

"For now."

Voss rolled her eyes. "Fine. It'll be worth it." She took her piña colada with her as she left.

Pavarotti smiled. "Night, Rachael."

She bristled. Chauncey had wanted to know if Voss and Josh Hart were sleeping together, and she'd taken some satisfaction in being able to say no. But he'd never asked her if she was screwing Pavarotti, and for that she was glad. She didn't like to lie.

For his part, Pavarotti apparently thought a single sex-filled, post-case victory celebration made him her lover, made it okay for him to use her given name. And it was okay . . . in bed. But on the job, things were different. Soon she would have to make absolutely certain she had disabused him of that notion. Six years earlier, her younger brother Ethan had developed cancer that spread rapidly through his body and killed him forty-seven days after its discovery. Since then, there was only one man in the world she cared for, and right now he was out in the middle of the Caribbean with people who might well kill him if they learned his identity.

Belowdecks, she lay down on a rack and closed her eyes, knowing she would never be able to sleep.

And yet, somehow, she did.

-25--

In the morning, Tori's quarters still smelled like the food Josh had cooked her. It wasn't just the food, though. The room still had the slightest trace of sex in the air.

She propped open her door and sat on her rack, drinking warm pomegranate juice and staring out at the lightening sky. Dawn came early in the islands, but she thought there must be at least an hour before sunrise. She needed it desperately. Not just daylight, but strong coffee and the heat of a Caribbean morning. Her eyes burned, her thoughts were soft and muddy, and her bones ached, but she knew the sunshine would help.

She tried not to think about Josh, both because she didn't want to worry about him, and because she despised the resentment that surged up inside her when she did. Tori hated the position he had put her in, hated him for making love to her, and for how wonderful he had made her feel. Awful dreams had chased her down into sleep for the scant hours she had spent with her head on the pillow, and now whenever she closed her eyes she imagined him in a bloody heap, neck twisted at an impossible angle, or floating bloated and blue-skinned on the waves. She wanted to scream at him, but she hoped Gabe and Boggs hadn't killed him, either.

Remnants of her dreams lingered. She'd woken with

clenched fists and the feeling that she had to fight off hands that were reaching for her, trying to restrain her. Self-analysis had never been her favorite pastime, but she didn't need a psych degree to recognize the origins of those feelings. The FBI was lurking somewhere close, just beyond their perceptions, and they didn't even have their vital cargo. If they returned to Miami without the guns, they might all lose their jobs—though the job wasn't really what troubled her. She might have just sailed home, but Gabe Rio wasn't about to do that, which meant that though they were out on the open sea, they were trapped by circumstance. Tori could feel her muscles constrict at the thought.

They needed to be swift, and lucky.

Tori reached up to rub her itchy eyes, and when she lowered her hand, Dwyer was standing in her open doorway, silhouetted in the pre-dawn light, his red hair limned with a golden glow.

Startled, she spilled her pomegranate juice.

"Shit," she whispered, setting her glass on the floor. "What's going on?"

Though shadow covered his face, Tori could make out a strange expression on Dwyer's face. The young guy—she was trying to stop thinking of him as a kid—looked confused and a little antsy. She'd known addicts in her life, and they always seemed lost and desperate when they were craving. Dwyer had a bit of that in him now, though she had a feeling drugs weren't responsible.

"Captain wants you up top," he said. He glanced back out the door, looking at something out on the water, in the distance. "We're here."

Tori slipped on a pair of rubber-soled deck shoes, then grabbed a face cloth from a shelf in the corner of the room and wiped the juice off the back of her hand.

"Why do you look so worried?"

Dwyer's soft, dark laugh took her by surprise.

"Aside from the total clusterfuck this thing is turning out to be, y'mean?"

"Yeah. Aside from that."

Instead of answering he stepped backward, out onto the deck, and once more glanced out over the water, toward something she couldn't see. "Come and have a look. See if you don't wanna click your heels and wake up home in bed."

With his face now washed in the glimmer of imminent morning, Dwyer seemed almost an apparition. The dark water behind him had a kind of haze upon it, a strange condition of the light, like the gauzy texture of the world right before a twilight summer storm.

Tori didn't want to go out there. Her mind started to manufacture reasons—she needed to change, needed to shower, needed to pee—but except for putting on clean clothes, she'd have to leave her quarters for any of those things.

"Come on," Dwyer urged. "The captain's waiting."

She nodded, feeling foolish. Snatching a thin white hooded sweater, she slipped it on. "No sign of the FBI?" she asked as she zipped it.

"Not yet."

Tori stepped up to the threshold, stared into Dwyer's blue eyes. "Show me."

He only pointed to a spot off the starboard bow, like the silent ghost of Christmas yet to come. Frustrated and dragging from lack of sleep, Tori stepped out onto the walkway, two levels up from the deck, and peered through the slowly dispersing darkness at a tiny island perhaps three-quarters of a mile away. Yet it wasn't the island that made her blink and catch her breath.

"What the hell?" she whispered, forgetting Dwyer entirely.

She started along the walkway, picking up speed, hurrying toward the stairs. As she turned to start up, she saw Dwyer behind her. At the same moment, she realized that the *Antoinette* felt quiet and still, save for the gentle roll of the sea.

"We've stopped. The engines are idle."

Dwyer tore his focus from the horizon. "You're just noticing?"

Tori hurried up the stairs, hands sliding on the railings. "You must've seen this on the radar a while ago."

"The island, yeah. The rest we just figured for rock formations or something," Dwyer explained, following.

On the third level of the accommodations block she paused on the landing for another look. This high off the water, there could be no mistaking the extent of what she saw. Still, she kept climbing, both because Captain Rio had sent Dwyer to fetch her and because she wanted to see it from up top, to make sense of it in her head. At night the view would have been eerie, and even now, as the horizon began to burn brightly with the impending dawn, it made her want to cross herself and keep sailing right on past, the way she'd always done as a little girl when her parents would drive past a cemetery with her in the backseat.

Only when she reached the metal landing just outside the wheelhouse did Tori stop, and peer, and try to understand. With a bright flash, the sun came over the eastern horizon and the shadows swiftly retreated toward the west. In the warm light of day, there could be no mistake.

The island couldn't have been more than a mile and a half long. The trees were tall and thin near the shore, but thicker toward the hilly inland. The shores were soft sand, except where dark rock jutted out from the land in jagged formations. And in the shallows all around the island were sunken ships.

The prow of a fishing boat thrust from the gentle waves beside the mast of some rich man's pride and joy. A rusting freighter, a quarter the size of the *Antoinette,* loomed out of the water like a man-made breakwater. A schooner at least forty or fifty years old lay on its side, one of its two masts snapped off and the other bleached white in the sun, tattered sail drooping, thin and torn as cheesecloth.

And there were others. More fishing boats. Several sleek white cabin cruisers and larger yachts that looked like they ought to have been moored in the marina of some tourist mecca. As the morning sun spread farther, Tori could make out smaller boats washed up on the shore, or jutting half out of the surf—rowboats and little Boston Whalers that must have come off larger ships.

"It's a cemetery," Dwyer said.

Tori shivered, eyes scanning the island. A lot of the boats

were clustered in the center where there was a natural cove thanks to the jetties created by the formations of dark rock. But there were others all along the shore.

"I don't get it," Tori said. "What did this? Storms?"

Even as she said it, she knew it didn't make sense. The trade winds seemed gentle enough here, and the waves were low and lapped the sandy shores of the island. The rock formations jarred a bit with what she expected from this part of the world, which got her thinking about volcanoes and tectonic plates and weird theories about the Bermuda Triangle causing electromagnetic problems with ships' instruments.

"Hurricanes, you mean? I doubt it. The rich bastards who used to own those fancy boats wouldn't have just left them out here. They'd want 'em repaired, don't you think?"

"Maybe not. They've got insurance. This far from anything, they'd probably just radio for help and be happy they got off the island."

"I'm thinking currents, actually."

Dwyer stood one step below the landing, and she glanced down at him. "You mean they drifted here?"

The Irishman shrugged. "Could be. Engine trouble, derelict ships. Maybe the currents sort of converge here or something."

"Derelict ships?" Tori repeated, looking out across the gently swaying masts and wheelhouses and bows. "Then what sank them?"

"Fuck if I know. It's a mystery, isn't it?"

But Dwyer's voice had a little tremor when he said it and she turned to him, eyes narrowed. He didn't look at her, and Tori had a feeling he was purposely avoiding her gaze. The ship graveyard unnerved her, but it had gotten much further under Dwyer's skin.

"This has to do with the *Mariposa*. What aren't you telling me?"

Dwyer cocked his head. "They were attacked here. Put our cargo ashore."

Tori's eyes still burned and her head still felt stuffed with cotton. She blamed tiredness for not making these connections earlier. Trying to wake up, desperate for coffee, she took a fresh look at the island and realized that, in among the trees and the brush and the thicker vegetation of the small island's interior, there would be plenty of places for people to hide.

"So you think there are people living on the island? Someone attacked them from there?"

"Dunno," Dwyer said, shrugging. "Could be pirates. Not Johnny bloody Depp, but the real sort, with guns and knives and a buyer waiting back in port. But radar isn't picking up any ships nearby. Could be people on the island—"

"Or they could be on the boats," Tori whispered.

Dwyer turned to look at her. "What?"

Tori nodded toward the half-sunken derelicts. "Add up all the space that's still above water on those boats . . . cabins and wheelhouses and stuff . . . and you could have dry shelter for dozens of people."

They stared at the ships together, and Tori felt like she was seeing the potential there for the first time. Many of them were so close together that a good jump would carry someone from one deck to the next. Some had been tied to others with rope or rotting sail. One large fishing trawler had been plowed right into the side of a little cargo ship, so that they were essentially the same structure.

The door into the wheelhouse opened. Tori turned to see Gabe Rio staring at her, grim and urgent.

"You coming in or what? We've got business to take care of."

"Sorry, Captain," Dwyer said, hustling up onto the landing.

"All right," Tori said, following Gabe into the wheelhouse with Dwyer right behind her. Miguel and Suarez were both on the bridge as well. "What's the story? Is the FBI coming?"

Gabe stared out through the windows at the island and its halo of dead ships. "Not yet."

Tori felt her skin prickle with the flush of heat. She knew what was coming, and she wished he wouldn't say it. But she had to ask.

"So, what's the next move?"

Gabe looked at her. "We're going ashore to find the guns. And you're coming with us."

Tori blinked at him. "Why's that, exactly?"

Miguel snickered. "I told you, Gabriel. She wanted in yesterday when we went over to the *Mariposa,* but now that there might be danger, the girl's all reluctant."

Captain Rio ignored him, gaze locked on Tori.

"I'm not going to make you come," he told her, "but a lot is riding on this. You said you were Viscaya's eyes and ears out here, right? If we can't find the guns, or this all goes to shit, I want someone to be able to tell them we did everything we could."

Tori glanced around at the men in the wheelhouse, took in the way they were looking at her, and she understood that this wasn't just about Gabe Rio. If Miguel lost this job and word got out about what had happened, he might never get another job. Yet the captain's concern extended further than Miguel for once. Staying out of prison would be cold comfort if they all ended up out of a job. If they brought Tori along, she might be the one person who could speak on their behalf, if it came to that.

"What happens to Josh while we're on the island?" she asked.

"Nothing yet," Gabe replied, his voice cold.

Tori nodded. "All right. Then what are we waiting for?"

-26--

Josh lay on his side on the floor of the rec room. If he'd had the strength, he would have climbed onto one of the two ugly sofas. Their cushions might be faded and stained, but at least they would be soft. On the other hand, the fabric felt like sandpaper on a normal day, and right now the cold floor felt good on his swollen, bloody cheek. Dirty boot prints didn't bother him. Pain had pushed him past such concerns.

He wished he still had the gun Miguel had let him carry during the night.

Fucking Miguel. Josh figured that once the chief mate had figured out something was amiss—that the new cook was something other than what he seemed—Miguel had been waiting for the moment he could take that gun back. And once he had, things had swiftly unraveled.

His right hand tensed, fingers instinctively clutching at the weapon he yearned for. If he'd had the gun, though, it wouldn't have been Miguel Rio who caught the first bullet— he'd marked that for Hank Boggs. That son of a bitch had a reckoning in his future, and Josh figured it was only a matter of time. Really, the only chance Gabe had of getting the *Antoinette* free of the noose that was drawing close around it would be to throw the whole goddamn galley stove overboard and leave immediately, before Voss and the rest of Josh's squad got restless and figured out that someone had spoiled their plans. Otherwise, Voss would run out of patience, real- ize something had gone wrong, and the FBI would move in.

The Rio brothers had twenty-four hours, give or take, and instead of using that time to slip quietly away, Gabe wanted to retrieve the guns, drag them back to Miami, and put them on Viscaya's doorstep like a cat bringing its master a dead bird. The captain was a stubborn son of a bitch, but that was all right with Josh. The more time they wasted trying to get those guns back, the better his odds of survival.

Josh had been emphatic about the squad not moving in until he set off the personal locator beacon he'd hidden be- hind the stove, but he knew his partner all too well. He'd called in on the sat-phone to tell them the *Antoinette* was about to rendezvous with the *Mariposa*. Already Voss would be wondering how come he hadn't called in again or set off the PLB. She'd be tempted to throw out the plan they'd made, and to ignore the cautions he'd given to wait for his signal. All Josh had to do was manage to stay alive until Voss ran out of patience.

The smell of his own blood filled his nostrils. He could feel a little pool of it growing tacky as it dried under his cheek. His jaw throbbed and his whole face felt swollen. His left eye had swollen up so much that he couldn't open it all the way. Gently, he ran his tongue over his teeth, probing to see if any were broken. One tooth on the lower left side of his mouth felt loose, but otherwise they were all intact.

He doubted the same could be said of his ribs. They probably weren't broken, but given the way his right side felt when he breathed, he thought several must be badly bruised. Boggs had started with his fists, but once Josh had slid to the floor, the chief engineer had started kicking. Now there were places all over his body that were numb, and far too many others he wished he could not feel.

As far as he was aware, Josh had been on the floor for about an hour, perhaps more. But he couldn't deny the possibility that he had lain there longer, unconscious. His head still swam a little, and he figured he had a mild concussion.

"Get up," he whispered to himself. His lips felt numb and the words were little more than a mumble.

If Boggs comes back, he might kill you.

The thought raced through him like a jolt of adrenaline. Captain Rio didn't seem inclined to kill him yet, but Josh knew that could change without warning. If he wanted to live, he ought to find some way to defend himself. If he could fashion some kind of weapon, even a club adapted from the leg of the Ping-Pong table, then all the better. Boggs had it coming, one way or another.

Josh had given his loyalty to the FBI. Maybe not his heart and soul, but at the very least his mind and body. He knew the law, and throwing the big bald engineer over the side or shivving him in the throat with some makeshift blade snapped off a piece of rec room furniture would be frowned upon by the U.S. government. Josh wouldn't be proud of it, either. That kind of justice didn't fit with how he viewed himself or his job.

But no one had ever beaten him for their own entertainment before, so his views were adjusting accordingly. When the shit hit the fan, if he couldn't arrange for Boggs to catch a bullet, he would be severely disappointed.

He took a thin breath, wary of his aching ribs, and lifted his head. The blood on his face had started to dry to the floor and it tugged painfully as he pulled his cheek away. Propping himself up with his left arm, right hand pressed to his bruised ribs, he managed to roll slowly and rise to his knees. His jaw still felt swollen and he blew a pained exhalation out through his teeth.

Then he paused, taking stock. No jutting bones. Nothing punctured internally as far as he could tell. Just pain, all over. Breathing through his nose now—the way he did when he felt nauseous and was trying to stave off the urge to vomit—he put a hand on the chair he'd been sitting in when Boggs had started to work him over. Shaky as a newborn colt, he rose and slid into the chair, settling back gingerly, closing his eyes as he let out another breath.

So much for looking for a weapon. If Boggs came back now, Josh would barely be able to lift a hand, never mind defend himself.

A few more minutes. Just take it easy. Don't rush. A few more minutes and he would get up from the chair, find something that he could hurt the chief engineer with.

He let his eyes close and started to drift. The adrenaline rush started to subside and all he wanted to do was crash—just sleep, and heal. But Josh couldn't afford to do that. Inhaling sharply, he opened his eyes and stared at the bright Caribbean light coming through the small windows on either side of the door. No telling when Boggs or the captain would return.

"Up," he whispered, wary now of how much the guards outside the two doors might hear. Valente and Tupper had been posted last night, one at either entrance, but he had no idea who might be out there now. Best to be quiet.

Pushing himself up from the chair, he sucked in a painful breath, then crossed his arms in front of his chest. He hesitated, steadying his breathing, then forced his eyes open wider, steeling his nerves, focusing on the task at hand. He glanced around the rec room, moving his whole body instead of just his head, not wanting to twist anything too far just in case the muscles were torn. He didn't have the strength to break up a chair or snap a leg off the Ping-Pong table, though he considered that for a moment.

No, it had to be something he could hide, something sharp and quick.

Shuffling around, right arm held against his ribs, he checked out the card table, the various bits of furniture, the crappy pool table. His eyes had glanced right past the Ping-Pong table for at least the third time before he paused to stare at the net, and the silver metal brackets that held it up on either side.

The metal was thin. Worked back and forth, it would likely snap off, leaving a sharp end. It would take a bit of leverage, but if he took it slowly and was careful, he could manage any pain. If Boggs came for him again, and got in close enough, Josh would do the bastard as much damage as possible.

He grabbed the net and had started to tear it off when the starboard door clicked open behind him.

Josh turned quickly, instinctively putting a protective hand over his ribs, and was surprised when the only pain was a dull throbbing ache rather than the sharp jab he'd expected. Perhaps the bones were intact after all.

The door swung inward and Angie Tyree poked her head in, wary and furtive. She glanced back out onto the walkway, then slid into the rec room, closing the door quickly behind her.

"What the hell—" Josh began.

Eyes widening, she put a finger to her lips to shush him, glancing past him at the port side door as though afraid someone would come to investigate. Josh stood quietly as she approached, studying the engineer. Despite her oil-stained tank top and jeans and the clunky work boots she had on, Angela Tyree was a beautiful woman. Her skin was a rich, dark coffee, and she had lovely eyes above full, sensual lips. But in the time they'd been at sea together, Josh had seen how hard she could be, which detracted both from her beauty and from how far he would be willing to trust her.

Yet the fear in her eyes pleaded for his trust. It was clear she wasn't supposed to be here, and didn't want to be discovered.

"How did you get in here?" he whispered, hating the mumble that his swollen mouth and aching jaw made of his words.

"I'm supposed to be guarding the door."

Josh frowned. Angie didn't have a weapon, and she was all that stood between him and freedom. He started toward the door she'd come through.

"No," she said, grabbing his arm. "Where are you gonna go? For a swim?"

He paused, thinking about the layout of the ship, the distance to the galley, the chances of running into other members of the crew, some of whom would no doubt be armed. Every muscle urged him toward the door, but if Angie had other thoughts, he wanted to hear them.

"You have a better idea?" he asked.

"Just listen," she said, glancing over her shoulder at the door through which she'd entered. Then she locked her eyes on him, sizing him up as though for the first time. "I'm third assistant engineer on a container ship. It's just my job. Yes, I knew the Rios made some stops along the way sometimes, and that whatever they picked up couldn't be legal if it was so secret. But I swear I've never been part of any of it. I just do my job and mind my own business."

Josh saw the desperation etched in her face and decided that Angie couldn't be that good an actress. He nodded. "Go on."

Angie licked her lips and shrugged. "Nothing. I just . . . I'm not part of it."

"You knew and kept quiet. You could've turned them in. You could've at least quit the job if you were worried about going to jail."

He understood what she was fishing for, but he twisted the knife anyway. The more terrified she was, the more useful she'd be.

"Look, I can help you get out of here . . ."

Josh held up a hand to hush her, cocking his head slightly

as though he'd heard something. The effect on her was instantaneous, erasing any lingering suspicions he might have had that Gabe Rio had sent her in here trying to find out if Josh had any information that Hank Boggs's fists hadn't been able to extract.

"What did you hear?" she asked, taking a step toward the door.

"Nothing. Just the boat. Everything creaks. Listen, Angie, if you're as blameless as you say, that'll come out during the prosecution. But if you can bring me a gun and get me to the galley—or get us both to one of the lifeboats—I'll do everything I can to protect you."

She gnawed her lower lip, more vulnerable than he'd ever seen her, looking almost like a little girl.

"I wouldn't have to be in jail?"

Josh considered lying, but only for a second. "I can't make any promises. There's only so much I can do. But I can tell you this much—I think there's a very good chance that if you help me, you'll stay out of prison."

She might not have gone to prison at all, regardless, but Josh didn't have to tell her that. Angie scratched below her right eye, glancing back and forth at the doors before staring at him again.

"I've got trust issues, Josh, but I don't guess I have much of a choice. And you always seemed like a decent guy, before I knew you were lying."

"It wasn't all a lie. I'm a damned good cook."

He smiled to set her at ease and pain hammered both sides of his swollen face. Josh hissed and brought a hand up, gingerly touching his jaw. When he glanced at Angie, he saw the sympathy in her eyes, and surprised himself by both liking and trusting her.

"As soon as it's dark—" she began.

Josh shook his head. "No good. The sun's only been up an hour or two."

"We'll get caught."

"We only need to get to the . . ." Josh let his words trail off, then gave a soft shake of his head, chuckling at how slowly his brain was working. He'd told Gabe and Boggs about the PLB, but he'd also told them the holster was rigged so that if they tried to remove the beacon without entering the right code, they'd set it off.

As lies went, it wasn't a very good one, and it wouldn't hold up for long. But right now, all Captain Rio wanted was to get those guns, and with Josh locked up, maybe he wouldn't have dared remove the PLB yet. It was worth a shot.

"All right. Let's try a different approach. Get to the stove in the galley. Behind it there's a small rubber holster, inside of which you'll find a black and yellow thing that looks like a small walkie-talkie. If you open its face, there are two blue buttons and a red one. Ignore the red one. Don't touch it. Press the two blue buttons down simultaneously and hold them until you hear a beep. Then take it and hide it somewhere else on the ship."

Angie bit her lip again. "What is it? Some kind of signal?"

"Exactly. If you do that, I'll do what I can for you. And if we're all still here by nightfall, you come get me, and we'll get out of here in one of the enclosed lifeboats."

The idea of leaving the *Antoinette* seemed to scare the crap out of her, but she took another breath and nodded. "Okay."

"And, Angie?"

She looked up at him, some of the toughness coming back into her eyes.

"The PLB—the walkie-talkie thing—it might not be there. The captain knows about it, but I told him if he messes with it too much, tries to take it out of its sheath, it's rigged to go off automatically."

"Is it?" Angie asked.

He debated quickly, calculating whether or not he could afford to trust her. Then he took a breath and shook his head. "No. That's bullshit. Still, he might hesitate. If it's already gone from where I hid it, you're going to have to check Gabe's quarters, and probably Miguel's. Try the wheelhouse first, though."

Angie deflated a little, gaze dropping, no doubt thinking about getting caught snooping around the captain's quarters, or—even worse, given Miguel's temper—the chief mate's.

"Jesus, how did I get into this? If they catch me—"

"Don't let them."

After a moment she lifted her eyes, her expression grim. She nodded. "I'll see you soon."

-27--

The *Antoinette* carried ten lifeboats, five on either side. Some were enclosed, designed for tropical storms and worse, mostly used by the Navy but growing more common in the private sector during recent years. Though there were usually only about two dozen people aboard the ship, at least twice a year they sailed with an additional maintenance crew, who made improvements, painted, and cleaned while under way, so that the ship would not have to waste time in port while it could be sailing, making money for its owners. There were never more than fifty people on board. Maritime rules indicated that there should be lifeboats enough on each side of the vessel to carry everyone, so that if the *Antoinette* listed to port, they could all escape using the lifeboats on the starboard side, or vice versa.

The company—and often enough the crew—might cut corners in some areas, but never when it came to lifeboats. In fact, in recent years, Viscaya Shipping had invested in the enclosed lifeboats that had first been used by the military. The entrance was a hatch that could be sealed from within, making the boat into a watertight escape pod, in case of rough seas.

But of the ten lifeboats on board the *Antoinette,* only four were enclosed. Frank Esper at Viscaya had priced out the cost of replacing all ten of the traditional open boats, but Tori had been there when he had brought it up to the Rio brothers. She remembered the way they had scoffed at the idea. Lifeboats were vital in an emergency, but in practice they were used far more often to ferry people and materials to and from the ship when it wasn't convenient to make port.

Morning had come on in full by the time they set off from the *Antoinette*. Tori rode in the first lifeboat to hit the water, along with the captain and three able-bodied seamen. Two of them she didn't know very well, but the third—Kevonne Royce—had worked for Viscaya for three years, and Tori liked him a great deal. Kevonne worked hard and followed orders when he was on duty, and off duty he never failed to lighten the mood around him. He had a baby girl named Violet at home, and she had changed his life. Kevonne had grown up a club kid in Miami, hanging with rappers and dancers who came from nothing but found themselves what they called "dumb, stupid rich." He'd deejayed for a couple of years, partied hard and ugly, and then one of his girlfriends had turned up pregnant. Violet's birth had been an epiphany for Kevonne, and her mother was now his fiancée. All he wanted out of his life was to take care of his family.

He still had the charm that had helped him blaze his way through Miami, but Kevonne didn't seem charming today. Nothing could lighten the mood.

The wind seemed reluctant to blow, only the barest hint of a breeze sweeping across the waves. From the look of the trees, it was not even enough to rustle the leaves and fronds. The sun had felt like a gift at daybreak, but now it beat down on them, promising a blistering day. They had been blessed with beautiful weather the past week or so, but it was barely after nine o'clock and already it was clear that today would be different.

Tori glanced back at the second lifeboat, saw Hank Boggs staring at her, and turned to face forward again.

"What is it?" Gabe asked.

She hesitated. How much might she say to the captain before he would think she had overstepped her bounds? It had taken him so long to get past the idea that Viscaya had put her on board because they didn't trust him that she didn't want to give him any reason to think she doubted him now.

But silence would be worse. Gabe would read something negative into a lack of response.

"I just wish you hadn't brought him along," she admitted.

"Boggs?"

Tori nodded. "He gives me the creeps."

Gabe glanced back. The second lifeboat carried the chief engineer and another two able-bodied seamen whose jobs were to do whatever the captain needed them to do. In this case, it would be hauling and carrying crates of guns . . . if they could find the damned things.

"He's useful," the captain said.

"He's dangerous," Tori replied, then glanced up at Gabe. "Sorry. No disrespect intended. You're the captain. But you asked, and he does creep me out."

"If there's trouble, you'll be glad he's along."

Tori opened her mouth, forming words without even thinking. *You're expecting trouble?* But the question died on her lips. She scanned the ruined, derelict ships that crowded the water ahead of them, half-sunken, blocking much of their view of the island.

Stupid question.

The guttural roar of the motor echoed back off the hulls of the half-sunken ships as they approached. Spray from the prow of the lifeboat misted on her arms and face, sprinkling her sunglasses. She licked salt from her lips and removed the glasses, cleaning them on her shirt, but the moment she put them back on, the spray began to dot the lenses again and she abandoned any effort to keep her vision clear.

A dreadful silence descended upon the passengers on the lifeboat—the noise of the motor and the water remained, but none of them seemed willing to speak. No one knew what to say. The two sailors who sat with Kevonne were a study in opposites—one a stubbled and bedraggled California surfer boy who went by the name of Bone, and the other an acutely professional Vietnamese man called Pang.

Bone and Kevonne were known to cultivate magnificently potent marijuana, with which they were generous to a fault. All Tori knew about Pang was that he had been a musician of some kind—or perhaps still was. She'd rarely seen him without his iPod, the white buds in his ears. Even now, as the lifeboat plowed through the water, Pang sat listening to his music. Sunlight glinted off his mirrored glasses. If not for the curious smile on his face as they slowed, navigating through a break among the derelict ships, he would have looked more like an off-duty Secret Service agent than a sailor. What the hell he had to smile about, Tori had no idea. Maybe, to Pang, their situation seemed like some kind of adventure. If so, then he must have been the only one among them that could not feel the strange heaviness of the island air, the wrongness of everything around them.

Tori doubted she'd ever seen Bone without an amiable grin and a slightly stoned glaze in his eyes. His easy charm often made him seem a bit stupid or foolish, but now he gripped the side of the lifeboat and stared at the ruined vessels around them as they maneuvered around the wrecks, and his gaze held a darkly intelligent spark. The man might be friendly and open, but that didn't make him an idiot. He knew enough to fear the unknown.

Yes, if they went back to Miami without the guns, things would get ugly. But by going ashore now, they were taking the risk that the FBI would catch up to them before they could get clear of the area. Gabe seemed to think they could pull it off—get the guns on board, keep Josh locked up until they got closer to U.S. waters, radio ahead to Viscaya, and get the guns off-loaded before they made port. There would be arrests and probably criminal charges, maybe court hearings, but in the end the Feds would have zero evidence of anything except that Josh had been beaten and locked up. And, for that, lies could obfuscate the truth. Tori had suggested several of these herself—that he'd assaulted Miguel, raved about them being terrorists, and that they'd locked him up for their safety and for his own. Since he had no proof of his claims that he was an FBI agent and had seemed so unstable, they couldn't take the risk he might be lying.

Bullshit, and no judge would be stupid enough not to smell it. But the law was all about what could be proven, and Viscaya could afford excellent lawyers.

To Tori, it sounded like a fairy-tale future, but she needed Gabe to tell her fairy tales right now. As long as they had a plan that didn't include killing Josh or going to prison, she would go along with the Rios. There were no good options left. Out on the ocean, she could run away from her conflicted feelings about Josh, but not from their situation.

"This is fucked," Kevonne said.

Tori blinked, startled from her reverie. She glanced at Gabe, but his focus remained on the island, as though he didn't even notice the wrecks they were navigating past. Pang steered them carefully, throttling down even as he gazed around with the smile of a teenager discovering the world's coolest video game.

Kevonne glanced from Tori to the captain and back again, expecting a reply. When none came, he swore under his breath and peered at the nearest of the wrecks. Tori wondered what he wanted her to say.

"Slow down," Gabe said.

Pang throttled down even further and they all got a better look at the derelict ships around them. Though it forced them to approach at an angle, a clear path—perhaps fifty feet wide—lay open before them. The cove seemed ordinary enough, save for the jagged black rocks that jutted out to either side. Once they cleared the graveyard of ships, their course would be simple and swift.

Tori understood why Gabe had wanted a better look at the wrecks, though. The ships were weathered to varying degrees, depending upon how long they had lain off the island's coast. They passed a fishing boat whose cabin had partially rotted. The hull had several holes in it, each two or three feet wide. But adjacent to it—nearer to the lifeboat—was the sort of pleasure craft that rich men hired crews for just so that they could call themselves *captain*. The wheelhouse had been damaged by fire, but otherwise it seemed in excellent shape until they passed close by. Under the crystal blue water, they could see a broad dark area on the white hull.

"Did you—?" Bone began, then stopped himself.

Gabe looked at him. "What?"

"Nothing. Just fish."

But Tori had seen something darting back into that hole as well. "An eel, maybe?"

Bone nodded. "Probably."

To their left lay the sailboat they'd seen earlier, its twin masts canted over the top of a small, rusty freighter. Tori stared at it as they passed, noticing that all but one of the lifeboat berths were empty, and wondering where the rest of them had gone. Against the vividness of the blue sky and the crystal water, and washed by the brilliant sunlight, the conjoined wrecks looked bleached and lifeless. Yet the morning made the shadowy interiors of both vessels that much darker, and a stray thought ran through Tori's mind about rats leaving sinking ships.

But not these, she thought, nonsensically. *They didn't leave these.*

And that was it, she realized. The ships were derelict wrecks, half-sunk and ruined, but they didn't feel abandoned. She glanced again at the pleasure craft and tipped her head back, staring at the trawling nets that had been roped together and strung from the prow across the fifty-foot span that separated it from the twin-masted sailboat. Pang piloted the lifeboat beneath that high-wire array of nets. They had all noticed many other ropes and chains that had been used to connect some of the wrecks to others like some kind of web. The one above their heads hadn't sagged much, which meant it hadn't been there very long.

"It just doesn't feel like we're alone," she said, her voice small.

Gabe shot her a dark look.

"Thank you!" Kevonne threw up his hands. "That's what I'm saying. It's freaky. The back of my neck is itching something fierce, like someone's watching me."

Bone looked up at Gabe. "My skin's crawling, Captain. I'm with them. Think we ought to hail whoever's here?"

Gabe looked like he was going to argue the point, and Tori felt sure he would say he hadn't felt it at all.

"There *could* be people on the island," she said quickly. "Or out on some of these wrecks. Might be survivors from the *Mariposa,* or whoever attacked them."

The captain shook his head. "You guys are spooked, that's all. None of these ships are seaworthy, and whoever attacked the *Mariposa*'s crew wouldn't just be hanging out here. They'd have taken the guns and gone."

"If they found the guns," Bone said, shifting in the lifeboat, looking like he'd never needed a joint more in all his days. "If they didn't, maybe they're still on the island, man. Maybe they left some guys here to look and are coming back for them."

"You're getting paranoid," Gabe said.

Bone gave a little laugh and turned, wide-eyed. "Dude, I'm freaking out, okay? Someone killed all those guys, we got an FBI on the boat, and fucking look around you! Paranoia's the healthiest reaction I can muster, okay?"

Gabe's nostrils flared.

"Dude," Kevonne said. "Captain."

Bone gave a sheepish smile and an apologetic shrug and looked at Gabe. "Sorry, Captain. Sure as hell feels like we're not alone, that's all."

Gabe relented. "Go on, then. Hail them, if you think they're here."

Bone nodded and licked his lips, then got on his knees in the lifeboat and started to call out to the wrecks as they passed. His voice echoed off hulls, sometimes drifting away on an errant breeze or hissing into the shush of water against the boat or the roar of the motor. He kept calling as Pang— lost in his music—steered them clear of the graveyard of ships and then upped the throttle, churning them faster into the cove and toward the shore.

No one called back. Tori didn't see any movement on any of the boats, or on shore. Bone finally relented and quieted down, and for a few seconds, no one said anything at all.

Then Tori shuddered, her spine stiffening, a chill dancing up the back of her neck.

"Do you hear that?" she asked.

Gabe, Kevonne, and Bone all looked at her.

"What?" the captain asked.

She frowned, glanced back over her shoulder. Pang sat behind her, and past him Hank Boggs and the other two sailors they'd brought followed in the second lifeboat, making their way through the derelict ships.

"Nothing now," she said, studying the shadows aboard those wrecks again. "For a second, I thought I heard singing."

"Pang's got his damn iPod up too loud," Kevonne said.

Tori glanced at the smiling sailor, hidden behind his sunglasses. She listened hard, but she couldn't hear a single note of his music, and couldn't believe that bit of singing had been an errant snatch of a tune from his iPod. She considered asking if she could listen a moment, but told herself she was being foolish. Of course the music had come from Pang's iPod.

But when Tori turned toward the island again, she found Bone watching her anxiously, eyes wide with a fear that made him look like a small boy. Had he heard the singing, too?

"Here we go," Gabe said, gesturing to Pang.

The lifeboat knifed through the shallows and bottomed out, sliding onto the shore even as Pang raised the motor blades out of the water. Gabe jumped into the shallows and Kevonne stepped out onto the sand.

They'd arrived.

-28--

Angie stood outside the rec room on the starboard side of the accommodations block's third story, one hand shielding her eyes from the sun as she watched the two lifeboats run aground on the island's sandy shore. She wondered if she could make it down to the galley where Josh had hidden his locator beacon without anyone noticing that she'd left the door unguarded. Captain Rio and that bastard Boggs were gone, and they were her two greatest concerns. Miguel Rio worried her, too, but not as much as the captain. The chief mate could be a real bastard, but he wasn't as smart as his brother.

With Gabe, Boggs, Tori, and half of the deckhands off on

their errand, the *Antoinette* felt like a ghost ship. Tupper and Valente were on duty in the engine room—or they were supposed to be. After guarding Josh all night, no doubt they were trading naps. They were assholes, but neither of them was irresponsible enough to completely abandon their shift.

The fourth assistant engineer was a guy named Oscar Jimenez. He and Angie had taken over guarding Josh early this morning, which meant she knew he was there, standing watch over the port side rec room door, but she couldn't see him and he couldn't see her. If Angie slipped away for a little while, Oscar would never know she was gone.

Still, she couldn't risk it. If Dwyer or Miguel came down the stairs and found that she'd left the door unguarded, there would be hell to pay. If she had any chance at all of helping Josh escape and earning herself a Get Out of Jail Free card, she dared not risk leaving the door unguarded. She needed someone to take over for her, just for a while.

The minutes ticked by and the sun beat down, a strange stillness to the sea air. Her skin crawled with impatience. She studied the sunken ships that sprawled in the water off the island's coast, then shifted her focus to the lifeboats that had been abandoned in the cove. She swore quietly to herself, then retreated into the shade provided by the walkway above her head.

She was standing in this shelter, hidden from above and below, when she heard someone clomping down the metal stairs. Stepping out to the railing, she squinted against the sunlight and looked up to see a very tired-looking Dwyer descending. He paused and hung out over the railing above her.

"Hello, darlin'," Dwyer said. With his red hair and broad grin, he looked like a little boy.

"You don't look nearly tired enough," Angie said, heart skipping nervously. "Did you sleep?"

The grin widened. "Only a couple of hours."

He tromped down the last flight of stairs and turned onto the level three walkway. Angie wondered if he could see the fear and deceit in her eyes. She had spent years developing a tough-girl facade, and hoped she could maintain it.

"That's a couple more than I've had," she said.

Dwyer reached out and took both of her hands, kissed her forehead. "That's a lie."

Angie feigned a tentative smile. "All right. I had a couple, too, but I'm exhausted and starving and I need to pee."

In the time they had been sleeping together, she and Dwyer had never pretended what they had was a romance. They genuinely liked each other and they satisfied each other's urges—sometimes very well, and sometimes merely well enough—but they weren't in love. Still, there was a sweet tenderness in his eyes now and he softened, reaching out to touch her cheek.

"By all means, angel, go and take care of that. I was just off to the mess myself. Our cook may be locked up, but someone's got to have prepared something for breakfast. Bring me something back?"

Angie gave a soft laugh. If Dwyer had slept a while, maybe Miguel had as well. It was possible that they hadn't gotten to the personal locator beacon yet, or that they hadn't dared remove it. Maybe breakfast wasn't Dwyer's only purpose for going down to the galley.

"Thanks, babe," she said, and kissed his cheek.

He caught her face in his hands and brushed her mouth with his. She wondered if he could taste the deception on her lips.

"I'll be quick," Angie said, and hurried away from the rec room.

The back of her neck prickled and her face felt flushed as she made her way down to the deck. The entire situation had seemed almost surreal to her, but now the crushing reality set in. How had she ever thought that she could go along with the sins of Viscaya Shipping and never pay the price? She'd told herself it had nothing to do with her, that she was just doing a job, but she had never denied the little thrill that ran through her whenever the Rio brothers indulged in their outlaw behavior.

It had sometimes felt like a bit of fantasy, as though she were playing at something dangerous. But now the danger had turned real and tangible, and playtime was over.

On the deck, she paused for a cleansing breath of salt air, then pushed open the door into the mess hall. Angie hadn't passed anyone on the stairs and the mess hall was empty as well, making the *Antoinette* seem more like a ghost ship than ever. She strode across the room and through the open doorway that led into the galley—the point of no return.

A pan clattered and she let out a tiny cry, raising a hand to cover her mouth.

Sal Pucillo jumped a bit as he spun from the sink, turning to face her. "Jesus, Angie, you scared me."

"The feeling's mutual." She offered a halfhearted smile, reminding herself that she was never very friendly to Pucillo and it would seem false if she changed that now. "What're you doing? Galley's not your usual gig."

Pucillo's eyes hardened and he picked up a soapy pan from the sink and continued scrubbing. The clatter she'd heard must have been the pan slipping from his hands.

"Someone's gotta pick up the slack if Tori and Josh aren't around to cook for us. I made breakfast, too. French toast and bacon. There's some left in the plastic over there," he said, nodding toward the refrigerator. On a shelf beside it was a covered rectangular plastic container.

"You don't mind if I take some? I'm starving."

"Go on ahead. I was just gonna put the rest in the fridge. The whole point of cooking it was so the crew could eat."

Angie went to the shelf and opened the container, surprised to find maybe twenty slices of bacon and half a dozen slices of French toast inside. Plenty left over, and her stomach rumbled at the aroma. She thought about heating it up, but didn't bother. A little maple syrup and two forks, and she and Dwyer could have breakfast together up on level three, standing guard over the man who could land them all in jail.

She glanced at the stove. When she'd first entered, she had avoided looking directly at it, not wanting Pucillo to notice anything. But now he busied himself with the greasy pan, so she let her gaze stray to the wide silver bulk of the stove, and felt her spirits tumble when she saw that it stood at a slight angle from the wall. Someone had moved it recently, and not been too meticulous about putting it back.

"Thanks for this." She searched the drawers and found two clean forks, then took a half-full bottle of orange juice from the fridge. As desperately as she needed coffee, she didn't have time to make it. "Very cool of you to step up."

"Someone had to," he replied without turning. Studiously keeping his back to her, he cleared his throat. "So is it true? Josh is FBI?"

Angie weighed the benefits of playing dumb, then decided there weren't any. "That's what I hear."

Pucillo's shoulders sagged. "Jesus. My wife's gonna . . ."

He didn't finish. Nor did he have to.

"You don't know anything, Sal. Nobody's going to tie you to whatever the Rios are up to. The whole crew knows you go out of your way to avoid even hearing anything illegal." A realization struck her. "Is that why you're down here?"

"Damn straight. Cooking. Cleaning. I'll live in the damn galley if I have to. See no evil, hear no evil, speak no evil. If I have to testify, I want to be able to tell the truth. That'll save me if anything can. I'm just down here, minding my own business."

Angie felt a flash of envy. "You'll be okay," she said. "I really believe that."

Pucillo kept scrubbing. The steel wool must have been practically gone by now, and the pan had to be clean, but he didn't stop. "I wish I did."

As they were talking, Angie had been moving over to the stove. Now she leaned against the wall, trying her best to be inconspicuous in case he should glance at her, and looked into the space between stove and wall.

Her heart sank and it was all she could do to keep from swearing aloud. Remnants of black electrical tape made it clear that something had been there, but the PLB was gone. She wondered where it was now. If it had been her, she'd have thrown it into the ocean, let it sink to the bottom. Even if it didn't short out, no signal would transmit from the depths of the Caribbean. But if there was a chance that the PLB was still on board, she had to find it, which meant searching the whole damn ship.

Or asking Dwyer.

Angie didn't like either option, but she knew she had to do something. It was too late to hide down here with Pucillo.

-29--

Gabe stopped about twenty feet up the beach and surveyed the island. From their approach they'd already gauged it at about half a mile wide and three times that in length—not much land, but it could still take all day and more to search if they weren't smart about it. He tried to think like Ruiz, the captain of the *Mariposa*. If he'd brought the guns ashore, worried about an attack come nightfall, where would he hole up?

Closest to the sand were towering skeletal palm trees, their heavy fronds barely rustling in the light morning breeze. At the bases of those trees grew a sparse sea grass. Farther inland there were other trees, green and tangled, and prickly-looking underbrush. Gabe didn't see any obvious footpaths, but there were natural patterns in the growth, almost like coves on the shore, inviting travelers with easier access. Now that he looked more closely, he realized that the island wasn't as flat as he'd imagined. A ridge of mounds—a sort of spine of natural rises—ran along its length.

"You ever seen breakers like that?" Bone asked, coming up beside Gabe. He wore a light pack and clutched a water bottle. "Black like that, I mean?"

Gabe glanced along the beach at the weird rock formations that jutted into the water. On either side of the cove there were places where jagged shards of the same ebony stone thrust up from the sand or the white foaming surf.

"Something like it," Gabe replied. "Looks volcanic."

"You think there's a volcano here?"

The captain studied the island again. "Hell if I know. I've seen a couple of volcanoes, and it doesn't look anything like that. But I'm not a geologist."

"It's weird, though, right?"

Gabe didn't bother to reply. Bone had answered his own question. He turned toward the others. Tori and Kevonne stood a little farther up the beach, well away from where Pang was helping Boggs and the other two sailors dig anchors into the sand to keep the lifeboats from floating away on the first big wave. They were wasting their time; the tide was as high as it would get. But they were good sailors and had procedures to follow.

"All right, let's go," he called.

Boggs reached into one of the lifeboats and pulled out a long vinyl bag, unzipped it, and withdrew the rifle from inside. He loaded it quickly, then slung the weapon over his shoulder.

"Do we really need guns? There's nobody here," Bone said, a pleading tone in his voice. Gabe wondered if he'd been this way back in California, if he'd left because he'd been getting on his surfer buddies' nerves.

"Maybe not. But the guys from the *Mariposa* are dead." The captain wore a nine-millimeter pistol in a holster on his right hip. He reached down and popped the snap that kept it in place. "I'd rather be prepared than join them."

Gabe walked down to meet Boggs and the others, who gathered around him.

Bone hurried to catch up. "Hey, Captain, do you think I could have one, then?"

"When we find our cargo, you can all have guns for all I care. But let's get to work. Four teams. Kevonne, take Pang and head west along the shore. Look for any sign of the *Mariposa*'s crew—footprints, guns, breaks in the tree line. Tori and I will head east."

He turned to Boggs. "The rest of you go with the chief. Head inland maybe a hundred yards, then split up, two in one direction, two in the other. Crisscross that section. They won't have taken the guns much deeper than that. Don't waste time with the overgrown areas or the hills."

"We should go in as far as the bottom of those hills, though, Captain," Boggs said. "There may be decent defensive positions there. If the *Mariposa*'s captain wanted a place to hide, or to fight from, he might have gone that far."

Gabe didn't like to be contradicted, especially by a man like Boggs, but he couldn't deny that the chief had a point.

"All right. Go in as far as the hills, but don't climb. Even if they wanted the high ground, they didn't lug crates of guns up those hills, and the guns are what we're looking for. They're all that matters. Make sure every team has at least one radio. Let me know the second you run across anything that's even a question mark. I'll decide for myself what is and isn't important. Got it?"

The men all began to move out. Tori knelt in the sand, double-checking her pack, making sure they had food and water. When they had first set out on this voyage, Gabe had hated the idea of some office girl coming along, looking over his shoulder, reporting back to Viscaya. Now he was glad to have her along.

Tori had surprised him with her resilience. The typical cubicle slave would be curled up in a weepy fetal ball back in their quarters right now. But Tori had steel in her, a survivor's edge, and he admired the hell out of that. He had brought her out to the island to make sure that he had a witness that Esper and the rest of his bosses at Viscaya would trust. Gabe would do whatever it took to get those guns, to finish the job, but if they ended up going home empty-handed, he wanted Tori to be able to tell them firsthand that he'd done everything possible.

True, Tori's eyes had a glint of fear, but they all looked afraid. The difference was that everyone else seemed content to let him lead, while Tori had an air of determination that had nothing to do with Gabe Rio or his orders. Terrified she might be, but she would do whatever it took to get the job done and get home safe. They were in it together, and he liked that.

"Thanks," she said as she shouldered her pack and they started east along the sand together.

"For what?"

"Not sending me with Boggs."

Gabe had been starting to search the sand and the tree line, but now he glanced at her. "You honestly think I'd have done that to you?"

"I thought maybe you'd see me as a liability," Tori said.

The irony of the comment, given what he'd just been thinking, made him shake his head. "I don't."

"Glad to hear it."

They walked near the tree line, where the sand did not give way so readily beneath their feet. Beyond the cove, the black rocks were not so prominent, but there were many places where patches of dark stone were visible under the sand, as though it had been worn away to reveal the rocks beneath, like the beach was only a disguise for the real island under it.

In one spot, they came upon a great hump in the sand, but as they drew closer Gabe saw that it was an old rowboat, overturned and half-buried in the sand, wood bleached white by time and sun. As they stood puzzling it out, Tori tapped his arm and pointed into the trees farther along the beach, where what had once been a small yacht—forty feet or so—lay among the trees and brush, partially overgrown, two downed palms evidence of its violent arrival on shore.

"Must have been a hell of a storm," Tori said.

"They're born around here all the time," Gabe replied, though when he glanced at the blue sky, felt the baking warmth of the sun and the bare whisper of the day's wind, it was hard to imagine a hurricane striking this tiny island.

Farther along they came upon another outcropping of the black rock where the remains of at least two lifeboats were scattered. There were derelict ships half-sunken—and some completely submerged—off the island here as well, but they were not as numerous away from the cove. In the surf, a small boat with an outboard—a Whaler no doubt used as a runabout by the rich owners of one of these ruined yachts—swayed back and forth with the waves.

"I don't see a thing," Tori said when they had gone perhaps three-quarters of a mile. "Are we even sure the *Mariposa* stopped here?"

Gabe glanced at her, a dozen harsh replies playing on his lips. What came out instead was honesty. "I'm not sure of anything, but it feels like someone's been here."

Tori actually laughed, and he glanced at her sharply, only to see her gesture toward the nearest offshore wreck. "It feels like plenty of people have been here. The place is like the Bermuda Triangle's backed-up drain."

He had been trying to avoid such thoughts. "I don't believe in that crap."

They walked half a dozen steps before Tori replied. "I don't, either. But the only other thing I can think of is pirates. Could be they attack these other ships, kill the crews, steal whatever they can, then take them here and scuttle them. Like home base or whatever."

"Could be," Gabe said.

But he didn't believe it. Not only did it feel like bullshit, but they had yet to see any sign of visitors. No remnants of a camp or a cooking fire or even prints in the sand. The weather could eradicate such things, but not if they were recent. And if it wasn't pirates, he didn't have the first clue what had happened to all of these ships.

Tori paused to check out a gap in the tree line, but only for a moment before moving on. Gabe started to do likewise, but the breeze lifted slightly and rustled the fronds of the palm trees, and he looked up.

The gap provided a perfect view of the nearest of the island's hills. They were green and brown and thick with vegetation in some places—making him wonder how far seabirds might carry seeds—but there were peaks and ridges made of that same glassy black, and he realized that his thoughts about the beach hadn't been completely off. Much of the island's spine consisted of that ebony stone. He'd never seen anything like it.

Tori had kept walking and now Gabe picked up his pace to catch her. They must have traveled nearly a mile by now— half the distance they'd need to meet up with Kevonne and Pang on the other side, with no sign of any visitors to the island except the ruined boats. None of it made any sense.

Gabe paused to examine an area of undergrowth that

seemed to have been disturbed, but the ground around it showed no sign of passersby, and he figured it had been bad weather or some kind of animal, though they hadn't seen anything at all so far.

"What is it, Captain?" Tori prodded.

He turned to her, raising an eyebrow. "You don't have to call me Captain out here, Tori."

"Okay. What's on your mind, Gabe? You're distracted, and it isn't just this."

Something about her cool brown eyes brought the truth out in him. "Just thinking about Maya. About how things ended."

Tori thrust her hands into her pockets as they continued along the sand. "It got ugly, huh?"

"Very. If I end up in prison over this, I don't think she'll care," Gabe said, thinking that Maya might even be happy. Then she could carry on fucking whoever she wanted and never have to worry about his jealousy again.

Wrapped up in his own thoughts, he missed the way Tori stiffened and the fear that flared in her eyes. But when she said his name, her voice had become so small that he looked at her anew.

"I can't go to prison, Gabe. Not even jail. Not for a single night."

Some of the respect he felt for her slipped away. "None of us wants to go to jail, Tori. It's definitely not part of my plan. I'll do whatever it takes—"

Tori shook her head, fixing him with hard eyes. "You don't understand. I can't go to jail. The cops will find out who I am, and then . . ."

Gabe frowned as her words trailed off. "What do you mean, who you are?"

She sighed, gnawed her lip a bit, and he saw in her eyes the moment when she decided to trust him. Tori started walking again and, sensing it was what she desired, Gabe fell in beside her. While they walked, she told him the story of her life before she came to Miami, of her cruel father and criminal husband, of her plan to escape, and the hideous coincidence that allowed her to do so without anyone realizing she had gone.

Tori told the story without ever mentioning her real name.

"He thinks I'm dead, Gabe," she said, turning to him once more, eyes pleading. "Everyone thinks I'm dead. But if I go to jail, he'll find out I'm alive, and that's the one thing I know I couldn't survive."

Gabe watched her a moment, absorbing her fear, and the truth of it. It frightened her more to imagine seeing her ex-husband again than it did to think of going to prison, or dying out here the way the crew of the *Mariposa* had.

"All right," he said. "Before we reach port, I'm going to get Viscaya to off-load the guns onto a smaller ship. No reason I can't off-load you, too. If you don't come into port, you can't be blamed for beating the crap out of an FBI agent and holding him captive."

"But Josh knows I was on the *Antoinette*."

Gabe shrugged. "The FBI can't arrest you if they can't find you, Tori. You've started over before. You can just vanish, like you did in New York."

Her eyes widened. Somehow, this option had never occurred to her.

"But none of that's going to work if we don't find the damn guns," he added.

She nodded and they picked up the pace. Just a few minutes later, the radio clipped to his belt chirped and he snatched it up.

"Go ahead," he said.

Boggs's voice came through with only a smattering of static. "Captain, we found something. A couple of caves in the base of a hill."

Caves. Could the *Mariposa*'s crew have hidden there, or at least stashed the guns there? The scenario spun out in his head and Gabe could see it was possible. The dying man on the fishing boat had said they thought they'd be safer on land, which Gabe figured meant whoever attacked them had greater numbers and they wanted to fight back from cover. The trees would provide some, but as a base, the caves would make perfect sense.

"Any sign of the guns? Or people?"

More static. "Not yet."

"All right. Keep looking. Call in if you find anything. If you see other caves, search them, too. And, Chief?"

"Yeah."

"Watch yourself."

"I hear that."

With a final blast of static, they signed off. Gabe put the radio back on his belt. Tori had slowed down to listen to the exchange, but was still a few paces ahead.

"You think they'll find anything?" she asked as he caught up.

"Them or us. We'll find something."

"What makes you so sure?"

Gabe shot her a sidelong glance. "Worst-case scenario, the pirates or whatever found the guns and took them, right? Which means they killed everyone on the island. If we don't find the guns, you can be damn sure we'll find the bodies."

"Well, *there's* a pleasant thought," Tori teased.

He had no reply. Gabe had always enjoyed her company, but—much as he would have liked to set her at ease—he couldn't find it within himself to make light of their situation. There was nothing pleasant about it.

So he said nothing, and they walked on in silence, with Gabe stealing occasional glances at Tori. He'd always flirted with her, found her attractive, even beautiful at times. But it had been a long while since he'd walked on the sand with a woman other than his wife, so despite the many other things on his mind, he found his thoughts straying to Maya. If he'd listened to her, he might have avoided all of this—the FBI, the murdered crew of the *Mariposa*, this island.

If you'd listened to her, she might not have started screwing someone else.

A ripple of anger passed through him, not at Maya but at himself for even entertaining such thoughts. She had known who he was, and how much he belonged to the ocean, when she married him. Gabe hadn't changed at all, but somehow her expectations had.

You'll get out of this, he told himself, as if that would show her how wrong she had been. It was a foolish instinct. Maya wouldn't care. Yes, he had a plan that just might keep him and Miguel from serving any real jail time, but after what Maya had done to him, did it matter? The question that settled in and gnawed at his heart was whether or not Viscaya would be able to give him a job when it was all over—whether *anyone* would hire him to crew a ship after the shitstorm that this would all bring.

Without Maya, he had nothing to go home to.

-30--

THREE MONTHS AGO . . .

Soft multicolored lights glowed from hidden sources all around the perimeter, casting the whole patio in a surreal glow reminiscent of a movie set. The palm trees that drooped over the top of the fence were real enough, but the setting made them seem artificial, except when the breeze rustled their fronds. The fountain in the middle of the patio, between the two bars that sat diagonal from each other, had a bright white light shining up from its center that made the water glisten. The perimeter lights were subdued, allowing the fountain to provide the main source of illumination.

Cinco had class. Most downtown Miami clubs and eateries catered to a drug-addled twentysomething crowd, or splayed their wares wide in an invitation to tourists. Cinco appealed to a slightly older demographic, somehow managing to be more upscale without costing any more than the palaces of youthful bacchanalia that dotted the city's nightscape. They served quality food in the restaurant, and out on the patio bar they kept a DJ spinning Latin sounds that ran the gamut from traditional to thumping club jams.

And oh my God, the women are beautiful.

Gabe Rio let this thought ricochet around his brain as he listened to a woman named Serafina talk about her work as a restaurant manager and how her family back in Tampa didn't understand what she saw in Miami. Serafina wore a cream-colored dress made of soft fabric that clung to her in lovely ways and hinted that it might well be the only piece of fabric she wore. Her heels were just high enough to draw attention to her long, shapely legs.

Silently, he thanked his cousin Louis, who tended bar at Cinco and had first dragged him down to the place. Louis had only wanted to have a drink and to introduce Gabe to some of his friends, and the first night, that had been exactly what had happened. But soon, Louis's friends had become his friends as well, and some of the crew and the regular bar patrons at Cinco would recognize him when he came in. Some of the girls would flirt with him. One night, a waitress named Anna had asked him, a glimmer in her eye, what it would take to put a smile on his face.

Just the question had been enough to earn her the smile she'd been looking for. But it was far from the only thing Anna had done to get a rise out of him. The first night they were together, Gabe had been out of his head after too much Grey Goose, his senses full up with the delicious scent of her, and he'd been able to push all thoughts of his wife aside right up until the moment he came.

He'd stayed away from Cinco for nearly a month after that, enveloped in a fog of guilt. Maya must have known something was wrong, but she had long since given up trying to decipher his moods. Often when he came home from being at sea, they would make love and he would lose himself in the soft curves of her coffee skin and the urgency and sadness of her eyes, and he would remember who they'd once been to each other, how he'd romanced her, how she'd laughed. But in the aftermath, they would draw apart from each other in bed and she would whisper that she was glad to have him home safe and ask him how it went, and how long he would be able to stay home this time.

Stay home and paint the walls. Stay home and fix the bathtub drain. Stay home and have a baby. Stay home.

Already he would be missing the water and the solitude, the strange sounds and sights and aromas of distant ports. Once she had told him that the only time he ever seemed to be home was when he was inside her, and otherwise his eyes were always gazing out to sea. Gabe hadn't argued the point.

The women he'd met at Cinco over the past few years never asked him to stay home. Some of them wanted him to come back, but they weren't fussy about when. They never needed anything from him that he couldn't give them in a single night. Hell, in a handful of hours.

And yet he loved Maya so much it hurt. He wanted to be the man she wished for, and when he knew he couldn't live a life away from the ocean, he tried at least to stay away from Cinco. But sometimes he just needed a break from disappointing Maya. Sometimes he just needed a woman who could be satisfied with what he gave her.

"Are you still with me, baby?" Serafina asked, the edges of her lips rising into something between a smile and a pout.

Gabe raised his frosty beer bottle in a quiet salute. "I'm not going anywhere."

Her eyelids fluttered and she launched into another story, reaching out now and again to touch his arm or adjust his shirt. He had ten years on her, at least, and flecks of gray in his hair, but Serafina either didn't notice or it was what had drawn her to him in the first place.

Out on the open patio, with the music thumping and the night sky washed in the lights of Miami, she told him about the affair she'd had with her teacher at a culinary school, and how those months had inextricably connected exquisite food with exquisite sex in her mind.

Her copper eyes lit with mischief. "The chef here makes a seared shrimp with lechon asado risotto. Have you ever had it?"

Gabe arched an eyebrow. "No. Is it good?"

Serafina sipped at her caipirinha, looking up at him over the rim of the glass. "Exquisite."

Gabe caught his breath. It felt like the space between them had just vanished, that he could slip the spaghetti straps of her dress off her shoulders and let it slide to the floor. The moment startled him with its intensity and he surprised himself with a small, soft laugh.

She pouted. "What's funny?"

"Suddenly I'm very hungry."

Reassured, she reached out to run her fingernails along his forearm, down to his wrist, then traced them across the back of his hand. "I know. Me, too. The thought of those shrimp has me salivating."

"Can I buy you dinner?"

"I'd like that."

Gabe smiled, took a sip from his beer, and reached down to take her hand, meaning to lead her off the patio, hoping to find a table in the restaurant but willing to settle for eating at the bar if it meant giving this woman what she craved. They threaded through the crowd on the patio, slid past the fountain, and a path opened up in front of them.

Maya stood just outside the door, scanning the crowd, eyes fierce. In a sleeveless peach blouse, black cotton pants, and heels, she seemed underdressed compared to the other women here, but no less beautiful.

And then she spotted Gabe, just as he tried to pull his hand away from Serafina's.

Most women would have made a scene. Having taken the time to seek out her wandering husband, finding him in an expensive bar with a woman like Serafina, she might have been expected to raise a little hell. It would have been so much easier for Gabe had Maya done just that.

Instead she only looked at him, first with rage in her eyes, and then a second later with terrible disappointment. He'd loved her long enough that the look on her face needed no interpretation. Their marriage had come to an impasse. Finding him here was not only proof of lies and infidelity she'd already accused him of, it was evidence that he had given up searching for compromise. He'd chosen his work over his marriage, and her wishes no longer entered the equation. She had to deal with it, or not.

Her eyes glistened, but she did not cry. She cocked her head, shook it once, and then turned. As she stepped back into the bar, a young, too-tanned white guy reached out and ran a hand over the small of her back and her rounded ass, saying something Gabe couldn't hear. Maya didn't slow down.

"Shit," Gabe whispered. He turned to Serafina.

"Your wife. I get it. I'm a big girl, Gabriel. Go on."

He squeezed her hand, set his beer on the low wall of the fountain, and rushed after Maya, calling her name. The music and the chatter of the people crowding the bar drowned out his voice. Bodies flowed together and he weaved through them as best he could. One cluster of people blocked his path entirely, talking loudly to one another to be heard over the music, and he brushed none too gently by them.

One of the guys, young and cocky, shouted and grabbed his shoulder. Another night Gabe might have stared him down, taught him respect for his elders, but he shook it off, slapped the hand away, and kept going, bulling his way through and finally breaking free of the crowd. In the foyer, the hostesses smiled at him and wished him good night even as he ran past them, slamming out through the double glass doors.

He practically spilled into the parking lot. The doors swung shut behind him, muffling the music. The night air felt warm and sticky, too close around him. The lights of downtown Miami gleamed in every direction. He swung his head from side to side, heart racing, cursing himself and Maya both as he looked for her car, but he saw no sign of her until he started running for his own car and spotted her white Corvette tearing out of the lot.

Gabe faltered. "Fuck!"

He only hesitated a moment before once more breaking into a run. Behind the wheel of his aging BMW, he fired up the engine, reversed out of the space, and headed for home. If he kept the pedal down, he wouldn't be far behind her, might even beat her into the parking garage.

But when he got home, Maya's parking space was empty.

Gabe waited up, apologies and promises on the tip of his tongue, but Maya never came home that night. By the time she finally returned—shortly before noon the next day—all of his regrets had been replaced by suspicion and anger.

She came in disheveled, still dressed in the clothes she'd worn the night before, her hair unruly. One look at her and all Gabe could think was that she looked as though she'd just rolled out of some other man's bed.

"Where the hell were you last night?"

Maya narrowed her eyes like she was seeing him for the first time. "I drove for a while, thinking about all the things I was going to say to you when I got home. Then I realized I don't have to say any of them. You know how I feel, and you don't care. So why should I bother?"

His heart clenched. He *did* care, but how could he argue with Maya? She was at least partly right. She'd made clear that she wanted him to change, to be a different man from the one she'd fallen in love with, and that wasn't going to happen.

The ache that had been building in his head all night turned into a vise. Wondering where she had been the night before stoked a raging fire in him.

"Fine. But where did you sleep?" he said, following her back through the hallway and into the bedroom.

She led him to the bathroom door and stopped, turning to face him. "At a friend's."

Gabe felt sick. "What friend?"

"No one you know."

She closed the bathroom door. He heard her lock it and just stood there, staring at the fake wood grain until he heard the shower come on.

31

Angie and Dwyer sat on the walkway, leaning against the railing, eating breakfast in the shade. The plastic jug of orange juice sat between them and Angie held the container of French toast and bacon. A voice inside her wanted to scream, but she squashed the urge. If she panicked, her fate would be entirely out of her hands.

"Cold French toast is disgusting," Dwyer said, holding a triangular slice up on his fork and biting into it.

"And yet you're eating it."

"I'm hungry," he said with a shrug.

Dwyer picked up the orange juice and took a swig. Sharing the bottle with him didn't trouble her. They had shared far more than that. Her relationship with Dwyer had been all about the sex, and the fact that she thought he was cute and fun to be around. Now, though, sitting here and deceiving him, planning for her own future without taking his into account at all, she realized she had been lying to herself. She felt something for Tom Dwyer. Not love, exactly, but a connection.

But Angie had been telling herself there were no strings attached for so long that she knew she could pretend for a little while longer that she didn't care. Long enough to do what had to be done.

"Hey," Dwyer said. "You okay?"

"Is that a joke?"

Dwyer smiled. "Maybe 'okay' is the wrong word. But I know that look, angel. What's on your mind?"

Angie tilted her head toward the door to the rec room. "Him. What are you all doing, Tom? What are you going to do with him?"

He looked almost hurt. "Nothing. Not me, anyway. With the captain ashore, Miguel's in charge. I'm fourth down the line after Suarez, love, but nobody's talking about doing worse to our guest than he's already gotten. Captain Rio's got a plan."

"You promise?"

Dwyer narrowed his eyes. "Why do you give a shit, all of a sudden?"

Angie's heart raced, wishing she could read his mind. "Why do I care if you guys kill a federal agent?" she whispered, glancing again at the rec room door. "I don't want any part of that."

"Neither do I, sweetheart. But we *are* part of this. Don't let yourself think otherwise. Nobody wants things to go that far, and if we're lucky and the captain's careful, it won't. But whatever happens, we're all a part of it."

Dwyer dropped his fork into the plastic container in her hand. Angie couldn't tell if he was angry or just as frightened as she was, but their conversation had obviously touched a nerve.

"I've got to get back up top. Suarez needs to get some sleep."

Angie nodded wordlessly and set down the container. She turned to gaze out at the ocean, letting Dwyer feel the distance he'd just put between them. As she'd hoped, it gave him pause, and he crouched by her and put a hand on her shoulder.

"Hey," he said, fingertips touching her chin, turning her to face him. "I know you're scared. I'm not going to let anything happen to you."

Something shifted in her then. Sex meant very little to her, but revealing her vulnerability was different. Dwyer liked that she seemed afraid, that she needed him, and Angie nursed a sudden resentment. But she couldn't let him see how much it pissed her off, thinking that she needed anyone to take care of her.

"Anton is going to take over for me in a couple of hours," she said. "Can I come up and see you?"

The Irishman's eyes lit up. Much as he had liked her oil-stained tough-girl exterior, he couldn't hide how much he relished this new facet of her. He smiled softly, and caressed her face again.

"Soon as you can," he said, kissing her forehead. "Don't worry. You've nothing to fear."

Right, she thought. *You'll see to that.*

Any guilt she might have felt evaporated as she watched him hurry along the walkway to the stairs. His boots clanged on the metal steps as he ascended toward the wheelhouse, and Angie let disdain replace her fear. If they really didn't plan to kill Josh, chances were good the PLB hadn't been destroyed or thrown overboard. They'd need to put it back where they'd gotten it at some point. Which meant they had it stashed somewhere. She supposed it might be in Miguel's cabin—at least while he was sleeping—but she thought the captain's quarters more likely, and the wheelhouse itself the most likely of all.

The clock was ticking, but Anton would come to replace her soon enough, and since they weren't ready to kill Josh, she could afford the extra time. As soon as she had the opportunity, she'd find the beacon and trigger it. The FBI would show up and the Rio brothers would go to jail, along with those most loyal to them. Like Dwyer.

If the cost of Angie taking care of herself was Dwyer ending up in prison, she could live with that.

I'm not going to let anything happen to you. You've nothing to fear, she thought, his words echoing in her mind. *Asshole*. She had everything to fear. And there wasn't a damn thing Dwyer could do about it.

32

"What the hell *is* this place?" Tori whispered, more to herself than to Gabe.

The sun beat down on the back of her neck and her shoes were full of sand, but those small discomforts were pushed out of her head by the view they had literally stumbled upon. They'd walked around to the south side of the island, surprised to find that the ridge of hills came all the way to the shore. The slope down to the beach had grown steeper, rising to a peak seventy or eighty feet above the water. The waves lapped against a tumble of rocks and a jagged cliff face, or so it had seemed at first.

Tori and Gabe had followed the land, climbing upward until the ground gave way entirely to rough black stone. The sound had reached them first. Tori had hesitated, then proceeded with more caution, and a few steps later they had realized the source of the echoing whisper of tides, the muffled ripple of water over rocks.

They stood now, staring down into a massive crack in the cliff, as though some ancient god had hacked it in two. Enormous shards had fallen into the surf like chunks calving off an iceberg, but the split in the cliff face was so deep and wide it created a secret cove, and in the shadows where the sun did not reach, it certainly appeared that the opening reached far back into the cliff—into the ridge of hills.

The tide had begun to recede, but the waves swept deep into the hidden grotto, black stones and shells gleaming wetly in the shallow surf. White bits of coral rolled with the ebb and flow. Something shifted under the water in the shadowed cleft and she narrowed her eyes, looking closer.

"Come on," Gabe said, grabbing her arm just enough to turn her.

He started moving inland, toward the head of the cliff. Tori glanced back once and caught a glimpse of white in the surf, caught amidst the jagged black breakers that had fallen away from the cliff years, perhaps decades or centuries, before. The white rocks seemed strange against the black.

"Do you think a storm did this?" she asked as they climbed.

"Over time, I guess," Gabe replied.

They made their way up to the peak, then continued on another fifty yards, instinctively avoiding the edge. At the grotto's roof, the black stone must have been twenty feet thick or more, but Tori feared that it would give way underfoot and they would fall all the way down to the rocky inlet below.

"I don't think it was just a storm," she said as they began to descend on the other side, picking their way carefully down the rocky slope on the west side of the cleft.

"How do you mean?"

Tori turned it over like a puzzle in her head. "Boggs said there were caves in the hills, right? As deep as this thing goes, maybe there was a cave there already. A big one. You get years of erosion and then a big enough storm surge, and the wall between the water and the cave just comes down."

Gabe lost his footing and nearly fell, put down one hand to brace himself, then shook it off, brow furrowed.

"Maybe," he said.

But Tori had already decided that was how the grotto had been formed. It made sense to her. Not that it mattered; they'd be out of here soon, one way or another, and she never wanted to come back. But with that black, volcanic-looking stone, the grotto had an eerie beauty. She wished she had a camera.

At the bottom, the rocks formed a kind of cracked path toward the mouth of the grotto. Curious, Tori started making her way out on them, jumping up to one flat angled stone and dropping down to the next. Once, as a child, her parents had let her go to Maine with her friend Ellen's family, and there had been rocks jumbled on the shore like this.

"What are you doing?" Gabe snapped.

Tori turned, surprised at his tone. "Just getting a closer look."

"You think we're on vacation? You're wasting time." He looked annoyed, but then his gaze shifted past her, toward the grotto, and he turned away. Tori knew the expression on his face all too well—she'd seen it on men all her life. He was hiding something.

"I only need a minute. What don't you want me to see?"

Gabe just shrugged. "Go ahead, then. But make it quick."

More curious than ever, Tori continued picking her way across the rocks, but with every step she grew more uneasy. Waves struck the scattered rocks to her right and salt spray misted the air. Where she'd set off, the rocks had sloped down at a manageable angle, but now the jagged stone became sheer cliff.

Fifteen feet ahead, the sea water rushed into and slipped out of the mouth of the grotto. The stones she walked on now were slick with spray, and Tori moved more cautiously. When she came to a gap, she considered turning back, but instead leaped forward, landing on an angled stone with both feet and steadying herself with a hand. Her pack bounced against her back.

As she started to rise from a crouch, she glimpsed a strange pattern in the black rock and paused to study it. Balancing precariously, she stretched out one leg to prop herself between that stone and the next so that she was able to see between them. The angled stone upon which she stood was etched on two sides with whorls and symbols that might have been the letters of some strange alphabet. Some reminded her of ancient Greek, while others were entirely unfamiliar.

Her stomach tightened with sudden nausea and gooseflesh broke out all over her skin. Tori tried to swallow and found she could not. A dreadful chill went up the back of her neck and she shuddered and lost her footing, then threw out her hands to catch herself as she fell. One foot splashed into the water between two stones and her knees came down hard on the edge of another in front of her.

She wasn't aware of crying out, but she must have, for a second later, Gabe was calling her name and she could hear him making his way along the rocks behind her.

"Are you all right?"

"I'm fine," she said.

But was she? The nausea she'd felt seemed to be passing, but the chill remained and her skin prickled with something that was neither heat nor cold. Tori recognized it. How could she not? She'd spent long spans of her life afraid, and knew the touch of fear all too well.

Now she pulled her foot from the water, cursing her clumsiness, and sat on one of the rocks as she stared again at the odd symbols carved into the stone. Who had put them there, and why? Did that mean people had once lived on the island? Had they been a part of some kind of ancient temple?

Gabe made his way over the stones more gracefully than she would have expected. He might be a bit older than she was, but the captain was a capable man, in excellent shape.

"You've got to take a look at these," Tori said. She'd pulled her hair back into a ponytail, but stray damp locks had fallen in front of her eyes and she tucked them behind her ears as she leaned in to get a better look at the engravings.

"I've seen them already. Let's just go, Tori. We're running out of morning."

Tori stared at the symbols, surprised to find her heart still jittering and her stomach still uneasy. Just looking at those weird letters made her afraid, which made no sense at all, considering she had no idea what they meant. It took a moment for Gabe's words to sink in, but when they did, she looked up at him.

"How did you see them? You couldn't have, from all the way up there. Were there more on the other side?"

The confusion on his face made her realize that he had no idea what she was talking about. Gabe hadn't been referring to the strange symbols on the black stone. But if not that, then what?

Tori turned to scan behind her. The rocks went on for another five feet, beyond which was the mouth of the hidden grotto. The surf rushed over a forty-foot section of rocks and shells. At first, nothing caught her eyes, but then she caught a glimpse of white in the water and remembered having noticed several similar shapes from above, white rocks out of place among the black.

A wave flowed in, and the bleached stone rolled. Not rock, then. To move so easily in the surf it must be brittle coral or some kind of heavy shell. Then the wave slid back out and for just a moment—a breath between ebb and flow—the top inch or so of the white thing was visible above the water. In the sun, and with the white froth of the surf calm for a fraction of a second, she saw it clearly.

A human skull.

Tori made a small noise at the back of her throat and struggled to stand. She scanned the shallow water of the grotto. Now that she knew what she was looking for, she spotted three other skulls right away. She breathed through her nose, trying not to panic, even as she realized that what she'd thought was coral might well be shards of bone instead.

"Who are they?" she said.

"Not from the *Mariposa*," Gabe replied. "None of this is recent."

Tori stared at the skulls. Obviously they weren't from the *Mariposa*'s crew. They were bleached and smooth from being in the water, almost like driftwood now, so they had been in the grotto a long time. But knowing who they weren't was entirely different from figuring out who they were.

"Hey," Gabe said.

She looked at him.

"It's not our puzzle to solve, Tori. We've gotta get—"

His radio crackled, startling them both. Gabe snatched it off his belt.

"Rio," he said.

"It's Kevonne, boss. You on your way?" His voice came through a hiss of static.

Gabe thumbed a button on the radio. "We're getting there. You got something?"

"Damn right," Kevonne said. "Plenty of tracks, and two of the guys who made them. But they're not gonna be making any more. DOA, Captain. Both of 'em."

Tori exhaled a soft prayer to a God she'd lost faith in as a little girl.

"Dead how?" Gabe asked.

The answer came back fast. "Bullets. But this wasn't a gunfight, boss. I'm thinking self-inflicted."

"They killed themselves?" Tori said. "Why?"

Gabe held up a hand to hush her. "Any sign of the guns?" he said into the radio.

"No. But if they're here, they probably aren't far."

"We're coming," Gabe replied, turning to make his way back along the rocks, hurrying westward even as he put the radio back on his belt.

Tori scrambled over the rocks, her right foot squelching in her wet shoe. "Why would they kill themselves?"

Gabe didn't turn or slow. "Fuck if I know. Despair? Maybe they figured they were gonna starve to death or something."

"They were only here for a day. Seriously, that doesn't freak you out? Why would anyone put a bullet in their head if they had any hope at all they could be rescued? A few hours wouldn't be enough to take that hope away, Gabe. They wouldn't even have been that hungry yet!"

Gabe had reached the end of the rocks and started onto the sandy shore, but now he turned to face her, shaking his head.

"I don't really care, all right? Can you just move your ass so we can get the damn guns and get off this island? Whatever happened to these guys, it doesn't matter."

With that, he started off again.

She hurried to catch up, the two of them marching quickly over the rough ground and eventually onto soft beach again. With every step, she wanted to break into a run, and the fear she'd felt while looking at that weird engraving still lingered.

Gabe wanted to get off the island as quickly as possible, and Tori didn't blame him. But he also thought the suicide of two stranded fishermen didn't matter and, on that count, Tori felt sure he was wrong. If they'd really killed themselves, it wouldn't have been out of despair. Only fear could drive someone to desperation that quickly. More than fear, really. Terror.

But what could have made them so afraid?

She glanced back toward the grotto for a moment, then

up at the sun. How long until midday? How long until afternoon, when the shadows of the hills and trees would grow long and the ocean would darken? Tori quickened her pace even more, and Gabe matched her speed without question.

She no longer cared if they managed to find the guns, and she had a feeling that pretty soon even Gabe would be willing to go home without them, as long as it meant getting the hell off the island.

-33--

David Boudreau strolled along the brick sidewalk of M Street, a cup of hazelnut coffee in his right hand and the morning edition of *The Washington Post* in his left. He only read the paper to amuse himself, trying to figure out which reporters were actually clueless and which were actively involved in major cover-ups. He studied the sky, intrigued by the day's curious weather. Sunlight splashed the sidewalk and shone down the entire length of M Street, but the horizon in every direction revealed clusters of low-slung gray clouds, a pattern of light and dark that covered the entirety of the DC area.

Apropos, he thought.

His cell phone erupted in a snatch of angry music from Flogging Molly—a nod to the Irish heritage he'd inherited from his late father. The music had worn a groove in his brain and he realized it was time to change his ring tone. With a sigh, David tucked the newspaper under his right arm and managed to fish the cell from his pocket right before it could go to voice mail.

"What's up?" he said, phone pressed to his ear. "I've sort of got my hands full."

"With what? You haven't been to the office in two days."

"I've been available by phone and e-mail. Working from home."

He heard the sigh on the other end of the line, heavy and theatrical. But that was Henry Wagner, his titular employer, on a typical day.

"What are you working on, David?" Wagner asked.

"It's a pet project, General. But I hope you'll trust me when I say that it falls squarely within our mission parameters."

"You do that on purpose, don't you?" Wagner said.

"Do what?"

"'Mission parameters'? Seriously, kid. The military jargon isn't funny."

David bristled. All right, he was riding General Wagner a little, but the man knew how much he hated being called *kid*. At twenty-four years old, he hardly qualified as a child, and considering he had achieved several advanced degrees while still in his teens, he hadn't been a kid in a long time.

"General, I use terms like 'mission parameters' because I want to make sure I'm understood, and such jargon falls within your comfort zone. If you'd prefer I not use such terms, I'll do my best to avoid them in the future. Now, to your original question—when things are quiet at the office, I've been spending a little time on a pet project of mine which, if it pans out, will absolutely fall under our operational brief."

"'If it pans out,' huh?" Wagner said. "So it's not pressing then. I'm glad to hear it, because we've got a situation I'd like you to look into right away."

Almost without David noticing it, the sun had hidden behind a bank of clouds, and he shivered now as he paused in front of a brick row house. The whole street had been gentrified ages ago, and remained one of the loveliest in Georgetown. Storefronts were festooned with American flags, shaded by awnings, and marked by antique-scripted signs hanging from wrought iron rods. Non-brick surfaces were painted in dark greens and burgundies and rich creams— only colors that would have been used in Colonial times. People walked their dogs and jogged and pushed baby carriages and actually smiled when they passed each other on the street. In Washington, DC, that was a thing of wonder and beauty.

"What is it?" David asked.

"Something that requires your attention," Wagner replied.

David paused on the brick sidewalk, wishing he could sip his coffee without dropping the newspaper tucked under his arm. He stepped over to a lamppost to get out of the way of foot traffic.

"I'm listening, General. What, exactly?"

Another heavy sigh. "You're familiar with the discovery of . . . *Homo floresiensis?*"

He said it as if he were reading it from a file, and David knew that was exactly what he was doing.

"The 'hobbit' skeleton they found in that limestone cave in Ling Bua. Yes, I'm familiar with it, as I am with every single investigation in Alena's files. You know that. Three-foot adult female, a separate human species that lived concurrently with what we consider modern humans, as recently as ten thousand years ago. Have they found something else?"

"Mount Kazbek in the Caucasus Mountains, dormant volcano. Ice on the top, hot springs on the bottom. A month ago, a small earthquake opened fissures in the base that revealed an ancient cave system. A number of partial skeletons were found inside that present a lot of similarities to *Homo floresiensis*."

David started walking again, aiming for a patch of sunshine ahead. Three blocks farther and he'd be home.

"You're boring me, General. Anyone can examine those bones—"

"They have horns."

David held the phone away from his ear and stared at it a second, as though there might be something wrong with it.

"Did you say horns?"

"Vestigial horns, yes. Small pointed protrusions from the skull."

"Interesting, but I'm not sure why it interests you," David said. "Where's the upside for . . ." He almost said the DOD, but caught himself. The Department of Defense didn't like their secrets aired on open phone lines. Officially, David worked for the NSF, but he knew where his funding and his projects came from.

"They were cave painters. The paintings indicate that they had some kind of ritualized weapon—there's obviously an occult component—that could make their enemies . . . well, the team on-site isn't sure if 'melt' or 'vanish' would be a better term, but—"

"You've got a team on-site."

"No," Wagner said quickly. "There are a couple of U.S. scientists there observing, but I'm talking about the Georgian team. The cave's on the Georgia side of the mountain, not the Russian side."

"Uh-huh. Look, have your observers get some hi-res, well-lit shots of all the cave paintings and upload them to the secure FTP. I promise I'll give them my immediate attention as soon as they arrive, but I haven't heard a reason yet for me to go to Georgia."

"Your grandmother—" Wagner began, in protest.

"Is in Croatia, as you well know. And much as she would want to see a little human skull with horns on it, you wouldn't even have bothered her with this unless you had something more to go on, or she volunteered to go."

Wagner snorted derisively. "That's because your grandmother always has something better to do. What's your excuse, World of Warcraft?"

"Trust me, General. I also have better things to do," David said, happy to see the flowerpots hanging from the front of the brick row house he shared with Alena come into view. "Now if you don't mind, my coffee's getting cold."

"David—"

He ended the call, silenced the phone, and slid it into his pocket. It was a perfect day for delicious coffee, the morning paper, and a mystery, and he had all three. No way would he let General Wagner pull him away today.

34

Kevonne and Pang were waiting on the beach. Tori caught sight of them before Gabe did. She and the captain had followed the shoreline away from the hidden grotto and come around a spit of dirt and black rock, when Tori spotted the two sailors sitting on a white sand beach about a quarter mile ahead.

"What are they doing just sitting there?" Gabe said, picking up the pace.

Tori hurried to keep up with him. "Waiting for you, obviously. The dead guys aren't going anywhere."

Even as she said it, a chill went through her. The words sounded so cavalier, but inside she felt anything but. More than ever before, she felt the weight of someone's attention on her—that cold, familiar feeling of being watched by some unseen observer. Tori knew it was probably foolish. The trees were more sparse on this side, with sand scattered deep among them, and the only places anyone could really be hiding to observe them were among the half-sunken ships just offshore. She had glanced at the boats over and over as she walked and not seen so much as a hint of movement. No, they were alone, for now. But she wanted off the island in the worst way.

Kevonne jumped up, tapping Pang, who had pulled the audio buds out of his ears for once. He clicked off his iPod as he stood. Pang's sunglasses were still in place, but something—perhaps finding the dead men, or simply the general sense of unease they all felt—had wiped the smile off his face at last.

"Hey, Captain," Kevonne said.

"Where are they?" Gabe asked.

Pang nodded a respectful hello to both Gabe and Tori. "This way."

He went first, and Kevonne hesitated a second before following. His dark brown skin seemed to have a hint of sickly gray. Going back to see those bodies was the last thing he wanted to do. Pang and Kevonne led them to the tree line, where Pang crouched and pointed to a place where the sand had been recently disturbed.

"You said there were footprints or whatever, right?" Tori asked.

Kevonne nodded and pointed farther along the beach. "Down that way. But it's just what you'd think. A lot of prints from a bunch of different people. Plus, where the sand is soft, you can see where crates were set down and then dragged."

Gabe stood up straighter. "The guns?"

"Probably. We've got a decent trajectory for where they went into the trees at least," Kevonne said.

Pang shoved his hands in his pockets and looked at them. With his sunglasses hiding his eyes, it was impossible to be sure who he focused on, but she assumed his words were for Gabe.

"We wanted to make sure you got a look at these dead guys first," Pang said.

Tori made a face, eyes wide. "Gee, thanks."

No one so much as smiled.

"Let's go, then," Gabe said.

Without another word, Pang and Kevonne stepped into the trees, trampling more sea grass themselves. Tori followed, with the captain coming last. When she looked back she saw Gabe glancing around, taking in their surroundings, eyes narrowed. He seemed to be searching for some indication as to what had happened here. Tori ignored him after that, focused on the sailors in front of her. If something in their surroundings was odd or out of place, she wouldn't notice it unless it was ridiculously hard to miss.

Like the two dead men crumpled on the ground amidst their own blood, for instance.

"Oh," Tori said, more a sound than a word. She covered her

mouth and stepped to one side to let Gabe pass by. Instead, he came to a stop right next to her, eight or nine feet from the dead men.

One of them had been heavyset and bald, with tattoos on his back and arms, and snaking up one side of his neck into a serpentine design over his left ear. He had no shirt, and his copper-hued skin was flecked with dark spots of dry blood. The other corpse belonged to a man short and thin enough to have been a thirteen-year-old boy. Only the sagging of his skin and the roughness of his hands gave away his age. They couldn't tell anything by his features, because he had no face to speak of.

The little man still held a pistol in his right hand. His heavyset shipmate must have dropped his own gun, for it lay in the brush a foot from his left hand, which was open, palm up, though in death the fingers had curled in like the legs of a crab. They had been dead no more than two days, but already their remains had begun to stink.

Tori looked away.

"These weren't suicides," she said quietly. "Not really."

"What?" Kevonne asked. "You think someone set it up to look that way, like in some cop show, out here on this island in the middle of goddamn nowhere?"

"She's right," Gabe said.

Tori glanced at him, saw him pointing at the dead men, but didn't look herself. She had seen enough.

"Same end result, though," the captain said. "They must have counted to three or something, then shot each other in the face. Either way, they were set on dying."

Pang cleared his throat, drawing Tori's attention. He was nodding. "Okay," he said, "but why? They didn't even hold out for a rescue? Couple of wrecks we've seen still had lifeboats on 'em, but these dudes didn't even try to get to them."

Tori thought about the skulls she and Gabe had seen rolling in the surf in the hidden grotto. She glanced at the captain and saw from his eyes that he must have been thinking the same thing.

"Maybe they were saving each other from something worse than getting shot," she said.

Kevonne swore. Pang whistled and took off his sunglasses, studying the bodies more closely. Wide-eyed denial was in both their faces.

"Come on, now," Kevonne said. "Don't start shit like that. What are you even talking about?"

Pang ran both hands through his hair, glasses dangling from the fingers of his right. "Save the last two bullets for us."

Gabe crouched and picked up the pistol the tattooed corpse had dropped. He racked the slide, checked the magazine, and popped it back in before he stood.

"They didn't wait for the last two bullets," he said. "These guys were in a hurry." The captain clicked on the safety and slid the gun into his waistband, then gestured to the other pistol, still clutched in the hand of the tiny dead man. "Pang, take that one."

Pang hesitated, gaze shifting all around, so much fear in his eyes that Tori was glad when he slid his glasses back on. He smiled nervously, but now that she knew the smiles were a mask, looking at him made a little trickle of dread run down the back of her neck.

"I'd rather not, Captain."

Kevonne swore, bent down, and pulled the other pistol out of the dead man's hand. The fingers were stiff enough to resist, but Kevonne twisted the gun until it came free. He followed Gabe's lead, checking the clip, then putting on the safety, but he didn't bother putting the gun away.

"Can we get the hell away from the dead guys now?" he asked.

Gabe took one more look at the corpses, then nodded. Tori let out a sigh of relief and started back through the trees, leading the way to the beach. The others followed her, but by the time she reached the sand she was nearly running. When she hit the beach, she had expected some of her anxiety to abate, but it did not fade at all. Her pulse throbbed in her ears and she breathed evenly, getting control of herself as best she could. Offshore, a bit more of the sunken ships was visible— the tide had started to go down. Above their heads, the sun had reached, or perhaps passed, its apex.

Tori kept walking, and the guys followed her.

Gabe grabbed his radio off his belt. "Chief, you read me?" he asked.

In a soft whisper of static, Boggs's voice came back. "I'm here."

"Any luck?"

"Still checking caves."

"Come out to the beach, pretty much right opposite the cove where we came in. We've got tracks. Should be able to narrow down the search."

"On the way."

Tori, Gabe, Kevonne, and Pang waited, adding their own footprints to the ones the crew of the *Mariposa* had left behind. They talked about trying to go into the trees to meet Boggs and the others halfway, but the captain shut them down. The last thing they needed to do was waste their time wandering around the island looking for one another.

Perhaps fifteen minutes passed before they heard someone approaching, and moments later, Bone emerged from among the trees. He had a thin scratch on his face from a sharp branch or thorn, and he dabbed at the little drips of blood on his cheek with his shirt, as though they were tears.

"Bone?" Gabe said.

The surfer's eyes had darkened to grim acceptance, his fear not gone but apparently put aside for now.

"Sorry to keep you waiting, Captain," Bone said. "But good news. We crossed their path on our way to you. The chief's tracking it back with the other guys right now."

Before Gabe could reply, his radio crackled.

It was Boggs, announcing that they'd found the guns.

Tori felt a surge of relief and started toward Bone. "Show us the way."

35

Gabe wasn't happy when they found the guns. The crew of the *Mariposa* had tramped through the brush, sometimes carrying and sometimes dragging the thick plastic trunks loaded with assault rifles, illegal ammunition, and exquisitely manufactured semiauto pistols made from nonmetals, which would not be picked up by the typical security scan. The latter weren't likely to get on airplanes in the U.S.—not after 9/11—but there were plenty of other places where metal detectors were still the safeguard of choice.

Boggs had found the cave directly inland from where the men of the *Mariposa* had come ashore, maybe a hundred and fifty yards from the beach. According to the chief, this particular cave had no features that distinguished it from the others on the island, so it had to have been chosen for its proximity to the place they'd made landfall. Having never seen the other caves, Gabe only had the grotto to compare it to. This cleft in the base of the hill looked to have been formed by a shifting of the earth—some kind of underground tremor, maybe even a quake. Not that he knew the first thing about earthquakes, really. But since it was more a split in the face of the hill than the sort of cave he thought of, that felt reasonable. More than anything, it looked like the gleaming ebony rock that formed the foundation of the island had cracked open. And if the number of caves was any evidence, it seemed to have cracked open in a great many places.

He wondered if Tori had been wrong about the grotto. Maybe it hadn't been a storm at all that had broken through into the huge chamber inside that coastal cliff; maybe an earthquake had brought it down. But whatever it was, that chamber—and the weird writing they'd found engraved on parts of the shattered wall—were evidence that some of the caves had been on the island a very long time.

"Gather them up," Gabe said, staring at the ground.

The weapons were scattered around the mouth of the cave, discarded or dropped or unpacked but never used. He knelt and picked up an assault rifle. The weapon was light as a feather but he didn't take that to mean much, since they were built to be lightweight. When he popped the clip, however, he found it empty.

"Shit."

"This one's unopened," Kevonne said, as he and Pang dragged one of the plastic cases out of the cave. It measured about four feet by two feet, black plastic with steel locks, no markings at all.

Two more of the cases had been shoved aside just outside the cave, open, their contents either missing or among the weapons arrayed on the ground. Gabe knew some of the weapons would simply be gone, lost in the hands of the members of the crew of the *Mariposa,* wherever they had vanished to. The bottom of the ocean, probably. The weapons scattered on the ground would fill maybe two-thirds of a case if they consolidated into one.

Boggs came out of the cave, running a hand over the stubble on his scalp. Sweat beaded up on his forehead and ran down his neck.

"Three more inside, all of them open, but it doesn't look like they took any guns out of them. Just ammo. Reloading, I'd guess."

Tori gave a little laugh, just off to Gabe's right, and he shot her a look. He didn't like the sound of that laugh; it had the faint edge of crazy in it. But Tori just shrugged her shoulders.

"Yeah, reloading, why not?" she said. "But what were they shooting at, Gabe?"

Who, he thought. *Who were they shooting at?* But he felt certain Tori's word choice hadn't been accidental, so he didn't attempt to correct her.

"Help me with these," he told her, getting down on his knees and reaching for the nearest of the weapons. "You want to get out of here, so let's make it quick."

As Tori joined him on the ground and started helping him repack the guns that lay scattered around into a single case, Gabe looked up at Boggs and the others.

"Get the rest packed up in there, close the cases, and drag them out here. We'll have to make two trips back to the cove, I think."

Boggs hesitated.

"What is it, Chief?" Gabe asked, impatient to be moving.

"Just wondering why we don't radio the *Antoinette,* ask the chief mate to bring her around to this side of the island," Boggs said.

Gabe swallowed, then glanced back the way they'd come, toward the two men who'd shot each other rather than face whatever had made the rest of the *Mariposa*'s crew vanish.

"It didn't work out real well for the last guys who tried it. Anyway, it's not even half a mile, Chief. Just get moving and we'll be fine."

That last bit, about them being fine, rang a little hollow in his ears, but if the others felt the same way, no one dared to mention it. They set about dragging the other cases out of the cave and packing the guns away. Inside, in the dark, Gabe heard the dripping, and beneath it the shushing sound of water in motion, ebb and flow. This cave went deep and somehow the ocean had gotten in. It seemed the grotto wasn't the only place where the sea had found its way underground. If the island had really been shifting and cracking for as long as he imagined, there might be dozens of such tunnels down there.

He wondered for a moment if some of the *Mariposa*'s crew might still be ashore, hiding down in those caves. But the two dead guys on the beach and the abandoned guns in the dirt suggested otherwise, and Gabe wasn't in the mood to go exploring. He was just here for the guns.

They'd found six of the plastic crates altogether out of ten that the *Antoinette* had been expecting to pick up from the *Mariposa*. What had happened to the other four, Gabe had no idea, but now that they had found these six, he had no intention of spending more time searching this damned island for them.

With the scattered guns consolidated into a single case, he would only return with five, and his employers would want to know what had happened. Gabe would tell them the other crates must be with the *Mariposa*'s crew, wherever those men had gone. No one would debate the story. They'd just be happy to have recovered anything. And maybe, if he could pull off the crazy plan he'd committed himself to, he would still be able to hold on to his job after all the arrest and court proceedings were through. Gabe told himself that if he showed Viscaya loyalty, the company would be loyal in return.

He only half believed it, but he didn't see any other choices.

There were eight of them. They could have taken four of the five cases, but the damn things were so heavy they would have been stopping every hundred yards to rest, and he did not like that idea at all. Gabe Rio wanted a little hustle out of his crew, so he made them work in teams. They took three crates on the first run, intending to come back for the other two. While two people walked alongside, the other six carried the weapons cases, two to a case. Each team would be spelled for a little while by whichever two weren't currently carrying anything, and in that way they made decent time.

The trees and brush forced them to alter course more than once, but in just under an hour, they reached the cove where their lifeboats were moored.

In the hours since they had first landed here, the tide had receded enough so that the lifeboats were stranded on the sand. Gabe didn't give it a second thought—it would be simple enough for them to slide the boats down the wet sand and into the surf.

But the tide had stranded other things on the beach as well. The sand fell away steeply just twenty feet from the high tide line, revealing a wide swath of seashells and doomed jellyfish. Among them were smooth, timeworn shards of bone, and a dozen or more skulls. Like the few in the grotto, they were old things, but no less human. No less dead.

"Jesus!" Boggs shouted, dropping his end of a case.

Kevonne stared, gape-mouthed. "What the fuck is this shit?"

Tori reached out and took Gabe's hand.

That was when Bone started to cry.

-36--

Tupper had already done his rounds for this shift as duty engineer, and until the captain, the chief, and the others came back from the island, he had nothing to do belowdecks. The duty engineer was always on call, just in case anything should go wrong. And, sure, he ought to do his rounds more frequently. Instead, he had retreated to the farthest, most hidden corner of the engineering section, in the shadows behind the boilers.

Not that he was hiding. Tupper didn't hide from anything or anyone. Never had, and never would. No, he came back here whenever he needed some solitude, or room to think, or to have a private place to get a little high. The rules didn't allow smoking down here, and the captain would not have been pleased to discover Tupper puffing on a fat joint in the boiler room. Fortunately, none of the other engineers cared as long as he occasionally shared. Even the chief would only have been pissed if he wasn't invited, but Chief Boggs was ashore at the moment, so Tupper had the smoke all to himself.

God, he needed it.

After this, he'd head to the galley and fix himself an iced coffee. Josh didn't like anyone messing up his work space, but fuck him. Dude was FBI. Nobody cared what he liked and didn't like. Josh ought to count himself lucky just to be alive.

Tupper sighed, took a long drag on the joint, held the sweet smoke in his lungs for a few seconds, then blew it out slow.

He closed his eyes and rested the back of his head against the starboard hull.

FBI on board, rendezvous ship full of dead guys, guns missing, a third of the damn crew gone ashore to find them. Tupper considered himself a simple enough guy—beer and grass, pussy, sunshine, decent music, and cheeseburgers were all he required. Simple guy, simple life. But his life had just turned into a colossal clusterfuck.

"Shiiiiiit," he whispered.

Sweat trickled down his forehead and he let it run. With the boilers chugging, it was like a steam room full of clanking pipes. Hot as hell. But he liked being belowdecks, down deep enough that he was cradled by the ocean. The back of his head felt cool, in spite of the boiler room's heat.

Tupper took another long drag, relishing the smoke. At last the tension in his shoulders had started to subside.

At first, the knocking sounded far away, just one more clank and thump from the pipes and the chugging boilers. Slowly, though, a crease formed in his forehead. What was that noise? He knew the workings of the *Antoinette*'s innards better than anyone except the chief, but he didn't recognize this sound.

His eyes opened. Something going wrong with the boilers, maybe? He was duty engineer, which made it his responsibility.

Tupper listened hard, the burning ember dimming at the end of the joint. His senses were pleasantly dulled and he felt sleepy, but he shook it off as best he could. The knocking came again, and he turned to look along the wall to his left. A pipe down there, maybe? He squinted in the gloom, slowly accepting that he would have to get up and check it out. Now was definitely not the time to piss off Captain Rio.

With a sigh, he put a hand against the hull and started to rise.

Something thumped the hull from the outside.

Tupper yanked his hand back as though burned. He stared at the hull, and jumped when the sound came again—a knock against the metal that resounded in the boiler room. It quickened—half a dozen blows striking the hull in as many seconds. Then it stopped, leaving only low echoes in the midst of the clanking and the heat. Tupper cocked his head, staring, waiting for it to come again, wondering what the hell had been hammering on the hull out there, underwater. Sharks or dolphins, maybe? Fucking blind or stupid sharks, if they were, trying to attack the hull of a freighter.

He pinched the end of the joint, licked his thumb and forefinger, and did it again to make sure it was out. Then he slipped the roach into his pocket and started slowly out of the boiler room.

Two more quick thumps rang against the hull and he quickened his pace, their echoes following him out.

-37--

A little after two o'clock, Angie finally made her way up the metal stairs to the wheelhouse. She'd been up these stairs dozens of times, and often thought about how much the tower of living spaces that sat on the back of the *Antoinette* reminded her of whitewashed Miami apartment buildings. The stairs only added to the illusion.

She climbed the last few steps carrying two cups of coffee, careful to keep her balance. On the metal landing she paused to take a deep breath and rebuild the smile she'd manufactured on her way up. No matter how many times she plastered it on, that smile kept cracking and falling away. Right now, she needed it more than ever.

Forcing herself not to falter—in expression or in balance—she reached out with the tip of her shoe and kicked at the base of the wheelhouse door. This ought to have been the most mundane of tasks, going to visit Dwyer in the wheelhouse, bringing her boyfriend—or whatever they were supposed to be to each other—a cup of coffee. But her skin prickled with the anxiety of deception.

Suck it up, Ange, she thought. *This is how you stay out of jail.*

The Caribbean sun had been beating down on the *Antoinette* all day and there'd been little wind, and almost no chop on the water. Now an oddly cool breeze gusted past her, chilling the beads of sweat on the back of her neck, and she shivered.

Through the windows, she watched Dwyer stride toward her. He turned to say something to Suarez, who stood by the wheel and the instruments, watching the radar like a hawk. Angie could only remember a couple of times when she had visited the bridge and *not* seen Suarez there, but today his normally laid-back demeanor had been replaced by a tightly coiled tension that unsettled her.

Watching for other boats, she thought. *Waiting for the FBI.*

Despite her deal with Josh, she couldn't help silently urging Gabe and Tori and the others to hurry. How hard could it be to get the guns and get the hell back to the ship?

Dwyer pulled the door open, grinning, and stepped aside to let her in. "If those are iced coffees, you've just fulfilled my two greatest wishes at the same time."

For a precious few seconds, Angie didn't have to fake her smile. She handed him the iced coffee, loaded with sugar the way he liked it, and slid her hand behind his neck, pulling him down to kiss her. But as soon as the kiss broke off, she remembered his earlier condescension, and why she'd come, and her smile turned false again.

"What took you so long?" he asked, glancing at the clock.

"Fucking Anton didn't show up to relieve me until about twenty minutes ago. He 'overslept,'" she said. "I almost chucked his ass overboard. My eyes are burning and I'm dead on my feet, but he overslept? Fucker."

Dwyer laughed, kissed her again, and took a sip of his coffee. Even Suarez glanced up from his vigil over the instruments to smile at her frustration.

"I'm funny to you guys now?" Angie said, nostrils flaring. "You're goin' over the railing right after Anton."

That made Suarez break out in an actual grin. He must

have been tired to let his guard down like that. Dwyer knew better than to push her buttons any further, though. He only took another sip of coffee, ice clinking in his cup.

"I'm glad you came up to see me, love," Dwyer said, "but maybe you ought to try to get a little sleep while Anton's on guard duty."

Angie almost pouted. If she wanted to manipulate Dwyer, that would be the way to go. But he knew her well enough to know the pout wasn't really part of her repertoire, and she didn't want him to start wondering what she really wanted.

"In a little bit," she said, raising her cup. "After our coffee. What about you? How long until someone spells you guys?"

Dwyer glanced at Suarez, but the white-haired old Cuban didn't even glance up from the radar this time.

"Miguel's taking three hours, then me, then Suarez," Dwyer said.

Angie frowned. "You don't think they'll be back by then? What the hell is taking so long?"

"They found 'em," Dwyer said. "Now it's a matter of getting 'em back to—"

Suarez cut him off. "It takes as long as it takes, Angela. We stick until Captain Rio says otherwise."

The old man had an edge in his voice and a hard glint in his eyes that Angie had never seen there before, and for a second she feared that Suarez had somehow sensed she was hiding something. But then he went back to staring at the radar screen, jaw set, leaning forward in his seat, and she understood. Suarez had stoic down to a science, but their current dilemma had him rattled.

"You won't get an argument from me," she said. "I just wish things could go a little faster. I want to get out of here before Josh's friends show up."

Suarez glanced up at her with a look that let her know he regretted snapping at her, just a little. "Don't worry. We'll be long gone."

"Absolutely," Dwyer agreed, a little too emphatically. He touched her face and kissed her forehead. Once upon a time she'd have been charmed by the gestures. Today she wanted to punch him.

"Good," Angie said, walking toward Suarez, sipping her iced coffee.

Suarez sat in one of the two chairs in front of the wheel and the instrument array. Angie didn't have the first clue how to pilot the ship, but she had a feeling she could figure it out if necessary. The wheel was literally nothing more than that—a metal steering wheel that stuck out of a black control box. Crazy to think that something so simple could guide the entire ship. It was more complicated than that, of course. But in truth, with the collision avoidance system built into the *Antoinette*'s computer guidance programming, plus radar, and people like Angie herself doing their jobs down in the engine room, a monkey could get the ship moving.

She leaned on the back of the empty chair and gazed out the windshield at the sea. It was barely mid-afternoon, but already the water had begun to darken. The sunlight hit it at a different angle as the day grew long.

Dwyer stood beside her, slipped an arm around her, and sipped his coffee.

"I'm with you, angel. I hope they hurry."

But Angie had stopped listening. Stopped breathing. A low hiss of static came from the radio, a row of green and yellow lights flickering across its face. And right on top of it, out in the open, sat Josh's lifeline, the personal locator beacon. It remained in its rubber holster, and she suspected that nobody had tried taking it out yet, just in case Josh had been telling the truth about it being rigged to go off automatically. The black and yellow plastic made it look like a nouveau walkie-talkie or a bulky cell phone.

Dwyer took her free hand, squeezed her fingers, trying to lend her comfort.

Angie looked up at him, stood on her toes and kissed his freckled nose, smiling as she began to breathe again.

Exhausted as she was, she had no intention of leaving the wheelhouse just yet. All she had to do was bide her time, and she'd get the chance to set off the beacon. And if the opportunity didn't arise, she'd have to create one.

The door banged open, and all three of them turned to see Tupper standing in the doorway.

"Dude, what the hell are you doing up here? Last I checked, you're the duty engineer at the moment," Angie said.

Tupper didn't spare her so much as a scowl. He looked genuinely spooked, even skittish, and large sweat stains had formed under his arms and at the neck of his T-shirt. For a second, Angie thought he'd seen the Feds closing in, but that was ridiculous. Suarez would have seen them coming on the radar.

"Mr. Dwyer," Tupper said, "can you come down to the engine room?"

Dwyer and Suarez glanced at each other.

"You came all the way up here to ask that?" Suarez said. "You could've called from belowdecks, saved yourself a trip, and not left your post unattended."

If Suarez expected some kind of explanation or apology, he didn't get it.

"There's something you need to hear," Tupper said.

A flicker of alarm crossed Dwyer's face. "Something wrong with the engines?"

"No. Nothing like that. Just . . . humor me, man."

Again, the second and third mates exchanged a look. Then Suarez shrugged. "Go ahead. Miguel will be up in a little while."

Dwyer drained the rest of his iced coffee and tossed the cup in a trash bin. He smiled at Angie as if to say, *Damn, Tupper's gone over the edge,* and then he nodded toward the engineer.

"All right, Tup. Lead the way."

They exited the wheelhouse, leaving Angie and Suarez alone. She knew she ought to go. Without Dwyer there, she had no reason to stay. But she might never get a better chance at the beacon. All she needed was for Suarez to be distracted for a few seconds. Immediately, she thought of several ways she could distract him, but most of them involved seduction, nudity, or sex to one degree or another, and she had too much self-respect to resort to something that would make her feel like a whore.

Think of something else, she told herself.

But nothing was coming to her.

Josh had torn the net off the Ping-Pong table and now lay stretched out on top of it. With the doors closed, the temperature in the rec room had gotten more than a little uncomfortable as the day wore on. Elevated by the Ping-Pong table, he was perfectly situated to catch every breeze that came through the open windows. He had shut the lights off and gotten a cold soda out of the machine, and he lay with the can pressed against his throbbing face, keeping his breathing steady, trying to let himself slip into a meditative state so that the passage of time wouldn't drive him nuts.

It wasn't working very well.

Angie had seemed frightened by the prospect of going to prison, but he had little confidence in the woman. When it came time to betray her captain, her crewmates, and the guy she'd been screwing, would she have the guts to do it? Josh wasn't sure. If he was being honest with himself, he wasn't sure of much these days. Despite his better judgment, he had let himself fall for Tori, all the while knowing that in order to do his job he would have to betray her. He would do whatever he could, short of becoming a criminal himself, to help her, but he knew that would mean nothing. She must hate him now, and that certainty tore him up inside. He wasn't accustomed to feeling ashamed.

Meanwhile, all he could do was hope that Angie cared more about saving her own ass than she did about Dwyer. All she had to do was trigger the PLB. Not break him out, not even bring the beacon to him. If she could find it, she could signal Voss and have the FBI, Coast Guard, and ICE here in a couple of hours at most.

But that was a big "if." And if she got caught, or the Rio

brothers even suspected she was trying to help him, Angie would end up in the rec room with him.

"Shit."

Josh rolled onto his side and swung his legs off the Ping-Pong table. With deep regret, he set down the soda can. It had started to lose some of its chill, but still his battered face throbbed painfully the instant he took the cold metal away. A couple of hours ago, it had been so swollen that it almost felt like the skin would split. In comparison, the pain didn't seem quite so bad now.

He cracked the Mountain Dew can and took a long drink, gulping down half the can in seconds, then rested it on the table again. Quietly, he walked to the corner of the room and pressed his face to the louvered shutters, trying to get a glimpse of whoever had been posted as his latest guard.

At first he thought the door had been left unattended, but then he heard a low sigh and readjusted his position so that he had a slitted view of the walkway in front of the door. Anton Pinsky lay stretched out, eyes hidden behind sunglasses, five days' stubble instead of a beard, and a tall plastic bottle of water by his head. Anton was a little guy, no more than five foot six, with eyes that always seemed to hint he'd rather be elsewhere.

Josh knew he could get past Anton. He had planned to wait until dark to try something stupid, but if Angie didn't at least get some kind of word back to him in the next couple of hours, something stupid might have to be bumped up on his list of things to do.

-39--

Special Agent Rachael Voss stood on the deck of her squad's seized drug boat and tried to tell herself that Josh Hart was still alive. She'd known agents who claimed to have a kind of sixth sense about such things, that they'd know if something had happened to their partner or their wife or child. It would have been a comfort to believe such a thing, but she'd always thought those people sounded like assholes when they spouted off about spiritual connections and psychic rapports and crap like that.

For all Voss knew, Josh might be floating somewhere out on the Caribbean, feeding the fish. She didn't want to believe that, but she had to accept it as a possibility. Standing out there in the merciless sun, sweat trickling down her back and between her breasts, eyes squinted against the glare off the water, amounted to Voss punishing herself for not wanting to accept it.

The only reason for Josh not to have set off the PLB by now—so many long hours after signaling that the *Antoinette* would rendezvous with their gun seller—was that his cover had been blown. Josh was either dead or in no shape to be setting off any beacon. Voss considered the possibility that the Rio brothers had found both the sat-phone and the PLB and tossed them overboard instead of throwing Josh over, but that seemed like wishful thinking.

Her hands started to shake and she crossed her arms to still them.

Last time she'd checked her watch, it had been after two p.m. The Colombian drug lord's yacht floated in the same waters where the *Antoinette* had been sailing when Josh had called in on the satellite phone. That meant they weren't that far from the rendezvous point for the gun buy. How far away was the *Antoinette* now? The only things on their radar were tiny, scattered islands. Nothing moving. No sign of the container ship.

Standing out on the deck meant more than one kind of torment for Voss. The scorching heat was hot enough, but the glare of the people on the other boats around hers burned her just as badly. There were four Coast Guard craft and two Immigration and Customs Enforcement ships, and the commanders of those vessels were getting more than a little impatient.

"Rachael."

Voss hung her head and surprised herself by laughing, but she didn't turn around.

"Christ," Pavarotti muttered. "Special Agent Voss."

She turned to look at him. The younger agent had taken a lot of crap from her this time out, and he'd put up with all of it. Now, though, even Pavarotti looked like he was on edge. And why not? They were all tired and ragged, wondering if this deal was going to fall apart, and if they'd left an agent out in the field to die.

"What's up?" she asked.

Pavarotti stood up straight, like he was a jarhead reporting to his commanding officer. "Supervisory Special Agent Bosworth contacted me and asked me to pass along a message."

Voss sighed, and gritted her teeth. "Go on, Joe. What did Chauncey say?"

"Supervisory Special Agent Bosworth—"

"I'm gonna break your nose, Plausky."

Pavarotti allowed her a smile. "I quote, 'Tell Voss if she doesn't answer her phone I'm going to come out there and shove it down her throat.' He also mentioned that SAC Del-Rosso would be on the line the next time your phone rang."

Voss had continued to communicate with the guys coordinating the interagency efforts for the Coast Guard and ICE, but she had stopped picking up Chauncey's calls a little before noon. Now she looked at Pavarotti.

"We're not leaving Josh out here," she said.

Pavarotti nodded once. "I'm with you. But at some point, the rest of these guys are gonna be called away."

"What else did Chauncey have to say?"

"He had other choice words for you, but honestly, Rachael, they were halfhearted. He's got more on his mind than just being pissed off at you for not responding."

Voss shook her head and looked out to sea, back turned to Pavarotti and all of the other ships who had gathered there to wait for some signal, any indication that Josh Hart might still be alive, so they could rush in and save his ass and bust some assholes responsible for putting automatic weapons on the streets of America.

DelRosso was the special agent in charge. The only reason Chauncey would get him involved was to hammer home a point, or to take this case away from her. Probably both. And that meant only one thing.

"Ed Turcotte's come to town?" she asked. But it wasn't really a question.

"He and his squad left St. Croix an hour ago," Pavarotti said.

Voss swore under her breath, then turned to him. As she did, her phone began to ring. She flinched, her heart racing, and started to reach for it. Her hand froze.

"You've got to answer it, Special Agent Voss," Pavarotti said.

The boat swayed under them. Voss stared at him. "Oh, now you're all fucking official?" she asked bitterly. "DelRosso's going to tell me to stand down, Joe. He's going to tell me to wait for Counter-Terrorism to get here and turn the case over to Turcotte the second they arrive."

"Answer it, Rachael. Tell him whatever he wants to hear. Turcotte's not here yet. It'll be hours yet. Until then, we do whatever we have to do to take care of Josh."

Taking a deep breath, Voss answered the phone.

-40--

You're a survivor, Tori. That's what you do. You make it through.

She held such thoughts close to her, repeating them over and over like a mantra. Whatever had happened to the people whose bones now rolled in the surf as the tide went out, Tori refused to end up like them.

"Hey," Gabe said quietly, stepping up beside her. "It'll be okay."

Tori nodded, but would take no comfort from him. She kept her distance now from all of them. When they had discovered that the FBI was onto them, that Josh was an agent and they might all be going to prison, she had thought they were screwed right then. But whatever this was, she knew it was worse. They had scoured half the island and seen no sign of anyone living, and if the *Antoinette* had picked up ships returning—pirates or raiders or whoever had killed the *Mariposa*'s crew—Miguel would have signaled Gabe. As the shadows grew longer and the breeze off the water picked up, the sense of foreboding she'd had for hours now only increased.

Despite who he was, Tori liked Gabe Rio. Ironically enough, she also liked Josh. If she thought about it, she'd grown fond of most of the *Antoinette*'s crew during the voyage. Boggs, Tupper, Angie Tyree, and a few others she could do without, but guys like Dwyer and Kevonne and Bone made her smile. They were in this together, and she'd do whatever she could to help get them all out of it.

But she had felt herself closing off the doors between herself and the others ever since she and Gabe had seen those bones in the grotto. As they had lugged the gun cases through the trees, she had thought about her father's cruelty, and the way her mother had turned a blind eye, and she knew that had been a lesson. Marrying Ted had been another. Tori could not rely on anyone except herself. When she had found kindhearted George online and he had helped her to escape from Ted, she had thought of him as her rescuer. But *she* had found George, and asked for his help, and she had taken what he had to offer and then moved on.

Tori had finally reached a place of peace and confidence inside her head, and a moment in her life when she felt she really could start over. The intensity of her attraction to Josh and the chemistry between them had felt like the result of that, or even a reward for finding her own inner strength. How long had she dreamed of a man she could really trust and believe in?

Now, with the new life she'd been trying to build falling apart around her, and with a heart full of dread like she had never known, she had to learn the lesson all over again.

Was she a damsel in distress? Damn right. Her whole cursed life.

But there were no heroes on this beach, and none on the *Antoinette,* Josh included. So she would go along with whatever Gabe wanted to do, and help where she could, as long as her best interests matched his. But the only person she could rely on was herself.

Standing on the beach, just a few feet from where the waves swept across the sand, she thrust her hands into her pockets to keep them steady. Tori could taste the fear on her lips, but she didn't mind so much anymore. She'd known fear intimately in the past, and thus far it had kept her alive.

"Watch it, you idiots!" Gabe shouted, storming down to the water.

Boggs had left his two lackeys to move the three boxes of guns from the beach to his lifeboat, heading back into the trees with Pang, Kevonne, and Bone, to retrieve the last two cases. Gabe had let the two sailors rest for a while, since it would take time for the others to return with the rest of their salvaged cargo.

Now they'd nearly dumped one of the cases into the water, and Gabe waded into the surf, looking like he might be itching to use one of those guns himself. The two sailors apologized profusely as Gabe steadied the heavy case and they finished loading it. Tori had been feeling bad because she didn't know their names, but from the way he dealt with them, she got the idea that Gabe wasn't quite sure what to call them, either, and he was the captain. She didn't blame him, or herself. The two guys—she thought one of them was called Mitchell—kept quiet, and mostly to themselves.

Once they had all three cases loaded, they stayed in the lifeboat, talking quietly, stealing nervous glances between the island and the *Antoinette.* Tori understood those glances. *What are we waiting for?* they said. *Let's get the fuck out of here.*

They were still sitting like that, and Gabe and Tori were together on the beach, talking about everything except their tense circumstances, when Pang and Bone staggered out of the trees with the fourth case.

"Thank God." Tori sighed.

"For Christ's sake, Bone, what took so long?" Gabe asked.

As he spoke, Boggs and Kevonne trudged out of the brush with the last of the salvaged cases. The chief's face had turned bright red and sweat dripped down his forehead and scalp. He looked like a steamed lobster.

"All due respect, Captain," Boggs said, "but we were moving our goddamn asses."

Tori happened to agree with him. The four men had really not been gone that long, all things considered. But since she hated Boggs, she wasn't about to defend him. Gabe spent a couple of seconds looking like he might get pissed off at Boggs for the back talk, but then he waved a hand and the moment passed.

"All right. Let's just get going."

Grunting, sweating, looking altogether like they might just collapse there on the sand, the four of them struggled down the beach. They made it a dozen feet before Kevonne stumbled.

"Watch it!" Boggs snapped.

"Hey, Chief, can we just set these down for a minute?" Bone asked. "Get a better grip, okay? I don't want to end up dropping these guns in the drink."

By that point, Bone and Pang were already lowering their case to the ground. Even if the chief wanted to yell at them, it'd be too late. Instead, Boggs started to lower his case as well. When he and Kevonne set it on the sand, his groan of relief made him sound like an old man.

Tori glanced at Gabe. She could feel his impatience, and she shared it. By silent, mutual understanding, they had all avoided talking about the bones and skulls that rolled in the waves just offshore, but each of them was anxious to get back to the ship.

"Chief," Gabe said. "Your lifeboat's ready to go. Start back. We're right behind you."

Boggs visibly relaxed. "Yessir, Captain."

He headed for the lifeboat. The two sailors, Mitchell and not-Mitchell, straightened up, jumped out of the lifeboat, and started pushing it back from shore before Boggs had even reached them. The chief snapped at them, but even his ire didn't slow them down, so anxious were they to get out of there. Tori envied them, and from the looks of exasperation on the faces of the others, she knew she wasn't alone.

Gabe took Boggs's place and nodded at Kevonne. "You ready?"

"Ready, Captain."

They lifted together, and started, stiff-legged, toward the other lifeboat. Bone and Pang did the same with the final case. Tori felt fairly useless, but she didn't feel like she had anything to prove. She had done her share of the lugging with the first three boxes of guns and her biceps and forearms ached from it. If the four guys—all of whom were stronger than she—wanted to volunteer, she wouldn't argue with them. Gender bias didn't even make it onto the list of her current concerns.

The motor of Boggs's lifeboat roared loudly for a second, but then it dropped to a low drone as the chief throttled down. He still had to navigate the graveyard of ships that separated the beach from the open water. Tori watched them go, wishing she had thought to go with them. Much as she hated Boggs, getting off the island quicker would've been worth spending ten minutes with him.

"Tori, come hold her steady, will you?" Gabe called.

With a nod, she started toward the men who were gathered around the remaining lifeboat. The gentle surf swayed it only a little. The tide had withdrawn enough so that the front half of the boat sat on the sand now, the anchor line stretched out across damp beach. When they'd landed, one of the guys had dug in the anchor as far ashore as the tether line would reach. Now they didn't even need the anchor. The lifeboat wouldn't be drifting anywhere until the tide came back in.

Tori hurried up and grabbed the side of the lifeboat, even as Kevonne stepped into it from the other side. He set the edge of the gun case on the edge of the boat and it tilted hard. Tori used all her weight to provide a counter, tilting it back up again, and Kevonne and Gabe muscled the heavy plastic case into the lifeboat.

The captain helped her keep it steady as Pang and Bone slid the last case into the boat, and Kevonne dragged both of them around on the floor of the lifeboat a bit, arranging room for all five of them to sit. It would be cramped, but they'd manage. Nobody was going to be waiting around on the island for a second trip.

"All aboard," Gabe said.

"Damn straight. And full speed ahead," Bone muttered.

Tori climbed into the lifeboat from the front. Pang went up the beach and tugged the anchor out of the sand, then carried it back to the boat, looping the rope around his forearm. He dumped it in beside the gun cases, then braced both hands against the prow. Gabe and Bone flanked him on either side, and the three of them began to push. The lifeboat rocked a little, but its rear end was still afloat, and it started to slide into the water.

Bone gave a little groan of revulsion and dragged himself aboard, turning to look back down at the water he'd just been trudging in. Tori didn't look. She knew from the look on his face that the shush and rattle she heard were bones in the surf. The only other sound was the other lifeboat's engine just offshore, like the growl of a neighbor's lawn mower on a summer day.

Gabe kept pushing, wading out a little, stoic as ever, either untroubled or unwilling to reveal it if he was. Pang had hidden his own fears behind his sunglasses again, but he'd stashed his iPod somewhere.

He was the first to look up, frowning deeply, realizing something was wrong. The other lifeboat's engine had started to rev higher, whining.

"What the hell—" Kevonne started to say.

Tori turned just as shouts began to carry across the water to the island. The graveyard of ships filled her field of vision, tangled and jutting and jagged like some bizarre bit of modern art. The angled gap among the derelict ships was like a corridor back out to open sea, and Boggs's lifeboat had just begun to traverse the gap.

One of the sailors shouted again, the word *fuck* echoing back to the beach. The motor whined louder. Chief Boggs shoved one of the men aside and knelt at the back, staring down into the water at the propeller, trying to figure out what the hell they had snagged on.

"Chief?" Gabe called from the shore. "What is it?"

Pang hauled himself up beside Tori. Only the captain remained standing—waist-deep now—in the waves. But they were all focused on the other lifeboat, out there amid the ruined ships.

"Goddamn, did you see that?" Boggs cried, turning to the two who'd accompanied him. Mitchell and not-Mitchell, as Tori thought of them.

The one at the prow leaned way out over the water, gazing down, and even from that distance Tori thought he looked like he was about to puke into the sea. He swayed a bit, then started to shake his head and fell back into the boat, scrambling away. He bumped right up against the other side of the lifeboat—there wasn't much room for retreat.

"Chief?" Gabe shouted again.

Boggs looked up at the captain, and at Tori and the others. His features were slack with shock. Then the lifeboat flipped, the port side dipping down into the water as though a massive wave had swept up beneath it—except no such wave disrupted the coolly rippling sea. Boggs hurtled through the air and splashed into the water nine or ten feet from the lifeboat. Mitchell—Tori felt sure he must be Mitchell—dropped just beside the upturned boat, but not-Mitchell had been lying sprawled on the bottom of the craft, and it turned over so fast that it covered him completely. He must have fallen out then, along with the three plastic crates of guns.

"Jesus Christ!" Gabe shouted, wading farther into the water, their own lifeboat forgotten for a moment. "The fucking guns! You assholes, what are you—"

Mitchell came up screaming, a four-inch swathe of his face turned to ragged, bloody mess. He scrabbled for the edge of the lifeboat, but something cracked in the boat itself, and it buckled and began to sink, half-submerged in seconds. Tori held her breath, felt herself waiting for obscene cursing or prayers to an uncaring God, but whatever had hold of Mitchell filled him with enough pain and terror that he uttered not a single intelligible word, and somehow that was worse.

He screamed again, still trying to pull himself up on the

remnant of the boat, and then he stopped and juddered in the water as though in the grip of seizure. Like the lifeboat, something in him cracked, then he vanished below the water, swift as a hanged man down the throat of the gallows. The crystal blue Caribbean waters blossomed with crimson.

"Swim!" Tori shouted, standing up in her own lifeboat. "Chief, swim for it!"

Boggs had been staring along with the rest of them, but they were near the shore and he was bobbing out there in the gap amid the graveyard of ships. Shaken from his entrancement by Tori's voice, or Mitchell's blood on the water, he turned and started kicking for the nearest derelict ship.

Pang and Bone were shouting for Boggs to swim as well. Tori tore her eyes away from the chief and looked at Kevonne, who stared back as they shared a sudden realization. He lunged for the starter, got the motor coughing, and grabbed the throttle.

"Gabe!" Tori yelled.

But the captain could not look away from the sight of Boggs frantically thrashing in the water. Tori glanced that way, saw a ripple on the surface of the water, and knew that whatever had dragged Mitchell down was now aiming for Boggs.

The chief reached the wrecked cabin cruiser. He grabbed hold of the frame of a shattered window and hauled himself out of the sea, got his footing on a railing, and climbed higher on a ladder of empty window frames. Only then did he turn and stare down at the water.

The third man, not-Mitchell, never emerged from the overturned ruin of the lifeboat. The ripple in the water vanished, whatever had caused it swimming deeper or falling still.

"Gabe!" Tori screamed. The captain snapped his head around to stare at her. "Get back on shore!"

Kevonne throttled up and the lifeboat roared toward the beach. They'd only drifted a dozen feet from the island, but Kevonne gunned the motor and drove the boat right up onto the sand. Tori collided with Pang as they hit the beach. Bone leaped out, jumping around, clutching at his head with both hands like it might break apart.

"Come on," Tori said, grabbing Kevonne's hand.

Pang scrambled so madly to get out of the lifeboat that he fell over the edge, splashing in the shallows. When he came up, spitting water, his sunglasses had fallen off, revealing his terrified eyes. Tori and Kevonne jumped after him.

Gabe slogged to shore, eyes wide with some mix of fear and fury.

"What the hell are you doing?" the captain screamed at Kevonne. Then he looked at Tori. "Get back in the fucking lifeboat."

"Are you crazy?" Tori snapped, heart racing, face flushed. "Didn't you see what just happened? Something's out there!"

Gabe rounded on her. "No shit. I'm not fucking blind. But we can't just stay here. If we don't get back to the *Antoinette,* we're as good as dead."

"What?" Kevonne said. "Why? We're on land, Captain. That thing, whatever it is, that's in the water. No, man, we gotta stay here, figure something out. We got guns. We got—"

"So did the crew from the *Mariposa,*" Gabe said, his words clipped and his eyes cold. "And where are they?"

Silently, all five of them turned to look out to sea—at the graveyard of ships, and at Hank Boggs, stranded among the wrecks, and at the *Antoinette,* which sat waiting for them less than half a mile offshore.

-41--

Dwyer hated going down into the bowels of a ship, with the engines and boilers, the sweat and the heat close around him. He never visited Angie when she was on duty be-lowdecks, and was glad that she had never asked him why. How could he admit to her that it frightened him? More than frightened him, really. With the metal closing around him and the water beyond that, he felt as though he would be crushed. Once, while visiting New York, he'd been trapped for over an hour on a broken elevator. Panic had closed off his throat and amped up his adrenaline so that he thought he was suffocating and having a heart attack, all at the same time. But he'd been claustrophobic long before that elevator ride.

He followed Tupper down the metal steps into the engine room. His eardrums were unused to the noise level and he winced as it pressed around him. The heat embraced him, but Dwyer clenched his jaw and kept moving, down through the engine room, out into another corridor, and then into the boiler room, where humidity blanketed him in an instant.

"Tupper!" he barked.

The engineer had gotten ten feet ahead of him, but turned now, wide-eyed and anxious. "Come on, man."

Dwyer wiped sweat from his forehead, then ran both hands through his red hair, spiking it, wishing for a shower. "Tell me again what we're doing down here? 'Cause I'll tell you, boyo, you seem like you've gone off your rocker."

Off your rocker. One of his Gram's favorite sayings, from back when he was a boy. Stress had a way of making him regress, and always had, as though subconsciously he wished he could go back to a simpler time. Dwyer figured everybody felt that way sometimes.

The suggestion pissed Tupper off. The engineer narrowed his eyes, nostrils flaring. If they were in a bar, Dwyer would have thought he was squaring off for a fight.

"Haven't you been listening to a word I said?" Tupper demanded.

"A bit difficult when you're muttering half of it."

Tupper squeezed his eyes shut and took a deep breath. When he opened them, he spoke with barely controlled anger. Yet Dwyer thought the anger itself was a kind of control, and what it held the reins on was fear.

"Look, the whole ship's on edge," Tupper said. "I get that. But you've gotta listen to me, man. Better yet, don't listen to me. Listen to the ship."

Dwyer hesitated. Even the arch of an eyebrow right now might be enough to set Tupper off, and he really didn't relish the idea of a fistfight down here. As it was he had to force himself to keep his breathing steady, keep his heart from racing, and he wasn't succeeding completely. But Tupper was really losing it.

"Listen to the ship?" Dwyer said, carefully.

Tupper rolled his eyes. "Fuck! I'm not crazy, Dwyer. Come over here."

He stepped into a narrow space between two large boiler tanks. Dwyer started to follow, then froze. The gap held only shadows, not even wide enough for light to pass through. The boilers hummed. His hands clenched into fists and his throat felt tight. He managed to swallow, then took a long, labored breath.

"Dwyer!" Tupper called from the darkness.

Dwyer took a step back instead of forward. Yet in the space of long seconds, he heard a loud thump. He frowned, distracted by the sound. It came again and he stepped forward.

"Tupper?"

The engineer popped out of the narrow space, and Dwyer jerked backward, startled. The thump came a third and fourth time, in rapid succession, muffled but still echoing low and deep in the boiler room.

"There. Did you hear it?"

Dwyer nodded. "What the hell is that? Is something wrong with the boilers?"

"No, man. It's not the boilers. That's what I'm telling you."

Then the engineer's rant came back to him, his mutterings about something in the water, banging on the hull.

"That's coming from outside?" Dwyer asked, incredulous, as he pushed past Tupper and slid between the boilers. His skin crawled and panic threatened, but he kept on.

"Damn right it is," Tupper said, right behind him. "Something's knocking. And it wants to come in."

Past the boilers, Dwyer stopped, waiting, thinking for a second that the sound wouldn't come again, that Tupper had been wrong and it really was something to do with the engines and the boilers. And how the hell would they get out of there if the boilers exploded?

He laid his hands on the inner surface of the hull.

The knock came again, louder than ever, and he jumped back. "Jesus!"

"What do you think it is?" Tupper asked.

Dwyer stared at his palms, which still tingled from contact with the metal. He backed away farther, pushed past Tupper, slid quickly between the boilers, and quickened his pace as he threaded back through the *Antoinette*'s heart.

"Dude!" Tupper called, rushing to catch up with him, keeping pace just behind him. "What do you think that is?"

Dwyer still didn't answer. He hadn't a clue what could be banging on the *Antoinette*'s hull, but he had the terrible feeling Tupper was right; it wanted in. And no way did he want to be trapped in the narrow labyrinth belowdecks if it got its wish.

-42--

Angie sat beside Suarez, up in the wheelhouse, looking out over the hundreds of metal containers stacked on the deck in front of them, and at the ocean beyond. Every few seconds she caught herself glancing to the right, where the windows offered a view of the island and the ruined, sunken ships that clustered around it. But Suarez never wavered. His focus remained on the radar screen, where the image continued to refresh, scanning for any approaching ships. She had thought that he would ask her why she had remained when Dwyer had gone below, but Suarez seemed content to ignore her. Eventually, Angie couldn't stand the silence.

"Aren't you scared at all?" she asked.

The old Cuban cocked his head to one side and looked at her. "Pardon me?"

"I mean, you just sit there looking at the radar, calm as anything. We could go to prison. The FBI is probably moving in on us right now. And what happened to the guys with the guns, anyway? 'Cause it sounds like a clusterfuck. That doesn't make you nervous?"

Angie hadn't meant to ramble on like that. She only wanted to make conversation, to set Suarez at ease with her presence, hoping he'd step away from the command console and the wheel long enough for her to grab the PLB and set off the beacon. But her fear came tumbling out in the form of words.

Suarez raised his eyebrows. "You gotta be serene, Angela."

"So you're a wise old man, now?"

"Not so old," he said. And maybe he wasn't at that. The white hair and his innate gravity gave him the appearance of being sixty or more, but his eyes were bright and alive and his skin not so deeply lined. He might actually have been no more than fifty.

"I think serene's out of reach for me right now," she admitted.

"Then pray," Suarez told her.

Angie arched an eyebrow, surprised, but then it occurred to her that she really knew nothing at all about the man.

"You've never heard of the Serenity Prayer?"

She shook her head.

" 'God, grant me the serenity to accept the things I cannot change, the courage to change the things I can, and the wisdom to know the difference.' "

A smile stole across her face. "See? You are a wise old man."

Suarez chuckled. "Don't push your luck with that 'old' business."

But while they joked about it, the words of the Serenity Prayer were working their way into Angie's heart and mind. Suarez wanted her to surrender herself to some higher power, to accept that their situation was not only completely fucked, but totally out of their control. Maybe that was true for him, but not for her. She had already taken steps to change her circumstances, and serenity be damned.

"Thanks," she said. "I'm not so afraid anymore."

"My pleasure."

He nodded, but his attention had returned to the radar

screen. Angie glanced past him at the PLB, and knew the time had come. Single-minded and loyal, Suarez would not be easily distracted, which called for a more direct approach. With real regret, she looked around the wheelhouse for something to hit him with. If she knocked him out, she could set off the beacon and then go find somewhere to hide until the FBI showed up. There were a hundred little corners she could hole up in belowdecks, around the ballast tanks and boilers and engines. She could hide in a lifeboat, maybe even find a place among the containers out on the deck, or slip into an unlocked one.

A metal fire extinguisher hung by the door. The moment she laid her eyes on it, Angie felt a pang of regret. Her hands already began to cringe away from the action. But thoughts of prison could overcome a great deal of reluctance, and she forced herself out of the seat.

"I'll see you later," she said. "Thanks."

Suarez only grunted, barely glancing up to acknowledge her departure.

Angie walked toward the door. Halfway there she froze, as Miguel Rio appeared on the landing outside the wheelhouse. He spotted her and frowned as he yanked the door open and stepped inside.

"What are you doing up here?" he asked. "Shouldn't you be off banging Dwyer somewhere?"

A rush of anger flooded through her and Angie gratefully let it carry her away. This was familiar territory.

"Fuck you. Who woke you up on the asshole side of bed this morning?" she snapped, cocking her head and crossing her arms, daring him to fight back.

Miguel took a deep breath, shaking his head, then stopped himself from saying whatever he wanted.

"Sorry. Just freaking out a little."

"We all are," Angie said, forcing herself to put on a face that would pass as forgiveness, when what she wanted to do was lash out at the chief mate. How would she get hold of the PLB now? It wasn't as though she could knock them both out, and when would she have another chance to get to the beacon?

The awkward moment stretched out between them. Eventually, Angie relented.

"I guess I'd better—"

Someone began shouting outside the wheelhouse. Miguel frowned and turned away from her, hauling the door open. Angie glanced back at Suarez, who'd looked up from the radar screen at last. Then the shouting came again, and this time she knew who that voice belonged to.

"Dwyer?"

Miguel stepped out onto the landing and Angie followed, practically colliding with him as she rushed out. They hung over the railing and looked down to see Dwyer hustling up the last flight of stairs to reach the wheelhouse.

"What's the matter with you?" Miguel asked as Dwyer arrived on the landing.

Dwyer bent over, one hand up to gesture for patience as he caught his breath. "Down in the boiler room . . . something's banging . . . on the hull."

Angie didn't think she had ever seen Dwyer frightened, but he looked scared now.

"What do you mean?" she asked. "Someone's—"

"Not from the inside," Dwyer said, his frantic eyes silencing her. He turned to Miguel. "There's something in the water, Miguel. It's ramming against the ship."

"Something what? Like a shark?" Miguel asked. "Or you think we got FBI divers down there?"

Dwyer steadied his breathing and leaned back against the railing. He'd settled down a bit now, but he still looked spooked. Beads of sweat stood out on his forehead.

"It's not the FBI. But there's something down there, that's for sure."

Miguel ran a hand through his hair. Angie had always thought him good-looking—though never as good-looking as Miguel obviously considered himself—but he looked like crap now. Too much stubble, not enough sleep. He must have been a competent first mate, but in that moment it was clear that Gabe Rio had been made captain over Miguel by virtue of more than being the older brother.

"All right, listen—" Miguel started.

Only to be interrupted by distant shouts.

"What the hell is that?" Angie said.

All three of them turned toward the island. Standing just outside the wheelhouse, they were high enough to see over the derelict ships half-sunken in the water around the island. One of the lifeboats had made it partway through the maze of wrecks, but it had overturned.

As they watched, a sailor tried to grab hold of the overturned lifeboat. He screamed, attempting to haul himself up, then somehow the lifeboat broke apart in his hands.

"Jesus Christ," Dwyer muttered, his brogue emerging.

The sailor vanished beneath the water.

"Did something just . . ." Miguel began, but trailed off, as though unwilling to finish the thought.

"Pull him down?" Angie said. "That's what it looked like."

Dwyer seemed to shrink, leaning on the railing for support. "Told you, man. Something's in the water. And not just out there. It's right here, too. Around us."

They watched Hank Boggs pull himself out of the water onto a sunken cabin cruiser, and saw Gabe and Tori and a few others scramble back onto shore from the other lifeboat. For perhaps a minute, the three of them said nothing.

Then Suarez opened the door behind them. "Miguel. Radio."

Angie could hear the static crackling inside. Miguel took one last look toward the island, then hurried into the wheelhouse. Suarez stayed out there with Angie and Dwyer, and as the door swung shut behind Miguel, they watched the water around the broken-up lifeboat turn dark with blood.

"Lord help them," Suarez muttered.

Angie agreed. If there was ever a time for prayers, it had arrived.

She ran for the stairs. Dwyer called after her, wanting to know where she was going, but she didn't slow down. They needed help, and she could only think of one way to get it. There were things she couldn't do anything about, but she could damn well bring about change.

For twenty or thirty seconds after he'd spoken to his brother on the radio, Gabe didn't want to be the captain anymore. His heart seemed to have shrunken in his chest, and memories flooded his mind. Maya liked to lie in bed on rainy mornings, tucked beneath his arm, her head on his chest, just listening to his heartbeat. Gabe could watch an old movie or a baseball game and she'd be entirely content just to cling to him like that. In happier times, she had always told him it made her feel safe. Protected.

When they wanted to escape, they would drive south to the Keys, find a place on the water, drink margaritas, and listen to Bob Marley. Hell, sometimes he and Maya would even listen to Jimmy Buffett, the hero to middle-aged white stoners everywhere. Buffett knew something about relaxing. Like margaritas, that music made him feel like he was on vacation.

At home, Maya relished the days when neither of them had to work. She always had some project for him to do—putting up a floral border in the spare bedroom or repainting the bathroom or reorganizing the furniture in the living room just so she'd have the perfect place to hang the new painting she'd bought. Gabe had bitched about it, but he had loved it, too, turning up the radio and singing along as they created and re-created their home together.

The home he spent most of his time leaving, out of fear that one day he would become too comfortable and become trapped there.

For that half-minute, Gabe lost himself in thoughts and memories and regrets.

"Captain!" Kevonne shouted. "What the hell are we going to do?"

Sweat beaded on his forehead and he gesticulated wildly, pointing at the reef of sunken ships and at the *Antoinette* in the distance, then at their lifeboat and at Bone and Pang and Tori. He kept shouting, but Gabe found himself unable to focus. *Shock,* he thought. *It's shock.*

It occurred to him that they were in paradise. Perfect blue sky. Sun moving lower, throwing the long shadows of palm trees across the sand. All the ingredients were there. If he had a margarita, Maya, and Bob Marley, it would have been like heaven.

A small sound—half-chuckle and half-grunt—came from his throat and he shook his head in disbelief.

"Gabriel-fucking-Rio!" Tori shouted.

She gave him a shove with both hands and he staggered back, then narrowed his eyes, glaring at her. Tori stood in front of him, somehow managing to look more angry than afraid. With her hair back in a ponytail and her bronzed skin and tight tank top, she only added to the illusion of some tropical vacation. But Gabe had woken from that dream.

Bone had dropped to the sand twenty feet from the water and hugged his knees to his chest, muttering "what the fuck" over and over again. Pang strode along the shore, alternately staring out at the place where the other lifeboat had just gone down and peering into the shallow surf for some sign of anything that might threaten them.

Kevonne still shouted at Gabe. "Captain. Come on, man! What do we do?"

Gabe locked eyes with Tori. "Sorry. I was just thinking. I'm okay now."

Tori barked a dry laugh. "Are you? Me, I'm not so much okay as scared out of my mind. We've got to get off this island and back to the *Antoinette,* and I'm pretty sure it's got to be now, Gabe. Before nightfall."

That woke Bone from his shock-coma. The boy looked dreadfully old as he turned toward them. "Are you nuts? I'm not going out there, Tori. Something's under the water. You see all those bones? It's what killed them. That's why all those boats are sunk out there. People came ashore, to do a little fishing or take a swim or whatever. Tiny little island in the Caribbean, right? But once they're here, they can't leave. That was the mistake they made, don't you get it? Trying to leave! We're safe here. Here is good."

Kevonne rounded on him. "And what are we gonna eat, dumbass? Or drink? I didn't see any water fountains, did you?"

Gabe put a hand on his shoulder. "That's enough." He glanced at Tori. "What do you mean, 'before nightfall'? Where do you get that?"

"It's the only thing that makes sense. We know they can come on land or there'd be survivors here on the island. So why aren't they on us *right now*? Something's keeping them in the water at the moment, and it's gotta be the sun. They let us get to the island. Now they want to keep us here until sundown."

Gabe turned to Bone and Pang. "She's right. Sorry, Bone, but it does make sense. Whatever just happened—whatever's in the water—it won't *stay* in the water."

"How can you be sure?" Bone asked frantically, determined to be right.

"Look around you. You see anyone else? You think you're the only one who's ever assumed that being on land is safe? Tori thinks it doesn't like the sun, and if it spends most of its time underwater, maybe that's true. But it means that, at best, we've got until dark to get back to the *Antoinette*."

"Captain," Tori said, stepping up close beside him, diminishing the space between them almost to the point of intimacy. "The other boats—they were scuttled. They had to be. The people on board wouldn't have put holes in the hulls. Which means that whatever's out there is doing it."

Pang started pacing along the water's edge. "Oh, that's just beautiful."

"No, no," Kevonne said, waving him silent. "The *Antoinette*'s a beast, man. It isn't some rich boy's toy or a damn fishing boat. She'll be okay. We just have to get out there."

Gabe nodded. "Right. So put your heads together, and let's figure out how."

They all fell silent. Tori's eyes lowered, the weight of gravity pressing down on her. Gabe looked out at the graveyard of ships and saw it anew. The stretched netting, the ropes, the way some of them seemed to have crashed into others—it wasn't the result of pirates building some kind of village out of the wrecks, any more than that the ships themselves had been sunk by hurricanes. The tethers between ships had been previous attempts to escape. He tried to tell himself that some of those escapes must have been successful, but the logic didn't hold up. If anyone had gotten out of here alive, would the graveyard of ships still be there?

There were thirty years or more of derelict vessels, whose captains had come across the island and been drawn into its trap. And if they managed to radio for help, then whoever came looking either didn't find the island or were also drawn in. Maybe he was wrong and others had survived, and for whatever reason had never spoken of their ordeal. After all, the *Mariposa* had managed to get away from the island. Granted, only one man had been aboard, and he had been wounded so badly he died. The fishing boat's captain must have assumed they were trapped, that they would be better able to defend themselves with their cargo of guns if they brought them ashore. Like Bone, he must have assumed the creature or creatures in the water couldn't reach them there. Perhaps he had even thought they could kill them all, and then they would be able to get away.

He'd been a fool. Which raised a dreadful question in Gabe's mind—how, exactly, had the *Mariposa* managed to escape? It made no sense, unless whatever lurked out there, under the water, had allowed the dying sailor to take the *Mariposa* back out onto the open sea. The idea suggested two awful conclusions: first, that the *Mariposa* had been cast out into the Caribbean as a lure, to draw more victims to the island, and second, that whatever had killed its crew was intelligent enough to use the fishing boat to lure others into its grasp.

Not thoughts you want to share, he told himself, looking at the fear in the eyes of those still on the island with him.

"Kevonne, Bone, unload the gun cases from the lifeboat. We're gonna match ammo with weapons, load every gun we've got ammunition for. That way, we don't have to take the time to reload. When a gun is empty, you discard it, right over the side, and grab another one."

"Viscaya—" Tori started to say.

"Fuck Viscaya," Gabe said.

"So we're just going to make a break for it? That's it?" Bone asked. He looked like he might be about to cry.

"You got a better idea?" Kevonne asked.

"I'm not going," Bone said.

Pang laughed—an edgy, disturbing sound. "Yeah, good plan. Stay here and die."

Bone buried his face in his hands, pushed his fingers through his shaggy blond hair, and started to rock back and forth.

"Come on," Tori said softly. "You get one chance to live, Bone, and this is it. We've got a few hours before it gets dark. After that . . ."

The surfer started to nod, drew a long, shuddering breath, and pushed himself up off the sand. He went to help Kevonne start unloading the guns, both of them wary about stepping into the water.

"Captain, what about Chief Boggs?" Pang asked, shielding his eyes from the sun.

Gabe hadn't thought that far ahead. "We'll try to reach him on our way out."

Pang seemed satisfied with that, and went to help with the guns. They were falling back on habit now, taking orders from their captain. In some ways, it would be easier that way for all of them, but it weighed on Gabe. Their lives were in his hands. If he screwed up, they were all dead.

Don't flatter yourself, he thought. *You're probably all dead anyway.*

Tori moved closer as the guys moved off, and Gabe gave her a sidelong glance. The guys might fall apart, but Tori seemed to be holding it together better than any of them.

"Where do you think they came from?" she asked. "Whatever they are, out there?"

He thought of ocean storms and shattered walls and glass-smooth black stone engraved with strange writing.

"You're thinking the grotto," Gabe said.

Tori returned the intensity of his gaze. "Aren't you?"

He looked to the west, saw the sun had sunken farther than he had thought. Gabe strode away from her, kicking up sand as he hurried to help unpack the guns. He knew that whatever awaited them just offshore, it would only wait until sunset.

Again he thought of Maya. Would it have been so bad to have given her the life she wanted, with a baby and a husband who spent more time at home than at sea? Would it have been so difficult for him to be content with that fate? The questions lingered, but the answers didn't matter unless he managed to keep himself alive long enough to get back to Miami.

-44--

TWO MONTHS AGO . . .

Streetlights strafed the windshield as Gabe drove his aging BMW through Miami traffic. Gleaming neon and pastels flashed across the hood in a blurred reflection of the shops and bars and restaurants. Night had fallen a couple of hours ago, but the streets were still busy for a Tuesday night, and the traffic clogged the center lanes thanks to vehicles parked and double-parked on either side.

He gripped the steering wheel tightly, somehow both muddled and focused by the four bottles of hard iced tea he'd had at Jamie's Reel Life—a divey little fish joint a few miles from his apartment building. Jamie's had a streetside patio, where exhaust fumes mixed with the flavor of the mojitos and fried lobster tails that had made the place a local favorite. No one seemed to care.

Gabe had eaten dinner—popcorn shrimp and fries, just something to soak up the alcohol—but his stomach felt all twisted up anyway. He tried to tell himself it was the hard iced tea, but knew better. Nearly a month had gone by since that night Maya had caught him at Cinco, the night she hadn't come home. Ever since, he'd been on edge, flush with anger and resentment that were directed just as much at himself as at his wife. It had been difficult enough the morning after, when she'd told him she had slept at a friend's, her eyes like flint and that challenge in her voice daring him to ask for more details. Gabe had bit his tongue. He'd been the one cheating, after all. She had every right to be furious, and the truth was that if she had gone out to even the score and had sex with some guy, he really didn't want to know.

Or so he'd thought.

For the first few days, they had barely spoken to each other, the air between them thick with bitterness. Gabe had swung wildly back and forth between rage and guilt, between jealousy and self-loathing. Then, the night before he was headed out on a voyage for Viscaya, he had tried to talk to her, only to have it degenerate into a tirade in which he blamed her for having driven him to stray with the weight of her expectations.

Maya had smiled for the first time in days, but it was all teeth and cruel eyes. "Oh, no. You don't get to put it on me, Gabriel. *You* changed the rules, *papi*. Make sure you remember that."

His heart had sunk and he'd tried to get her to elaborate on what she'd meant. Why did he need to remember? What had she done? But Maya had said all she would say. When he woke early the next morning, he tried to talk to her before the *Antoinette* sailed—a short jaunt before the South American trip that was coming up—but Maya pretended to be sleeping. Even when he called her on it, and whispered to her, and tried to apologize, she kept her eyes firmly closed and her breathing even.

Half-drunk, Gabe pulled the BMW onto the side road— little more than an alley—that led to the back of his building. The car slid through darkness and then into the splash of light from the lampposts that lined the drive. He slowed at the entrance to the underground parking garage, steadying his breathing, fingers still tight on the wheel.

You didn't want to know, he thought.

But he needed to know—*want* had nothing to do with it—because the rules had changed again. In the ten days since he had returned from that brief voyage, Maya had transformed. The night he had come home, she had been quiet and depressed and had slept on the sofa, breathing softly, only half-covered by a thin cotton sheet, the bronze curve of her exposed calf making his heart ache.

"You did this," he had whispered into the darkened room, the new carpet crushed under his bare feet, the wall clock ticking loudly and impatiently. "You expected me to give up everything for you."

But Maya had slept on, her expression peaceful. If she dreamed, there were only pleasant things in her subconscious that night, and he had envied her that peace. Speaking those words aloud, Gabe felt a storm of conflicting emotions raging inside him. He blamed her—damn right he did. But how could he hate her when the worst thing she had done was want him home with her more often?

The following evening, when she had stayed out all night for the second time, all his guilt and hesitation vanished. When she finally showed up at the apartment looking freshly showered but still in her clothes from the night before, he had flown into a rage. Instead of fighting with him, she had apologized, smiled sweetly, and lied smoothly.

Gabe had been sleeping with other women. Now, Maya was either cheating on him in return, or she wanted him to think she was. And all he'd been able to think was, *You fucking started it, you bitch.*

Since then, she had been in their bed every night, but there were long periods during the day—while he was at the Viscaya offices or out after work—when she didn't answer her cell phone. He had come back to the apartment at six or seven o'clock to find her not yet home. Gabe had inquired at first, but she brushed off all of his questions with that same smile, the same denials.

Tonight, that would end.

Gabe had told her he had a meeting with Frank Esper down at the Viscaya offices. More than likely, Maya would not believe him. Many times before he had claimed to be at meetings and found his way to Cinco instead. Thoughts of Cinco made him think of Serafina, the woman he had been flirting with when Maya had caught him, a month ago. Serafina had been exquisite. He became wistful whenever he thought about that lost opportunity, remembering her seductive smile and the delicious scent of her. But there would be no Cinco for Gabe tonight.

On Friday night, the last time he'd gone out, he had come home to find Maya in the shower, singing quietly to herself, a private moment of bliss. The bedclothes had been a mess. She had stepped out of the shower, toweling off her hair, still singing. It had been at least a couple of months since he had seen her naked and a wave of desire swept through him.

Maya had turned and seen him standing there, watching her, and she had mustered that infuriating smile. But there had been an instant between her solitude and that smile, a fraction of a moment when she had been startled by his presence, during which he had seen a different emotion flicker across her features. Fear.

And then his suspicions had turned to certainty. Until then it had been possible that she might only be pretending to have an affair to torment him, out of vengeance. But that glimpse of fear in her eyes had given her away. Gabe had not asked her why she was showering so late, or why the bed was a mess— she would only have made up some story about a migraine and a nap. But he had heard it all before.

That night, while she slept beside him, he lay awake, convinced he could smell the stink of another man in his bed.

The BMW idled at the top of the ramp that led down into the garage. Light washed across his rearview mirror and he glanced up to see a mini-SUV pulling up the drive behind him. It wouldn't do to have horns blowing out here. If he got into some kind of argument, he might draw attention and give himself away.

"No more," he whispered, hands wrapped around the wheel.

The alcohol rode quietly along at the back of his thoughts now, urging him on, comforting and antagonizing him in equal measure. Gabe lifted his foot off the brake and drove down the ramp. The gate opened for him and he let the BMW roll, purring, into the garage, then pulled the car into his spot, right next to Maya's Corvette. His wife was home, just as he had known she would be. But she wasn't home alone.

Who the fuck is he, Maya? Gabe thought. *Who'd fucking dare?*

A cold numbness filled him then, and he moved as though he no longer had any control over his body. In the back of his mind, somewhere behind the alcohol, a small voice still warned him not to go home in this condition. As long as he didn't know the truth, he wouldn't have to do anything about it. Maya might forgive him someday. They might be able to go back to the way things had been when they had been able to laugh together, and the days seemed longer and the sky bluer. Romantic bullshit, he chided himself, and wondered which of his urges was more fueled by the drinks—the need to confront her, or the temptation to turn away.

He rode up the elevator, the keys gripped tightly in his hand.

The corridor smelled like disinfectant, and he heard the DeSimones' baby crying as he passed their door. The smell of frying fajitas drifted from one of the apartments. Mixed with the stink of the disinfectant the maintenance staff used, it made his stomach roil. Outside his own apartment door, he gripped his keys. His breathing sounded very loud, though he tried to be quiet.

Gabe slipped the key into the lock, turned it silently, and rotated the door handle. He held his breath, thinking: *You changed the rules, not me. You knew what you were getting when you married me.* The door slid open and he saw the antique mirror he'd bought her with money he'd made breaking the law, and the gourmet kitchen he'd put in himself, and the glass-top table in the eat-in. On the table were a cell phone and a key ring that didn't belong to Maya.

And he heard her laugh, soft and girlish, like she had laughed for him in better days.

Lost in fury and despair, he clapped both hands to the sides of his head and squeezed his eyes tightly shut. Alarms were going off in his mind as though to drive him out, to force him to flee before the imminent catastrophe could unfold. What he saw now he could never unsee.

But then a horrid sound began to build in his chest and throat—a bestial roar. Gabe had been frozen to the spot, but now he stormed through the foyer and the eat-in kitchen and turned through the archway into the living room, big hands curled into fists, tasting violence on his tongue.

"You made a big fucking mistake, having him here, *puta*! Whatever happens now, it's on your goddamn . . ."

He couldn't finish the sentence. Gabe stood mutely, just inside the living room, staring at the scene before him. Maya sat cross-legged in a plush chair. On the sofa, a beer on the coffee table in front of him, Miguel stared back at Gabe in obvious dismay. What broke Gabe, though, was the pity in his brother's eyes.

"Bro," Miguel said. "What the hell are you doing?"

Gabe's fists opened and he shook his head. "No. Don't you do it. Don't you take her side." His voice grew louder once more, rising to a shout. "She's a lying whore, man! She's been fucking some guy, doing it in my own damn bed!"

Maya lct out a long, disgusted sigh and shook her head. "That's enough."

"It's not nearly enough!" Gabe yelled. Then he turned on his brother. "And what the hell are you even doing here?"

Miguel stood up, decades of sibling fireworks coming into play. "Trying to help, you asshole. Maya called me, looking for advice. I was trying to help save your marriage."

"You were wasting your time," Gabe sneered.

Miguel threw up his hands. "I can see that now."

He started to leave. Maya reached out and grabbed his wrist, held him in place.

"Miguel, wait," she said, and her gaze shifted to Gabe. "Take him with you."

Gabe started to argue. He had been wrong tonight, but that didn't erase the past month. He knew she had been cheating on him.

Maya shook her head. "Just leave. You want to spend your life on the ocean, banging girls in clubs whenever you're in port, have fun with that. I tried to give you a home."

"I wanted a wife, not a home."

Maya's upper lip curled and her eyes nailed him to the spot. "Well, now you don't have either."

-45--

Josh's eyes snapped open, but it took a few seconds before he realized that he had been sleeping. He sat in the stained, ugly stuffed chair he'd been in when Captain Rio had decided to have Hank Boggs beat the crap out of him.

With a low groan he sat up straighter, wincing at a brand-new kink in his back. The skin on his face felt tight where he'd been struck, but it didn't pulsate the way it had before. What remained was a deep ache, and an aversion to making any complicated facial expressions. A smile would hurt like hell. Fortunately, he didn't foresee having any reason to smile in the near future.

"This sucks!" a voice said, just outside the starboard side door.

Josh frowned, then hissed through his teeth at the pain that shot through his swollen, cut-up face, and wondered if it would be possible to avoid facial expressions altogether. Slowly, bones popping from napping in a contorted position, he got up from the chair and started toward that door.

He had woken abruptly. That probably meant this wasn't the first outburst from the other side of the door. Last he had checked, Anton had been guarding the port side door and Jimenez had returned for a second shift on the starboard side. Now, though, he heard a familiar voice outside.

"Look, I don't like it any more than you do," Angie Tyree was saying, "but Tupper's got something going on down below, and they need you to take over as duty engineer. That means I'm back on guard duty. Believe me, I'm thrilled."

Josh peeked through the louvered shutters. A tired and annoyed Jimenez faced off with Angie on the walkway outside the door.

"I'm not pissed at you, Angie," Jimenez said. "I just need a break, you know? I had, what, three hours? I slept for one, and the other two I was on duty until Tupper came on. I've been either guarding the damn cook or down below since before the sun came up. Now I'm back on duty?"

"Practically half the crew's ashore, and someone's got to watch Josh. We're all in this, Oscar."

The big man sighed and nodded. "I know. I know. I'm going. You have fun. Shoulda brought a magazine or something, though. I'm bringing a book up next time. A little while longer, I'd have been in there playing Ping-Pong with Mr. FBI."

Josh watched through the shutters as Angie smiled. She gave away nothing. Moments later, Jimenez walked over to the stairs and started down. Angie waved over the railing, smiling at him for a few seconds. Then her smile vanished and she took a step back, looked around, and rushed for the door.

When Angie came into the rec room, her eyes were frantic.

"Did you find it?" Josh whispered, fearful that Anton might overhear them through the other door. "Did you set off the beacon?"

Angie shook her head. "It's in the wheelhouse, but I couldn't get to it."

"Then what are you—"

A flash of anger crossed her face. "Just shut up and listen. We're out of time."

"You mean they're going to—"

"Just. Shut. Up." Angie looked around, stepped up to the window and peeked through the louvers, then spun toward him again. "Something's happening. Something crazy. They found the guns, and one of the lifeboats was coming back."

She described what she'd seen—the lifeboat upended, a sailor trying to drag himself from the water until he was dragged under, blood in the water. The lifeboat destroyed.

Josh stared at her. "This is true? This really happened?"

Angie nodded, and swallowed hard. "Something's in the water, Josh. And not just near the island. Dwyer and Tupper, they heard something slamming into the hull from outside, down belowdecks."

Josh tried to process it, figure out what it meant. But Angie didn't give him time. She put one hand behind her back, tugged up her shirt, and pulled out a pistol, which she handed over to him. He took it, checked the clip and the chamber out of habit, then looked up at her.

"We need to set off that beacon right now," Angie said. "We need help."

Josh nodded. "Don't worry. We'll get it."

-46--

Dwyer felt like a cornered animal, tensed to bolt but with nowhere to run. Minutes had passed since his run up from belowdecks to the wheelhouse—all those goddamn stairs—and he should have recovered by now, but his chest rose and fell and his breath came too fast, and he knew it wasn't about the exertion at all.

Miguel and Suarez were talking in quick, clipped tones, both of them just as tense as Dwyer felt. They looked like boxers waiting for the bell.

"Think," Miguel said, staring at Suarez like he expected the guy to do a magic trick. "Come up with something. We can't just leave them out there."

"I'm thinking," Suarez said. Another time he might've taken offense at Miguel's tone—Dwyer had seen it before—but now he was focused. "The only thing we've got that can get to them is more lifeboats, and you saw that one go down. We send anyone else out there, the same thing could happen."

Miguel rested his hands on the wheel, stared out at the water. "Shit, shit, shit." He spun and strode over to the door, then stared out at the island, where his brother and the other four crew members were busy doing something on the beach. "What does that? Goddamn sharks don't flip boats. Maybe an alligator would drag somebody down from below like that, but we're in the Caribbean, not the fuckin' Everglades. And the boat's wrecked now. Whatever flipped it—and killed those guys—trashed the boat, too. What *does* that?"

Silence engulfed the three men in the wheelhouse.

Dwyer cleared his throat. "There's only one thing we can do."

Miguel and Suarez pivoted to look at him.

"What?" Suarez asked.

Dwyer fixed Miguel with a hard look. "We get our asses out of here. We fire up the engines and get on our way."

Miguel looked more disgusted than angry. "Yeah, that's helpful. You think I'm going to leave my brother out there?"

Dwyer gazed out at the island, pressed his forehead against the glass, and took a breath.

"The FBI are on our asses. They could show up at any time. We can't send anybody else to the island without risking their lives, too. And whatever's in the water, it's hammering at our hull. I thought maybe it was just stupid, but now I wonder if maybe it—or they—think they can actually get through. So I think you have two choices, Miguel. You can get us all out of here, save the lives you can, or you can keep us here while you watch your brother die trying to get back to the ship, and risk the rest of our lives in the bargain."

He heard Miguel coming for him, but didn't turn in time. Miguel's fist slammed into his temple, and as Miguel tried to follow up with another blow, Dwyer stumbled backward then sprawled on the floor. He looked up in time to see Miguel drawing the gun he carried holstered at the small of his back.

"You listen to me, you Irish prick," Miguel snarled, upper lip trembling. "My brother's worth a hundred of you. I'm not leaving here without him, and if I do decide to send another lifeboat out there, you'll be its goddamn captain."

Dwyer didn't try to get up. He didn't want to set Miguel

off. Instead he glanced at Suarez, who seemed contemplative as ever, just taking it all in.

"Talk to him, Suarez."

Suarez only shook his head.

"No?" Dwyer said. "You want to shoot me? Go on and do it, then. Better a bullet than dying the way those poor bastards did."

Miguel gritted his teeth, nostrils flaring. For a second, Dwyer thought he would actually pull the trigger, but then he swore under his breath and lowered the pistol.

"You want to get out of here," Miguel said, staring down at Dwyer, "and I'm not leaving without Gabe. So I guess you better start figuring out how we can both get what we want."

Dwyer wanted to throw him through the windshield. Instead he held up his hands to make sure Miguel knew he wasn't about to try anything stupid, and climbed back to his feet.

"You're the man with the gun," he said. "All right. I'm goin' to assume Captain Rio isn't going to just sit around out there. He'll make a try, won't he?"

Miguel frowned. "He's not stupid. Why would he do that instead of waiting for us to figure out a way to get to him?"

Suarez slid his hands into his pockets. Somehow, he managed to look relaxed. "No, Dwyer's right. The captain's got a lot of guns. He'll try to get back to the *Antoinette* as soon as possible."

"I don't get it," Miguel said. "He should just—"

"There should be other survivors," Dwyer explained. "From the *Mariposa,* or one of those other tubs, yeah? But there aren't. Which tells us that those things in the water don't always *stay* in the water."

Suarez went to the wheel. "First things first then. We get this ship as close to shore as we can without running aground."

Dwyer watched as this new information filtered into Miguel's mind, and new fear blossomed behind his eyes. If the man hadn't knocked him on his ass and then held a gun on him a minute ago, Dwyer might even have felt bad for him.

"Yeah," Miguel said to Suarez. "Do it."

Then he holstered his gun and went to grab the radio, probably for another conversation with his brother. As he picked it up, the door swung open, and all three of them turned to look.

Josh stepped into the wheelhouse, gun in hand.

"Fuck," Miguel snapped, drawing his own weapon again.

The chief mate and the FBI man faced off across the wheelhouse, pistols aimed. As they did, Angie followed Josh through the door, her eyes haunted by guilt and terror.

Dwyer stared at her. "You treacherous bitch."

She started to lower her eyes, then straightened up, raising her chin, meeting his glare with one of her own.

Josh backed into a corner where he could cover them all at once, but his focus remained on Miguel, who had the only other gun in the wheelhouse.

"Your timing sucks," Miguel told him. "What now?"

"I think we need to talk."

Dwyer glanced out the window, toward the island, and his eyes widened. Captain Rio had gotten the others onto the surviving lifeboat and they were pushing off from shore.

"Sorry to break it to you, guys," he said, "but it may be too late for talking."

-47--

Tori knelt in the prow of the lifeboat, taking deep, steady breaths as Gabe climbed aboard. Kevonne throttled gently forward, turning out to sea, and they all trained their guns on the water around them. Though the angle of the sunlight had changed, and the water did not have the same crystal clarity it had at midday, it was shallow enough here that they could see the sandy bottom, and they watched for any sign of movement below the surface.

Pang prayed under his breath, swinging the barrel of his machine gun, or assault rifle, or whatever the hell it was; he scanned the water, ready to fire. Gabe arranged several guns on the floor of the lifeboat around him, but they didn't have a lot of room. There were five of them and two big cases of weapons. Anything they didn't have ammunition for had been left back on the beach. The guns remaining in the crates were all loaded. Tori had two pistols stuffed into the waist of her shorts, the metal strangely warm against her skin. She had learned to fire a gun without falling in love with them. The assault rifle in her hands had felt very light until she'd loaded a clip of bullets into it, and now it hung heavily on the strap over her shoulder.

"Oh, fuck, look out!" Bone said, practically choking. He aimed a deadly little machine pistol at the water, wire stock against his shoulder, taking aim.

"Dude!" Pang snapped, grabbing his arm. "It's a fish."

Bone's chest was heaving and he actually laughed as he relaxed slightly. Tori didn't laugh, and neither did Gabe. Fear lodged in her throat and for a second she had stopped breathing.

"Jesus, Kevonne, please hurry," she said.

He glanced at her, nodded once, but said nothing. She wondered if he kept his mouth clamped tightly shut to keep his own fear inside, and how long that would work. Kevonne focused on the water ahead, keeping on course. They'd moved the lifeboat thirty yards down the beach before setting off from the shore. Gabe had spent long minutes studying the arrangement of the wrecked vessels that comprised the graveyard of ships and had chosen their course carefully.

The biggest tangle of wreckage—including a fishing trawler, a fifty-foot rich boy's toy, the two-masted schooner, and the rusty freighter they'd seen from the *Antoinette*'s deck—had the tightest conglomeration of vessels. It reached the closest to the island, and thrust farthest from the shore. Gabe claimed that he wanted to stick as close to the derelict ships as possible in hopes that whatever was down there might think they were just another part of the wreckage. Tori didn't buy that for a second. Gabe wanted to stay close to the sunken ships so that if necessary they could swim to safety the way Boggs had done. And she agreed completely.

Kevonne went slowly, hoping that keeping the noise level low would be less likely to draw attention. Tori's heart hammered against her rib cage and she trembled with every breath. They were moving closer to the *Antoinette,* but not fast enough.

"Captain," Pang said, his voice low and even. "Have a look at this."

Gabe shifted slightly, and peered over the side where Pang aimed his weapon. Tori looked as well. Perhaps fifteen feet to port, a ripple had appeared on the surface that had nothing to do with tide or undertow. Something long and white moved, serpentine, in the darkness of the steadily deepening water.

"That's not a fish," Pang said in that same flat monotone.

"No," Gabe agreed. "It's not."

Bone grunted. Instead of the whimpering he'd done before, his demeanor shifted to a kind of grim humor. "Well, do you think maybe you could *fucking shoot it, now*?"

"More to starboard, Captain," Kevonne said.

Tori twisted around, still on her knees, and lifted her weapon, scanning the water. Twin ripples paced the boat on that side, but she thought she saw more than two silver-white streaks down in the deep. She wanted to run, but the ocean surrounded them. She wanted to cry, but she couldn't afford to lose her focus. A cool, detached numbness began to spread through her—a feeling she hadn't had since the last time Ted had beaten her, when she had known that her only choices were to leave him or die.

"Wait for my word," Gabe said.

The ripples vanished, the things going deeper.

"They're gone!" Bone cried.

"Not gone. They're gonna come up under us!" Pang said.

"Kevonne, gun it, then dead stop," Gabe snapped. "Everyone hold on."

Tori steadied herself with one hand on the gunwale as Kevonne opened up the throttle. The lifeboat punched forward across the waves—fifteen, twenty feet—then Kevonne dropped the throttle back to neutral for a heartbeat before throwing it in reverse long enough to stop them dead.

Ripples traced the water behind them, for a moment looking almost like part of their wake.

"Fire!" Gabe shouted, even as he pulled the trigger.

Pang and Bone strafed the water, bullets punching the surface in tiny plinking splashes. Gabe emptied an entire clip in seconds and tossed the gun aside, snatching another up from the floor of the boat.

"Tori!" Kevonne yelled.

She spun, caught a glimpse of something white underwater, just off the prow, and pulled the trigger. The recoil pushed her back but she steadied herself and kept firing, breathing evenly, drawing deep within herself. Adrenaline made her skin flush and prickle and she kept firing.

"Jesus, look at it! What the fuck is it?" Bone shouted.

He'd been firing off the starboard side and Tori whipped around to see the thing floating on the surface. For a second she thought it was a human body, maybe the corpse of one of the *Mariposa*'s crew. It had arms and a head, skin that was fish-belly white, and its long fingers were covered with suckers like the tentacles of an octopus. Then she caught a glimpse of its face—multiple gill-like slits where a nose ought to be, round black eyes, and a wide mouthful of needle-sharp piranha teeth. Its lower body had a silver-green hue, thick and tapered like a serpent or an eel, and ended in the same kind of suckers that covered its fingers.

Where it bobbed above the water, it began to blister and boil and burn in the sun, the flesh melting away.

Gunfire punched the water again as Tori stared at it.

"Kevonne, hit it!" Gabe screamed.

The lifeboat jumped forward, surging through the water and then racing over the surface. Something slammed into them from beneath and the boat rocked but didn't tip. They'd glanced off it, but more were coming.

Tori picked her way toward the back. Gabe, Bone, and Pang kept firing, discarding weapons. Hundreds of rounds plinked the water, the reports slamming her ears. But she found a spot and started firing as well. Three shots and she hit an empty chamber and tossed the gun overboard, grabbing another from the nearest crate.

"How we doin', Kevonne?" she called.

"Good! We're good!" he shouted, the words stolen away by the wind, which buffeted all of them as the lifeboat shot across the water.

Out of the corner of her eye Tori saw that they'd entered the alleyway among the graveyard of ships, hugging the lee of the sunken vessels to starboard. Boggs was across the gap, on their port side, but they were too busy trying to stay alive to worry about reaching him now. They skipped right past the fifty-foot yacht, coming up on the fishing trawler.

"Not good!" Kevonne yelled.

His tone told her all she needed to know. Beside her, Pang tried to turn. Bone kept firing into the water behind them. Instinct made Tori hunker down and grab hold of the side of the boat, just before the impact took them from below, slamming up beneath the bow on the port side.

Gabe jumped from the boat, lunging over the side, even as they shot upward, boat twisting in the air. She heard the motor whine as the blades spun in open air, and then she plunged into the water.

No. God, please no.

Tori thrashed in the water, eyes tightly closed against the salt. She sucked in a lungful of water and began to choke, getting her bearings, breaching the surface. Coughing, frantic, she whipped around and saw the lopsided deck of the fishing trawler a dozen feet away. She swam for it—choking up water, desperate to scream, every inch of her flesh burning with the expectation of attack.

Her fingers struck wood. The deck of the trawler. Something splashed just behind her and now she did scream, glancing around, chest pounding, spotting the deck railing nearby. A hand grasped her wrist and she screamed again, thinking they had caught her. She looked up to see Gabe above her. He lay across a metal trunk that had been bolted to the deck. She grabbed his other hand and he pulled her out of the water.

Tori had time only to mumble a muffled thanks as they

stood atop the trunk. Then Gabe scrambled over to the deck railing. Tori hesitated, then leaped to the railing on the opposite side, wanting to leave room for the others. Latching on, she climbed the deck rail like a ladder. The wheelhouse was half underwater, but she could get above it, stand on top of it.

"Come on, Bone! Swim!" Pang shouted.

Tori stopped, ten feet above the water now. Across from her, on the other railing, Pang had climbed onto the ruined trawler to perch just below Gabe, but Bone hadn't reached the boat yet. He swam toward them, blond hair slick against his skull, eyes wide with fear, despair, and a terrible knowledge.

Ripples circled him.

"Bone, hurry!" Tori cried.

Gabe screamed for him to swim. Pang joined in, and then Kevonne added to the chorus from a tangle of thick netting that hung off one side of the wreck like a spiderweb. He'd climbed halfway up, just six feet out of the water, but now hung with one hand lowered.

"Come on, man!" Kevonne screamed. "You can make it. Take my hand!"

Bone reached for him, still a few feet away. Kevonne hung lower, hope in his eyes. Then Bone stopped short, grunting with sudden pain, and he was tugged backward and down. His hands broke the surface, thrashing, and he bucked against what held him, his face emerging from the water.

A long hand snaked up from the water and clasped his face, suckers attaching to his flesh. Those fingers began to burn in the sun, even as they dragged Bone down into the darkness of the ocean.

For a few seconds, none of them spoke or moved. Then, as one, Tori, Gabe, Pang, and Kevonne dragged themselves farther up the wreckage of the trawler, as high out of the water as they could manage. They came together at what had once been the bow of the boat, staring at each other.

"What are they?" Tori asked.

Kevonne hung his head. "Does it matter?"

Tori stared at him, angry for a moment, then her shoulders sagged. "No. I guess it doesn't."

She looked at Gabe, but the captain wouldn't meet her gaze. Pang slid down the deck a little to stand on the peak of the portion of the wheelhouse that was still above water.

"Watch your step," Tori told him.

Pang gave a sick laugh. "You think?" Then he pointed out across the alleyway they'd been trying to travel through to get back out into open water. "I see the chief."

That woke Gabe up. He blinked, a fierce determination flickering to life in his eyes. He looked at Tori, then slid down to join Pang. Tori didn't need to get that close to the water to see Boggs, who stood framed in the broken wheelhouse window of a scuttled cabin cruiser just across from them. His wreck was separated from theirs by maybe thirty yards of ocean. It lay canted to one side, and Boggs perched inside the lower half of the wheelhouse, almost underneath the ship, ten feet above the water.

"Chief!" Gabe shouted. "We need to figure out a way to get you over here with us!" His voice echoed off the hulls and decks of dead men's ships.

Boggs cocked his head, listening, and then shouted in return. "Why? You're just as stranded as I am!"

Gabe sat back a bit and looked around. He didn't say it, but he didn't have to. Tori had eyes, and so did the others. Boggs was right. They were all stranded. It was only a matter of time, now.

"We were right, weren't we?" she said.

The captain looked at her. "About what?"

"The sunlight. You saw them burn. They're, like, some kind of underwater vampires. They like it down there, dark and cool, but they don't need to stay in the water. Not once the sun goes down."

Pang and Kevonne stared at her, but Gabe nodded.

"Yeah. I think that's exactly what they are," he said.

The *Antoinette* was close, but not nearly close enough. Tori glanced at the horizon, where the sun had dropped even farther in the sky.

"We have to think of something," she said. "And fast."

Gabe unclipped the radio from his belt. Its leather holster had been dampened, but when he thumbed the button, the radio crackled.

"Miguel? Listen up, brother."

-48--

"Oh, my God," Angie said, barely aware she'd spoken.

She stared out the wheelhouse window, watching the people from the lifeboat climb onto a half-sunken fishing trawler. A few feet away, Josh and Miguel shuffled into new positions so both of them could glance out at the island, even as they kept their guns aimed at each other. Suarez and Dwyer stood by the instrument panel. Dwyer had positioned himself near the wheel and the radio, as though he thought that gave him some kind of control, but now he tried to get a look as well.

"Can you see who made it out of the water?" Miguel asked.

It took Angie a second to realize he'd meant the question for her. Josh didn't even glance at her, so she looked out the window again, counting heads.

"The captain, for sure," she said.

Miguel exhaled, bright eyes going dull, closing off whatever emotion he might have felt.

"Tori and what's his name, Pang, too," Angie went on. She glanced at Josh, but if Tori's survival meant anything to him, he didn't show it. "Someone else is there, hanging on a net, but I can't . . ." She let the words drift, but then the man on the net climbed higher and she saw he was black. "Kevonne. The other one's Kevonne."

"So the one in the water, that was Bone?" Josh asked.

"Had to be," Angie said.

"That sucks. He was a good kid."

Miguel spat on the ground, raised the barrel of his pistol. "Fuck you. Good kid? You'd have put him in prison."

"It's not up to me who goes to jail, Miguel. But you can bet you and Gabe will end up there. Maybe you could be cellmates?"

Miguel's hand trembled and his lips pressed into a tight line. "If I'm going to prison anyway, tell me why I shouldn't shoot you."

"Hang on," Suarez started, but Miguel silenced him with a glance.

Angie tensed. She didn't know how much Josh knew about the Rio brothers, but he must at least realize that pushing Miguel would be unwise. Angie looked at Dwyer, trying to plead with him with her eyes. But his gaze had turned bitter, and she knew there would be no help from him.

Josh's shoulders rose and fell as he took a long breath. He cocked his head, cracking the bones in his neck. His aim never wavered and he had stopped glancing out at the survivors stranded on those ruined ships.

"You don't want to go to prison," Josh said. "I get it. But I'm guessing your brother's life might be worth it."

"What the fuck are you talking about?" Miguel sneered.

Josh tilted his head, gesturing toward the personal locator beacon, where it still sat on the instrument panel, right by the wheel.

"Give that to me. I set it off. FBI and Coast Guard come and get us. We get your brother and the others out of there, kill whatever's in the water—"

"And Gabe and me go to prison," Miguel finished.

Josh shrugged, gun barrel bobbing. "You can pick what happens next in this story, Mr. Rio, but you can't choose how it ends. That's going to be up to a judge and jury."

Miguel fixed him with a glare of such hatred that Angie flinched and turned away. But when she looked back, a strange calm had come over him, as though he might actually be listening to reason.

The radio crackled. Captain Rio's voice filled the wheelhouse. "Miguel? Listen up, brother."

Nobody moved. Frozen, they stared at one another, locked in the paralysis wrought by the presence of guns.

"Josh, let him answer," Angie said. "You can't leave them out there."

Miguel, Suarez, and Dwyer all stared at the FBI agent.

"I don't intend to," Josh said, after a moment. He gestured toward the radio with his gun. "Go ahead. Tell him you're trying to decide between going to prison and keeping him alive."

Miguel actually laughed. "You don't know shit. Gabe would rather be dead."

"You want to give him his wish?" Josh replied.

"Idiots," Suarez muttered. He picked up the radio and thumbed the button. "Glad to hear your voice, Captain. You had us worried."

The radio crackled again. "Had myself worried, *mi amigo*. Miguel there?"

Suarez held out the radio and Miguel took it from him, using his left hand, keeping the gun in his right as steady as he could. He kept it pointed at Josh. Angie glanced at the PLB, sitting there on the panel, no one paying it any attention at all, though it might be the one thing that could save them all. She could try for it, but Dwyer and Suarez were both in the way.

"I'm here, Gabriel," Miguel said, ignoring Josh. "Just trying to figure out what we can do to help you. It doesn't look like more lifeboats would do the job."

The button clicked as he let it go. The radio hissed.

"You're right. They might get here, but probably not back," Gabe replied.

Miguel glared at Josh as he growled into the radio. "Our options are limited, *hermano*. We've got a situation in the wheelhouse."

Click. Hiss. "Got a little situation out here, too, Mikey. What's going on?"

"The cook's up here, and he's got a gun pointed at me right now. Fucker stabbed us in the back, and right now he's standing in the way of me doing anything to help—"

Josh interrupted with a snort of laughter. "Right, so I'm the villain now? Who's the bad guy, Captain?" he called. "The FBI agent doing his job, or the asshole who's fucking his brother's wife?"

Angie's mouth dropped open. Dwyer and Suarez swiveled around to stare at Miguel. He'd been annoyed, waiting to finish what he'd been saying to Gabe, his thumb still on the button. Now it slipped off.

Click. Hiss. Nothing.

Then, Gabe's voice. "What did he just say?"

Miguel's face contorted into a mask of rage and shame. "You bastard! Why the fuck . . . ?" But he couldn't even finish. Instead he started to shake his head and he opened his mouth in an awful scream.

And pulled the trigger.

Angie yelped and threw herself against the window, cracking the glass. The bullet punched through Josh's shoulder and exited his back in a spray of blood.

The gun flew out of Josh's hand and clattered on the floor. Angie pushed off from the wall and ran for it, but Dwyer got there first, stamped his foot down on it, and backhanded her across the face. She staggered back, and all her fear evaporated in a burst of fury. Lunging, she punched him in the throat. As he tried to grapple with her, she slipped inside his reach and took a fistful of his red hair, then drove her knee up into his groin.

Angie had been hurt before, and she had learned how to hurt back.

Dwyer twisted just enough to block most of the strength of her knee-shot, but still let out a grunt of pain and staggered back, stepping off the gun. She reached for it, but a second gunshot rang out against the metal and glass inside the wheelhouse and she jerked back, looking up to see Miguel now leveling his gun at her.

"That's enough," he said.

Slightly bent, Dwyer walked gingerly toward her, lips upturned in a sneer. He reached for the gun.

"Not you, either," Miguel said. He gestured for Dwyer to back up with a wave of the gun. "Suarez, pick it up."

The old Cuban walked over, casual as ever, and picked up the gun. He clicked on the safety and tucked it into the front of his pants. On the ground, Josh lay bleeding, but conscious. He slid back to the wall, leaving a streak of blood on the floor, then sat up, staring expectantly at the officers of the *Antoinette*.

"What now?" he asked Miguel.

Miguel looked out at the island, and the graveyard of ships. Then he glanced out the front windows at the cargo and the ocean beyond, maybe trying to decide whether to leave his brother there after all.

He clicked the button on the radio. "Gabe, listen. If you can make it to the schooner, the way she's laying, you can get across to that old freighter out there."

He hesitated, then let go of the button. The hiss went on a few seconds.

"Miguel?" the captain asked, his voice full of pain and threat and uncertainty.

"I have a plan, bro," Miguel said, ignoring the questions inherent in his brother's tone. "It might take a while, but I have an idea."

This time he did not hesitate before taking his thumb off the button, but the wait for the captain's reply went on three times as long. Angie held her breath during the long, wordless hiss, and she felt certain Miguel did as well. Perhaps they all did.

"Make it fast," Captain Rio said at last. "Whatever it is, it's gotta happen before the sun goes down. Otherwise, you'll be too late."

The hiss returned to the radio.

Miguel looked around the wheelhouse. "Dwyer, come with me. Suarez, you watch the cook."

Angie stepped forward. "What about me?"

Dwyer had one hand over his throat, and when he spoke, his voice was a rasp. "Feel free to shoot her."

Suarez sniffed. "I don't take orders from you, boy."

Miguel laughed. "Just watch them, Hector."

Then he and Dwyer were out the door. Josh sat against the wall, bleeding. Angie and Suarez stared at each other for a moment, and then the old Cuban rolled his eyes dismissively and went back to watching the radar screen.

Hank Boggs crouched inside the empty frame of a window in the cabin cruiser's wheelhouse and watched Captain Rio, Kevonne, Pang, and that bitch, Tori, as they scrambled for better purchase on the tilted deck of the half-sunken fishing trawler. He'd watched as they'd set off from the island, praying that they'd stop and pick him up, or at least get back to the *Antoinette* and send help.

Then he'd seen the water rippling around them and he'd known his prayers fell on deaf ears. If God existed, up in the heavens, he wasn't listening. Or perhaps this place—any place where things like this could exist—was in his blind spot.

Bone had died the same way Mitchell had, dragged down into a blossoming pool of his own blood. A goddamned shame. Bone had been a decent guy.

Now all five of them were stranded, but at least the captain and the others were together. Boggs was on his own, separated from them by a gap way too wide to even think about swimming while those things were in the water. *And what about them? What are they, anyway?* Boggs pushed the questions away, saving them for another time. He didn't want to think about it, because the few answers that danced at the periphery of his thoughts only frightened him more.

The wreck he'd swum to lay at an angle in the water, maybe forty-five degrees, and he crouched inside, looking down through the open window frame at the water below. He might have been better off on top of the lopsided ship, but from here he had a better view of the island and of the others, stranded across from him.

Little shards of glass still in the window frame crunched under his shoes as Boggs straightened up, careful with his footing. If he fell, he would tumble into the water, and though he could see no disturbance on the water, he thought he could feel them there, waiting down in the dark.

He studied the arrangement of the wrecks near his position, as well as those on the other side of the alley they had sailed through to get to the beach. He needed to get to a higher vantage point to take a look at the sunken ships that were nearest to him. One of these boats must still have a working lifeboat on it, and much as he didn't want to risk it, that might be his only shot at getting out to the *Antoinette*. The container ship's draft was much too deep to get in this close.

Yet even as the thought crossed his mind, he saw something odd out of the corner of his eye, and turned to see that the *Antoinette* had begun to turn. Though slowly, the ship had begun to move toward shore.

"What the hell?" Boggs muttered to himself.

Then he got it. The *Antoinette* couldn't come and get them, but Miguel could sure as hell get her *closer,* giving them all a better shot at reaching the ship alive.

A terrible thought filled him. Miguel wasn't coming for Hank Boggs—he was coming for his brother, the goddamned captain. Whatever rescue efforts the crew of the *Antoinette* would be making, they were going to be focused on the other side of the gulf that separated his position from the others.

Panic flared in his chest. Boggs hadn't been scared of much in his adult life, but the thought of being out here alone when the sun went down filled him with a terror so profound that for several long seconds he could not move. He had heard people talk about getting a chill, but had never felt anything like the sudden icy cold that enveloped him. For a few moments, he felt as though he'd been locked in a freezer.

When the chill passed, the panic remained.

They might not leave him behind, but Boggs knew he wasn't their priority. They weren't hurrying to get to him, and weren't likely to reach him before nightfall. Keenly aware of the dark water below, he looked over at the fishing trawler and at the double-masted schooner that lay on its side. Gabe and Tori and the others were on the move now, looking for a way to cross to the schooner.

Boggs looked up. Above him and to the left, a thick tangle of netting and rope had been stretched from the bow of the cabin cruiser all the way to the broken mast of the schooner. In places, curtains of net hung down, but the central line was fairly taut. Even where it sagged in the middle, it must still have been at least thirty feet above the water.

He had known it was there, of course. They had all noticed it on the way in, and wondered at its use and origin. Mitchell had said it looked like some kid's idea of a pirate tree house, the way some of the ships were tethered together. But Boggs wasn't some circus tightrope walker. He had the strength to shimmy out along the rope and netting and hang on, but ninety feet? Could he make it that far? Once, maybe, when he was younger. But he was older now, and heavier, and as taut as it looked, there was no way of telling how well the rope had been tied off on either side, or how much the sun and salt might have rotted it.

Boggs closed his eyes, took a deep breath, and when he opened them, he gazed at the western horizon. How many hours before dark? Three? Four? Best not to count on four.

Which meant he had to get started.

The cabin cruiser sat, half-submerged, canted sideways in the water. The angle wasn't so extreme that he couldn't manage, but still he was really beneath the wheelhouse. He'd never be able to climb up to the bow from down there. One missed grip or a slip of the foot and he'd fall. It made a hell of a lot more sense to go up through the wheelhouse and get on top of the cruiser. Up there he could scale the port side railing like a jungle gym, all the way to the bow.

Boggs glanced at the *Antoinette,* sliding nearer to the reef of ruined ships, and then at the horizon one more time. The whole ship creaked and the breeze coming through the broken windows whistled softly. He slid down the inner wall of the wheelhouse to the V where the wall met the floor. On his hands and knees, he began to climb the slanted floor like Spider-Man, the toes of his shoes finding traction, hands giving him balance. Boggs picked his way across the wheelhouse, scaling the tilted floor, headed for the broken windows on the port side—the high side, now.

His left foot slipped and went out from under him. His knee slammed down, and he slid toward the water at the submerged rear of the wheelhouse. His heart raced as his hands scrabbled for purchase. He shoved his right foot out, flat on his belly, slowing down, turning sideways, slipping toward the water.

It's not deep, he told himself. *A couple of feet. If anything was there, I'd see it.*

His left hand caught the upright balustrade fixed to the floor around the stairs that led down into the cabin below. Hope filled him, but momentum slid him farther, and first his left foot and then his right plunged into the water. His shoes struck the back wall of the wheelhouse, and he was in water up to his knees. The way the ship sat, tipped over in the water like that, the sun struck the roof, and only ambient daylight made it through the windows. Down there where the water had flooded in, all was in shadow.

"Please, no," he gasped, tightening his grip on the balustrade and—now that his feet had purchase—pulling himself up to the stairs that led belowdecks. He straddled the top stair, which was a peak, of sorts, like the top of a roof. He thought of sitting on his roof back when he was a boy, up on hot tar shingles, drinking grape soda and waiting for his mother to come home from work.

The thought calmed him. The water that had collected at the rear of the wheelhouse was only that—water. And not very deep. The floor sloped down in front of him; the stairs did the same behind him. But the railings around the stairs would give him a good head start for climbing again, making his way up to the port side where it stuck out of the water. He just had to reach a broken window and get out of the wheelhouse on top, and then it would be easy climbing the outside of the ship.

He caught his breath, taking a moment. The sound of the sea lapping the sides of the ship—so close now that he was near the waterline—made him uneasy. And he could hear, down in the cabin belowdecks, the slosh of the water that had filled the sunken portion of the cruiser.

Bracing himself, he grabbed the railing—more like a ladder at this angle—and stood up on the peak of the top tilted stair. With his right hand he tugged on the balustrade, testing its strength.

Boggs paused, frowning, then cocked his head. He heard singing, like a far-off lullaby. Could that be Tori, all the way over on the trawler or the schooner? The sound comforted him, relaxing his thundering heart.

But then it grew louder, and he realized that it did not come from outside the cruiser, but from within. From below him, down those stairs, inside the flooded cabin.

An awful sorrow filled him—not fear, but profound sadness. As Boggs glanced down into the darkness of the cabin, he began to weep, as he had not done in the better part of thirty years.

Three sets of black eyes gazed up at him from the throat of the stairwell. A single hand slid upward, fingers wrapping around his ankle. He hung his head in surrender.

Only when they began to pull him down the stairs did Boggs begin, at last, to scream.

-50--

Tired but grateful to be home, Alena Boudreau unlocked the door to the brickfront row house on M Street. It had been her residence since 1975, when her father had passed away and she had taken the money from the sale of her parents' house in New Hampshire, given up her apartment, and decided to make a permanent home for herself and her daughter in Washington, DC. A decade or so later, Marie had graduated college and had a child of her own, and the two women had raised the boy, David, together.

Marie lived in California now, where she worked for a green energy company, and she kept in touch only sporadically. When she did bother to call or e-mail, Marie always made sure to express her disapproval of David's choice to work with his grandmother. Even as a teenager, she had never been able to accept that her education, her clothes, even her meals, had been paid for by money her mother earned in the employ of the U.S. government, and the idea that her son now used his brilliance toiling for the same paymasters got under Marie's skin. Sometimes Alena thought his mother's irritation was what kept David working for the DOD.

From the time Marie had been ten or eleven years old, Alena had understood that she and her daughter were wired differently, and she had spent years trying to find a common ground between them so that they could enjoy each other's company instead of grating on each other's nerves. Alena still hadn't found that common ground, and it hurt her heart, but so much time had gone by that she tried her best not to think about it now.

She had David. Or she had him as much as anyone did. They were very much alike, she and her grandson, but that also meant that they were two people of very solitary nature still living under the same roof. He would go, eventually; Alena was resigned to that. David could not live in the shelter of his family forever. When the day came, it would be bittersweet. But for now, Alena liked having her grandson around almost as much as she appreciated having someone of his intellect with whom she could share ideas and theories.

She stepped into the house, set down her travel bag, and dropped her keys on the little table at the bottom of the stairs. As she closed the door, she frowned—there were lights on, which meant David was home, but not the slightest scent of cooking lingered in the house.

Alena smiled indulgently and shook her head. She and David both lost themselves in work far too frequently, and much too completely. But Alena rarely became so distracted that her growling stomach couldn't budge her, while David often had to be reminded to eat.

She climbed the stairs, passing by her own quarters on the

second floor. They had arranged the house this way when David had been an infant, he and his mother taking the third floor and Alena the second, each with their own bedrooms, bathrooms, sitting rooms, and offices. The first floor consisted of a kitchen, a dining room, and an old-fashioned parlor, where grandmother and grandson often played cards with the news on in the background. When they were wrestling with an intriguing puzzle, trying to make sense of what their research had discovered, the rhythm of poker often eased their minds, let their subconscious thoughts consider the puzzle at hand.

Their real offices were elsewhere, of course, but much of the contemplation that went into their investigations happened when they weren't surrounded by other people, bright lights, and ringing phones.

Outside the windows, the wan light of early evening had begun to retreat. Night would fall soon, but David would not have noticed. She reached the third floor and turned right, knowing exactly where to find him. The door to his office stood open, a pile of books stacked against it to keep the breeze from the open windows from blowing it shut. David's office seemed to get the least sunlight of any room in the house, and she thought he liked it that way. The shade on the single window always hung halfway down. He kept a green glass banker's lamp on his desk and two brass floor lamps with hand-painted rose crystal globes around the bulbs. They looked almost like gas lamps.

David wasn't at his cluttered desk. The computer screen, dormant and unattended, showed fish swimming back and forth. Rather, he stood over a long oak table on the other side of the room, examining maps spread out beneath a hanging stained-glass lamp that would have looked more at home in a pool hall. The only thing it shared in common with the others was its antique status; David had little room in his life for material things, but had somehow acquired a love for antique glass lamps.

Though he dressed impeccably in crisp jeans and a tailored shirt, her grandson kept himself stylishly ungroomed, his hair artfully ruffled and his chin stubble trimmed so short it seemed almost the ghost of a beard. That he cared about such things always surprised her, particularly when he wouldn't take the time to eat.

The wall beyond the table looked like something from a police detective's squad room, covered with newspaper clippings whose headlines announced missing boats and vanished travelers. She recognized pages and photographs from the files of two cases from her own past, one off the coast of Africa and the other a remote island in the South Pacific. David had been along with her for the latter, at the age of seventeen, and had never quite recovered from the things he had seen. Alena understood the reaction; she had felt much the same after that African case. The details remained fresh in her mind even though the events had occurred in September 1967.

The original discovery, in the sixties, had been unsettling enough. Far more so when a second similar site had been found on an uncharted South Pacific island just eight years ago. The coincidence had been too much for David, and now he spent every spare moment scouring news reports and maritime journals for evidence of additional sites, even as they both prayed he would never find one.

"I'm sure you haven't eaten. Why don't we get some dinner?" Alena said. "Il Bacio. My treat."

As if waking from a trance, David blinked and turned to look at her. Then he smiled in that disarming way he had perfected as a child. Turned away from the lamp, his blue eyes seemed almost luminescent in the gathering gloom.

"Alena, how did you get here?"

"Teleported," she said, arching an eyebrow. "What do you think? Airplane. They fly, you know."

"Don't tell me the general rushed you home to look at hobbit weaponry."

She laughed. "What are you talking about?"

He smiled in return, finally seeming to become aware of his surroundings, then pulled away from the items he had unrolled on the table. Alena saw now that they were not maps but maritime charts.

"Never mind," David said, waving the comment away. He came over and kissed her cheek. "I'm glad you're home."

"Looks like you've been avoiding the office," she observed.

He nodded, gaze drifting back to the charts. He often lost himself in them, and his brow grew troubled every time. David reached out and picked up a small rock, no larger than a baseball, that had been holding down one side of a chart. The paper curled up when he lifted the weight off it.

"What do you make of this?" he asked, placing it in her hand.

Alena got a little queasy feeling in her belly as she went to the table to examine the rock in the light, turned it over in her hands, ran her fingers over the smooth, glassy black surface.

"I think it's exactly what you think it is. Where did it come from?"

"A Dominican fisherman dragged that and some larger pieces up in nets he wasn't supposed to be using, somewhere in the Caribbean. I've only got a vague idea of where they were found."

"When was this?"

David looked sheepish. "1982."

Alena sighed and nodded. "Decades ago." She set the rock back down on the table and reached out to touch his cheek. "Your eyes are red and I can practically hear your stomach shrinking. You need rest and food, and I would really like a nice veal saltimbocca and a glass of red at Il Bacio. Come, have dinner with your grandmother. I'll tell you about the Donika Cave."

"I am a little hungry, but . . ." He hesitated and looked back at the charts on the table.

"1982, David. If there's a third island there, it's waited this long to be discovered. One more night won't make a difference."

The day had metamorphosed into a nightmare. The dead crew of the *Mariposa* and the missing guns were no more than a nuisance now, after the horrors of that ancient, crumbling grotto, and the things Gabe believed had come from deep within the glassy, black volcanic rock that lined the cavern within. He imagined a hellish tunnel, straight down through the water, and things still swimming in unknown depths. But even those images were not the worst part of his nightmare. The worst came when he heard Hank Boggs begin to scream.

It wasn't the screams that got him—they weren't the day's first—nor the death of Chief Boggs. The most heinous moment for Gabe came when he recognized the feeling rising up inside him as relief. With Boggs dead, things were simpler. They didn't have to worry about retrieving him, didn't have to risk any foolish heroics beyond saving their own skins.

The realization staggered him and he faltered, standing on the precipitous edge of the trawler's nose. Tori grabbed his arm to steady him.

"Hey," she said. "Watch it. You okay?"

He peered at her. She was frightened, but rock steady and determined. Gabe wondered where this woman had come from, because the smart, pretty, flirty girl from the offices back in Miami had vanished completely.

"There's nothing you could have done for him," Tori said.

She thought he'd been upset, or grieving for Boggs, when in truth he had been glad the man was no longer his problem. Gabe gently tugged his arm free of her touch, unworthy of her concern.

"Go on, Tori. You next," he said.

Kevonne and Pang already stood on the weathered hull of the schooner's starboard side, which had spent many years exposed to the elements. The two sailors had considered it a minor miracle to discover that the winch cables at the aft end of the trawler—which had once hauled its nets—were already strung across the gap between the fishing boat and the schooner. Gabe saw it as an ugly omen. Lives had probably been lost just getting from one ship to the next, but someone had succeeded in turning those winch arms toward the schooner and tying the cables off somewhere on its deck. But he couldn't make himself believe that whoever had done that had managed to make it away from the island alive. The fact that the things were still in the water suggested that no one had come here in force, and that no one had ever gotten away and lived long enough to do anything about the bizarre Venus flytrap this paradise had become.

"Come on!" Kevonne shouted across the gap. "The *Antoinette*'s coming!"

He sounded so excited, as though he thought Miguel might actually try bringing the *Antoinette* up close to the rusty freighter. Gabe knew that wasn't the case. The water just wasn't deep enough, especially now, with the tide out.

But Miguel said he had a plan.

Gabe looked down into the gap between the trawler and the schooner. At the bottom, only seven or eight feet of water showed. But they needed to cross to a place far enough up the side of the lopsided ship's hull that they could stand without slipping off. Once Kevonne and Pang had been able to put their feet down, they had used the cables as guide wires to move up farther. Now they were almost at the deck—which would be practically a sheer drop-off into the water on that side.

"What if I fall?" Tori asked.

He looked at her, almost relieved to see that her steely resolve had cracks in it. It shook him from his reverie. Tori needed him to step up, to be the captain.

"You'll be fine. You saw the guys do it. Just shimmy, and don't let go."

Tori arched an eyebrow. "Easy for you to say."

Gabe glanced at the horizon, feeling the urgency of the dwindling afternoon. Tori caught the look and nodded, as though trying to convince herself. She put her back to the schooner and grabbed hold of the cable, hoisted herself up and wrapped her legs around it. Hanging upside down, she started to haul herself as quickly as she could, hand over hand, across the gap between ships.

"Don't stop for anything," Gabe said.

"Thanks," Tori huffed, the muscles in her arms standing out from the effort. "Now . . . shut up."

Gabe watched her, holding his breath. Across from him, on the hull of the sunken schooner, Pang and Kevonne stared in silence, waiting to help. None of them looked down, not even when something splashed below them, between the trawler and the two-masted sailing ship. At the start, Kevonne had wanted to go feetfirst, so he could look ahead and see where he was going. Gabe and Pang had immediately nixed that idea. Headfirst, pulling themselves along, would be much faster, and lugging your own body weight that far, speed was of the essence.

Three-quarters of the way across, Tori paused to rest.

"Don't stop!" Gabe called.

Kevonne held on to the cable and worked his way toward her. The angle of the hull wasn't steep, but it did slant, and the wood was smooth, and if he slipped he would end up in the water.

"Tori?" Kevonne called.

"I know!" she snapped. Her arms were wrapped around the cable, giving her hands a rest. She flexed her fingers, took a breath, and then grabbed hold and started moving again, hanging down, muscles straining.

Twenty seconds later, Kevonne was helping her down off the cable. Together they started moving back to the flatter area at the top of the hull, holding on to the cable as an anchor and guide. At the highest vantage point on the schooner, the way it laid in the water, the hull was as flat as the deck would have been had the ship been upright, while the actual deck had become a sheer drop down into the water.

The three of them stood waiting. Gabe felt very old,

suddenly, and exhausted. For a few seconds, he almost gave
up. Angry with himself, he shook it off. Miguel said he had
a plan, and Gabe would have to rely on that. Whatever it
took, he would make it back to the *Antoinette*. No way in hell
would he let himself die before he got a chance to look his
brother in the eye and ask if the FBI agent had been telling
the truth about Miguel and Maya.

Idiot. He's not lying. What did he have to gain?

Anguish filled him, overpowering his fear. He thought of
Maya's bronze skin, the softness of her hair, and the gentle
curve at the small of her back. He thought of the way her eyes
sparkled when he made her laugh, and the way they dimmed
when he made her cry, and he couldn't decide in that moment
who he hated more, his brother or himself.

Gabe crossed himself, kissed the tips of his fingers, and
glanced into the sky. If God took any notice, perhaps he would
also take pity.

He hooked his left arm over the cable, then pulled his legs
up, troubled at having to support his own weight. It wasn't
something he'd be able to do for very long. Heart fluttering, he
began to move across the gap between ships. The cable bit into
his hands, but he'd been at sea for years, and the calluses were
thick. Working his legs, keeping them hooked over the cable
as he made his way, was much more difficult. At twenty it
would have been simple enough. Gabe didn't usually think of
himself as very old, but his muscles weren't as limber as they'd
once been.

His arms strained, his shoulders burned, and his hands
stung, despite their calluses. A terrible certainty filled him that
his strength would give out before he reached the other side,
that the extra weight he carried from years of indulgences—
not a lot, really, but perhaps enough—would drag him down.

"Captain!" Kevonne yelled. "Put your feet down!"

The words broke through his concentration and he listened
carefully, afraid he'd misunderstood. But then Tori spoke,
much closer than Kevonne.

"Gabe. You're here."

She reached him, touched his arm. Tentatively, blinking

with amazement, he let his legs drop down to the schooner's hull, holding tightly to the cable, and turned to look at Tori. She had walked out to guide him in, just as Kevonne had done for her.

"Thanks," he said.

Tori squeezed his wrist. "Let's move."

The two of them made their way to where Kevonne and Pang waited, and they all rested a few seconds. Gabe had to take a step back from the edge, where the deck dropped straight down to the water. He had never been afraid of heights, but any time he stood on a balcony or even the walkway along the *Antoinette*'s accommodations block, the physical urge to jump tugged him forward. He'd read about that feeling. *Thanatos,* they called it. The death urge. Fortunately the instinct to stay alive overrode his body's strange desire to succumb to gravity.

"The rest should be easy," Kevonne said.

Pang snorted, glancing at him. "You think?"

Kevonne shrugged, gestured back the way they'd come. "Compared to that, yeah."

Gabe wasn't quite so sure. He lay on his stomach on the wooden hull and looked over the edge, getting a better look. Tori lay down beside him, close enough that he could hear her quickened breathing. Adrenaline still drove them all. Without it, Gabe figured they'd be dead already.

The deck angled down into the water, but now that he looked at it, he realized it wasn't exactly ninety degrees. Perhaps eighty. Close enough. Without something to hold on to, they'd just slide down into the water, and the space that separated the schooner from the sunken freighter had already filled with shadows. The sunlight came skimming across the surface of the water now, and didn't reach into that gap.

One of the masts had broken off perhaps a third of the way up its length. The other lay on the tilted deck of the rusty sunken freighter, creating a bridge to that ship from the schooner. They would have to slide down the deck to reach the base of the mast. Once again, however, whoever had come before them had paved the way. The cable from the trawler's winch had been tied off on the mast itself. If they were careful, they ought to be able to guide their descent.

"Who did all of this?" Tori asked, staring down at where the cable had been wound around the mast and hooked back onto itself.

"Dead motherfuckers," Pang said, voice flat.

Gabe, Tori, and Kevonne all looked at him.

Pang shrugged. "What? We were all thinking it."

Kevonne stripped off his shirt, wrapped it around his right hand, and sat down on the edge. Traversing the gap had been one thing, and hard on the hands, but the cable wasn't a fire pole. If they weren't careful, they'd tear the skin on their fingers and palms.

He didn't wait for them to wish him luck, just slid over the edge and slowly rappelled down the deck, coming to rest on the thickness of the mast. Kevonne had made it look easy, which prompted Pang to pull his own shirt over his head and follow suit. Halfway down his hands slipped and he nearly fell. Catching himself cost him. He gripped the cable tight enough to stop his descent and cried out as the metal dug into his flesh. His left hand was wrapped with cloth, but the right had been bare. Now it would be slick with blood.

Gabe said nothing to hurry him.

Down in the space between the schooner and the freighter—in the gathering shadows—the water sloshed, slapping the sides of the ships. Tori's focus was entirely on Pang, and she did not react at all. But Gabe looked down, peering into the dark, and saw the eyes staring back at him. The splash had come from off to the right, and when he looked in that direction it only took him a moment to make out a second set of eyes and the pale, glistening white hump of a head. The creatures watched them like crocodiles, so still, waiting for them to make a mistake.

Pang reached the mast. By then, Kevonne had crept on hands and knees across ten feet of the thick mast. For the last three or four feet, where the mast began to thin, he had to straddle the wood and drag himself forward, keeping balanced, twenty-five feet above the water.

"Shit," Tori said.

With a look of determination, she started to peel off her tank top. Gabe grabbed her arm to stop her.

"Hold on," he said. As she watched, he unbuttoned his own, a cotton short-sleeve with a faded scallop pattern. Maya had bought it for him two years before, during better times.

Better times, Gabe thought. *Hell, they were all better times.* Perspective could be a bitch. Pushing away thoughts of Maya, he held the shirt by its bottom hem and tore it down the middle, then handed half to Tori.

"A weird time to get all chivalrous on me," she said.

Gabe surprised himself by smiling. "It's not that I don't want to see you naked. I just don't want you distracting the rest of us."

Tori nodded. "Good. You had me worried."

She went down much faster than either of the guys, but by the time she landed on the mast, Kevonne and Pang were both safe on the rusty freighter. Tori started making her way across the mast-bridge without hesitation, driven by the lengthening shadows of late afternoon. If she had noticed the things down in the water, watching her, she made no mention of them.

When a third one appeared and reached out of the water to press its hands against the rusted freighter, then began to slither up the metal hull, Gabe wanted to scream. The suckers on its hands somehow allowed it to stick like a salamander to the side of the freighter, and it slithered upward until the top half of its pearlescent body was out of the water. Then it paused, clinging to the hull, as if testing out the shadows.

Dark enough, Gabe thought, glancing quickly at the horizon.

Sunlight still washed the deck of the freighter. Tori, Kevonne, and Pang were safe there, for now. But down there between the ships, the day had already fled. The creature seemed frozen for several seconds, then it slid farther up the hull, its serpentine lower body curled against the metal, suckers holding it in place.

"Gabe!" Tori called. "What are you waiting for? What's wrong?"

Kevonne joined in. "Captain?"

But it wasn't their urging that got him moving. Another pair of long-fingered hands rose from the gentle, lapping waves, and a second creature began to climb up the freighter's hull. How far would they venture from the shadows? How much light was enough to hold them back?

His hands were oddly steady but his throat went dry and he felt twitchy. He dropped down to sit on the edge of the sideways schooner, no longer able to hear the questions and urgent shouts from the others because his heart pounded so loudly in his ears. Twisting around, he gripped the cable with his torn shirt and pressed his feet against the deck. Then he pushed off, just a bit, and let his hands slide on the cable, the shirt tearing further, wearing thin. He tightened his grip and the cloth tugged away, metal scouring his palms and fingers. His jaws clamped shut in pain and his hands became slippery. With two fingers, he pulled the remnant of his shirt down into his hands, wrapped it as best he could, then moved more slowly.

He couldn't do it. The rag his shirt had become tore away, metal bit into his palms, and after a few more feet he froze. Gritting his teeth he looked down, saw the mast not that far below, and turned around, letting his legs hang down below him. With the wood just five feet away, he let go.

Falling, he felt despair fill him. If not for the square metal fitting around the base of the mast, he would likely have slipped right off and fallen into the water. But his shoes hit that flat surface, jarring his bones, and he let his momentum carry him forward. Steadied by his landing, he went down on his hands and knees on the mast. His hands stung and they were slippery with his blood, but Gabe did not slow. He hustled across the mast, the exhortations of the others finally reaching him.

His skin prickled with fear, but he did not look down, unwilling to learn how close they might be, or how many.

When he reached the place where the mast thinned enough that he should have straddled it, he could not bear to hang his legs over the sides. Instead, he stood. Refusing to look at Tori or his sailors, Gabe ran the last half dozen feet and leaped to the sun-washed deck of the rusting freighter.

He clapped his hands to his forehead and doubled over, heart slamming against his chest, breath too fast. Forcing himself to calm down, building walls around the fear inside of him, he straightened up, first pressing his hands together as if in prayer and then dropping them to his sides. Telling himself he was the captain no longer made any difference. Gabe Rio wanted to live, captain or not. Yes, he and Miguel needed to be eye to eye, and he needed answers, and despite it all he still wanted to see Maya again.

"What the hell, Captain?" Kevonne said.

Pang shook his head, dumbstruck. "One wrong step and you would've—"

Tori cut him off. "They're down there, aren't they?" Staring at him, studying his eyes.

Gabe nodded. "On the hull."

"Oh, fuck me," Pang said with such sadness that the profanity sounded almost like a prayer.

From down in the shadows between ships, a lone voice rose in a slow, ethereal melody, and a second joined it. Revulsion rippled through him.

"Sirens," Kevonne said. "They're sirens. Like in the legends."

"I don't remember anything about flesh-eating monsters with octopus fingers from my Greek mythology," Gabe said.

"Maybe not," Tori said, "but every legend starts somewhere."

But by then Gabe was barely listening. He stared past Kevonne, out to sea, and now Tori was turning, too. Then Kevonne and Pang both looked to see what had drawn their attention. The *Antoinette* glided closer—as close as they could take her without running aground.

Not that it would matter. The ship couldn't come alongside the old freighter, and any gap would be too far. But Miguel had said he had a plan, and as Gabe watched his ship slip through the water, he began to get an inkling just what that plan might entail.

The crane at the *Antoinette*'s bow was in motion. Already, one of the twenty-foot metal containers had been hooked up, and the crane lifted it slowly into the air.

52

Tori and the guys stood on the far edge of the rusty freighter's deck, away from the wheelhouse and the stairs—away from anything that might allow access from the darkness of the flooded cargo hold. Kevonne and Pang talked animatedly, both excited at the prospect of rescue and anxious about the waning sunlight. Gabe glared at the *Antoinette,* waiting in grim silence for the moment when he could confront Miguel. They had all heard Josh's accusation, and understood what it meant. Miguel had been sleeping with his brother's wife.

On board the *Antoinette,* people ran around on the deck, shouting to one another, working quickly. The crane swung out, metal containers dangling in the air. Normally Sal Pucillo operated the crane, but Tori wondered if Miguel had taken the controls. Surely, under the circumstances, Pucillo would put aside any objections he had and do whatever it took to save their lives, but Miguel might not want to trust him with it. Tori suspected the chief mate would want to do this job himself.

Whoever held the controls, the crane lowered the latest container out over the water. The container swayed, like the trailer of an eighteen-wheeler twisting on the end of a string, and the crane operator lowered it over the side of the ship. The cable began to play out. Up on the deck, Tori could see Dwyer talking into a handheld radio, probably guiding whoever operated the crane.

When the container was just above the water, Dwyer gave a hand signal and the crane released the huge metal case. It splashed into the water, tilted slightly, then settled and began to sink. Abruptly it came to a halt, slightly askew, the side nearest them above the water.

"This might actually work," Kevonne said.

"Might?" Pang snapped. "Fuck might. It's gonna work."

The first container the crane had dropped into the water had vanished beneath the waves. So had the second. They were on the sixth now, and two of those managed to rise partway above the water. Miguel had begun to build them a bridge back to the *Antoinette*. One container had popped open, boxes spilling out, floating to the surface. Another had slid off to the side and disappeared, but Tori thought if they dumped enough of the containers, the crazy plan might just work.

As the thought took shape in her mind, she heard Kevonne and Pang start to laugh. The crane operator had taken a new approach. The crane itself had dipped down between two stacks of containers, each half a dozen high, and now it swung. Tori took a step back in surprise as the top four in the pile nearest the edge toppled off the deck and into the water.

"That's it," Gabe said. "No time for precision."

Even so, Tori kept glancing at the western horizon and then at the work in progress, silently urging Miguel and the others on the *Antoinette* to hurry. Sunset seemed to be approaching much faster than they could build their bridge. Dusk would come too soon.

Once again, her fate had been taken out of her hands, and Tori hated it. She stood on the edge of the freighter's deck, washed in golden, late afternoon sunlight, and stared back the way they had come, at the opposite side of the deck. Darkness yawned in the space between freighter and lopsided schooner, and Tori watched intently, waiting for the moment when those long, hideous fingers would come up from the shadows and the creatures would slither onto the deck.

At sunset, they would come.

53

Josh opened his eyes, unsure at first what had woken him. He'd been out for a few minutes, maybe longer. Not asleep, but unconscious. That didn't bode well. With Angie's help he had torn up his shirt and bound the gunshot wound in his shoulder, but whenever he moved he paid for it with searing pain that brought beads of sweat out on his forehead.

Now he looked down, saw that blood had soaked through the shirt, but when he touched the cloth with his good hand it felt tacky, like it had begun to dry. The bleeding seemed to have slowed or stopped. He might not die from the gunshot after all—the bullet had passed all the way through, and that was a plus—but infection could still get him.

Off to his left, in the dimming light inside the wheelhouse, someone shifted. He glanced over and saw Angie unclip a heavy duty emergency flashlight from the charger where it was mounted near the port side door. She moved casually, but with purpose, walking toward Suarez, who sat by the wheel, watching the progress Miguel and the others were making with the crane.

Suarez sensed her coming and turned, starting to frown, perhaps to chastise her. A flicker of alarm crossed his features as Angie came too close and his hand began to move toward the gun in his waistband.

Angie struck him with the heavy flashlight, right across the bridge of his nose. Suarez let out a grunt as blood gushed from his nostrils. Angie kept moving, driving him into the control panel and the wheel. She let the flashlight drop from her grip and it shattered as it hit the ground, and then they were grappling together, both of them reaching for his gun. Angie got it first, pulling it out, raising the barrel, but Suarez slapped it out of her hand and it skittered across the floor toward the back of the wheelhouse.

They went down, grunting, hands tangled in hair or closing around throats.

"Stupid woman. What the hell you think you—"

"I don't want to die, you asshole!" Angie screamed in Suarez's face.

He tried to reason with her as they continued grappling. Suarez slipped her grasp and crawled toward the gun, but Angie grabbed him by the belt and drove her fist into his crotch. With a cry of pain, Suarez doubled up. Angie tried to get past him, but despite his pain he got his fingers wrapped in her hair again and grabbed her arm, pulling her back.

Josh forced himself to stand, sliding up the wall. Pain set off fireworks in his head and he swayed, breathing through his teeth, nearly collapsing again. Then he staggered across the wheelhouse to the two chairs that were affixed to the floor in front of the wheel. He snatched the PLB from the console, but his left arm hung useless and he could not slide it from its rubber holster.

As Angie and Suarez fought, he set the PLB back on the console, rested his hand on it, and managed to slip it out of the holster. He flipped open the faceplate, blinking back the pain, and pressed the two blue buttons there simultaneously, holding them down until the little gadget issued a long beep.

"You can stop now," he said.

Suarez and Angie had barely noticed him moving, but now they dragged themselves away from each other, scratched and bloody and wearing foolish expressions. Then Angie grinned.

"You set it off?" she asked.

Josh nodded, staring at Suarez. "No point in shooting anyone now, Mr. Suarez. The signal is sent. My people will follow the beacon. They'll be coming."

Suarez seemed to deflate. He knelt on the floor, looking somehow much older than he had before, and then slumped back to sit, legs sprawled in front of him, as though in surrender.

Then he looked up at Josh and said, "Thank God."

54

A helicopter, Rachael Voss thought. The ship that the FBI gave Ed Turcotte's Counter-Terrorism squad had its own helicopter. Voss wasn't generally the jealous type, but she couldn't help envying that, thinking about all the cases she'd worked where it would've been handy to have her own helicopter.

Turcotte had caught up with her little cluster of Coast Guard, ICE, and FBI boats forty-five minutes ago, and in the time since then he had managed to talk to the commanders of every vessel except for hers. It had been Voss's case from the beginning, her command, but Turcotte wanted to send her a message, let her know that she wasn't at the helm anymore. Counter-Terrorism had taken over. It didn't matter that nobody had a single shred of evidence that Viscaya's operations had supported or aided terrorism within or outside the United States. They wanted the bust—wanted to make a big splash on the news about a terrorist cell operating out of Miami, and how Homeland Security was keeping America safe—and they would take it.

Voss might have been able to hold them off longer, but with Josh out of contact for so long, Chauncey and DelRosso couldn't argue anymore. They'd put it down as her fuckup, her op, and if Special Agent Joshua Hart turned up dead, that would be on her as well.

Rachael's heart felt cracked in half. Maybe they were all right; maybe she had lost perspective, and Ed Turcotte taking over this case was the only way to salvage anything out of it—arrests, smuggled guns, any tiny victory for the FBI, and maybe, if they were lucky, Josh's life.

He's not dead, Voss told herself. Insisted to herself.

But so much time had passed, even she had stopped believing it.

Her cell phone trilled. She glanced down at the screen and saw that it was Turcotte himself calling. Out there on his ship—a loan from the goddamned military, with its shiny black helicopter—he had finally deigned to speak with her, just to tell her she could fuck off and go home now if she wanted, that she was relieved of command.

Pavarotti came up from below, hustling, feet pounding the steps. "Rachael!"

She sighed. How many times did she have to tell him?

Her cell phone kept ringing. She punched TALK, raised it to her ear. "This is Voss."

As she did, Pavarotti grabbed her arm, spun her around. She would have screamed at him, maybe decked him, but then she saw the smile on his face, the light dancing in his eyes. They'd only had sex the one time, but right then she thought maybe seconds were in order.

"Rachael, it's Ed Turcotte," the voice said in her ear. Presumptuous with her first name, the asshole. "Your squad has done all you can. We're going to take it from here. I'll want you to stick around in a support capacity. Here's the plan—"

"Actually, Ed, there's a new plan," she said, grinning at Pavarotti. "Special Agent Hart just set off his beacon. We've got the tracking system set up, and we're heading out. Feel free to follow along."

She gestured to Pavarotti, pointed toward the wheelhouse, and he set off running. He'd get them moving, tracing the beacon.

"Hang on a second, Rachael," Turcotte said, sounding all pissy. "It isn't for you to say—"

"You can have the bust, Ed. I couldn't give a shit. You can say they're Martian jihadists for all I care. I just want my partner back safe. Now, we're the ones set up to track the beacon, so unless you're going to order us to stand down while we've got an agent in deep cover signaling us to come get his ass out of danger, not to mention a boatload of suspects in a two-year investigation waiting for you to arrest them, I'd like to get going. Maybe you'll even get to play with your helicopter."

Turcotte didn't reply for a second, and Voss feared he had hung up on her. When he did speak, his voice was low and even.

"By all means, lead the way."

-55--

Tori twisted her ankle jumping from the freighter's deck. The drop couldn't have been more than ten feet, but she had to leap straight out to reach the makeshift bridge created by the haphazardly placed containers. She landed badly, tipping to the right, and let momentum carry her forward, fresh sparks of fear erupting in her mind. How close was the edge? She spread out her hands, slowed her slide, and came to rest facedown on the warm metal roof of a freshly painted container, chest heaving.

Her right hand hung out over the edge, fifteen feet above the water.

With a strangled cry, she brought her hand in and rolled onto her back. A loud clang sounded as Gabe landed a few feet back, stumbling onto all fours. He stood immediately, grimacing as his knees popped. Dark circles had formed under his eyes and his expression had gone slack.

"Tori!" he snapped.

"I know!"

She flipped over, scrambled to her feet, and started moving. The metal rang with every footfall, echoing inside the container. Gabe kept pace just a few steps behind, his heavier tread thunderous. He was breathing hard, and she imagined she could feel his breath on the back of her neck.

Ahead, Pang and Kevonne had already jumped to the next container. A glance at them made Tori gasp. It had taken more than two hours for Miguel to finish laying the containers down for this rudimentary bridge. Some of the metal boxes were tilted, and others were separated by gaps that might well be too wide for them to jump. But they were out of time now, and it would have to do.

Twilight had come.

On the western horizon, the sun shimmered just above the water. To her right, the sides of the containers above the water were still washed with a warm golden light, but the waves—splashing higher now—had gone dark.

Tori wouldn't even look to her left. She knew better. On the eastern side of that makeshift metal walkway, the creatures had started to crawl up out of the water, clinging to the sides of the containers in the indigo gloom. Their singing had grown louder.

Up on the deck of the *Antoinette,* silhouettes shouted down at them to hurry, to run, and she wanted to scream back at them and tell them how totally unhelpful they were. With the spray from the sea, the smooth metal of the container was slippery, and she moved as fast as she could. A wrong step now would slide her right off into the water and she wouldn't let that happen; she had to stay in control. Looking at the sinking sun terrified her almost as much as the thought of glimpsing the sickly things lurking just out of reach of the daylight to her left, but she could not afford to run.

The first gap was only a few feet, and she and Gabe both cleared it with ease, slipping a little, but then hurrying on. When Tori came to the end of the second container, she paused, hands fluttering up to clutch the sides of her head, glancing around as she tried to figure out how to cross. The next container slanted down, away from them. The gap here must have been four or five feet.

"Just jump!" Gabe said.

Tori glanced down to the left. White, translucent fingers clutched at the edge of the next container, down in the shadows just above the water.

"I'll slide right down," she said.

"Good! It'll be faster!" Gabe snapped. "Go, or let me by!"

She knew he meant it. What got her moving, though, was

the sight of Kevonne and Pang up ahead, nearly to the end of the container she was about to jump onto. It slanted down toward the water, coming within half a dozen feet of the waves—and whatever lurked beneath them. But the next container was a good four feet higher, and the one after that—though angled badly—even higher. Miguel had started dumping whole stacks of them overboard closer to the *Antoinette,* so the containers were like a jumble of huge stones, providing several possible paths to the ship. As she watched, Pang jumped up, grabbed the edge of one of the higher containers, and hauled himself on top of it.

"Tori, the sun!" Gabe shouted.

She backed up seven paces, took a breath, stared down at her feet a second—and saw that twilight had truly arrived. The gloom had begun to gather, making everything in her perception vague and golden.

"Oh, my God," she whispered, suddenly sure they would not make it.

Tori ran and leaped, pulling her feet up, and landed on the next container, sliding down it much faster than she'd expected. Her heart pounded as she slid to the left and she put a hand down, trying to stop her slide, twisting around. Her legs were out in front of her, and she kept them straight as she collided with the next container, the impact ringing out over the waves.

The opening between the two containers might only have been twenty inches or so, but she was only six feet above the water. Frantic, she scrambled back up a little ways, pulling her legs away, staring at the darkness of that narrow gap as she jumped to her feet.

Kevonne and Pang had been here moments ago. They would reach the *Antoinette* first. Tori wanted to be with them. She wanted to be safe, locked in her quarters, surrounded by metal. A prison cell would do, at this point. She ran two steps and jumped up, grabbed hold of the top of the next container as she had seen Pang do, and pulled herself up. For a second she didn't think she had the strength, but panic gave her a boost and she dragged herself onto the container's roof. Still only ten feet off the water, but better.

Until she heard Pang shout just ahead, and the people up on the deck of the *Antoinette* screaming frantically down at them, and then the shriek of a voice that barely sounded human. Tori faltered, staring straight ahead, where Pang now stood alone at the edge of a container.

"Kevonne!" he shouted, stalking back and forth, jittery, gazing into the water. "Jesus, Kevonne!"

As Tori hurried toward him, Pang glanced at her, then at the setting sun. He shook his head, stepped back, and leaped to the next container. Only one more to go beyond that, and he would be at the ship. The crew of the *Antoinette* was lowering a lifeboat on its cables. If they could reach it, the crew would haul them up to safety.

Gabe pounded along behind her; she could feel the tremors in the metal beneath her feet. Tori raced after Pang, but he had become almost a silhouette himself. She glanced at the horizon and saw that the sun had begun to melt into the water, gliding down over the edge of the world.

"No, please," she whispered, her chest aching with a thousand regrets.

Biting her lip, she kept on. The sirens' voices grew louder, the song rising. Tori slipped, threw her arms out, steadied herself, and reached the next gap. The containers had landed at odd angles. She went to the right corner, took a breath, and jumped up. Her foot slipped and her shin cracked against the edge of the container's roof, but momentum carried her forward and she regained her feet in seconds.

"Out of the way!" Gabe shouted.

Tori twisted around to see him jumping. She stepped back as he landed, fell, and spilled off to the side, his left leg shooting out into space. Into darkness.

Long, sickly white fingers wrapped around his ankle, suckers sinking into the flesh. Gabe's eyes went wide as he screamed and tried to pull his leg from its grasp. The thing held on, its head rising just above the edge of the container. The last dim glow of daylight made its hand and face steam and blister and its song went silent. But it did not let go.

"Get off!" Gabe shouted, as it dragged him nearer the edge. He looked up, eyes wide, and stared at Tori. "Help me!"

"Pang!" she cried. "Pang, come back!"

But she knew Pang would not come back, not with the sun vanishing on the horizon. Knowing she should be running, saving herself, Tori grabbed Gabe's outstretched hand and braced herself, giving him something to hang on to, some leverage.

"Pull!" she screamed.

Gabe's face had gone red with pain and effort, but he couldn't free himself. Tori knew she didn't have the strength, and neither did he. One of the guns she'd had on the lifeboat had been lost when she'd landed in the water, but she reached behind her and tugged out the other. Holding Gabe's wrist with one hand, she pointed at the creature's oil-black eyes and pulled the trigger, expecting a kick. Nothing happened.

Swearing, she cast the gun aside, realizing it had been fouled with seawater when she'd had to swim for the trawler. But Gabe hadn't gone under the water. She needed the small pistol whose handle even now jutted from Gabe's rear waistband.

She threw herself on top of him, heard the thump of his forehead against metal and his grunt of pain and surprise. Then she snatched the gun from his belt, thumbed the safety, and took aim. The creature opened its jaw impossibly wide, darted hundreds of tiny fangs toward her hand, toward the gun.

Tori put a bullet through its throat, then a second through its head.

Creamy ichor, laced with red, burst out the back of its skull, and it slipped off Gabe, detaching from his flesh and the container. The suckers pulled away from metal with a disgusting wet smacking, but where the fingers had wrapped around Gabe's leg, they pulled skin away with them. Gabe let out a roar of pain even as he dragged his leg in and staggered to his feet.

"Thanks," he said, throwing an arm around her, limping as they hustled toward the last container.

"Yeah." She couldn't think of anything else to say. She'd spent her life depending on men and, at last, the tables had been turned. Now she just wanted to live long enough not to regret it.

The gap separating them from the last container was no longer than a ruler. Miguel had gotten that part right. They jumped it. Up ahead, Pang had already climbed into the lifeboat, which dangled tantalizingly close. On the deck above them, someone stood by to hit the controls, ready to winch them up.

Pang twisted around in the lifeboat as though he was having some kind of seizure. "They're coming! Run, Captain! Jesus, they're coming!"

Tori didn't look back. Gabe's labored breathing filled her ears. She thought she could feel his heart pounding beside her, just as she felt her own. To her left, white hands appeared, heads rising, as two of the creatures began to slither up onto the container.

This time, no smoke rose from their flesh, and no blisters appeared. She glanced to her right, to the west, just in time to see the last sliver of the sun vanish into the ocean. A flash of green light flickered on the horizon, and then the darkness swept in.

Night had fallen.

She and Gabe practically threw themselves into the lifeboat. The winches cried out from above, in chorus with the creatures' song.

"It'll be okay," Gabe said, sliding an arm around her. "It's gonna be okay now."

Tori went cold. "The hell it is," she said.

For even as the cables drew them up toward the deck of the *Antoinette,* sickly white shapes slithered up her hull in the moonlight.

-56--

Night had fallen.

Miguel stood on the deck of the *Antoinette,* Heckler & Koch assault rifle slung over his shoulder and the Sig Sauer holstered at his hip. He'd handed over the controls of the crane to Dwyer for the last half containers or so and now he waited at the railing, watching the lifeboat ascend toward the deck with Gabe, Tori, and Pang on board. He held his breath, a sick twisting in his gut as he prayed for them to reach the deck. The ship had lightened considerably—he'd dumped half their cargo over the side—so they'd be out of here at speed, if the fuckers would get down to the engine room and do their jobs.

"Tupper!" he shouted, turning to the assistant engineer. "Get below, goddammit! We need to be under way, now!"

The thuggish Tupper looked at him with idiot eyes. "Jimenez is down there now. We're ready to go!"

Other members of the crew were arrayed along the railing as well, watching the lifeboat's ascent, but Miguel paid no attention to them. He leaned over the edge, glimpsed his brother crouched in the boat, and then turned to seek out Dwyer. The young Irishman, face pale in the moonlight in spite of his seemingly eternal sunburn, hustled toward him from the direction of the crane.

"What's going on?" Dwyer asked.

"Kevonne's dead. The others are coming up. Get your ass up to the wheelhouse and find out what Suarez is waiting for. Set course anywhere but fucking here, and full ahead."

Dwyer nodded and started for the stairs before he faltered, head jerking back in confusion as he stared up at the accommodations block. Miguel spun to see what had so astonished him, and saw Angie Tyree helping the FBI man down the stairs toward the deck. Josh leaned heavily on her, the bloodstains on his shirt a potent black in the moonlight.

Angie and Josh. Which begged the question, what had happened to Suarez? Something glinted in Josh's hand, and Miguel didn't need to look any closer to know it had to be the gun he'd left with Suarez. That didn't bode well for the old Cuban, or for any of them. But Miguel didn't much care anymore. Maybe Gabe would have a plan that would sort all this out, a story to tell Viscaya about rough seas, losing half their cargo, and dead crew members, but whatever Gabe had planned, Miguel had decided it would have to include an explanation that covered the death of an FBI agent. As soon as they were safely away, he would put a bullet in the guy's skull himself.

"What do you want me to—" Dwyer started to ask.

A question interrupted by screams from below, shouts from the lifeboat. Tori and Pang cried out for them to bring the lifeboat up faster. Gabe's deep voice provided a counterpoint, but at first Miguel couldn't make out the words, so intertwined were they with the screams of the others. He thought Gabe was saying, "We're coming up." He blinked a couple of times, processing, and sorted out where he'd gone wrong.

Not *we're*. "They're." *They* were coming up.

Even as this information clicked in, Tupper let out a shriek that tore the air, just a dozen feet along the deck to Miguel's right. He swung the barrel of the H&K in that direction and saw Tupper go down. Miguel hadn't seen one of the things up close before and for a second could only stare at its sickeningly white skin, oily and slightly jaundiced by the moonlight, and its puckered, serpentine lower body. Its long fingers dragged Tupper down and wrapped around his head, stifling his screams. Its jaws went so wide they seemed almost to unhinge and then it thrust its face at Tupper's chest.

People cursed and screamed and got the hell away from the thing and their dead crewmate, but there were more. One of them flopped onto the deck and slithered toward Valente with hideous speed. It knocked him down and sprawled on top of him, too fast for any of them to do anything.

Miguel opened fire on the one that had killed Tupper, the bullets ripping it apart, then swung the gun toward Valente. But there were people running, too much chaos, and he hesitated in fear of killing one of his crew.

Then there were more—too many—slithering onto the deck, and he turned to Dwyer. "Get up top! Get us out of here!"

He heard the whine of the winch cables as they brought the lifeboat to the top and spun around to see Gabe, Tori, and Pang climbing onto the deck. Pang supported Gabe, whose left leg was torn and bloody. Miguel started to run toward his brother, but then Gabe turned to look at him, eyes full of anguish that had nothing to do with his wounded leg, and Miguel faltered. Even in the midst of blood and death and inhuman horrors, Gabe saw *him* as the monster.

-57--

When Gabe saw the guilt in his brother's eyes, his first instinct was to shoot him. He had taken his gun back from Tori, and in one swift motion he raised it and swept the barrel around to aim at Miguel's head. In that fraction of a moment, conscience overrode instinct and anguish; he thought of their mother, and what it would do to her to learn that one of her sons had killed the other. But he didn't lower the pistol.

"Drop it," he said.

Miguel slid the H&K assault rifle to the deck and took a step back.

Screams drifted off across the ship and out over the Caribbean, swept away by the wind—cries of help in a place where no one would ever hear, or answer. The sirens—ancient things, Gabe thought, from a time before the world had surrendered its mysteries—came up the hull with a damp, dragging sound, and boarded the *Antoinette*. His ship. Once his pride.

Pang let loose a cry of such terror—the nighttime fears of prehistoric children, when the whole world was unknown— that both Rio brothers glanced over. One siren wrapped around his legs while a second coiled its lower body around his head, crushing his skull. The gun he'd been holding flew from his hand, skittering across the deck.

"Jesus," Miguel whispered. "Gabe, we have to—"

Gabe cocked the pistol. "Why?"

People were running, climbing the stairs of the accommodations block or vanishing below, slamming doors, bolting locks.

How long they'd be able to keep the things out, Gabe didn't know. But he and his brother were staying where they were.

Until Tori grabbed Gabe's arm and twisted him halfway around.

"Stop!" she snapped. "What are you doing? We've got to hide!"

"You heard—" he began.

Miguel lunged for him. Gabe shoved Tori away, turned, and struck his brother across the cheek with the barrel of the gun, laying the skin open to the bone. Miguel staggered to his knees and scrambled up again, starting to back away. He snatched the H&K up from the deck.

"I'm sorry, Gabriel," he said, only half-aiming the weapon. "You don't understand. Maya needed me. You hurt her so much, and then it was like she was invisible to you, like you didn't even see her anymore."

The things were coming for them, sliding along the deck.

"Stop!" Tori screamed.

Gabe lunged at Miguel, grabbed the barrel of the H&K with one hand, and cracked the pistol over his head with the other. He tugged the assault rifle out of Miguel's grasp, turned, and tossed it to Tori, who caught the gun as though it might burn her.

"Don't you fucking talk about her," Gabe rasped, low in his throat, not even sure his brother could hear him.

Miguel collapsed into his arms, begging for forgiveness.

Gabe held him close, heart breaking. "Sorry won't do it, *hermano*."

Then he turned, aimed just past Tori, and put a bullet into the open mouth of a siren, blowing out jagged teeth and the back of its head. He fired again, taking it in the chest as it reared up, cobra-style, to attack her.

Tori turned, swung the H&K, and strafed three others that were slithering toward them. Gabe and Miguel stood, together, then stepped up on either side of her.

When Tori crouched to pick up the gun Pang had dropped, Miguel took the assault rifle back, and Gabe didn't stop him. There would be no forgiveness, but they had no time for re-crimination, either. Time had run out.

58

Angie flinched with every gunshot, held her breath with every scream. She wanted to run, to abandon Josh and just go, but she couldn't bring herself to leave him. It wasn't that she was afraid of prison—not anymore. But without Josh, she would have been alone. So she let him put an arm around her and hustled him as fast as she could across the deck. They moved along the accommodations block, afraid of being out in the open, and when they reached the far side of the structure—with only bare deck between them and the port side railing—they hesitated a second.

Long enough to hear the shuffle of footsteps behind them.

Josh twisted, grunting in pain from the wound in his shoulder, and aimed the gun. Angie held him up, but prepared to bolt if they got to him, then realized that footsteps meant something human giving chase.

Even out of the moonlight, in the overhanging shadows of the walkway above, she saw orange highlights in Dwyer's hair.

"You were supposed to get the ship out of here," Angie said.

Dwyer scowled. "No time. I saw you two and wondered where you were headed. Then I figured it out—the covered lifeboats."

Angie held her breath. Was he trying to stop them? "I'm sorry, Tom. I never wanted to lie. I just couldn't go to prison, and—"

Dwyer gave a short laugh. "Fuck 'sorry.' Let's get out of here."

Josh nodded, turning painfully, urging Angie on. "Go."

The three of them hurried away from the shelter of the

accommodations block, out into the moonlight, on the open deck.

"They're coming from the island, or around it," Josh told Dwyer. "They might not be in the water on this side yet."

"Let's hope," Dwyer replied.

Their every step punctuated by gunshots, they reached the winch controls for the lifeboat Angie had in mind. They'd been built for high seas, for terrible storms, and perfected by the military. She didn't know if it would keep the creatures out, but it was their only shot.

Dwyer tore the tarp off the lifeboat as Angie worked the controls, raising the boat up, the crane arms swinging it out over the edge of the railing.

"Listen," Josh said, a bit dreamily. He'd lost a lot of blood.

The gunshots and screaming had stopped, and now they could hear voices rising, singing in an eerie chorus. Dwyer froze, staring. Angie tracked his gaze to the accommodations block. In the moonlight she could see at least three of the things clinging to the walls, their tails coiled like snakes. One hung from a walkway railing.

The singing stopped, and all four of them attacked, smashing through windows and locked doors.

"Oh, Jaysus," Dwyer said.

Angie turned and saw one of the pearly white things gliding across the deck toward them. Another hung from the second-story walkway on the accommodations tower.

"Josh, get in," Angie whispered.

The FBI agent raised his gun, barely able to stand, and took aim. "The hell with that. You get in."

Dwyer grabbed Angie's hand and started pulling her toward the open hatch.

Josh fired.

59

Tori aimed at a siren and pulled the trigger.

"Good, now run!" Gabe snapped.

Together, she and the Rio brothers raced across the deck, firing at the creatures that came too close or tried to block the way. The gun in her hand had been Pang's, and she only had it now because the sirens had killed him. If he'd still been alive, she might be dead. Was that luck, or fate? The question seemed important now, because she had a terrible feeling that fate had caught up with her. She had escaped it once, three years before, down in the tunnel underneath Penn Station. Now she wondered if she had been meant to board that train, to die in that explosion. Tori feared that death had come for her, but her body wouldn't allow her to surrender.

"Move your asses!" she screamed at the Rios.

Miguel twisted, sighted on a creature darting toward them from the stern, and fired four rounds into it, practically obliterating its head. Tori and the Rio brothers crossed the vast, empty space where the stacks of containers had been before. Most of the cargo had been sacrificed to save her and Gabe and Pang, but now Pang was dead, and she and Gabe would be, too, if they didn't find someplace to hole up where the creatures couldn't get at them.

Screams and gunshots echoed across the deck, followed by the shattering of glass and splintering of wood, and the squeal of warping metal.

"I'm not hearing as much chaos," Miguel said, with a hint of hope in his voice.

"That's not good," Gabe replied. "When it all goes quiet, it'll mean nobody's left alive to make any noise."

More gunshots, then, muffled and distant. Tori took off in a sprint, mustering all the strength she had left, and the Rio brothers did their best to keep up. The railing glinted in moonlight. To the left, the accommodations block loomed, but she could see silver-white things way up on the wall, climbing higher.

"Suarez," Gabe muttered, spotting the creatures moving toward the wheelhouse.

But he didn't slow down. None of them did.

Silhouettes moved on the deck. A man screamed. A gun barked. Miguel grabbed Tori's wrist and hauled her to a stop. Gabe faltered, turning to stare at them.

"This is bullshit," Miguel whispered. "We've gotta find an unlocked container, hide inside."

Gabe looked doubtful.

"They'll get in," Tori said. "You've seen them. They will get in, and we'll have nowhere left to run."

Anger flashed in Miguel's eyes. "You got a better idea?"

Another noise came from up ahead and the moon seemed to grow brighter, the scene clearer. The scene playing out at the railing resolved itself. Angie and a staggering man tried to get into one of the enclosed lifeboats. Smart. Really smart. The things were like little submarines, almost. They weren't meant to travel underwater, but they wouldn't flood and they were swift. If they were fast, and most of the things were still on the *Antoinette,* they might get away.

But Angie and Josh weren't alone. Things writhed on the deck nearby as they scrambled to reach the lifeboat. How they were going to lower her down, Tori had no idea, and the question vanished from her mind when she heard the cry of a shredded voice, and saw that one of the creatures writhing on the deck was Tom Dwyer. A siren had dragged him down. Dwyer fought, his skin gleaming as sickly as the creature's, and they rolled and twisted. He tried to drag himself away.

"Move!" Gabe snapped.

As Tori and the Rio brothers ran up, Gabe shot both of the grappling figures. Dwyer slumped to the deck immediately, bullet through his chest, but the siren flopped wretchedly on the deck for several seconds until the captain shot it again. Tori gave it a wide berth as she ran up to the winch controls, took in the cables, the way Josh leaned against the lifeboat, the blood on his shirt, and understood he'd been shot. He threw something into the open lifeboat hatch, but Tori had no idea what it might be.

Angie stood frozen, staring at Gabe, half-crouched, as though grief might have felled her. "You killed him!"

"I saved him," Gabe replied. "Neither of you were going to do it."

The words chilled Tori, but she couldn't deny that they were true. She glanced over at Josh, terror and regret and anger roiling inside her, but she tamped all of those emotions down when she saw how bad he looked. Josh held a gun in one hand but seemed barely able to stand, only still conscious by sheer force of will. Still, he focused on her, and a gentle sorrow touched his face.

"Hey," Josh said, reaching out for her.

"Get in the goddamn lifeboat!" Angie barked.

Josh ignored her. Alarmingly pale, he touched Tori's arm, then pulled her to him in a weird embrace full of fear and blood and handicapped by the grips they had on their guns.

"Fuck this!" Angie said, and lowered herself through the lifeboat hatch. "Who's coming?"

Gabe and Miguel moved toward the lifeboat.

"I'm sorry I lied to you," Josh whispered in Tori's ear, breath brushing her neck. "It wasn't all pretend."

She stiffened in confusion—pleased and furious and hopeless in equal measure. "Do it," she said. "Get in."

More shouting came out of the night, down alongside the accommodations block—someone else trying to get a lifeboat into the water. Tori looked along the port side and saw people struggling, falling, trying to rise, as sirens attacked them.

Josh nudged her away from the lifeboat controls, eyes glazed but still standing. Gun dangling at his side, he started the lifeboat on its slow descent.

"I go last. Part of the job," he said.

Tori nearly slapped him. From the moment things had gone wrong, she had been looking for a man—hell, anyone—to save her, but she was sick of being saved. She had spent three years as a secret survivor, lost between the cracks of the world, no real name and no more idea of who she really was than she'd had at the age of nine.

She stopped the lifeboat from lowering.

Josh swayed on his feet, and then collapsed to his knees, weak from blood loss.

"No!" Tori cried as she grabbed him to keep him from toppling completely. She tried to get him back on his feet, to move him toward the hatch, but did not have the strength. She twisted round and spotted the captain.

"Gabe, help me!" she said.

Tori saw the hesitation in Gabe's eyes. Angie shouted at them from inside the lifeboat, in a terrified frenzy to depart.

"Please," she said. "He's just a guy doing his job, no different from you."

Gabe Rio swore as he stepped away from the hatch, rushed to her side, and began to help lift Josh to his feet.

"Goddammit!" Miguel Rio roared. "What the fuck is the matter with you?" But he stepped out of the way as Gabe and Tori half-dragged Josh to the lifeboat. Gabe stepped through the hatch and reached up, awkwardly pulling Josh in after him.

A scream filled the air, carried by the wind, and Tori twisted round to see Sal Pucillo racing toward them. She was glad to see him, glad that yet another of the *Antoinette*'s crew would survive the night.

The thing came out of the dark so swiftly that Tori had only just clocked it in her peripheral vision before it hit Pucillo, knocking him to the deck. Tori and Miguel raised their guns, but fired wide for fear of hitting Sal. The creature twisted round, two rows of nostrils flaring, rippling like gills. Its lower body coiled around Pucillo and it grabbed the deck, hurling itself toward the railing and over the side.

Pucillo screamed all the way down, silenced only by the splash as they struck the water and it dragged him under.

"Give me your gun!" Miguel said.

Tori glanced at him, saw him staring, and turned to see two, three, five of the things whipping across the deck toward them. Others hung, cocoon-like, from the catwalks around the accommodations block.

Miguel snatched her gun from her hand. Raising both, he began to fire, but there wouldn't be bullets enough, and he had to know that. Tori stared for a sliver of a moment, and understood. Miguel had betrayed his brother, destroyed their bond. He could never make up for what he'd done, but this much he could do. He could give up his life for his brother.

Gabe began shouting from the open hatch of the lifeboat, going from English to rapid-fire Spanish. Miguel ignored him.

Tori hit the control, started the lifeboat descending again, and grabbed his wrist.

"Come on!" she said, a giddy exhilaration filling her.

She ran to the edge of the deck and Miguel staggered with her, still shooting. One of the guns dry-fired and he tossed it aside. The things slithered faster. He'd killed three of them, but there were so many more. Tori glanced up in a last moment of uncontrollable curiosity, overwhelmed by that strange hysteria, and saw one of the sirens atop the wheelhouse, outlined against the night sky.

Miguel gave her a shove.

If she hadn't leaped for the hatch, she'd have fallen all the way down to the water. As it was, she struck her ankle on the hatch rim and heard the crack of bone even as she landed on the floor of the lifeboat, slamming the back of her skull.

Josh reached out and took her hand, and held on tight.

"Close it!" Miguel screamed.

Angie tried to hold on to Gabe but the captain shoved her aside, pushing up through the hatch as though he thought he could fly back up to the deck of his ship.

"Miguel, no! Jump, *hermano*!" Gabe screamed.

But Miguel stood by the winch controls, staring down at them as the lifeboat lowered toward the water. Tori stared past Gabe, up through the hatch. Miguel seemed to grow smaller. Long, cratered fingers wrapped around his face from behind. He screamed again, but there were no words.

Angie pulled Gabe away, and this time he did not fight her. Tori watched as she tugged the hatch closed, dropped the bar to secure it, and before they could settle into a seat, the cables holding the lifeboat let go and they were falling.

Josh swore, and she lost her grip on his fingers. Gabe crashed into the hatch. Tori's head hit the ceiling and then the boat struck the water and she crashed to the floor. The lifeboat swayed from side to side but then righted itself. Disoriented, she watched as Gabe started to rise and move toward the pilot seat.

Something struck the roof. Another loud splash came from outside. The lifeboat rocked again and Gabe fell over.

"They're coming after us," Angie whispered.

Tori glanced over at Josh and saw that he'd succumbed at last. His shirt was soaked with blood, but she thought he was still breathing. Things scrabbled at the outside of the lifeboat and she felt ice spreading inside of her. She pressed her lips together, brushed away tears before they could fall, then willed them not to come.

She dragged herself into the pilot seat and strapped in as they started to slam into the lifeboat's hull, but it had been built to withstand hurricanes. Then the boat tipped over and they were upside down, rolling in the water. The others cried out as they were tossed around behind her. Tori stared out through the windows, trying to get a sense of their direction. Suckers scraped the hull. A thick, snakelike tail slammed the windshield and she shrank back, thinking it would shatter.

Not even a crack. Then she knew fate had other plans for her. But not if she stayed here. If she stayed, they would find a way in eventually.

Upside down in the water, she looked through the windshield and saw two of those slitted devil faces staring back. Tori locked gazes with the nearest one and fired up the motor, tugged the throttle down just a bit.

The engine coughed, the rotors chopping into something, and they let go of the lifeboat. It righted itself in the water and lurched forward, swinging side to side before settling down. Tori throttled up quick and the lifeboat roared across the sea, skimming waves, leaving the island behind.

Moments later, Gabe relieved her. She resisted giving up the wheel but he spoke softly, told her she was injured, and she couldn't argue. Tori surrendered the pilot seat to him and stretched out on the floor beside an unconscious Josh, with

Angie huddled at the back of the lifeboat. But only after long minutes had passed and her heartbeat began to slow to normal did Tori realize the numbness spreading through her was not solely due to shock. Blood matted her hair, where she'd struck her head, and her vision blurred from that blow. Concussion; maybe worse.

She tried to stay conscious, but the harder she focused, the more difficult it became. Something beeped softly in the cramped confines of the lifeboat and as she lay there, she glanced to her right and saw what appeared to be some kind of walkie-talkie on the floor, green light blinking. An image of Josh, tossing something into the lifeboat, swam up into her consciousness. When it slipped away again, Tori went with it.

—60——

Special Agent Rachael Voss had never been so tired in her life. She'd managed an hour and a half of fitful sleep sometime between three and five a.m., and since then, had been sitting out on the deck of a Coast Guard cutter, with no cigarettes, and no cell phone. Voss didn't feel like talking.

They'd found the lifeboat shortly before eleven p.m. Voss would always remember the way her heart had seized, and the way her breath had caught in her throat, when they had opened the hatch and she'd seen that Josh was aboard. Now he lay in the Coast Guard cutter's infirmary, unconscious. The other passengers on board the lifeboat had made the whole thing a gruesome puzzle. Angie Tyree, a ship's engineer, had spoken not a word, staring with blank eyes anytime a question had been posed. Tori Austin, pale despite her tan, hair matted with blood, muttered about sirens.

And Gabe Rio. Gabriel fucking Rio, captain of the *Antoinette,* told a story that seemed to explain the condition of the lifeboat's four passengers but could not possibly be true. When Voss had tried to ask the engineer, Tyree, about it, the woman had curled into a fetal ball.

After which Voss had not been allowed to ask any more questions. Josh and Tori Austin were taken to the infirmary for medical attention, and there they remained. The commander of the Coast Guard unit that had been tasked to the mission had been in to see them, and so had Ed Turcotte, but they were shutting Voss out and wouldn't even let her see her own partner.

Turcotte had figured out the lifeboat's speed and did the math, based on how much fuel remained in its tank. Some of the Coast Guard people had traced its trajectory backward, adjusted for current and other variables, and come up with a triangle of open sea that they believed contained the origin point for the lifeboat's launch. But whether or not the *Antoinette* would still be there when they found it was another question.

So while Josh slipped in and out of consciousness, the little fleet of would-be rescuers that Rachael Voss had gathered continued sailing, searching the area the Coast Guard techs had laid out for them.

An hour before dawn, as the sky had begun to lighten, Turcotte had ordered his chopper into the air, and the helicopter had begun its own search of the arc. But Voss had been up before that, unable to sleep.

Ed Turcotte came out onto the cutter's deck. He was an interesting-looking man, with his enormous bald spot and square jaw and hangdog face, like some cross between SWAT team leader and certified public accountant. Voss smiled to herself at the aptness of the comparison.

Turcotte didn't smile, and her own vanished.

"Josh is awake," Voss said.

"You could say that."

"What does that mean?"

Turcotte lifted his chin defiantly. He wanted to remind her who was running this mission. At the same time, she thought his eyes looked a bit spooked, and that worried her. What the hell spooked Ed Turcotte?

"It all sounds pretty wild," he said.

Voss stared at him, head cocked. "You mean he's confirmed Gabriel Rio's story?"

"A secret island. Monsters in the water killing everyone. Every detail."

Voss swallowed, her throat going dry. "So much for our little turf war over this case. It's about to get much bigger than either of us."

Turcotte looked away, squinting slightly. "Agreed."

"Do you believe any of it? Monsters, Ed? I mean, that's a far cry from Counter-Terrorism, isn't it?"

Turcotte twitched. One corner of his lip turned upward and she knew the conversation was about to turn ugly. But instead of chastising her, he surprised her by holding out his hand.

"Whatever happened out there, it doesn't sound like any of us are experts on it. We'll need to be able to work together."

Voss saw the grim determination in his eyes. Turcotte was an arrogant prick, but he had earned his position leading the Counter-Terrorism unit. The man knew how to do his job.

She shook his hand, sealing a pact.

A lanky agent—far too awake at this time in the morning, and young enough to be fresh out of Quantico—hurried out on deck. He came to a quick halt and glanced back and forth between them, afraid to interrupt.

"What've you got, Lavallee?" Turcotte asked.

"The *Antoinette*, sir," the young agent replied. "The chopper just radioed in. She's moored off a small island, twelve miles north/northeast."

Turcotte looked at Voss. "I don't know about you, Rachael, but I'd like to know what the hell went on out here. You ready?"

Voss looked out to the east, where the sun now rose, burning off the halo of night and mist that lingered over the water. Dawn, but it did not feel like a new day to her— not with Josh in the infirmary, and the nightmare he had only barely survived still going on. She looked down at the deep water, at the ocean dark, and it seemed to her as though it went down forever.

"Hell, yeah. Full ahead."

61

Overnight, the weather turned. Alena had slept fitfully, rousing several times to hear the patter of rain against her windows and the way the old windows rattled in their frames with every gust of wind. As a young woman she had traveled the world and rarely suffered from jet lag or insomnia or, God forbid, homesickness. She loved the adventure, even now. But no matter how fit her travels and the gym might have kept her body, her spirit sometimes grew tired. The time shift from Croatia to Washington, DC, had unsettled her, so she had not slept well and had risen just after four a.m. to find herself entirely awake.

In the kitchen, she fixed herself a cup of strong coffee and then sat at the small table by the window that looked out on M Street and watched the dawn arrive. The sky lightened, though the sun hadn't a hope of even peeking out from behind the heavy clouds, and rain dappled the lilies in the flower box just outside the window. General Wagner would expect her in the office today, writing reports and taking meetings, but Alena decided that she could write reports here at home and take any meetings by phone. It was a day for staying in, for swaddling herself in a blanket on the sofa, drinking coffee and listening to all the handsome twenty-something singer-songwriters that David teased her so much about.

The phone startled her into spilling her coffee.

"Damn it!" she muttered, then she shot an accusing glare at the offending instrument. It jangled in its cradle on the countertop, face lit up with the number of the incoming call, but she couldn't make out the digits from across the room.

As she rose, it occurred to her to check the clock on the microwave: 5:47 a.m. That was when she knew her day would not be spent on the sofa. Hank Wagner had worked with civilians long enough to know that even a general didn't call at 0600 hours and expect a warm reception.

Hoping that the phone would not wake David, she snatched it up and thumbed the button to talk. "This had better be good, General."

"Hello, Alena," Wagner replied. "And you know it isn't. For something 'good,' I'd let you sleep. I only wake you up when it's something ugly."

David woke to a banging on his bedroom door. His eyes snapped open and he stumbled out of bed with the sheet wrapped modestly around him, barely awake but filled with panic. As he oriented himself, he wondered what had happened. Fire? An intruder?

"Up and at 'em, David!" his grandmother called from the hallway. "Come on. Get your ass out of bed."

The bedroom door stood half-open and as he stumbled toward it he saw Alena hurry by, then abruptly reverse course as though she'd forgotten something.

"What is it?" he asked. "What's happened?"

She paused in the hall to look in at him, and it struck him that she had been up for quite some time. His grandmother had showered and dressed in black trousers and a white tailored blouse. She'd done her makeup and hair. But the shoes were a dead giveaway, flat and practical, perfect for traveling.

"Pack a bag," she said, then wrinkled her nose. "And take a shower. Your room reeks of man-smell. But hurry."

Before he could argue—or ask what else men should smell like—she set off again, vanishing beyond the narrow view his half-open door provided. David knew Alena did not exaggerate, that if she wanted him to hurry there must be a reason, but he'd just been roughly woken from too-brief slumber and he wanted to know what the hell was going on.

He pulled the door open and went into the hall, dragging the sheet around and behind him like the train of a wedding dress. When he didn't see Alena in the hall he blinked, then realized that she had gone into his office. The door hung open and she had turned on a light to brighten up the gloomy morning.

He started to ask what she was up to, but the moment he saw her bent over the table, peering at his ocean charts, he knew. His first instinct brought a rush of triumph, but then his stomach gave a sick twist and he shivered as nightmare images sprang up in the back of his head—memories that had haunted him both awake and asleep for years.

"Someone found another island," he said, approaching his grandmother from behind. "Who found it? And where?"

She did not turn to face him. "Gun smugglers, believe it or not. Followed quickly by FBI and Coast Guard. And in the Caribbean."

"Jesus." David came up beside her and stared down at the chart, at the tiny red X she had made. Over the past few months, comparing reports of missing pleasure craft, fishing boats, and other ships, he had been creating an incident map on the chart, trying to pinpoint a probability triangle, an area where those events indicated such a habitat would likely be found. Alena's X fell within his probability triangle.

"I was on the right track," he said, but the realization did not feel like a victory. He wondered how many people had already died.

Alena turned to him, rose on her toes, and kissed his temple. "You were. Now get in the shower. There's a plane waiting, and the car will be here to fetch us in twenty minutes."

She left the room, and a moment later he heard her soft tread as she descended the stairs. David glanced over at the wall where he had posted dozens of newspaper articles about missing ships, as well as case notes about the two previously discovered habitats. A strange feeling spread through him, and he hefted the chunk of glassy black stone in his hand as he tried to identify the unfamiliar tremor inside him. Staring at the smiling faces of a fiftyish couple who had vanished on their sailboat, David blinked in surprise.

He wasn't used to fear.

62

When the men and women in their Coast Guard uniforms had helped Gabe Rio out of the lifeboat and he'd seen the two grim bastards in FBI jackets waiting for him, he had felt something go out of him. At first it had felt like will, or purpose, or some reason to go on. Only later did he realize that the weight that had been lifted from him was responsibility. Whatever happened next would be out of his hands, and it shocked him how grateful that made him feel.

In those first moments, hustled on board the Coast Guard ship, he had been tempted to spill every detail he could remember about the crimes he had committed for Viscaya. With Miguel dead, he had no one left to protect. He could turn state's evidence, testify against Esper and the others, do a little time and then start a new life somewhere.

Then he had seen the smug look on the face of the grim, square-jawed FBI man—obviously the boss—and that made the decision for him. The FBI could go fuck themselves. The only two people Gabe really loved had betrayed him. His marriage lay in ruin and those things—*don't think about them*—had killed his brother. He'd lost his ship and most of his crew was dead. What more could they do to him than that?

Maybe twelve hours had passed since the Coast Guard ship had found them on the lifeboat the night before. Gabe had asked after the others—Angie and Tori and even Josh—but no one would give him any answers. The Coast Guard officers stationed outside his door would not speak to him. His only contact had been with the FBI, who had questioned him last night, allowed him four or five hours' sleep, and then questioned him again this morning. Now they were back for round three, only with a twist.

A female twist. A new face. As though that would make some kind of difference.

"Let's try this again, Mr. Rio." The words came from Special Agent O'Connell. Thinning silver hair, fiftyish, salt-and-pepper mustache. They had spent too many hours together already, and Gabe had tired of his voice.

"Captain Rio," Gabe corrected.

O'Connell sighed and exchanged a glance and a theatrical head-shake with his superior officer, Supervisory Special Agent Ed Turcotte. Gabe loved that the assholes introduced themselves like that, as if he gave a shit what brand of agent they might be.

"Are you kidding?"

This question came from the attractive blond woman who had appeared in the room with Turcotte and O'Connell this morning, as though she had been there all along. Of course she hadn't. Gabe had been exhausted and grieving—he still was—but he could never have encountered Rachael Voss and forgotten her. Not with that small, lithe body and the way she almost flaunted the pistol holstered at her waist. Not with the fire in her eyes and the tension in her every motion, and certainly not with the way she prowled the room side to side like a lioness about to pounce. The woman had smiled at him, introduced herself by name instead of title, but Gabe took one look at her and knew that, in her eyes, he was prey. Ed Turcotte might be running this show, and O'Connell might be his attack dog interrogator, but Rachael Voss had been the one hunting him, which meant that Josh Hart came from her team. Turcotte had already said he was Counter-Terrorism, but the dynamic in the room made it obvious that Voss didn't work for him.

"Excuse me?" Gabe said.

Voss leaned against the door frame and crossed her arms, trying to act aloof and failing. "I said you must be kidding with this 'captain' shit. I'm pretty sure your days as captain of anything but your cell block are over."

Gabe leaned back and shrugged. "I'm afraid I don't know what you're talking about, Agent Voss. I mean, I've heard all these accusations, but I haven't seen any evidence. I told you what happened to my ship—"

"You've told us shit," O'Connell interjected. "Wake up, Gabriel. You were just doing a job, man, and look what it cost you. Your brother, your crew, and you can bet your ass it's going to get you some jail time. The question is, how much? Do you really want to take this hit alone? Give us Viscaya, and we can help you."

Gabe shook his head, images of Miguel playing across his mind. His brother had grown up to be a trouble magnet, always dragging Gabe into his shit. As boys they had been inseparable, constantly in fistfights with other kids or with each other, sticking together no matter how ugly the scrape. Even then, Miguel's mouth got them into tight spots, but Gabe had never minded. The first time he'd fallen in love, with a girl named Elena, Miguel had stolen a gold necklace for Gabe to give to her. It made him a thief, yes, but a thoughtful one. He could still remember the gleam of mischief in Miguel's eyes when he showed Gabe the necklace, not to mention the delicious reward he'd received from Elena in return.

Gabe had loved his brother, even when that love—and his desire to help Miguel keep his job—had made Gabe into a criminal himself. And now he hated him, too. If Miguel had lived, perhaps one day they might have come to terms with what had happened, but now they would never have that chance.

"There's nothing you can do to help me," he said. "Can you bring Miguel back to life? I don't think so."

Voss stepped away from the wall and walked toward him. She moved easily, despite the gentle bob of the ship on the ocean, and he knew she'd spent a lot of time at sea. *Yeah, chasing guys like me,* he thought, and was surprised to find that he could not muster up any hatred for her. *Jesus. Miguel is dead.*

He exhaled and felt himself deflate.

"No one can help your brother now, Captain Rio," Voss said, and her use of the word made him lift his head. He studied her eyes, trying to figure out her angle. "Everyone you left behind on the *Antoinette* is past helping now. The best thing you can do is help yourself. Special Agent Hart says you helped save his life last night, that you could have left him—"

"Agent Voss!" Turcotte warned, glaring like the damned Grim Reaper.

"—that you could have left him there, and that if you hadn't given him a hand, it's possible your brother would still be alive. That action is going to speak well of you at trial. But you are obviously a smart man, Captain. You know there is going to be a trial, and that you are going to prison."

Gabe glanced at O'Connell and Turcotte, both of whom looked ticked. He liked that Voss had pissed them off.

"You don't have any evidence," he said.

Voss rolled her eyes. "Come on, Gabe. Before this is over, we'll get evidence off your ship and off the island. Even without it, we'll have testimony from Agent Hart, as well as from Tori Austin and Angela Tyree. You don't think they'll give you up to make things easier on themselves? I don't know why you'd bother trying to protect the guys you work for. They sure as hell aren't going to hire you back when you get out of prison. We've got you, Captain. So why are you still fighting us?"

Gabe stared at Voss. Then he laughed. He couldn't help it.

"Fighting's the only thing I've ever done well." But that only brought more thoughts of Miguel, grim nightmare images that wiped away all traces of his smile. A fresh wave of anger rushed through him and he turned to Turcotte.

"Look, if Josh—if Agent Hart—is awake, then you know everything I said about the island is true. Why are you even bothering with me? Dozens of people died last night. My people. My crew. Maybe they don't mean anything to you, but what happens next time someone finds that island?"

"We're here to talk about you, Mr. Rio. Nothing else," O'Connell said. He had a file open in front of him. "Let's go back to this fishing boat that Miss Austin told us about. How did you—"

"Dan," Turcotte said. "Leave it, for now. There'll be plenty of time later."

Rachael Voss's eyes turned stormy and Gabe thought she would argue, but then she relented. When Turcotte and

O'Connell stood, the latter closing his file and tucking it under his arm, she moved with them toward the door.

"Turcotte," Gabe said.

The Counter-Terrorism agent turned to look at him. They all did.

"You don't want to believe me, I get it. But at least check it out."

"We did," Turcotte said. "Scratch that. We are. We're here now, Mr. Rio. If you had a window to look out of, you'd be able to see the *Antoinette* just off to starboard. I've got a boarding team on the way out to her right now."

Gabe slid back in his chair, fear welling up inside him. He glanced around, knowing he had nowhere to run.

"You idiots. What the fuck are you . . . I thought you were taking me back to Miami! Jesus!" he shouted. "Call them back, man. Keep your people away from the ship and don't go near that fucking island!"

He stared at them, saw the shock and disdain in their eyes, and understood how his terror must appear to them.

"You wanted us to check it out," Turcotte said, eyes narrowed. "We're checking it out."

Gabe sank into his chair. Whatever weight might have lifted from him before, another took its place now. He thought he had survived the nightmare, but they had brought him right back into it.

"If you do go out to the island, you'd better use the helicopter," he said. "They won't let you leave by water. And whatever you do, get all of your ships away from the island by nightfall."

"We've got FBI and Coast Guard here, Mr. Rio," Turcotte said. "These people are well-trained, and if it comes to that, well-armed."

Gabe cocked his head and stared at Turcotte. "Yeah. So were we."

Angie Tyree saw them every time she closed her eyes. Images played across her mind of the legless things hanging from the walkways of the *Antoinette*'s accommodations block, or slithering over the railings, pale and luminescent, as though their flesh consisted only of scars. She could still hear the echoes of Dwyer's screams, still see the things driving Miguel to the deck and tearing him apart.

She couldn't stop crying and she hated that. All her life she had prided herself on being the tough girl. But all of that had been stripped away and she felt raw and jagged inside. The doctor hadn't found anything physically wrong with her, but she knew that she would never be okay again. The fear had gotten deep inside her, not just under the skin but down to the bone, and it nested in her marrow like a cancer.

So when the door opened, the click of the latch alone was enough to make Angie let out a soft cry and slide across the cot, jamming herself into the corner, hugging herself protectively, wondering if she would die now. The sunlight streaming in through the window and the bright blue Caribbean sky did nothing to lessen her terror.

When the FBI agent entered the room, she let out a breath and her eyes fluttered closed for a second. She allowed herself to sit on the cot instead of crouching in the corner, but her muscles remained tensed, ready to fight or run. Angie told herself she would not die quietly, that she would scream the way Dwyer had, so that her screams would ring in the ears of those who heard them for the rest of their lives. In that way, for a time, at least, she would be remembered. Someone would know she had been on this damned planet.

The agent had a plate of food, rice and black beans or something. When he spotted her perched uncomfortably on the cot, his eyes were filled with such humanity that Angie began to cry harder. She tried to staunch the flow of tears, tried to summon the inner bitch she had always worn as a mask at her own convenience, but it wouldn't come.

"Ms. Tyree," the agent said. He was a big guy, and decent-looking—not one of the agents who had questioned her earlier. "I'm Special Agent Plausky. I thought you must be hungry. I don't know when you ate last—"

"Why are we still here?" she asked, hearing the numbness of her own voice but unable to do anything about it.

Plausky set the plate on a little table in a corner opposite the cot, never taking his eyes off her. The FBI body language spoke clearly—he wore his gun in an armpit holster like a cop in some eighties movie, and was aware both of the weapon and of the crying woman in his custody. He would not turn his back on her, give her a chance to try for the gun. Angie figured it must just be training, because the idea that she might attempt such a thing felt absurd.

"Ms. Tyree, this is a major FBI investigation. The operation is not going to be over any time soon. When my superiors feel like they're done with you, and if opportunity arises, I'll do my best to have you transported either back to St. Croix or to Miami. You'll remain in federal custody until someone decides to let you go."

The words fell upon her like icy rain. Angie shivered, shaking her head.

"You don't get it. You don't get it," she said, hugging her knees to her chest and rocking back and forth. She glanced at the window and turned quickly away, afraid of what might appear there, despite the sunshine. "I can't stay here. None of us can stay here."

Plausky sighed and dragged the chair over from the small table. He perched on the edge of the chair, maybe trying to make her feel comfortable by moving down to her level, but still not letting his guard down.

"Ms. Tyree—Angie—trust me when I say you're not in any danger now."

She laughed, but the laugh became a sob and she broke

down, bowing her head. "Are you kidding me? Are you fucking kidding?"

Again, Plausky sighed. "Look, I'm trying to be polite here, but you've got to get it together. A real conversation wouldn't be a bad place to start. If you want to help yourself, you could start by talking about the Rio brothers and Viscaya, and what you know about the guns."

Angie shuddered, closed her eyes, and heard gunfire that made her flinch. But it wasn't happening now, only in her memory.

"The guns are gone." She opened her eyes and fixed him with a stare, breathing evenly, and managed to stop crying. Sniffling, she wiped at her nose. "You people are fucking crazy. The guns are *gone*."

"But you saw them?" Plausky asked, obviously interested now that she was talking about his precious investigation.

Angie took a long breath, steadying herself. "Yes. I saw them."

Plausky tried to keep a straight face so she wouldn't know how pleased he was with this. When he had tried to question her before, Angie had been unable to stop crying, had barely been able to speak. It had all been a blur to her, but she thought she had been screaming as well.

"Can you describe what you saw?" Plausky asked. "What type of guns, and how many?"

Angie hugged herself and glanced at the window. Forcing herself to stand, jaw tight with fear, she climbed off the bed and went to peer out through the glass. In the distance she could see the island. Closer—much closer—the *Antoinette* loomed in the water, dark and menacing. It looked abandoned, but she knew that was not the case.

"Not enough," she whispered.

"What's that?"

Heat rushing to her face, she rounded on him. "Not enough!" she screamed, fists clenched at her sides. "We didn't have enough guns, you stupid fucking *Fed*. These things were endless, like cockroaches. Bring all the guns you want; it won't make a difference!"

Plausky got up from his chair, backing away so quickly that he tipped it over. She saw the alarm in his eyes, saw his hand twitch toward his weapon and the way he tensed, and she started to fall apart all over again.

"Please," she said, slumping back against the wall. The images forced themselves into her head again, and now she did not even have to close her eyes. Dwyer's screams lingered in the air around her, following her, haunting her. "You've got to get me out of here. I don't care where you send me, but please don't make me stay. I'll say whatever you want, but please . . ."

Her body shook and she crawled back onto the bed, pushed herself into the corner, and watched the windows and the door and the shadowed corners, despair crushing her.

"Angela, listen," Plausky ventured. "You're totally safe here. I swear."

She turned from him, covered her face, and curled into a fetal ball. Words had failed her. All she could do now was wonder how many hours remained before nightfall. How many minutes were left for her to live.

-64--

Tori had a great many reasons to scream, but one overwhelming reason not to—her head ached fiercely, like someone had clamped a vise on the back of her skull. The Coast Guard ship—the *Kodiak*—had a doctor on board, and the man seemed to have stepped out of an old movie. Fiftyish, with a Jack Lemmon sort of everyman quality, Dr. Paul Dolan had a gentle smile and kind blue eyes, and made her feel like maybe her head hadn't actually cracked open. In the time he had spent with her, Dr. Dolan had also made her feel like she was not a prisoner.

But when Dr. Dolan left, the FBI agent in the hall had

glanced in at her and then nodded to the two Coast Guard officers, who had shut the door and locked it behind them, leaving her alone with her splitting headache, her blood-matted hair, stitches in her scalp, and a couple of lovely Percocets.

The painkillers had allowed her to sleep for a while, but they had worn off too quickly, and now the sunlight streaming through the window made her cringe. The doctor had told her she had a minor concussion, but it did not feel minor. There were scratches and bruises all over her body, but none of that hurt her. The pain in her skull overrode any other stimuli.

But she had other reasons to scream. Memories, to begin with. Kevonne, Bone, Pang, Pucillo, and so many others were dead. As much as she had come to despise Dwyer and Miguel, no one deserved to die like that. Despite how close she had come to death—or perhaps because of it—the images in Tori's head were jumbled. She remembered white flesh and black eyes and the way the creatures stuck to the sides of the derelict ships and slithered up onto the *Antoinette*. She remembered blood and thrashing and shrieks of agony. Yet somehow she could not form a real picture of one of the sirens in her mind. If she had a pencil and paper, she could not have drawn one.

Perhaps that was a mercy.

Yet even with her head splitting and the horrors fresh in her mind, her number-one reason to scream actually put a smile on her face. For as Tori stood at the window, squinting against the daylight, and stared out at the *Antoinette* and the island beyond it, she felt a sublime sense of bliss, a mad elation that soothed her even better than Percocet.

I'm alive, she thought. The FBI guy, Turcotte—the one so obviously in charge—had called her a survivor, and her heart had soared. Damn straight, she had survived. What the FBI did not know was that death had come for Tori twice in her life, and both times she had managed to elude its grasp by moments.

This morning, despite the splintering pain in her skull, she had found a new clarity of thought, epiphanies exploding like fireworks in her head. The first time she had narrowly avoided death, she had been so startled at her good fortune that she had been content to simply survive. Ted had presumed her dead and she wanted to stay that way, hidden, almost lurking on the periphery of her own life, afraid to really live just in case somebody noticed. Now, though, Tori felt as if she had woken from some kind of trance. She would have smiled, but she had found that it made her head hurt even more.

The irony was not lost on her. Here she was in FBI custody, certainly going to end up in court and possibly in prison, yet she felt more free, awake, and alive than she had at any time since the age of nine or ten.

It made no sense, really—especially since prison seemed so far away. Right now, it ought to have been the least of her concerns. She stood at the window and watched as a small boat skipped across the span of ocean that separated the Coast Guard ship from the *Antoinette*. On board were Coast Guard officers in uniform and what had to be FBI agents clothed like it was dress-down Friday at the office, except they also wore navy blue vests with *FBI* stenciled on the back. There were other ships around—Coast Guard cutters and a couple of smaller boats, including one that looked like a trust-fund baby's toy. But Tori could tell that the small craft that zipped toward the *Antoinette* had come from the ship she was on, the command vessel.

She had told them what had happened on the island and on board the container ship, and she had to imagine that Gabe and Angie and Josh had done the same. But still they were sending people to check it out. Tori supposed they were just following procedure, doing their jobs. And why not? They hadn't been with her last night, hadn't seen the things that she'd seen.

They'll learn, she thought.

Despite the proximity of the *Antoinette,* she felt only a queer uneasiness, and she wondered at her lack of fear. Perhaps it was a result of her concussion, or the exultation that flooded her in the wake of her survival, but Tori felt certain she had not escaped death twice only to have it catch up to her while in FBI custody.

She had studied the derelict ships surrounding the island. Everyone who had died there had died essentially alone, but Turcotte and his team had satellite communications with their home bases, and plenty of backup to call upon should they need it. This was the U.S. Coast Guard and the Federal Bureau of Investigation. They might not be prepared for what they were about to encounter, but that would change. The cavalry had come. The monsters would be destroyed.

Someone knocked on the door. Wincing at the sound, Tori turned, surprised that anyone would bother to knock.

"Come in."

The door opened and Josh stepped into the room, his left arm in a sling. His face was badly bruised, his lips split, and still a bit swollen in places, thanks to the beating Hank Boggs had given him, but he looked alert, and had obviously showered, shaved, and put on clean clothes. Tori herself wore the same jeans she'd had on the day before, but after her own shower this morning she had been given a clean gray T-shirt and a package of new underwear. Dr. Dolan had explained that every Coast Guard vessel carried such essentials in the event of an ocean rescue. The underpants had been a little small, but Tori didn't complain. At least they were clean.

"Good morning," Josh said, tentative and unsmiling.

Tori hated how happy it made her, seeing him. He had made love to her under false pretenses, but the memory of it still gave her a delicious shiver. She wondered if he regretted it, now. She wondered if *she* did.

"Not my best morning, actually," she replied.

Josh indicated his left shoulder. "Mine, either. But the doc says I'll be right as rain. Nothing broken. Just a hole where there shouldn't be one, and a whole lot of bruises from the tune-up Boggs gave me."

Tori hesitated, then nodded. "I'm glad."

Josh did smile, now, but it was self-deprecating. "I wasn't sure you would be."

"Neither was I." She glanced away, back out the window, saw figures moving on the deck of the *Antoinette*. "So what now?"

"It's complicated."

Tori gave a bitter laugh, then winced at the fresh spike of pain in her head.

"If you're in that much pain, I'm sure the doc will give you something for it. He's got me flying on Vicodin."

"That'd be good. But as far as 'complicated' goes, I'm talking about me. What happens to me, Josh?"

He pulled the door closed behind him and walked toward her. Tori stared at the door, aware of the significance. With the door closed, he wasn't Special Agent Josh Hart. At least, she didn't think so. But how could she really know, now, who she was talking to? How did she know the truth of anything where Josh was concerned?

Part of her hated him, but the rest of her was just too tired to think about it.

"In my report, I'm going to make it very clear that without both you and Angie, I would not have survived last night. If you cooperate with the investigation and testify against Viscaya and Gabe, you'll be all right. With the right lawyer, and as long as no terrorist connections can be made to the guns Viscaya's been smuggling, it's possible you won't ever see the inside of a cell."

Tori let out a long breath. She had resigned herself to fate, but now the idea that she might not have to spend any time in prison sparked a rush of hope. Though, oddly, that made her feel worse instead of better. Having hope gave her something to lose. And it made her feel grateful to someone for whom she harbored a great deal of anger.

Brows knitted, she studied him. "You lost a lot of blood last night. I wasn't sure you would make it."

"Neither was I," Josh replied.

"Maybe you don't remember, but you said something to me, right before we got into that lifeboat." Her throat felt dry and tight and she couldn't meet his eyes. "You said—"

"I said, 'It wasn't all pretend.'"

Tori stared at him. She wouldn't ask the question that hung between them. After a moment, Josh answered without her asking.

"I can't stop you from hating me, and I have no excuse for what I did, except that it wasn't something I planned. It never should have happened, but I can't say I regret it. I only regret that I hurt you." Josh shook his head, pushed the fingers of his good hand through his hair. "I screwed up pretty badly. I'll be investigated and I'll tell the truth. At the very least, I'll be forced on unpaid leave. But if they felt like it, they could fire me—"

"You expect me to feel sorry for you?"

"What?" He stared at her. "No. I'm just telling you that, even with all of this, I can't make myself regret it. What I said is true. It wasn't all pretend." With that, he turned and opened the door. "I'll ask the doctor to look in on you."

"Josh . . ."

Halfway out of the room, he paused and glanced back.

"You're staying on board, right? I mean, you're not going over to the *Antoinette,* are you?"

Josh gave a small shrug. "We're still waiting for official orders, but I'm not in a rush to get back on that ship, no."

Tori nodded, letting out a breath. "Good. I may want to kill you myself later on, and I don't want you getting killed before I get around to it."

For a second, he seemed unsure whether or not she was joking.

"I'll do my best," he said. Then he paused, a frown creasing his brow. "Wait, why would you think I was going back to the *Antoinette*?"

Tori half-turned toward the window. "Well, you've got FBI guys boarding her now. I just wanted to make sure you weren't going to be that stupid. I hope you all know what you're doing."

Josh's face went pale and he shook his head. "Fucking idiots."

Then he was gone, rushing into the corridor, leaving the door half-open behind him. Tori stared into the hall until one of the Coast Guard men shut the door.

"Shit," Tori whispered, turning to look out the window again.

The *Kodiak* had been commissioned out of Alaska, but re-assigned to port in Charleston, South Carolina, three years ago. A Hamilton Class cutter, she ran three hundred and seventy-eight feet at the waterline and had a fifteen-foot draft. With nearly one hundred and seventy men and women on board, a seventy-six-millimeter cannon, two twenty-five-millimeter chain guns capable of firing two hundred rounds per minute, and an automated missile defense system, the ship wasn't about search and rescue. The Coast Guard prided itself on that reputation, but they served the people of the United States in many capacities.

Josh had learned all of this from Lieutenant Commander Cornelius Sykes—one of the ranking officers on board the USCGC *Kodiak*. They had crossed paths before, as Josh's squad had often cooperated with the Coast Guard on ocean interdiction, and had an amiable enough acquaintance. Sykes had visited sick bay during the blood-loss-induced haze of the night before and then again this morning, in an attempt to keep Josh company. He didn't have much by way of a sense of humor, but Sykes was a good guy, intelligent and purposeful, and took obvious pride in his work.

While Dr. Dolan cleaned and dressed the bullet wound in Josh's shoulder, Sykes had taken it upon himself to educate Josh about the *Kodiak* and about the Coast Guard, and had picked up on the theme this morning. Josh had actually found the information about the ship interesting, and reassuring—especially considering there were two Island Class cutters and a two-hundred-and-seventy-foot Medium Endurance cutter in what Josh had started to think of as their "fleet." But when he stepped out onto the deck of the *Kodiak* and spotted

Sykes, he hoped the lieutenant commander had lost interest in lecturing.

"Hey, Josh," Sykes said, eyes narrowed with his usual intensity. "How's the shoulder?"

"Good, Cornelius, thanks. Listen, have you seen Agent Turcotte? One of your guys told me he was out on the deck."

Sykes nodded. "With the captain, just down to starboard. But do you really think you should be—"

"Thanks, man." Josh clapped him on the shoulder and strode away.

Sykes mumbled something but did not call after him. Josh hurried aft and quickly came in sight of a small gathering at the starboard railing. He shielded his eyes from the sun— it was another pristine blue Caribbean day—and could make out all six of the figures up ahead. His partner, Rachael Voss, stood with Ed Turcotte and Dan O'Connell from the Counter-Terrorism squad. They'd been joined by the *Kodiak*'s captain, Bud Rouleau, and a couple of his officers.

Two hundred yards off to starboard, the *Antoinette* loomed on the water, silent and apparently abandoned.

"Agent Turcotte!" Josh called as he hurried up. His shoulder ached and he blinked the sun from his eyes, craving caffeine.

Turcotte saw him and knitted his brows in disapproval, but Josh had no interest in pleasing him.

"Good morning, Agent Hart," Captain Rouleau said.

"And to you, sir," Josh replied, before focusing on Turcotte. "No disrespect, Ed, but what the hell are you doing?"

O'Connell scoffed. "No disrespect, huh?"

Voss glared at O'Connell, then turned a warning glance on Josh.

Turcotte raised his chin. "Shouldn't you still be in Dr. Dolan's sick bay?"

"I'll be fine," Josh snapped. "Which is a lot more than I can say for the poor bastards you sent over to the *Antoinette*. I told you the whole story, and still you've got a team boarding her with, what, sidearms? If any of those things are still on board—"

"First of all," Turcotte interrupted, "this isn't your case, Agent Hart. You're out of it. Second, even if these things are real—"

"Real enough to kill the whole fucking crew!"

"Boys," Voss said, trying to pacify them. O'Connell just rolled his eyes, but Captain Rouleau studied Josh intently.

Turcotte held up both hands. "Okay, okay. They're real, whatever they are, but you said they burn in the sun, and that they only come out at night. The others we pulled out of that lifeboat said the same thing. If you haven't noticed, it's pretty sunny out here. If they run into anything out there, they only have to retreat to sunlight—"

"If they get a chance," Josh said.

"Christ's sake, Hart, two seconds ago you said 'if' any of them are still on board! You don't even know. And if they are, we're the FBI, not the damn Cub Scouts!"

Voss sighed. "Ed. Cut him some slack. He's lucky to be alive."

What surprised Josh the most was not the almost friendly tone with which Rachael had addressed the leader of the squad that constantly attempted to snatch their cases, but that Turcotte actually relented. He gave a small shrug and a nod.

"Go on, then. Talk to him. I don't have time for this shit."

Voss led him a few steps away from the others, then stopped to study Josh. "You really okay? You did get shot last night, in case you've forgotten."

"The bullet went right through. Now are you going to tell me what's going on, or do I have to ask Pavarotti what you've let slip during pillow talk?"

She flinched. That irked her, and Josh was glad. He loved Rachael, but she needed to stop treating him like something fragile.

"You want to say that again?" Voss asked, the warning clear in her tone.

"Let's move on," Josh said. "Maybe start with, 'Hey, partner, I'm glad you're alive.'"

"Jesus, you're needy. I freakin' hugged you last night, and that's all the love you're getting. If you're on the job—which I want you to know I'm against—then you're on the job."

Josh smiled. "You missed me."

She rolled her eyes and glanced away. There had always been an intensity between them, but they had agreed early on to direct those feelings into their professional relationship. Voss tended to find distractions in short-lived romances, and Josh had gone through a numbing divorce. Now he had a new fascination, and new feelings—and though he would have to report it himself to avoid worse censure if it came out later, he still did not want Rachael to know about what had developed between him and Tori. She would tell him how stupid he had been, and she would be right.

"Seriously," he said. "You want to tell me what Turcotte's thinking, because this is incredibly stupid."

"He's thinking that, anytime now, this whole mess is going to be taken away from us and might just blow up in our faces," Voss said. "And if the guns the Rios were smuggling are on that ship, he wants to lay claim to them for the Bureau, and at least get that win on the books before the DOD starts hunting monsters."

Josh nodded. He did not agree, and knew that Turcotte would soon regret his choice, but he understood the motivation.

"Fine. But what's the DOD got to do with anything?"

"We're in a holding pattern right now," she said. "Turcotte and Captain Rouleau made their reports and in both cases—FBI and Coast Guard—we've been told to secure the area but otherwise stand down and await the arrival of some Navy ship. The ICE ships that were along with us on the hunt for the *Antoinette* have been called away. They're out of it. The Department of Defense is taking over."

Just a few feet away, Turcotte and the Coast Guard captain seemed to be commiserating on that very subject. Josh couldn't help but note the irony that someone had finally done to Turcotte what the Counter-Terrorism unit had so often done to everyone else in recent years. But he knew now wasn't the time to revel in that—not when he could see men moving on the deck of the *Antoinette* just a couple hundred yards away.

"That's good," Josh said. "If it was up to me, I'd order them to bomb the shit out of the island and be done with it."

Voss's expression softened and he saw a rare glimmer of fear in her eyes. "Me, too. If it's anything like what you said—"

"It's exactly like I said. You've got to get Turcotte to recall that team. Get those people off the ship."

She shook her head. "Look at him, Josh. That's not going to happen."

"Then people are going to die."

"Have a little faith," Voss chided him.

Josh sighed and ran a hand through his hair. "You're not listening, either. I lost my faith last night. We should sink that ship. Better yet, blow it apart."

He glanced at the *Antoinette* again. His shoulder throbbed and he wondered if it was too soon to take another Vicodin. He tried to pull together stray thoughts, to make sense of what he'd heard.

"Let me see if I've got this straight," he said. "We've got FBI, Coast Guard, and ICE on the case, but the DOD says, 'Screw Homeland Security and the Department of Justice, we call dibs'? And nobody argues?"

"We don't know if anyone argued, Josh. But you know if the Department of Defense wants in, they're in. All anyone has to tell the Joint Chiefs is that it's a matter of national security."

"*How* is it a matter of national security?"

"I wondered the same thing." Voss lowered her voice. "And I've wondered why, if Homeland Security pulled out ICE, they didn't pull out the Coast Guard as well. Not that I want them to abandon us out here, but still, it's odd, don't you think?"

Josh turned that one over for a moment. "No. Think about it. What does this Coast Guard ship have that the ICE guys didn't bring to the party?"

"You mean besides a helicopter?"

Josh nodded, turning to survey the deck of the *Kodiak*. "Yeah."

Voss looked to see what had caught his attention. "Ah. Of course. A big fucking cannon."

"Not to mention pulling ICE away from the scene limits

the number of people and agencies who will be exposed to the truth of what's on that island, once we have our marching orders."

"They're moving fast," Voss said. "Like they've got a plan."

"Maybe they do, but don't be surprised if it changes when they get a look at the things down there. It isn't going to be as simple as doing pest control."

Josh nodded toward Turcotte, Rouleau, and O'Connell. "What about this? If we have orders to secure and wait, where does Turcotte get off boarding the *Antoinette*?"

"Orders were to stay away from the island, but no one mentioned the *Antoinette*."

"And he's trying to use that loophole to close the case before the new boss shows up."

"That's about it."

Any other time, Josh would not have been surprised. Really, he wouldn't have blamed Turcotte at all. But the usual parameters did not apply here. FBI standard operating procedure had to be completely thrown out the window, and so did any concern for individual cases. They had discovered a new and deadly species. The things were smart enough to have used the *Mariposa* as bait, and Josh had to wonder if they had purposely let the lifeboat escape the night before for the same reason—to lure more prey back to the island. How many had they killed already? How many people had been on board the derelict ships that had been sunk in the island's shallows?

How did one gun-smuggling case matter in the face of that?

But Turcotte hadn't seen the creatures—the things Tori had called sirens—up close. If he had, he would have understood.

"He's got to call them back," Josh said.

"Wait," Voss replied.

Josh went to the railing and stared across the span of water that separated the *Kodiak* from the *Antoinette*. The small Coast Guard launch bobbed beside the massive container ship, waiting for the FBI team to return. No one moved up on the deck. Turcotte's people had either gone into the accommodations block or belowdecks.

"This is a huge mistake," he said.

O'Connell's radio crackled. "Come in, Dan. We're in."

"This is O'Connell," the older agent said into his hand-held. "Any sign of survivors?"

"Nada. It's quiet in here."

"Do a room by room search for the contraband. If you don't come up with anything, we'll start checking the containers out on deck. Check in every fifteen minutes."

"Will do."

At least he asked about survivors first, Josh thought. He watched the deck of the *Antoinette* expectantly, but after they had all stood in silence for several minutes, he began to breathe easier. Maybe the things had all retreated to the island before dawn, once they had gotten what they came for. Once they had fed.

"Maybe—" Voss started to say, but her words were interrupted by gunfire.

"Shit," Turcotte snarled.

O'Connell barked into his radio, but the only replies, amidst the static on the handheld, were screams.

-66--

Despite the sun bearing down on her, Rachael Voss felt cold. She stood with her arms crossed, staring across at the *Antoinette*. Nearly half an hour had passed while Coast Guard personnel boarded the container ship and approached every door without entering, under orders to stay out of any closed area. They were armed and careful and there were no more screams, but those of the FBI team Turcotte had sent over lingered in her mind.

Josh and Pavarotti stood behind her, talking quietly with Nadeau and McIlveen—two other members of their St. Croix field division squad. They were all spooked, eyes blank and haunted, and Voss knew their expressions mirrored her own. Only Josh seemed to have begun to recover, if the storm clouds in his eyes were any evidence. He had tried to warn Turcotte. Gabe Rio and the other survivors of the *Antoinette* had done the same.

Turcotte and O'Connell had barely moved from the place they had been standing when the shit hit the fan, but they were alone there now. Voss had moved up to the bow of the *Kodiak,* where several off-duty seamen were taking a cigarette break, and the rest of her team had joined her there. They came together in a crisis, her squad. If anything could make her feel safe under the circumstances, it was that.

She watched Turcotte, observed the slump of his shoulders, and felt sorry for him. The guy could be a total asshole, but he had tried to get clever, following orders to the letter but still attempting to hold on to his case. Voss suspected she might have done the same thing in his shoes, or at least considered it. Now most of Turcotte's squad was dead; only himself, O'Connell, and two others still lived. And all he could do was wait for the shitstorm that would no doubt result from his colossal fuckup, and grieve for good men.

Voss watched the Coast Guard launch surging in the water, returning from the *Antoinette* with only five people on board. She glanced across at the container ship and its blocky, rusty cargo, and shivered.

"Special Agent Voss?"

She turned to see Cornelius Sykes coming toward her. Behind her, Josh and the other guys came to attention and huddled close. Whatever news Sykes brought, they wanted in on it.

"Lieutenant Commander?" Voss said.

Sykes had about him the grim air of the consummate soldier. He viewed her as the commanding officer of her squad—which, technically, she was—and so he didn't even glance at the other agents.

"The captain has asked me to update you, ma'am."

Any other day she would have chided him for the *ma'am,* maybe even threatened to hurt him. Today it simply didn't seem important.

"All right. Let's have it."

For once, Sykes's severe manner seemed to relent and she saw the humanity in his face. "Our men who boarded the freighter called through every open door and window, but received no reply. They do believe they heard movement from at least two passages, but no voices." He hesitated a moment, then added, "No ordinary voices."

Josh stepped up beside Voss. "They heard singing."

"What the hell?" Tim Nadeau said. "Singing?"

They all stared at Josh, who had somehow become pale despite all the sun he'd had while undercover on the Viscaya case, and the dull purple and yellow tints of his bruises. Still, Voss thought he looked strong. Somehow, everything he'd been through had hardened him, burned away some of his cool, civilized exterior to reveal the real agent underneath— a man who finished what he started.

"It isn't singing," Josh said. "It only sounds like that. It could be their way of communicating with each other out of the water, or just a noise they make when they're . . . I don't know, hunting."

"Or hungry," McIlveen muttered.

"Mac, shut the fuck up," Voss snapped, and the agent shrugged.

Sykes nodded. "Whatever it is, they heard it. Some of the sirens are still on board the *Antoinette*."

"Sirens?" Nadeau asked.

Pavarotti glanced at him. "It's what the Austin woman and Gabe Rio began calling them when it all started going to hell. I was in with Turcotte and O'Connell when they talked to her this morning. In Greek myths—"

"I know the story," Nadeau said, waving Pavarotti off. "But they're not trying to say these things *are* sirens?"

Voss sighed. "It's just a word—something to call them. They sing, and they've lured enough sailors to their deaths." She gestured toward the shore of the island, where derelict ships thrust up out of the water at jagged angles. " 'Sirens' is as good a name as any."

"So we're assuming no survivors?" Pavarotti asked, shifting the conversation back to Lieutenant Commander Sykes.

Sykes glanced over his shoulder at Turcotte and O'Connell. "Your colleagues disagree, but Captain Rouleau has reported the incident and his belief that none of the agents who boarded are still alive."

"For their sake, let's hope not," Josh said.

His tone filled Voss with dread. She expected one of her squad to ask him what could be worse than death, and was grateful that none of them did.

"Anything else?" she asked.

Sykes inclined his head in an odd sort of salute. "Only that the captain will be out to update Special Agent Turcotte in a few minutes."

"Why tell me instead of Turcotte?"

The lieutenant commander wet his lips and blinked, and Voss realized that this part of the message had not really been meant for her. Sykes had his own reasons for passing it along.

"I've already informed him," Sykes said. "I just thought you might like to hear what the captain has to say."

Voss smiled, feeling the fakery of it and knowing Sykes must see it. "Thank you for that, Lieutenant Commander. I appreciate you keeping us in the loop."

With that, Sykes turned and strode purposefully back along the starboard deck and vanished through the nearest door, as though he couldn't wait to get out of there.

"What do you suppose that was about?" Josh asked.

Voss didn't look at him, or any of her squad. Instead, she focused again on Turcotte, studying the sag of his shoulders.

"I'd say Mr. Sykes is concerned about Turcotte's leadership and wants to make sure he's not the only FBI agent on this tub with a clue as to what's going on."

Pavarotti leaned over the railing, glancing sidelong toward Turcotte and O'Connell, who were fifty or sixty feet away. "Is Sykes concerned, or is the captain?"

They all looked at him, but quickly turned to Voss. She had seniority on the squad. There were nine of them altogether, but aside from Josh, who'd come on more recently, these guys had been with her the longest. The other four were back on the impounded drug lord's boat they'd used to get here, awaiting instructions.

Nadeau was a little guy, only five-five, whip-smart and whip-thin. Sometimes they called him Timmy because he seemed so young, but he was five years older than Rachael herself, and like the burly, ursine McIlveen, had been on the squad prior to her own arrival. Pavarotti was the only one she had slept with, and the only one who seemed like he wanted more from his life than just being FBI. Voss had screwed him because she wanted to, and because she had known right off that Pavarotti wouldn't let whatever happened between them interfere with the job. He didn't love her, so his heart wouldn't get in the way.

Josh, though . . . Voss looked in his eyes and knew that he would take a bullet for her, just as she would for him. It wasn't romance, but love could kill no matter what you wanted to call it. She knew those eyes all too well, and right now, she saw the doubt in them.

"This isn't going to go well, Rachael," he said.

Pavarotti leaned in, smiling, trying for some levity. "Special Agent Voss hates being called by her first name."

"Shut it, Opera Boy," Nadeau said. "No time for games."

"There's nothing Ed Turcotte hates more than not being in charge," Josh went on. "I don't know who's going to command this operation, but we're going to have to make sure Turcotte plays along."

Voss nodded. "He will. He just wanted to close out our end of things before the . . . extermination, or whatever, got under way."

McIlveen cocked his head, cracking his neck as he stretched. "You almost sound like you like him, boss. Did you forget how hard he worked to steal this case from us in the first place?"

"Fuck off, Mac. You really think I could forget that? It's only been hours since he even let us back into our own goddamn case. But he's a professional, and we're all FBI. Anyone they send down here is answering to the Joint Chiefs, and they answer to the president, so I don't think Turcotte's going to say anything but 'Yes, sir.' "

"I guess we'll find out soon," Josh said, nodding to port.

Voss turned to see the Navy ship approaching off the port

bow. It looked small in the distance, but it wouldn't be long before it had joined their little fleet, and they received their orders. She only hoped those orders consisted of something more than *Sit and wait*, or worse, *Go back to St. Croix*.

As far as Voss was concerned, it had started with her squad, and they would see it through to the end.

Her thoughts were interrupted by the arrival of Captain Rouleau, who emerged from the same door Sykes had vanished into a couple of minutes earlier, nodded to them, then turned to make for Turcotte and O'Connell.

Voss followed him, the squad falling in line behind her.

"Captain," she said, "any word on what'll happen next?"

"Not many specifics, I'm afraid," Rouleau replied as he headed for Turcotte, who nudged O'Connell, both men turning to greet the *Kodiak*'s captain.

"I guess we'll find out soon enough," Josh said, addressing the captain. "Any idea who's on that Navy ship? Who's taking command?"

Rouleau stopped, turning toward them, even as Turcotte and O'Connell strode up to join them all. The captain frowned.

"From what I've been told, Agent Hart, the commander of this operation is not on that ship."

Turcotte caught this and muttered a quiet and profane exclamation. He was frustrated, and Voss couldn't blame him.

"Then where is he?" Turcotte asked.

Even as the words left his lips, Voss frowned. Without her even realizing it, she had been hearing a new sound added to the mix of wind and ship's engines for a minute or more, growing from a subtle buzz to a kind of roar.

A second later, a helicopter passed above them and turned to circle around.

Captain Rouleau lifted his face toward the sky. "I believe this is her arriving now."

Alena Boudreau swept along a corridor aboard the USS *Hillstrom* with David at her side and Professors Ridge and Ernst, the four of them surrounded by a cadre of naval officers. The flight to St. Croix had given her time to think and plan, to spread out papers and focus on her laptop, but the chopper ride out to the location had been hours of wasted anticipation. She was ready to get to work.

A pair of sailors snapped off crisp salutes as they approached the open door to a large conference room—war room, muster room, whatever it really was on board a naval vessel—and she nodded to them as she went by, though of course the salute had not been intended for her. A pair of lieutenants—she'd already forgotten their names—led the way, but once inside they crossed the room and took seats in the back. Ridge and Ernst selected vacant spots in the first row.

Chairs had been fixed to the floor at the front of the room, lined up behind a long table. The *Hillstrom*'s captain, Arthur Siebalt, made for the table as every naval officer in the room stood and saluted. The Coast Guard officers rose to attention as well, and even the FBI agents stood out of respect. Alena took note of it, pleased. Right now she needed everyone in that meeting to understand and respond to authority. At the moment they perceived that authority to rest with Captain Siebalt, but she had long since become accustomed to such assumptions, and to shattering them.

"Please, take your seats," she said as she slid her laptop bag onto the table. "We've lost enough time as it is. The clock is ticking. The time is just after 1300 hours and every minute works against us if we hope to get this thing done today."

The FBI agents were the first to sit, shifting their focus to her. The Coast Guard and naval personnel hesitated, looking toward Captain Siebalt for leadership. To her right, David slid into the last chair at the table, reaching over for her laptop bag, unzipping it, and starting to slide it out, as if he were the only person in the room.

"Be seated," Captain Siebalt said. The man had an air of utter competence about him, and his uniform seemed freshly pressed. A professional officer, used to rank and hierarchy. The *Hillstrom* was a frigate, most frequently used as a support vessel accompanying carriers or amphibious strike groups, which was useful in two significant ways. First, the crew understood undersea warfare, including torpedoes, mines, and depth charges, and second, Siebalt was used to answering to a higher authority on missions.

As the meeting's attendees settled into their chairs, the captain began.

"Those of you who are guests on board the *Hillstrom*, welcome aboard. I am Captain Siebalt. This is my first officer, Commander Aaronson," he said, gesturing to the man on his left, who nodded a greeting to the small audience. "We will be helping to coordinate this operation, and the *Hillstrom* will be the command vessel for the duration."

Alena thought he might go on. Officers tended to feel that, when handing over authority, they had to subtly assert it by making a show, giving permission to their subordinates to obey someone else's orders. Her estimation of Siebalt had been correct, however. He only nodded to her and took his seat, with Aaronson settling into the chair beside him. Several of the *Hillstrom*'s other officers took their seats at the table, until she was the only one still on her feet and all eyes were upon her. Alena had worn a black ribbed cotton top and black trousers, which made her silver hair all the more striking. The outfit had been chosen purposefully. It had a kind of uniform-like quality that seemed to make military personnel more comfortable. And it did not hurt that she looked fantastic in black.

"My name is Dr. Alena Boudreau, and I'll be running this op," she said, studying their faces, cataloging their emotional responses to her authority in case any of them should become an issue later. Already, she saw that one of the FBI men—she presumed the ranking agent—had a tightness around the eyes and mouth. He'd bear watching.

"The operation will not have a name," she said. "There will be no log of the events that transpire, except the report that I will be preparing for my superiors. Captain Siebalt and Captain Rouleau will see to it that any log entries already written that make reference to the *Antoinette* and the situation on this island are eradicated—"

"Regulations are clear—" The Coast Guard captain, Rouleau, began to sputter.

"From this moment on, Captain, I make your regulations. If that makes you uncomfortable, you're welcome to confirm it with your own superiors. That goes for all of you. I want to have a cooperative interagency effort here, and I encourage you to speak to whomever you need to speak to immediately following this meeting in order to get comfortable with that. After that, you're either on the team or you're in the way. And if you're in the way, you'll be removed.

"To continue . . . I'm sorry, which one of you is Agent Turcotte?"

"I'm Special Agent Turcotte."

Just the one she'd thought. He sat up straighter in his chair. It did not escape her notice that he had corrected her use of his title. Alena was surprised that he hadn't gone so far as to use his full title of Supervisory Special Agent in Charge, but apparently he was at least self-aware enough to know how foolish that would have looked. She would have to keep him close, try to make him feel important, bend him to her own purposes. Or she would have to keep him out of it entirely. Attitude would cost lives.

"With apologies, Special Agent Turcotte, that goes for the FBI as well. No record of the *Antoinette,* case files expunged, et cetera."

His face darkened and Alena saw the bitterness start to spread to the other three FBI agents in the room. The least affected seemed to be the man wearing a sling on his left arm, his face badly bruised from some kind of altercation. That had to be Agent Hart, who had survived the previous night's horrors.

"I'm sorry," she said. "I know you have all worked hard on this case. But at the end of the day, every single person in this room—military, law enforcement, or civilian—works for the same employer, the United States government. Trust me when I say that making this case vanish will have a positive rather than negative impact on your career and future prospects, and that you will have the personal satisfaction of having dealt with a threat to human life and potentially national security."

That seemed to settle them down, so she forged ahead.

"The only record of this operation will be my own reports to my superiors. In order to reassure you, I am willing to allow Captains Rouleau and Siebalt and Special Agent Turcotte to review those reports before they are submitted."

Even Turcotte gave a grudging nod at that.

"This is going to be the strangest and probably the most dangerous day of your lives, with the exception of Agent Hart, who has already lived his," Alena said. They all sat a bit straighter, ready for the challenge or at least curious. "In extreme situations, I am empowered to extend limited intelligence clearance to anyone who I determine is vital to the success of an operation. I am extending that clearance to everyone in this room, effective immediately. When we're done here, you will not leave without providing your identification to David."

She nodded toward him, and David raised a hand in a semi-wave without ever looking up from the laptop. He tapped away at the keyboard.

"Dr. David Boudreau," she went on, indicating him again. "Nepotism at its finest. Yes, my grandson, but also smarter than anyone else in the room, myself included, and the only other person involved in this operation aside from myself who has encountered these particular bio-forms before."

A rumble of voices filled the room, mutters of surprise and astonished whispers.

"Excuse me," Agent Hart said. He wore a look of amazement that turned his handsome face boyish. "You've seen the sirens before?"

Alena arched an eyebrow. "Sirens? Ah, the bio-forms. Clever, but please don't think for a moment that these creatures are anything but an unknown species of marine life. As Dr. Ernst will tell you, they are unusual, dangerous, even terrifying, but they are hardly unnatural. Their 'song,' if you'd like to pursue the siren metaphor, is not dissimilar from bats' echolocation, aiding their sensory perception when out of the water."

She started to go on, but Agent Hart interrupted again. All eyes were now on him and the room seemed to have grown smaller.

"Wait. Seriously," he said, growing agitated. The one female FBI agent in the room, who Alena presumed must be his partner, put a hand on his arm, but Hart ignored her. "'Hardly unnatural'? They're underwater vampires, for fuck's sake. They burn in sunlight."

Alena frowned. She had gauged the potential problem that Turcotte might represent, but had not counted on Agent Hart posing difficulties. She knew the trauma he had been through, and she could see how shaken it had left him, but she had no time to comfort him.

"Sarah?" she said.

Professor Ernst stood. Attractive in a disheveled, academic sort of way, Sarah Ernst was forty-seven, her hair dyed an auburn just close enough to red to be serious and daring in equal turns.

"Dr. Ernst is a former MIT professor with PhDs in astrobiology and marine biology. She's been part of my team for three years."

"Thank you, Dr. Boudreau," Ernst said. She looked out over those gathered in the room, then focused on Hart. Alena had taught her well. Crisis management was often about personnel management. "Let's get this clear right up front. There is no evidence that anything remotely resembling horror movie vampires exists, or ever existed."

Professor Ernst smiled and they all seemed to relax. "Based upon the records I've read of the prior encounter with these . . . with the 'sirens,' the best reference point I can provide is a rare skin condition called xeroderma pigmentosum, in which the flesh is not protected from ultraviolet light and is therefore burned. With a lack of pigment, UV light damages DNA, causing cellular mutation that—in such cases—can cause the skin to burn or blacken. As the cells divide, the mutation spreads, and so does this burning effect. What happens with these creatures is obviously a radical example of this phenomenon—"

"They don't just blacken," Agent Hart interrupted. "They catch fire."

Ernst nodded. "So I'm told. Right now, I'm theorizing the presence of crystalline proteins in the skin that will burn on exposure to sunlight. Look, honestly, if I had read about the existence of these things, I would never have believed it. But there have been many things found in the ocean that nobody expected. And obviously, presented with them as a reality, I can only theorize until I have one of them to study. One thing I'm confident of, though . . ." She smiled. "There's no such thing as vampires."

"Thank you, Dr. Ernst," Alena said as the woman sat down. Then she gestured to the slender African-American man beside Ernst. "The final member of my team is Dr. Paul Ridge, whom I stole from the geology department at Northwestern. Thanks to his experience with primordial cave formations, I needed him more than his students did."

Professor Ridge waved a hand to identify himself, then cast an expectant look at Alena, silently urging her to move on. Ridge didn't like the spotlight at all.

"Now, normally I would have to mislead you about the nature of my employment, but this is a crisis management scenario, so there's to be no bullshit." Nobody flinched at her profanity and she nodded her approval. They weren't looking at her like an aging civilian anymore. "I'm a specialist in extraordinary discoveries. That's the best way to describe it. It's much more interesting than 'analyst,' which is the word I use when I want to bore people into not wondering about me anymore. My team is an under-the-radar division of the Defense Advanced Research Projects Agency, which is part of the DOD.

"Beyond that, all you need to know at the moment is this: The U.S. government has had two prior encounters with life-forms that sound substantially similar to what the crew of the *Antoinette* encountered on the island, and both of them were also island-based infestations. The first habitat was off the eastern coast of Africa and was eradicated. That was in 1967. Fishermen discovered the second habitat in the South Pacific only seven years ago. I was involved with both cases.

"As you can see, I survived. Both habitats were destroyed, along with their inhabitants. The sun will kill them, as you know, but so will firepower. Seven years ago, we tried to put to use lessons I learned in '67, but failed."

"Failed how?" Captain Siebalt asked, genuinely curious.

"Our job is twofold—destroy the threat, and learn everything we can about it. Most of my team died in '67 because we focused more on acquiring a research subject than on containing the threat. This time, things will be done differently. We will bring one of these things home to study, but eradication is our first priority."

"You want to bring one of these things back alive?" Agent Voss asked. "If you've seen these things, then you must know—"

Alena held up both hands to forestall any further interruption. "It won't be easy, of course. In order to fulfill that part of the mission, we will have to catch one in the dark. I'd prefer a living one, but a dead one will do. That means bagging one and then keeping it out of the sunlight long enough to get it back here and locked away in the dark. Just keep that in mind. If it helps, tell your people that there will be a reward for the first person to bring me—"

"Absolutely not!" Captain Rouleau said.

Alena narrowed her eyes. The old Coast Guard officer had reddened, either with anger or embarrassment.

"Captain?" she said.

"Pardon me, Dr. Boudreau," Captain Rouleau said, "but that sort of thing leads to competition, which is a distraction that could get good men and women killed."

She let out a breath, nodding. "I'm sorry, Captain. You're right, of course."

"Besides, Navy sailors don't need a reward to motivate

them," Captain Siebalt added, glancing sidelong at her from his place at the table. "If there's any way to bring one of those things back whole, you'll get one."

"That's all I can ask," Alena said. She glanced over at her grandson, who had paused and looked up from his laptop. "David, anything to contribute before we continue?"

He gave her his typical insouciant smile and scratched at his chin. "Only that you've been at this nearly ten minutes already. Tick, tick, Alena."

Little shit, she thought, with all the love in her heart. She couldn't help but chuckle, though she knew it would be her last for a while.

"All right," she said, turning to look at them all again. At Captain Siebalt and his officers to her left at the long table, at Captain Rouleau and his people, at the FBI agents who had more invested in this situation than any of them.

"What we've got ahead of us is little more than carefully executed destruction and extermination. You've all been drafted for pest control. These things can't be allowed to continue to thrive, and certainly can't be permitted to breed and spread.

"So here's the plan . . ."

-68--

"You're not going to throw me overboard, are you?" Tori asked, attempting a smile.

The serious little FBI guy, Nadeau, shook his head. "I don't think that's on the agenda. At least not today."

So he did have a sense of humor. It was just buried underneath an intense expression and the air of purpose that swept them both along the corridor and up the stairs. They passed an open door leading out on deck and the warm breeze helped her feel more awake and alert. But Agent

Nadeau opened an inner door and Tori reluctantly passed through it.

She had started to feel a little claustrophobic in the room they'd given her—not because of its size, but because they would not allow her to leave. If she had to use the bathroom, one of the Coast Guard seamen would accompany her and wait outside the door, but otherwise she remained a prisoner. After Josh had visited her, she had tried to rest, but as tired as she was, she only fidgeted and tossed and finally sat up again.

Nadeau's mysterious arrival had been a blessing.

"You still won't tell me where you're taking me?"

The agent preceded her down the hall, oblivious to any danger of attack from behind. She might be in custody, but obviously they didn't perceive her as much of a threat. Maybe that was because of Josh, or maybe it was because, even if she did try to get the jump on Nadeau and make a break for it, she didn't have anywhere to run.

"I'm taking you to a meeting," he said.

"About what?"

"Something to do with the operation, obviously. Beyond that, I have no idea, and wouldn't be able to tell you if I did. Can you stop asking now?"

Tori understood Nadeau's shtick now: cranky guy. Apparently he thought it was part of his charm.

He led her up another inner flight of stairs and then back toward starboard to a door flanked by yet another pair of seamen in the uniform of the U.S. Coast Guard. One of them rapped on the metal door and then unlatched it, swinging it open for them to enter.

"Very *Chamber of Secrets,*" she said.

But the room surprised her. Instead of the dreary, cheerless cell she had anticipated, she found herself in a small rec room a bit like those on board the *Antoinette*. Windows on the starboard wall let air and sunlight in and the smell of popcorn swirled on the breeze. Someone had used the microwave to pop some recently, but Tori doubted it was anyone in the room. She knew all but one of them, and she thought they had better things to do.

There were three FBI agents in the room—Josh, Rachael Voss, and the asshole Turcotte—and now Nadeau made four. Turcotte stood by one of the windows and did not even glance up when she and Nadeau entered and the door clanged shut behind them. The only person she did not recognize was a beautiful older woman with silver hair, whom she gauged at about sixty. The woman was dressed all in black and looked both stylish and serious, but she nodded to Tori, almost friendly.

"Please, Miss Austin," the woman said. "Take a seat."

In her current circumstances, she knew she shouldn't be making snap judgments, but Tori liked her immediately. Nobody else in the room had bothered to sit, but Tori went to one of the chairs around a round card table and slid into it, forcing herself not to even glance at Josh.

She hadn't forgiven him for lying to her, but as her anger had receded, she had begun to understand that he must be telling the truth. It couldn't all have been pretense. He would never have risked losing his job for her. That implied that either she meant something to him, or he'd wanted her so badly he couldn't control himself, or a little of both. And all of those options intrigued her, no matter how much it still stung.

Tori watched him as he spoke quietly to Agent Nadeau, loving his eyes and the line of his jaw, and feeling foolish to be thinking of such things in the midst of something so weird and awful.

She rolled her eyes a little and started to turn away, then caught both Rachael Voss and the silver-haired woman watching her. The older woman seemed interested and amused, but Voss's nostrils flared and her eyes narrowed in consternation. She had obviously seen something in the way Tori looked at Josh and didn't approve.

Someone rapped on the metal door. It was opened from outside and Tori blinked in surprise as Gabe Rio stepped into the room. The captain of the *Antoinette* looked ragged around the edges, with dark circles under his eyes, but he kept his chin high in defiance. No handcuffs, but they were obviously far more wary of him than they had been of her, for the broad-shouldered FBI agent who followed him into the room watched his every move. The seamen out in the hall closed and latched the door behind Gabe and the big agent.

"Thanks, Mac," Voss said to the big guy.

When Gabe saw the agents gathered there, he sized them up and then walked toward the card table.

"How you doing, Tori?" he asked, sliding into the chair beside her.

"I'm all right. You holding up?"

They both knew she wasn't talking about his bandaged leg or the harrowing experience they had shared, but about Miguel's death, and the revelation that his brother had been having an affair with Gabe's wife.

Gabe knocked his knuckles on the table. "I'm still here."

"And we're glad you are," the silver-haired woman said.

The FBI agents all focused on her as if she were a judge calling the court to order. Even Turcotte pulled his attention from the window. He crossed his arms and leaned against the wall, body language saying volumes about his disapproval of this situation, whatever it might be.

Since Tori and Gabe were sitting, the silver-haired woman joined them at the card table. The five FBI agents in the room remained standing, a few feet back, observing. None of them seemed particularly happy about being there—not even Josh.

"Miss Austin. Captain Rio. My name is Dr. Alena Boudreau and I am now in charge of all matters relating to this operation, including the events that transpired over the past twenty-four to forty-eight hours aboard the *Antoinette* and on the island."

As if in punctuation, a sudden roar filled the room. It took Tori a moment to realize the sound came from a helicopter that had just flown overhead.

Turcotte glanced back at the window. "Four choppers," he said, turning to look at Dr. Boudreau. "You're not wasting any time."

For her part, Dr. Boudreau adopted a serious expression, but Tori had a feeling the woman was only indulging Turcotte.

"The civilian helicopter will be returning to St. Croix in a couple of hours. They're loaning us their services in the meantime."

Dr. Boudreau turned back to Tori and Gabe. "Let me make this short and sweet. I've read the statements you gave about the creatures . . . the sirens, as you call them . . . and what happened to your crew. I'm sure the last thing either of you wants is to ever set foot on that island again. However, that's precisely what I'm asking."

Tori felt her mouth drop open and frigid air seemed to envelop her.

"You're crazy," Gabe said. "Out of your mind, lady."

"You can't possibly—" Turcotte began.

The woman shot him a dark look. "I have the authority to choose any team I want—to incorporate anyone, with any specialty, from any government agency, organization, or armed service, or to recruit any civilian who is necessary to the completion of the operation with which I am tasked. Do you want to argue this some more, Agent Turcotte, maybe give our people less time before nightfall, or can we get on with it?"

The buzz of helicopters outside grew momentarily louder and then receded once more.

Turcotte gestured for her to continue.

Dr. Boudreau sat up straighter in her chair and gazed at Tori and Gabe. Though still rational and open, her friendliness had vanished. "I'm in a bit of a hurry, so here's the deal. Captain Rio, those creatures killed your brother and almost your entire crew. They've taken away your livelihood. Your life will never be the same. Miss Austin, obviously you have no job to go back to. Both of you are headed for criminal trial, possibly prison. I can offer you something better. Significantly better."

Tori glanced at Josh, but he looked away. In fact, none of the FBI agents looked happy. That pleased her. Whatever might upset the FBI where this case was concerned had to be good for Tori Austin.

"We're listening," she said.

Gabe rocked back in his chair, arms crossed in defiance. "Go ahead."

Dr. Boudreau nodded, studying them. Sizing them up. "The United States government would like to keep these events, and the operation that is about to commence, a secret. Where the two of you are concerned, there are several ways that can be accomplished. First, they could simply have you killed."

She said it in such a casual and offhanded fashion that it took Tori a moment to process, then she flinched away from the older woman.

"That's not funny, I know," Dr. Boudreau continued. "But I know I have your attention now. The good news for me is that your criminal endeavors make any such measures unnecessary, even if that were the sort of thing I would ever be a party to, which it isn't. The bad news for you is that I can arrange to keep these events quiet by making sure you are both incarcerated for life in places where no one would ever believe a wild story such as this one. I would really rather not pursue that option."

"Then don't," Gabe said.

"That, I'm afraid, is entirely up to you."

Tori gnawed her lower lip. She could sense Gabe's anger and resistance and did not want to seem too eager, but she had resigned herself to prison or whatever else fate might bring, and the chance to avoid that had her heart soaring.

"What do you want from us?" she asked. Her gaze shifted past the silver-haired woman to Josh. He gave her an almost imperceptible nod. Beside him, Voss did not seem to notice, focused—as the others in the room were—on Dr. Boudreau.

"I'm capable of giving you a new life," the older woman said. "I'm offering you a chance to start over anywhere you like with a modest annual stipend and a new name. You only have to do two things for me. First, never speak of this island or the things you call sirens again, and second, come with me out to the island as part of my team."

Gabe actually laughed. "And why would we do that?"

Tori barely listened. The words were still echoing in her mind. A new start and a new name. She had tried for a fresh beginning in Miami, and that had led her here, and almost to prison. The idea that she might get yet another chance at wiping the slate blank seemed surreal.

Dr. Boudreau gestured toward Agent Turcotte, or, rather, beyond him. Out the window, Tori could see a helicopter in the distance, Coast Guard or Navy personnel landing on the island.

"I want to get this done today—"

"Why?" Gabe asked. "Today, tomorrow, next week, what difference does it make?"

Dr. Boudreau nodded as though in approval of the question, then slid her chair back. She walked over to the window and peered out, standing just a couple of feet away from Turcotte. As she turned to face the card table again, she gave Agent Turcotte a meaningful glance, as though the words to follow were meant for him as well.

"We have encountered these sirens before, but we know very little about them. Right now operation personnel are beginning an observational sweep of the island, but they are amphibious creatures. They will come up on land tonight, or at least they will if any of those people are still on the island come nightfall. I'd rather not begin the job only to have them interfere with it overnight. Beyond that, we cannot be certain how far beyond their main habitat they'll be willing to stray, so there's no way to accurately gauge what would be considered a 'safe distance' from the island. All in all, the best course is the most expeditious, and that is why I am willing to bring you both into the fold, and reward you afterward with your freedom.

"I'd like you to accompany me to the island and work with my people to point out any and all caves that you recall from your search yesterday—especially what Captain Rio called the 'kill sites' in his statement, and what you, Miss Austin, referred to as 'the grotto.' The faster we survey the island, the faster we can begin purging the island of these creatures.

"Now," she added, "time is of the essence. Your decisions?"

Tori glanced at Gabe, but he had lowered his gaze, staring at the table or perhaps at nothing, eyes haunted and distant. She did not look away and eventually, either noticing her in his peripheral vision or simply aware of the press of her attention, he lifted his chin. For several seconds, they regarded each other, and then Gabe turned toward Turcotte.

"And part of this whole Get Out of Jail Free card, this new life, would be testifying against Viscaya?"

Turcotte gave a curt nod.

Tori saw Josh blink and glance first at Voss and then at Turcotte, and she knew the man was lying. Dr. Boudreau kept her face blank.

"No, Gabe," Tori said, focusing on the older woman. "They're going to make the *Antoinette* disappear, and they're gonna make us disappear. We don't have to testify to anything as long as we play along and keep our mouths shut. Isn't that right, Dr. Boudreau?"

Turcotte glared daggers at the silver-haired woman, but Boudreau clearly had no interest in blowing smoke.

"That's right," she said. "No strings except your silence afterward."

"And what about Angie Tyree?" Gabe asked. "Where does she fit into all of this? 'Cause I don't see her in this room."

Tori felt bad that she hadn't even thought about Angie. The woman had never been her friend, but she was the only survivor of the *Antoinette* who had not been brought into this meeting.

Josh stepped closer to the table. His eyes had a glassy sheen from the Vicodin the shipboard doctor had given him.

"Angie's going to be given the same choice Dr. Boudreau just gave the two of you, but we don't want her on the island. She had a total mental breakdown last night and I don't think all the pieces are necessarily back together again. She'd be a liability."

Gabe kicked back and put his boots up on the table, crossing his arms. Though he spoke to Dr. Boudreau, his gaze rested on Agent Turcotte.

"So Angie gets to choose prison or silence, and we get to pick between prison and fucking suicide?" His brow furrowed deeply and Tori thought he had aged a great deal in the past day.

"You'll be off the island by nightfall," Dr. Boudreau said, her impatience growing.

"So you say," Gabe replied, then shook his head. "But the only way I can guarantee that is to not go at all. I've seen those things up close and I think I'll stay here, thank you."

Tori stared at him. "Gabe, they'll put you in prison. This is your chance to—"

His expression stopped her short. His sorrow pained her. He had always been a good man, involved in crimes he had never wished for on behalf of a brother who had never been grateful enough. Now he was paying for his crimes far more on the inside than he ever would in prison.

"Why do I care?" Gabe asked, small crinkles of pain around his eyes. "What can prison take away from me? I've got nothing left."

"Boo-fucking-hoo!" Turcotte snapped. He started toward the table, but Nadeau and Mac immediately stepped in his path. Turcotte rolled his eyes in disgust.

Tori looked around to see that the rest of them were watching her.

"What about you, Miss Austin?" Dr. Boudreau asked.

She felt almost guilty, not standing up to them. But unlike Gabe, she still felt like she had plenty to lose. Her future. Her freedom. A chance at tomorrow. Twice she'd been spared and, this time, she would not screw it up.

"I'm in," she said, lifting her chin, looking from Boudreau to Josh and Voss.

Dr. Boudreau thrust out her hand, a look of satisfaction on her face. "Thank you, Tori. You won't regret it."

The words sounded hollow. When Tori looked at Gabe, he lowered his gaze, either angry with her or just surrendering to his sorrow. He'd been broken up inside, but she was just happy to be alive. And if she did feel pangs of regret already beginning, what did it matter? Provided she survived, she would get over it.

Still, the thought of returning to the island, with its caves and its bones, made her feel sick. "Let's go before I chicken out."

And they were all moving, headed for the door. Mac accompanied Gabe, who would be locked up again. But Dr. Boudreau,

Josh, and Voss surrounded Tori, hustling her out of the room and down the corridor as though afraid she would change her mind.

"So, Tori," Dr. Boudreau said, "ever been in a helicopter?"

-69--

Angie sat on the edge of her cot and thought about bees.

More specifically, she thought about poking a stick into a nest of bees. Why the hell did the Coast Guard and the Navy and this Dr. Boudreau, whoever she was, want to be here in the first place? Angie did not understand why they couldn't just put a ring of buoys in the water a good distance from the island and mark STAY THE FUCK AWAY on every chart in existence. In ancient times, she knew, cartographers would create maps that illustrated the extent of their knowledge of the world, and in the margins—at the edges of what, to them, represented the unknown—they would write HERE THERE BE DRAGONS.

Same idea, she thought. *Stay the fuck away. Succinct and to the point.* As a plan, buoys and warnings on maps made a lot more sense to her than going back to the island, no matter what weapons you had.

Granted, there would be dumbasses—mostly rich pricks and skeptical fishermen—who would just have to go past the buoys and ignore the warnings. But if those people ended up eaten, didn't they have it coming to them?

One thing she knew, without any doubt whatsoever, was that no one should poke a stick into a beehive. Only they were.

Agent Plausky had told her about the offer from Dr. Boudreau—a free pass, as long as she vanished. No jail, and she could go wherever she wanted. They would pay for her to start over again back home in Honduras, or the Caribbean, or Europe, or anywhere in the USA—so long as she stayed out of the state of Florida and did not contact anyone involved with Viscaya Shipping. And as long as she didn't talk about the sirens.

Plausky, as professional and pleasant as could be, did not manage to be very convincing about that last part, which was how Angie realized that the government did not really care if she talked about the sirens. They were pretty sure nobody would believe her, and Angie figured they were right. The realization troubled her, but only a little. In truth, she wanted to get lost, to forget, and the idea of disappearing into a new life appealed to her. The only thing that appealed to her more—and it amazed her to find this particular truth hidden deep within herself—was the idea of going home.

All her life, Angie had wandered anywhere but home. But now the devil had come up close enough to whisper in her ear, and Angela Tyree did not want to die thousands of miles from home with no one even to grieve at her passing.

Home. She thought about it now as she sat on the cot, legs drawn up to her chest, rocking gently. The position made her a little self-conscious, considering it was the traditional pose of crazy people, but she knew she wasn't crazy. And anyway, nobody was watching.

When the wind shifted just right, breezing through the window, she felt sure she could smell her aunt Eugenia's cooking. It brought a smile to her face.

"I'll do anything you want," she had told Plausky. "I'll sign anything, testify to anything, and *forget* anything, on one condition. You have to get me out of here, away from all of this, today. I want to be on dry land somewhere civilized by the time the sun goes down."

Plausky had nodded immediately. "Actually, that's already in motion. The Bureau has a civilian chopper here on loan from St. Croix. It brought Dr. Boudreau out, and it'll be bringing you back in two, three hours, tops."

Angie had been euphoric.

Now she could not be sure the conversation had really happened. This, more than anything else, made her wonder just how badly the previous night had tilted her world off its axis. The doctor here on board the *Kodiak* had given her something last night, but she could not remember what it had been. Xanax, maybe. Something to bring her down from the panic and hyperventilation. This morning she had taken another pill, and now she wondered if her terror had truly begun to abate, or if her emotions were being chemically managed.

Not that she minded; she just wanted to know.

More than anything, she wondered if she would sleep tonight, and if she did, what might visit her dreams. It occurred to her that additional pills might be required.

Continuing her gentle rocking, Angie inhaled deeply. A frown creased her forehead, because instead of Auntie Eugenia's cooking, the air now smelled of burning. At first she thought it sprang from her imagination, but then the aroma became so powerful that there could be no mistaking it.

Something was on fire.

After a moment's consideration, Angie rose from the cot and went to the window. The *Antoinette* still loomed a couple hundred yards away from the Coast Guard ship, and off to the right of her window. But despite the way it floated, deadly and waiting, she barely noticed it.

The derelict ships were on fire. Flames roared up from that graveyard of half-sunken fishing boats and yachts and small freighters. The blaze spread hungrily from vessel to vessel, igniting in gusts and gouts of flame. The Coast Guard—or maybe the Navy—had covered and filled the boats with gasoline or something else that made the fire claw through wood, shatter fiberglass, and blacken steel. The sails and nets that had been stretched like a tall ship's rigging evaporated like spiderwebs, trailing strings of flame.

A helicopter buzzed past, flying low over the flickering flames and the waves of heat rising off the burning ships. It slowed above a cluster of several ships that had not yet begun to burn. A man hung partway out of the open side door of the helicopter, strapped in to keep him from falling. Angie realized that some of the sailors must have actually lowered themselves down to the boats earlier to plant whatever they were using to accelerate the fire, because now the guy in the chopper dropped a pair of burning flares that hit a fishing boat dead-on—one on the deck and one right into the wheelhouse—and fire blossomed upward even as the helicopter roared away.

It had begun.

The island had its devils, and the Navy had brought its own hell.

-70--

Josh sat on a table in the *Kodiak*'s sick bay with his shirt off. His sling hung from a chair, but he kept his left arm pressed to his body. Dr. Dolan changed the dressing on his wound.

"You're lucky the weapon was small caliber," the doctor said as he examined the back of Josh's shoulder. "Clean entry and exit, probably struck bone, but doesn't appear to have broken anything. Very lucky."

Josh grunted as the doctor gently touched the swollen skin around the wound, then pressed a fresh bandage over it. The one good thing he could say about the pain from that wound was that it had nearly obliterated the stings and aches left over from the beating Boggs had given him. Shifting his arm even a couple of inches made him forget all about bruised ribs.

"How is getting shot lucky, exactly?" he asked.

Dr. Dolan came around the front of the table, staring at him. "You're still breathing, Agent Hart. As I understand it, the man who shot you is dead. Who's luckier, would you say?"

Josh had not seen Miguel Rio die, but he knew the sirens had gotten him. And admittedly, the bullet wound seemed like a fair price to pay for not getting ripped apart by those things.

"Point taken," he said, sliding off the table. He reached for his shirt and gingerly slid his left arm into it. Pain erupted from his wound and radiated across his chest and up his arm.

Dr. Dolan saw him grimace. "I'm sure there's no point in my saying so, but you really shouldn't be going anywhere. You need rest to heal."

"I just need to get through today," Josh told him. "Four hours, maybe five. Then I can crash. Think you can pack me a picnic lunch for my trip ashore?"

Dolan's blue eyes were dark with disapproval. "You took some Vicodin less than three hours ago."

"Some," Josh agreed. "How about all of it?"

"Not funny," the doctor said. "Vicodin is powerful stuff, Agent Hart. Take enough of it, and you'll be able to function. Take too much, and you'll be less than useless to yourself and to everyone else. You're really better off staying on board."

"For a dozen reasons, at least," Josh admitted. Then his good humor vanished and he fixed Dr. Dolan with a look of such gravity that the man actually recoiled. "But I can't stay here while my squad is out there. None of them gave up on *me*, Doc. How can I do any less? They don't even know what they're facing."

Normally, Josh kept such feelings to himself, but the Vicodin made it seem entirely reasonable to say what was really on his mind.

Dr. Dolan studied him. "You think you need more Vicodin? That it isn't helping?"

"I'm not stupid, Doc. I know it's helping, but after the first couple of hours the pain starts coming back, deep down at first and then spreading, like a bomb exploding in slow motion."

"Pain is good," the doctor said. "It makes you careful, keeps you from doing anything really stupid. Pain reminds you to rest the arm so the wound can start to knit—"

"That's what the sling is for."

"It's not the same thing, and you know that," the doctor chided.

Josh sighed, regarding him grimly. "Look, Doc, I don't love the Vicodin. Seriously. Sure, part of it is wonderful.

It's like I'm a fish in a bowl, swimming around all content, and the things going on outside the bowl don't seem to matter that much. But the thing is, I've got some control issues, and when I manage to think about how much I'm liking my fishbowl . . . it worries me. So, like I said, I don't love the Vicodin. But right now, Dr. Dolan, it's my best damn friend in the world."

For several long moments, the doctor only looked at him. Then he sighed.

"All right," Dr. Dolan said. He hesitated, and then repeated it, as though trying to convince himself. "All right." He turned and opened the door, then flinched back as he discovered Rachael Voss outside.

"Oh. Something I can do for you, Agent?"

"Just need a minute with my partner, Doc," Voss replied.

Josh noted the tightness of her voice with curiosity, and the way her brows knitted together when she glanced at him over the doctor's shoulder. These things didn't trouble him, however. He had not been lying about the effects of the Vicodin. Rachael had something to talk to him about, and that was fine by him. Why wouldn't it be? If he didn't like what he heard, he could always swim deeper into his fishbowl—as long as Dolan came through with enough Vicodin to last him the day.

"Fine, fine," Dr. Dolan said. He glanced back at Josh. "I'll be back in a moment, Agent Hart."

Josh raised his right hand in a kind of wave.

Voss came into the room, pulling the door shut behind her. "What's up?" Josh asked.

"What's going on with you and Tori Austin? I saw the looks you two gave each other, and especially the way she looked at you. I know that look. I've given it to more than a few guys myself." Voss lowered her voice. "You're sleeping with her?"

Josh took a deep breath. He had hoped to save this conversation for later, but now he nodded slowly. "Once, yeah."

"Jesus!" Voss said, anger and confusion in her eyes.

"I know. And I know there could be serious repercussions. I'm going to put the whole thing in my report and face the music, whatever happens. It isn't something I meant to happen, Rachael."

She stared at him, cocking her head. "You care about her."

"I do." And he didn't think it was the Vicodin talking. "But it all happened under false pretenses. She thought I was someone else, just a nice guy who could cook. I hurt her pretty bad, and I—"

"Stop!" Voss said, holding up one hand. She shook her head, walked toward him, and gently slapped his face. "Wake up, Josh. Between this woman, that hole in your shoulder, and the drugs you're on, you are not thinking straight. No way are you going out to that island with her. I'll send Pavarotti instead."

Josh picked up his sling from the chair and carefully slipped it on. Fresh pain blossomed in his shoulder. What the hell was taking the doctor so long?

"Bullshit," he said, leaning against the examining table. "You're my best friend, Rachael. Maybe you're disappointed in me or worried about me, and maybe you're pissed off at me—"

"You could have told me!"

He blinked at the way she'd raised her voice. "And I planned to. It's not like we've had time for a heart-to-heart since you pulled me out of that lifeboat last night."

Voss seemed about to shout again, but then she deflated, letting out a long breath. "All right. Okay. I'm not going to pretend to understand, but it's something we can talk about later. And I am worried about you, Josh. You're compromised. If you have feelings for this woman, you shouldn't be the one out there with her."

Josh smiled and cocked his head, the pain abating for a moment. "I have feelings for you, Rachael. You're my best friend and my partner, and I love you, but that's never stopped me from thinking clearly when we're in the field."

She seemed taken aback by his words.

"Sorry," he said. "Vicodin makes me honest and too chatty. Anyway, this is your squad, yes. You're the boss. But Turcotte took over our case, and now this Alena Boudreau is in charge. She gets to decide who goes where. You could go talk to her, make it hard for me, but I'm really hoping you won't."

"You know I wouldn't."

And he did. Whatever disagreements they had, she would keep it between them.

"Thanks."

Voss looked like she had something else to say, but then, instead, she closed the gap between them and pulled Josh into a gentle embrace, resting her head on his chest. Pain flooded his shoulder, but he forced himself not to let it show or make a noise.

"Just don't die, okay? I already thought I'd lost you once."

Josh kissed the top of her head, feeling the bond between them more acutely than ever before—as if she had come to join him in his Vicodin fishbowl. In another world, they might have shared a love that went beyond friendship, but that would have required sacrificing the ability to work together, and the closeness that brought. No, their bond was as partners, not lovers.

"Dying is definitely not part of my plan."

Voss stepped back, seeming embarrassed by her show of emotion. "You have a plan?"

He pretended to think about it, then shook his head. "Actually, not dying is pretty much the entire plan."

For the first time since she had entered the room, Voss smiled. "Simple plans are always best. I like it."

A quick rap came at the door and then it opened. Dr. Dolan handed Josh a small white cup.

"Take two now," the doctor said as Josh rattled the pills in the cup. "In three hours, if you're not already back on board, take the other two. Come see me when you come back from the island and we'll change those dressings again. Then, if you're going to be resting for a while, I'll give you a bottle of Vicodin you can take with you when the operation is over."

"Why not give it to me now?" Josh asked.

"Because you want it now, and if you insist on staying upright today, I'm not going to let you do it so impaired that you can't put coherent thoughts together."

Josh arched an eyebrow and glanced at Voss, who did not

look amused. Somehow, it didn't make Josh himself any
less so.

"Spoilsport," he said to Dolan, then went to the sink, got a
cup of water, and washed down two pills. The other two he
crushed inside the paper cup, then slid the whole thing into
his pocket, promising himself that he would at least try to
wait the three hours.

Suspecting he would break the promise.

He made a mental note to try, should he survive the day,
to avoid getting shot in the future.

-71--

The gas mask fit too snugly over Voss's head, but she supposed snug was preferable to loose. The apparatus seemed
heavier to her than the masks she had worn before during
FBI operations, but maybe it was just a different manufacturer. The comm unit inside the mask had zero static, which
made it almost spooky when anyone on her channel spoke,
like the person had just snuck up behind her.

"Before we go in," David Boudreau said, "I want to make
sure we're all on the same page."

She turned to look at him, the sun's glare forcing her to
squint. It felt vaguely foolish to be parading around in these
masks in broad daylight, under a perfect blue sky. But everything about this case had turned surreal. Half-sunken ships
were burning in the shallow water off the island's shores. Flesh-
eating monsters—mermen or something equally whacked—
were darting away from the flames, quick pale flashes under
the water. They were also hiding in the quiet darkness of the
Antoinette's belly, waiting for nightfall.

Somehow, though, the conversation she'd had with Josh
half an hour ago—just before the chopper had dropped her,
Turcotte, and O'Connell onto the deck of the *Antoinette*,

where Boudreau and a combined Navy and Coast Guard strike team awaited—seemed the most surreal of all. This man she thought she knew, her partner and best friend, maybe the only real friend in her life, had not only had sex with a suspect, but admitted to having feelings for her. What world had she woken up in this morning?

"What page is that?" Turcotte asked as he slid his own gas mask on, adjusting the straps behind his head.

"We search the ship. Our primary objective is bringing a siren back for Alena and Dr. Ernst to study, alive if possible. Only when we've done that do we move on to secondary objectives."

Voss allowed herself a quiet chuckle, but apparently not quiet enough.

"What is it, Agent Voss?" David Boudreau asked. "Most people don't think I'm all that funny."

"I doubt that," Voss replied. "I'd bet you can be very charming when you want to."

She could see the comment threw him a little. That was good. She wanted to make sure he realized that his was not the only agenda at work here, no matter what orders he wanted to give. Not that the words had been a lie. The young professor, or whatever his title might be, was easy on the eyes. Good looks were part of it, but David also had what Voss and her college friends had always referred to as "Grrrr" back in the day—a certain confidence and sexual charisma.

"Are you flirting?" O'Connell asked. "Was that you flirting? Fucking pitiful."

Voss glared at him, knowing that through the mask, the death glare would not be nearly as effective.

"I'm not flirting, Special Agent O'Connell," she said, every word an icicle. "I made an observation because Dr. Boudreau Junior here is trying to be intimidating and I wish he'd get on with it so we can get this done before the damn gas wears off."

Through her comm, she heard David sigh. "Whatever. Look, I don't want to be an asshole, but the truth is you're over here as a courtesy. If you don't want to help, just stay out of the way until we're finished and then you can do your own search."

"And get eaten," O'Connell muttered.

Turcotte turned toward him, but if he gave his partner a dirty look, his gas mask shielded it from view.

"We know the priorities, Doctor," Turcotte said. "Let's move."

Voss had so many things she wanted to add. Did David Boudreau understand how much work they had put into the Viscaya investigation? Did he realize that the *Antoinette* could have helped them close the case and put dozens of people behind bars who were involved in drug and gun smuggling in the U.S.? Did he know they would now have to make their case without Gabe Rio and the *Antoinette*?

Probably he does, Voss thought. *But why should he care?*

And that was the crux of it. Eight FBI agents had boarded the freighter this morning, had gone below, and had not come out again. Voss figured some of them had walked over the same patch of deck where she now stood, and now they were dead, somewhere inside the ship.

He wanted to bring one of these sirens back alive, but all Voss and Turcotte and O'Connell wanted was to kill every last one of them.

"After you," she said, smiling at David through her gas mask.

The gas canisters had been fired into every open doorway and window and down stairwells. The strike team had done an admirable job, first scaling the accommodations block and clearing every room. David expressed little surprise that they had not encountered any of the sirens on those upper levels. The creatures would seek the darkest places, and perhaps also those below sea level, or so the young scientist believed.

Now, with wisps of gas snaking out from the open door ahead of them, Voss watched David hesitate. She did not blame him. Nor did she blame him when he raised the assault rifle he wore on a strap over his shoulder.

"Want me to go first, Doctor?" Turcotte asked, making the last word into an insult.

To his credit, David ignored the question. A pair of Coast

Guard seamen, both armed with assault rifles, stood just inside the door, there to make certain a retreat—if necessary—could not be blocked off. They nodded to David as he stepped through into the interior.

O'Connell drew his sidearm. Voss and Turcotte followed suit.

"This level has already been cleared," David said, as he led them into a low, drifting mist that represented what remained of the gas. It wouldn't be long before the Caribbean breeze swept it all away, but hopefully it had done its job. If not . . . Voss hesitated to think about it.

"Lieutenant Cryan, this is David Boudreau. Are you monitoring this channel?"

Voss heard a click on the comm and then a low hiss that hadn't been there before, followed by the lieutenant's voice. "I read you, Dr. Boudreau."

"Special Agent Turcotte and two of his people have arrived. We've entered the accommodations block on the deck level, port side. Where can we be most useful?"

"I'm right underneath you, Doctor—"

Over the comm, Voss heard a soft double thump followed by a hiss and realized they were still firing gas canisters into rooms down there. She faltered a little. Fresh canisters meant they were finding enclosed spaces where the sirens might be hiding. The things might well be conscious and waiting in the dark below.

"—if you want to take the aft stairs, I'll have someone waiting, and we'll put you all to work."

The lieutenant was as good as his word. When they reached the next level down, where pipes hissed and gas had gathered at the ceiling like a yellow-tinged cloud, a sailor awaited them. He gestured for them to follow and they did so, but Voss glanced warily through every doorway they passed—mostly storage and some electrical systems—and she noticed Turcotte and O'Connell and David himself doing the same.

Her own breath sounded much too loud inside the mask and her pulse throbbed in her temples.

And then they were at the top of another set of metal stairs in an open area where Lieutenant Cryan and three other men

waited. Perfunctory introductions were made, and then the
lieutenant gestured toward the metal stairs.

"Dr. Boudreau—"

"David."

Voss rolled her eyes in the gloom of the ship's innards.
First name basis during a government operation? Maybe she
had been wrong about him having charisma when he wasn't
being in charge. *Or he thinks of his grandmother as Dr.
Boudreau and wants to leave the name to her,* she thought,
and hoped that was the answer.

"David," the lieutenant confirmed, "we're headed down to
the engine rooms. I've got a team of four sailors on deck,
searching for open containers and checking any that are unlocked. The Coast Guard detachment—twelve seamen—are
searching the forward holds. You're welcome to join either of
those groups, or head down with us."

"We're with you, Lieutenant. The sirens' natural habitats
are dormant volcanic islands. They're going to seek out heat,
and the engine rooms are probably where they would find it."

The Navy officer glanced at the nine-millimeter pistols the
FBI agents carried.

"Then maybe you'd better take up the rear."

Turcotte started to argue, but he was interrupted by the appearance of a gas-masked head popping up from the stairwell. Voss and the others weren't on the same channel, but
she heard the man's muffled voice through his mask.

"Lieutenant, we've got a trail of blood down here."

Cryan glanced at David, then at Voss and the other two FBI
agents. "Switch your comms to channel three."

Then the lieutenant started for the stairs, following the sailor
down into the gloom. So far, everywhere they had walked, the
interior lights still worked. But as Voss looked deep into the
deck below them, she realized that most of the lights down
there were out—and if the electricity still worked, that meant
they had been broken in order to make it darker down there.

"Any bodies, Mr. Stone?" Lieutenant Cryan asked.

Voss followed Turcotte down, with O'Connell behind her.
She saw the Counter-Terrorism agent stiffen at the mention
of bodies.

"A little respect," Turcotte said. "These people were my squad."

"No disrespect intended," the lieutenant replied. "You didn't answer my question, Mr. Stone."

At the bottom of the stairs, they gathered in a pool of wan light that came down from above, surrounded by shadows. Voices and footfalls echoed from farther forward, the rest of the lieutenant's team.

"No bodies, sir," Stone said.

"But you found something?"

"Yes, sir. Bones, sir."

-72--

Tori had never been on a chopper before—she felt sort of silly even thinking of the thing as a "chopper"—but the experience turned out to be vastly different from what she expected. Instead of feeling in danger of falling, riding in the back of the helicopter with a handful of armed sailors gave her a sensation not unlike being on a bus. Sure, the chopper dipped and turned in ways a bus never could, but she felt safe and secure, even without being strapped in.

From the helicopter, the island had a pristine tropical beauty. Seeing it from above, she thought it looked like paradise—an island Eden—but she knew all too well that there were many things that seemed perfect and beautiful on the surface and turned out to be ugly and rotten inside.

"Are you all right?" Alena Boudreau asked.

Tori glanced over at the silver-haired woman, thinking Dr. Boudreau must be talking to her, but the question had actually been directed at Josh. He had laid his head back against the curve of the helicopter's inner wall and closed his eyes. Now he opened them, blinking in surprise.

"Me? I'm good, yeah. Thanks for asking, Doc."

His eyes were glassy. Tori had not noticed before, but now she stared at him, confirming it. She had seen the effects of drugs in the eyes of men too often to mistake it for anything else. Josh was high.

Of course he is, she thought. *He got shot yesterday, and had the shit kicked out of him. He must be doped to the gills.* Josh had already told her Dr. Dolan had given him painkillers, but she had been too focused on other things to wonder just how big a dose would be needed to numb the pain of a gunshot wound.

Now she was worried about him, and a part of her resented that. After the humiliation she'd felt upon learning of his deception, Josh Hart's well-being ought to have been the last thing on her mind. And yet she could not help it. Despite the painkiller haze he must be in, his eyes met hers across the helicopter's wide bay. They sat on benches opposite each other and she resisted the urge to look away. *Why did you even come with us?* she wanted to ask.

But she thought she knew the answer, and if she turned out to be right, it would only piss her off more. Better for her to tell herself he had come along for the helicopter ride, or because he wanted to see the island for himself, or to look out for the FBI's interest in the case, than to think he wanted to watch over her and keep her safe. To hell with that. Tori had looked for men to protect her long enough. Far too long.

Dr. Boudreau glanced back and forth between the two of them with obvious curiosity but said nothing. The woman intrigued Tori. How had she come to the place in her life where she could push around branches of the military, not to mention the FBI? Her confidence and the calm that radiated out from her filled Tori with admiration and envy. She had a grandson, but if Tori had to guess, she would have said the older woman was single. No ring, for starters, but beyond that, she seemed so full of purpose that Tori found it hard to imagine Alena Boudreau relying on anyone but herself.

"So, Dr. Boudreau," Josh said, "do you think Dr. Ernst will get a corpse for her dissection table?"

He had to practically shout to be heard over the helicopter's rotors. Tori raised her eyebrows, thinking the question odd and abrupt, and wondered if that was the painkillers talking or if Josh had sensed the woman's attention and hoped to deflect it.

"I hope so," the woman replied. "But that's a secondary priority."

Paul Ridge, who sat next to Tori, perked up at that. She had been quickly introduced to him on the deck of the *Kodiak*, just before they had climbed into the helicopter, and thought he seemed interesting. Ridge also radiated a fear and anxiety that Tori considered totally appropriate. No matter what he'd been told—or what any of them had been told—they couldn't imagine what they had gotten themselves into. Ridge knew enough to be afraid of the unknown.

"We're all secondary priorities," Ridge said, sharing a nervous smile. "The existence of these things creates so many questions that deserve answers, but pest control is job one, right, Alena?"

Dr. Boudreau nodded. "Unfortunately. But don't worry, Paul. I'll give you what time I can."

Ridge turned to look out the window at the island as the helicopter flew lower. "Not nearly enough time."

"I don't get what's so fascinating about this place. What makes it so different?" Tori asked.

Ridge, a handsome man to begin with, became even more so as soon as the topic turned to his chosen science. "On the surface, not much. Most Caribbean islands are volcanic or part of a system created by volcanic activity. The ridges and protrusions of black rock are volcanic, a combination of basalt and andesite. Lava flows formed the ridges when they cooled, and the rocks you see jutting out of the sand or the water are . . . well, chunks that were literally shot from the volcano during an eruption.

"But the samples that David has shown me also have trace elements that make the geology here quite different from the typical volcanic formations. There's a hydrologic chemistry at work that must be a factor related to the bio-forms—the sirens, I guess we're calling them—making the fissures and caves in the island's foundations habitable for them."

Tori smiled. "I think I only got about half of that."

Ridge began to reply, but Dr. Boudreau interrupted.

"You won't have time for the other half, Tori. I'm afraid I need you now. We're going to make several passes over the island and I want you to point out the locations of any caves you remember, including the grotto you talked about—"

"The sweep team must have found it by now," Josh cut in. "They've been on the island an hour or more."

Alena Boudreau nodded. "They're fairly certain they have, but I want to be sure we're in the right place and there isn't another similar location." She looked back to Tori. "Dr. Ridge is going to mark everything on a chart. If you have any observations, definitely share them. Any detail could be important in ways none of us understand as yet."

As she spoke, Ridge opened a sleek silver laptop and, with a touch of a button, pulled up a map he had already made of the island. The shape did not match entirely—apparently it was based on information the combined Navy/Coast Guard sweep team had gathered so far—but now Ridge would get to work refining it, starting with whatever Tori could tell him.

For the next quarter hour they circled the island and she shared what she remembered of the spots she had seen caves or any other protrusions of that black rock, including those that seemed to have split open the small mountain at the island's center—what had once been an active volcano but now lay dormant save for the traces of steam that lingered above those openings. If the others who had been on the island with her—Bone and Kevonne and Pang—had been alive, they could have provided much more information. Tori had not even set foot on the half of the island they had explored.

"What about the two bodies you and Captain Rio found yesterday?" Dr. Boudreau asked, her tone neutral. "The men from the *Mariposa*? Can you show us where they had been left?"

Tori frowned. "Why? Didn't you find them?"

"No. I'm afraid we didn't."

Frigid fingers seemed to trace along her spine and she shivered. "You mean they took the bodies away?"

Josh leaned forward, catching her eye, making her focus on him. "Hey. It's okay. The tide could have moved them."

Tori shook her head. "No. It was high tide when we found them, or near enough. They were well above the tide line. And those guys had been dead since at least the night before, so the sirens didn't take them just to . . . to eat. They wanted us to find the bodies yesterday, maybe to freak us out or confuse us or whatever. But then last night, when they attacked us, the bodies had served their purpose, so *then* they took them."

"Come on, Tori," Josh said. "These things are animals. They're primitive. They're not smart enough to want to just mess with your head."

"How do you know?" she demanded.

Josh had no reply to that. Neither did Dr. Boudreau, and that scared her most of all.

-73--

David Boudreau couldn't think of a damn thing to say.

He stood in the open hatchway, pipes hissing steam so quietly it almost sounded like they were breathing, just over his shoulder. Lieutenant Stone and his strike team had cleared the room, leaving one sailor—a tall, formidable woman whose eyes were emotionless behind her gas mask—to watch over them. Turcotte, O'Connell, and Voss stood in respectful silence around the pile of bones as though they were at a graveside funeral, and in some ways that was exactly what it was. No trace had yet been found of the *Antoinette*'s crew except for spatters and puddles of blood in various spots around the ship. But these bones came with shreds of clothing, bits of hair stuck to the skulls, and among them were at least two guns. Turcotte had said he suspected they would find others as well.

"It's a warning," Rachael Voss said, staring at the bones of her dead colleagues—members of Turcotte's Counter-Terrorism squad.

"Is it?" O'Connell asked. " 'Cause it seems to me it's more a big 'fuck you' than anything else."

"Jesus," Turcotte whispered, raising a hand to his forehead as he turned away. "Jesus Christ."

David had gotten a close look at the bones when they had first been led into the junction area, but he had retreated to a corner to give the FBI agents space to move and to grieve. Now he watched them and wondered if he should have left the room entirely, though it seemed too late now. The container ship creaked and hissed and pinged, and David felt claustrophobic, as though the freighter had begun to constrict around them. No matter what the FBI had wanted, he now regretted having brought these three on board, and part of him wished he had not come himself.

No matter how thick the metal hull of the *Antoinette* might be, he did not feel safe. If he had voiced his fears, others might have labeled them irrational. But they had not encountered the creatures up close before, and they did not wake in the dark with his nightmares. The last time Alena had led a DARPA team into one of these creatures' habitats, David had been an unofficial member of the expedition. At seventeen, he had already accomplished more than most other members of her team and Alena had been grooming him for a leadership position. But, though he pleaded with her, she refused to let him come ashore on the South Pacific island where the creatures nested.

Alena and her colleagues thought they had learned from their first encounter with the creatures in 1967. They kept all ships at a safe distance overnight, and even during the day would not allow even the largest vessels nearer than half a mile from shore. The *Gryphon,* an elegant refurbished schooner that Alena used as a research vessel, floated a full mile from the island, and David had been left behind with the *Gryphon*'s crew and half a dozen scientists, most of them people David had known all of his life.

Safely out of range.

Or so they'd thought until the things began to batter at the hull, splintering wooden beams, and the water started to rush in. And with the water, the monsters came. Even with the sun still shining outside, the creatures invaded the ship. The screams still echoed in David's head, even now, and the desperate cries of his dying friends lingered. Only a handful of those on board made it to the deck as the *Gryphon* took on water. The things would not come out into the sunlight, but with the ship listing, sinking, it would not be too long before they were all down in the dark together.

It had taken a handful of minutes for one of the operation's other ships, a metal-hulled military vessel, to come alongside and execute a rescue. Only David and two members of the *Gryphon*'s crew had survived. The creatures had killed the rest, and the schooner vanished under the waves. In his nightmares, David sometimes hung from a rescue line, white shapes flashing in the water below, and saw his own pale, dead features staring back up at him.

There were no wooden-hulled vessels on the current operation.

Yet that did not make David feel safe. Out here, with the things so close, he could never feel safe. Not with the sun shining, and no matter how far they kept offshore. The only way for him to ever feel safe, he knew, would be to destroy them all.

The sailor outside the door stepped in, knocking on the frame. "Dr. Boudreau. Lieutenant Stone says you're to come with me. We've found them."

The FBI agents all turned at once. Turcotte lifted his weapon and led the way. David nodded to him and then fell in behind them as they followed the female sailor through a narrow corridor, up a small flight of metal stairs, and down the other side. He knew he ought to be leading. Without Alena around, he had authority over all of these people. But David believed in letting people do their jobs without interfering—especially when those people were carrying guns and grudges.

Lieutenant Stone waited for them just inside a boiler room. David quick-counted eight other sailors, and every single one of them had an assault rifle raised and pointed at the darkness deeper into the room. If David had thought the pipes elsewhere in the ship breathed, then these must have been the *Antoinette*'s lungs. Mist from the gas canisters hazed the air and the only illumination came from amber emergency lights spaced at intervals along the ceiling.

Stone tapped his gas mask, indicating that they should switch back over to channel three—which they had left so that their conversation about the dead FBI agents would be private.

"The creatures are alive, but very much out of commission," the lieutenant said. "Some movement, but we're guessing it's involuntary."

"That could be a dangerous guess," Agent Voss said.

Stone shook his head. "If they were playing possum, they'd have attacked by now. Dr. Boudreau, my team is bagging one now. Are you still planning to use one of the containers for transport?"

David felt breathless and was tempted to take off his mask. He needed to be outside, up on deck, to breathe fresh air. But more than that, he needed to *see*.

"Yes," he said, moving forward, not even looking at Lieutenant Stone anymore. "Captain Siebalt's confirmed that one of the *Hillstrom*'s choppers will be able to transport it ship to ship."

He kept walking. Two of the sailors turned toward him in apparent alarm, raising the barrels of their weapons toward the ceiling to avoid shooting him.

"Hang on," Stone said, blocking his path. "What are you doing?"

David could feel them all looking at him then—the three FBI agents as well as the armed men and women under Stone's command.

"You said they were unconscious."

"As far as we can tell," Stone hedged.

"I want to see them, Lieutenant."

"And you'll get your chance when we get one of them into a lab on the *Hillstrom*. Until then, I have my orders, Doctor."

David spent most of his life on a happily even keel. Now

anger flared in him. How long had he studied the cases from Indonesia and the South Pacific? How long had he theorized the existence of other such islands and searched for proof? He wanted answers, and he needed to see these things up close.

"Stand down, Lieutenant Stone. You take your orders from Captain Siebalt, and right now, he takes his orders from the DOD. So get out of my way."

Even through the gas mask's plastic face screen, David saw how much he had pissed off Stone, and he understood why. Speaking that way to the man in front of his team had been a terrible idea, but David had only one concern right now and it wasn't mollifying Stone's hurt feelings.

"Yes, sir," the lieutenant said in icy tones, stepping aside.

David strode forward, moving between two rows of boilers until he saw another sailor, back to him, weapon aimed at something on the ground.

"Yerardi, let Dr. Boudreau pass," Lieutenant Stone called.

The sailor, Yerardi, glanced over his shoulder, spotted David, and slid out of the way. David silently thanked him, but his focus remained on the amber darkness ahead. Other sailors, masks strapped to their faces, had taken up similar positions in and around several of the boilers, aiming weapons at pale figures whose flesh gleamed like mother-of-pearl in the weird emergency light.

Remarkable. How many thousands of years had it taken for these things to evolve? How long had they remained hibernating in the guts of volcanoes before something—time or climate change, weather or earth tremor—had set them free? They were amphibious creatures, which explained the evolution of arms and hands in spite of their otherwise marine attributes. But how had they survived so long? Had these particular creatures lived for thousands of years, or had they been spawning down there in the subterranean volcanic chambers all this time?

They might well represent the greatest scientific find in centuries. Yet whatever research David might do, whatever discoveries he might make, could only be shared with the Department of Defense as they tried to figure out whether they could benefit from further knowledge of the creatures. The irony pained him deeply.

Two sailors hefted what looked to be a black body bag off the floor and started shuffling toward him. David stepped out of the way to let them pass, well aware of the burden they carried, wondering if it would remain unconscious long enough for them to lock it in one of the massive steel containers up on the deck.

He crouched to get a closer look at the siren nearest Yerardi. The suckers all over the thing's hands and serpentine lower body pouted open and shut like tiny mouths, searching for sustenance. David wondered if that had anything to do with how they breathed, but he knew those questions were best left to Dr. Ernst.

"Amazing," he whispered.

With a last glance at the creatures sprawled on the floor and the masked sailors standing watch over them, he rose and turned to follow the strange procession. Lieutenant Stone walked beside the men carrying the body bag. When their grotesque little parade reached the eight sailors standing guard at the front of the boiler room and the three agitated FBI agents, Stone turned to one of the sailors.

"Bring it up to Corriveau. He's got a container prepped," the lieutenant said.

The sailor shouldered his weapon and saluted. "Yes, sir."

"What about the others, Lieutenant?" asked another sailor, a bald man with charcoal-black skin. "Do we seal them in?"

Stone glanced at David. "What do you say, Dr. Boudreau? I know my orders. Do I get to carry them out?"

His tone dripped sarcasm, but the question lingered for a moment. David looked at Turcotte, then at Voss and O'Connell, before turning back to Lieutenant Stone.

"Are the charges set?"

"Yes, sir," Stone replied with a nod. "Throughout the accommodations block and all along the hull. She won't just sink, Doctor. She'll be wreckage and debris."

"Wait, what the hell are you—" Voss began.

David cut her off. "Good. I want it all underwater, just in case anyone ever comes looking."

"And the rest of the creatures?"

"Burn them," David said.

Lieutenant Stone gestured to his team. "You heard the man. Get to work."

"Hang on a second!" O'Connell shouted. The FBI agent grabbed David's arm. "Those are our guys back there, nothing but bones. You owe us our shot at this. You said we'd have time to go through the ship and try to come up with information that would help our case against Viscaya! You said we'd have time."

"You do have time," David said, looking from O'Connell to Voss to Turcotte, whose face still wore the expression of mixed sorrow and disgust that he'd had while standing over the bones of his dead agents. "You've got an hour to do all the searching you want. After that, we blow it apart. I don't want to leave them anywhere to run when things get hot on the island."

Voss watched David walk away, hating him a little. He had cooperated just enough to tell the DOD that he had accommodated the FBI's requests, but no more. They were going to set fire to the sirens down in the boiler room. It wasn't her area, but she had a feeling that might wreak serious havoc. Would the boilers explode? She had no idea.

"Let's go," she said, turning to Turcotte and O'Connell.

O'Connell took a step forward but faltered when Turcotte did not do the same. The eight sailors at the front of the boiler room followed Stone and the two men carrying the body bag, and David left in their wake. In moments, they'd be dousing the sirens' bodies with some kind of flame accelerant and then it would become insufferably hot in here.

"What's going on, Agent Turcotte?" Voss asked.

"Ed, let's go," O'Connell added. "We don't have a lot of time."

"We should at least search the captain's quarters and the wheelhouse before we give it all up," Voss went on.

Turcotte gave a hollow laugh. "Forget it, Rachael. Our part in this thing is over."

Turcotte went out through the metal hatchway. O'Connell

seemed pissed, but he followed. A moment later, after hearing a great deal of liquid sloshing toward the forward section of the boiler room, there came a great gasp of rising flames and the bright orange light of a blaze.

The burning sirens began to scream, the sound clawing at her eardrums. Voss froze, waiting to hear gunshots or the shouts of sailors under attack, but neither followed. With the anguished cry of dying monsters at her back, she sped from the room, wishing she had gone with Josh, wishing that she had never heard of Viscaya shipping or the Rio brothers.

Much as she hated to acknowledge it, Turcotte had been right. They were done here.

-74--

Alena Boudreau stood amidst the jagged rubble at the front of the grotto, where the surf roared in and out, and tried to get a sense of what the grotto had looked like prior to the collapse of its outer wall. At this corner of the island, a secondary volcano mouth had opened, creating the craterlike bowl. The lava outflow must have been massive, building up a small, jagged hill at the shore. Over the years, the lashing of waves had caused slabs of rock to break off and slide into the surf like the calving of an iceberg. What they now saw as a grotto had once been a black volcanic bowl. Over time, more and more of the mountain of volcanic rock had broken off and tumbled into the water, until the side of the bowl had collapsed, slicing an entrance into the chamber within. The tides had continued that work, carving and smoothing the opening and creating the grotto.

Or so it seemed. Ridge had confirmed within minutes of their arrival that ordinary erosion had not caused the side of the bowl to give way. A hurricane might have done the damage, but he had warned her that a volcanic tremor might have been the culprit, and that worried her. Aside from the steam that rose from various vents and caves and drifted up in some spots that seemed nothing but thick vegetation, the island gave every sign of being dormant. But Ridge would have to be the judge of that.

Alena took another step back, watching her team. Men and women from the *Hillstrom* worked quickly and efficiently. Several sailors were busy photographing every angle of the grotto. Others dredged human skulls and other bones from among the shells in the narrow grotto opening. Another team, under the command of Lieutenant Commander Cornelius Sykes—a serious man Alena had instantly warmed to—lined the top rim of the grotto and manned the lines from which others hung into the darkness below.

The descent team had gone to work immediately upon her arrival, planting explosives around the inner walls of the bowl, deep in the chamber, and the walls of the grotto. She liked working with experts, and relied upon Sykes's assertion that his explosives man knew what he was doing. Ridge had examined the geology and agreed that the deep placement of explosives, along with others higher up on the walls, would bring the whole thing down upon itself, filling the hole and closing the grotto off from the ocean for years. According to Ridge, it might be centuries before erosion brought the ocean back in—if ever.

It wasn't a perfect solution, but it would do.

"Dr. Boudreau, take a look at this," Ridge said.

She turned to find him crouched, staring at a chunk of volcanic rock among the rubble. The slab was inscribed with symbols and runic-style carvings unlike anything she had ever encountered before, and she bent slightly to study it more closely.

"What do you make of it?" Ridge asked.

"You're the geologist," she replied, straightening up. "What do *you* make of it?"

He uttered a soft laugh. "I study rocks, doesn't make me an anthropologist."

"I hired you, Paul, remember? I know what's on your

resume. You've studied tile mosaics in Pompeii and everything from Mayan ruins to hieroglyphics."

"Yes, but all from a geological perspective, mostly in helping to date the writings or art in question. I'm no expert on
the societies that made them." Ridge crouched and traced his
fingers over the symbols. "Did you find anything like this
in the other two habitats where you've located these things?"

Alena shook her head. "No. Plenty of evidence that humans had died on those two islands, but no sign that any had
ever lived there."

Ridge remained in a crouch but he had fallen silent. From
the way he held his head, cocked slightly to one side, she recognized that he was deep in contemplation. But Dr. Ridge
tended to work things out aloud, and his silence troubled her.

"What is it, Paul?"

He looked up at her, shielding his eyes from the sun. "Why
are you so sure that people did this?"

Alena stared at him, staggered by the suggestion. Could
the sirens have engraved these symbols in the black stone?
For several seconds, she let the question linger, but then the
arguments began cascading through her mind.

"The alternative is impossible," she began.

Ridge stood and glanced up into the grotto, then turned
toward her again. "Impossible?"

She nodded, relenting. "All right, highly improbable, then.
Think about what I just told you. We discovered no writings,
no engravings of any kind on either of the other two islands
where I've encountered these things. But more than that,
nothing I've seen so far has indicated that they have any kind
of culture. They don't build, or create anything resembling
society as far as we can tell. Humans are the only species on
Earth with written language, and it's a huge leap to think
these things are that developed. They seem utterly savage,
and we've never seen them use tools of any kind."

"But?" Ridge persisted.

Alena bit her lip for a second, studying the engraved stone.
"But these writings may well be ancient, and we have no way
of knowing what they were like a couple thousand years
ago."

Ridge nodded. "Yeah, but you're probably right."

"Almost certainly."

"Good. For some reason, I'm really spooked by the idea of them being able to write," Ridge said. "So, back to my question. What do you make of it?"

Alena looked up at the grotto. "Possibly a burial chamber, but there's no way to tell. The engravings could be story art, like cave paintings, though that doesn't feel right to me. Without more research and at least some translation, we can't know."

"What about worship?" Ridge asked.

"The thought had occurred to me," Alena replied. "If people did live here alongside the sirens at some point, they wouldn't be the first predators to be worshipped by the humans they preyed on."

"A lovely thought," Ridge said.

Alena smiled. "Hey, you asked."

"And on that note, I've got to get back topside. You coming? I've got a lot to show you."

Alena frowned. "A lot of what?"

Ridge gestured at the rock. "There's plenty more where this came from."

Alena took that in, then turned to one of the sailors taking pictures. "I want this rock."

The man, a heavily muscled Latino with bright, intelligent eyes, turned his camera toward the carvings she had been looking at.

"No, not a photo," she said. "I want the rock itself. Please have it brought back to the *Hillstrom*."

The sailor hesitated, bulky camera in his hands reminding Alena of crime scene photographers.

"I know it's not your assignment," she told him, "and I'm not making it your assignment. But I am tasking you with making certain that it gets done. Handle it for me, please."

Alena spoke to him politely and as charmingly as possible, but she also made sure that he knew that it wasn't a request.

"Yes, ma'am."

Satisfied, she nodded to Ridge, and the two of them started

to pick their way across the rockfall toward the other side of the grotto as the low surf rolled in around them. In the clear blue water, she would have seen any sign of movement, and the creatures would not come into the shallows while the sun still shone. Still, as they crossed, she treaded carefully on the rocks.

"Watch your step," she warned Ridge.

"Oh, I'm watching. No way am I putting even a toe in."

It couldn't have been any later than three p.m., so night was still hours away, but as they moved into the cooler shadow of the rock face, the presence of darkness unnerved her. The last time she had encountered these things—they had called them Bio-Form CMA-2 then, the CMA standing for Carnivorous Marine Amphibian—the sirens had left skeletons arrayed on the sandy shore of a South Pacific island as if to frighten people away. Some of those skeletons had been her friends, taken the day before, right out through the wooden hull of their research ship—an attack that young David had barely survived. Bio-Form CMA-2 had stripped the flesh and muscle from their bones in a single night.

These things—the ones the people from the *Antoinette* had christened "sirens"—would be Bio-Form CMA-3. She wondered how long they had been here, reproducing in the warren of watery caves in the subterranean heart of the island, until the outer wall of the chamber collapsed and freed them to spill out into the ocean. She could not believe that any single generation of a species could survive thousands of years, though David had suggested that volcanic activity might have woken them from some hibernating slumber.

Not that it mattered much to her how they managed to be alive. Alena wanted the sirens dead. If she could preserve one for study, and the Department of Defense could intuit or reverse engineer some deadly, controllable biowar effort from the creatures, that would be on their heads. For her own part, she knew she had to exterminate the things, to keep anyone else from dying like Harry Oliver and the others had, all those years ago.

David, though, wanted them dead for an entirely different

reason. Ever since his first glimpse of Bio-Form CMA-2, he had suffered from terrible recurring nightmares of drowning, during which he felt the presence of the things in the water. In his dreams he never saw them, but knew they were nearby, about to tear into him, and in those dreams he would hope to die from drowning before they touched him.

"This way," Ridge said. "You need a hand?"

Alena glanced up the steep, rough slope that would take her to the top rim of the grotto, where she spotted Tori Austin and Agent Hart watching her team at work.

"I'll race you," she said, not knowing whether to be pleased that Ridge thought her fit enough to make the climb, or to grumble about having to make it.

You can decide when you get to the top, she told herself, *depending on how your knees hold out.*

But her knees were just fine, and they made the climb in a handful of minutes. Tori and Agent Hart greeted them at the top, and then Alena turned to Ridge.

"All right," she said. "What've you got?"

Ridge stepped right up to the edge of the rim—which, here, sloped upward toward the back wall of the bowl—and gestured below. Alena followed his lead and noted with surprise that crude steps led downward. Once they might have been more substantial, before time and the elements had worn them away. The steps led down into the bowl.

And it truly was a bowl, sloping inward toward the center. The front of the grotto, where the oceanward wall of the chamber had collapsed, was only about twenty feet across. But that represented merely the opening in the bowl. The bowl itself stretched a good eighty feet from side to side. Twenty feet down from the rim, the slope began. But at its center—at the bottom of the bowl—there was only open space. A fifty-foot-wide drop into darkness, because far below the bowl itself was the yawning mouth of a massive cave.

Ridge pointed toward the grotto opening, where the waves rolled in and out.

"Notice the water level there," he said. "The tide's coming

in slowly, and right now the surf is fighting an uphill battle to get into the sub-chamber."

"The cave," Alena corrected.

Ridge nodded. "Exactly. It rolls up into the grotto, then back out. But when the tide gets higher, the water reaches the mouth of the cave and pours into it. Not long ago, let's say less than a century, but maybe even less than that, the water had no way of getting in or out. There was this upper bowl, and then the lower cave, the sub-chamber."

Alena looked at him. "We've established all this, Paul."

He smiled. Ridge did not smile often. He started carefully down the worn steps toward the bowl below and waved for her to follow. Alena hesitated. She trusted her balance and her own feet, but not those stairs.

"I've already been down here," Ridge reassured her. "Just watch your step and you'll be fine."

Warily, Alena started down. She risked a glance at the Navy personnel who had set up on the bottom shelf of the bowl. They had sunk anchors into the rock and were playing out ropes for the descent team, who had gone over the edge and lowered themselves partially into the sub-chamber— down in the dark where the sirens would be waiting out the sun—and it struck her how much courage that had to have taken.

Of course, none of them had ever seen the creatures.

But Tori and Agent Hart had. Alena glanced up at the rim and saw that they were not following her and Ridge down to the bowl.

"You two aren't coming?" she asked.

Tori shook her head. "I got you here. I don't need to get any closer."

Alena smiled. "I don't blame you."

As she picked her way carefully down those rough-hewn stairs, she let the fingers of her left hand trail on the inner wall of the bowl to steady her. Ridge reached the last step and paused to wait for her on the shelf of black, sloping rock that formed the bottom of the bowl. Movement off to her right caught her eye and she glanced over to see Lieutenant

Commander Sykes working his way around. The powerfully built officer moved purposefully back and forth from the sailors who were planting charges on the walls of the bowl to those who were at the edge of the shelf, anchoring the members of the descent team.

Sykes had a cool efficiency that she admired, not only doing his own job but making sure everyone else knew how to do theirs, pausing to make a quiet recommendation or adjustment here and there. In that fashion, he made his way around the open hole at the center of the bowl, so that by the time Alena reached the last step, Sykes had arrived at a spot perhaps a dozen feet away, where he checked the safety of several black ropes that vanished over the edge. Down below, the descent team would be setting other charges, and a kind of calm swept over Alena. With Sykes there, and the speed of the sailors working in the bowl and the sub-chamber below, they'd be out of the grotto in three-quarters of an hour at most. By then, many of the island's other caves would also have been lined with explosives.

This would work. A grim satisfaction took hold of her as she followed Ridge along the inner wall.

"I expected to find more of the writing on these walls," Ridge said, "but I confess I'm amazed by the extent."

At first glance, Alena had trouble making out much detail thanks to the angle of the sun, but when she shifted position, cutting the glare, she understood why Ridge had made her climb the hill and risk the stairs into the bowl. Whatever the language of the island's original inhabitants, it had been carved into an incredible expanse of glassy black rock at least fifteen feet high, and in apparent panels six to eight feet wide that stretched into the shadows at the rear of the bowl, and perhaps even around to the other side. There were images as well, and—though absent of any Egyptian influence—they communicated thoughts almost as well as hieroglyphics. Perhaps, after some study, they would prove even more eloquent than the Egyptian picture-writing.

"Alena?" Ridge prodded, awaiting her reaction.

She unclipped the two-way radio from her belt. "Lieutenant

Commander Sykes—" she began, before remembering that the officer was right behind her. She turned to see him glancing down at his own radio, then up at her. A moment's irritation creased the corners of his eyes, but then he must have seen something in her face, for he strode quickly over to join them.

"What is it, Doctor?" Sykes asked as he approached.

"The photographers who are documenting this," Alena said, gesturing to the wall. "I need them all up here on the bowl, and right now. I want pictures of every mark on these walls that nature didn't put here."

Sykes started to balk. "Is that really—"

Alena shot him a hard look—one that brought him up short. "This is the third time in my life I've encountered creatures like this, and I don't have any better idea of their history than I did the first time. What's on these walls could give us clues to finding other habitats, if they have any, and to exterminating them for good. For science, for history, and for national security, I need a record of all of this. And since we're going to blow it all to hell in a couple of hours—"

"I get it," Sykes said, holding up a hand in surrender. "Sorry, Dr. Boudreau. I wasn't thinking."

He unclipped his own radio and started barking orders. His gaze was fixed on a point behind her, and Alena turned to see that curiosity had gotten the better of Tori and Agent Hart, who were working their way down the stairs and trying to get a glimpse of what Ridge had called her up to see.

Alena turned to Ridge. "Paul, I want rubbings of as much of this as you can get before we have to dust off."

He nodded but did not turn, his focus entirely on the wall markings. "You got it."

The explosion shook the entire grotto, from sub-chamber up through the bowl to the rim. The stone shelf bucked beneath Alena, knocking her off her feet, and she let out a scream as the black rock splintered and gave way beneath her. A cloud of dust billowed up through the old volcano's throat and though the blast had muffled her hearing, the shouts and curses reached her even as she fell in a tangle of limbs and stone, flailing for a ledge that had been part of the broken shelf.

She held her breath as she fell, and a tiny, incoherent prayer filled her mind.

Then she hit the water and plunged into darkness, and the real fear began.

-75--

In the launch that carried her from the Coast Guard ship *Kodiak* to the USS *Hillstrom,* Angie Tyree stayed in the enclosed cabin behind the wheelhouse. The launch wasn't much bigger than the lifeboat that had saved her, but it sat higher on the water and must have had a deeper draft. Agent Plausky, who had been as kind to her as she supposed she could expect, watched her from the door that led to the aft deck, but Angie did not want to budge from the bench where she sat.

Still, she had a question. She had caught a glimpse of the *Antoinette* in the distance just before Plausky had taken her below to get her on board the launch.

"All of these ships are moving away from the island," she said. "What about the people you've sent ashore?"

Plausky glanced back toward the *Kodiak,* as though he could see right through it to the *Antoinette* and the island on the other side.

"The helicopters will bring them back. A half mile or so isn't going to cause any problems."

"So why pull back?" Angie asked.

"We're not getting distance from the island," the FBI agent explained. "We're retreating from the *Antoinette.*"

A shiver ran through Angie. "Why? Didn't you send people over there to kill the ones on board?"

Plausky nodded. "Yeah. And I guess they did the job. But

as long as the *Antoinette*'s there, it's going to be a safe haven for them. And if we left it there, it might draw undue attention. Someone might see it and want to explore the ship, and then the island. Probably a lot of salvage on board, not to mention inside the containers themselves. Better for everyone if it just goes away, like the wrecks Dr. Boudreau has the Navy and Coast Guard out there burning."

"You're going to burn it?" Angie asked.

"No. They're going to blow it up."

She stared at him, surprised to find herself sad at the idea of the *Antoinette*'s destruction. Not that the ship had ever been home, but it was a place for her to belong, and she doubted she would ever find such a place again.

The boat rocked under her and she hugged herself tightly. The conversation with Plausky helped keep her distracted, which was good. Sunlight or no, she couldn't help but think what might be swimming right beneath the launch. Everyone seemed to think the sirens didn't come this far from the island, but she didn't want to bet her life on it.

Through a side window she could just make out the Navy ship ahead and she let out a calming breath. Just three steps now. Get onto the *Hillstrom,* then onto the chopper, and fly back to St. Croix. Whatever they wanted after that, wherever they let her go, at least she would be away from here.

As if summoned by her anticipation, a low buzz that had been nagging at the edges of her hearing grew into a sudden roar, and she angled her head to peer into the sky above the launch. After today, she would always welcome the sound of a helicopter, but what she glimpsed as she looked up made her draw back in confusion.

"What the hell is that?" she asked. "Is it . . . wait . . ."

The helicopter passed above, headed for the deck of the enormous Navy ship. A long metal box hung on chains below the chopper, paint chipped and slightly rusted—one of the containers from the *Antoinette.*

"Agent Plausky," she said, hearing the tremor in her voice, "why is the Navy taking a container off my ship?"

The FBI agent came into the cabin and over to the bench where she now knelt. He bent over to look out, watching with her as the chopper took up a position above the *Hill-strom* and began to maneuver the container into place.

"One of the operation's goals is to have a creature for study. It seems a little extreme, but I guess they figured to keep it out of the sun and make sure it had no chance to escape, transporting it in a locked steel box made more sense than trying to chain it up."

The words hit her like blows. Angie flinched with each one, but Plausky seemed to barely notice. Only when she began to shake her head and slide down to the floor of the launch did he turn toward her.

"Alive?" Angie asked. "They're bringing one on board *alive*?"

Understanding lit his eyes. "Yeah. They are. But, listen, there are lots of guys with guns on that ship. And I'm not going to let anything happen to you. I'll get you on that helicopter and you get to leave."

"No," she said, shaking her head, feeling herself falling apart. "I can't . . . I'm not getting on board with one of those things."

Plausky crouched beside her. "Yeah, you are. Yes, Angie, just . . . Ssshhh, just listen. The sun's still shining. It's all right. Listen, all you wanted was to get out of here, and this is your shot at that. You'll be fine."

Frozen, she stared up at the window from where she'd landed on the floor. The sound of the chopper rotors filled her ears. She couldn't see the helicopter or the container or even the Navy ship, not from this angle.

Angie Tyree closed her eyes and tried to think of home, of the place where she'd been a little girl. But in the darkness inside her own mind, the sirens waited, and so she forced herself to keep her eyes open. And, silently, she prayed.

76

Special Agent Tim Nadeau had no love for profanity, but he cursed a blue streak as he picked himself up off the rocks in front of the grotto mouth, the surf rolling up to soak through his shoes and pants legs before he could rise. He'd torn a hole in the knee and blood had begun to soak into the fabric. When he'd thrown out his hands to catch himself, he'd scraped skin off his left palm and ended up hitting his head on a rock anyway. Now he felt the lump rising and winced at the tenderness of it, his fingers coming away streaked with red.

"What the fuck?" he whispered.

For those few seconds, the rest of the world had retreated. Now, like throwing a switch, the rest of his senses opened up and reality rushed in. He heard voices shouting in panic and looked up. That simple movement nearly made him lose his balance, and he understood that he had a concussion. But he understood other things as well.

The left side of the bowl had given way. One of the descent team, planting explosives on the walls of the sub-chamber, had screwed up royally and a charge had detonated. Whoever had fucked it up, it no longer mattered. The Navy would have a hard time finding enough pieces of him to put in a box for a funeral. But the running and shouting up on the rim—people were being careful not to get too close now that some of it had sheared off and fallen in—told him that the guy who'd exploded was the least of their concerns.

Nadeau grabbed his radio. "Josh, it's Tim. Come in."

Static hiss. No answer. "Agent Hart, this is Nadeau, do you read?"

Off balance, Nadeau started to scramble across the rocks toward the nearest sailor—a blond kid who looked completely frantic.

"Hey!" he shouted, and the sailor twisted toward him. "Any casualties?"

The sailor looked mystified, so Nadeau passed him, working his way over to a severe-looking dark-haired woman wearing an ensign's bars. She had a small comm unit tucked into her ear, the cord dangling past her cheek.

"What's the story?" Nadeau asked. "Ensign! I'm talking to you! Did we lose anyone?"

The woman turned to him, her eyes haunted, and threw a hand up toward the ruined bowl. "Take a look! What the hell do you think?"

Steadying himself, Nadeau put a hand up to the bloody lump on his skull, his head throbbing painfully. "You can do better than that."

The ensign shook her head. "Christ. Sorry, come with me."

As they climbed the steep, rough hill beside the grotto, she started talking. "At least one casualty—whoever set off that charge—but they're trying to figure out who it is. When the thing gave way, seven of my shipmates went with it, including Lieutenant Commander Sykes. Dr. Boudreau fell into the hole, too, along with the geologist she had with her."

"What about Agent Hart?"

The ensign gave him a blank look.

"The other FBI agent who was here? With his arm in a sling? He had the woman from the *Antoinette* with him?"

But the ensign's only reply was a shrug of apology.

Nadeau swore under his breath and kept climbing. When they reached the rim of what had once been the bowl, his heart sank. A third of the stone shelf that had made up the bottom of the bowl had given way, crumbling into the dark chamber far below. There was no sign of Josh and Tori, and he knew they must have fallen as well. Nadeau saw sailors moving, lowering lights into the darkness, and members of the descent team abandoning the explosives they had set on the walls below to work their way lower on their ropes, calling into the void, then pausing to listen.

Echoes were their only reply.

77

Voss stood in a cluster of Coast Guard officers and seamen on the deck of the *Kodiak* and watched as Lieutenant Stone switched on the detonator, under the watchful eyes of David Boudreau. A shuddery anger rattled through her with every breath and she glanced over at Ed Turcotte, who stood slightly apart from the rest of them, his eyes downcast.

"Asshole," she muttered.

David raised an eyebrow and gave her a sidelong glance, but Voss pressed her mouth shut and didn't say another word. She pushed away from the railing and threaded her way through the seamen, who separated to give her an exit.

"You don't have any fight left in you at all, huh?" she said, hands balled at her sides. Voss hadn't thrown a punch in a while and didn't intend to start today, but her fists ached.

Turcotte looked up. "Excuse me, Agent?"

"You heard me, Ed."

"Oh, it's Ed now, is it? We're friends?" Voss laughed. "Not fucking likely."

"I'm heartbroken."

"We had an hour, you son of a bitch!" she snapped, raising her voice to be heard above the growing roar of the Navy helicopter that even now moved toward the *Hillstrom,* long rusty container swaying on chains beneath it. The sight made her sick.

"An hour for what? What would have been the point?" Turcotte asked with a hollow laugh.

"The point? Do you have any idea how much time my squad put into this case? I almost lost my partner—"

Turcotte jabbed a finger at her. "Because you put him in jeopardy!"

Voss slapped the hand away. "Fuck you!" she shouted over

the helicopter's noise. "You think anyone could have seen this coming? The whole case is slipping through our fingers, but we had a chance to search Rio's ship, maybe salvage *something* to help us take down Viscaya, and you wouldn't even let us look! It's dereliction of duty, Ed. You turned your back on the job!"

With a sneer, he shook his head. "You kill me, Rachael. You're going to write me up? The DOD will eat you alive. Don't you get it? They're going to make this whole thing vanish! Stuck in a black box and put away, like it never happened. What evidence could we have found that they would have let us use? Nothing! You want Viscaya, you'll have to do it the hard way. And if you want to come at me, by all means, try your luck. But nobody's going to let you breathe a word about the *Antoinette* or this island or anything about this case, so you might want to think twice about what happens if they decide your little grudge against me is bad for national security."

She glared at him, but Turcotte turned and stared out across the blue water. They were nearly a mile out from the *Antoinette* now, a safe distance, and from here the island seemed so small and ordinary and unthreatening that the entire scene became unreal.

"Damn it," she whispered, dropping her gaze and staring at the small waves lapping against the side of the *Kodiak,* down below. "Damn you all."

The roar of the helicopter had diminished. By now, they'd be putting that container down on the deck of the *Hillstrom*. They'd brought the devil on board, and she was just glad Alena Boudreau had chosen the Navy ship as her base. Voss didn't want to be anywhere near one of those things.

The *Antoinette* detonated in three explosions, one on top of the next, a staccato eruption out on the open sea. Voss looked up to see fire and debris raining down around the swiftly sinking, ravaged remains of the container ship. It slid into the water in smoking pieces, all of its crimes and dark secrets engulfed by the blue Caribbean.

The thunder of the *Antoinette*'s destruction was still echoing in her ears when she heard someone shouting her name.

Voss and Turcotte turned as one to see McIlveen hurtling along the Coast Guard ship's deck toward them, with Dan O'Connell hustling along in his wake. Mac looked grim, but it was the shock on O'Connell's pale, drawn features that told her something awful had happened.

Off to her right, Lieutenant Stone had started to shout into his comm, and David Boudreau had turned deathly pale.

Something had gone wrong on the island.

Voss hung her head, running a hand through her hair.

"Josh," she whispered, or thought she did. Maybe she had only thought his name, along with the one other thing that swam up into her mind.

What now?

-78--

Josh broke the surface choking, coughing up water, and gasped for air. Shafts of sunlight made shining columns in the dark chamber, plenty of light to see by, and maybe enough to survive by; he didn't know. He threw out his right arm, pulling toward a rock ledge a dozen feet away, but his waterlogged clothes and boots dragged at him and he sensed the predatory abyss beneath him. Images flashed through his mind of white flesh, needle teeth snapping shut, and black eyes gleaming. He could feel them there, under him, and whether they were actually there mattered not at all.

Without both arms, he wouldn't be fast enough. And if the creatures didn't snag him from below, he might drown anyway. Struggling out of his sling, he cried out in pain as the knitting flesh of his bullet wound tore anew, but the pain drove him on. He set his jaws tight, hissed through his teeth, and swam, cursing the wound, the bullet, and the dead Miguel Rio for shooting him in the first place. The beautiful haze the Vicodin had provided had evaporated.

Something splashed behind him—maybe a rock falling from above, but maybe something else, something hungry. Ahead on the sun-splashed ledge, others were even now pulling themselves out of the water. Some were cradling injured limbs, one sailor bleeding from a gash on his face, and he saw Tori kneeling at the water's edge. Her eyes locked on him and he saw relief spill across her features. She urged him on.

Then he was there, at the ledge. He hooked his right arm onto the rocky outcropping and tried to climb, but he could not raise his left. His head and arms were in sunlight now, but the water remained dark and deep and he felt the vulnerability of his legs so keenly that a scream began to build inside him. Frantic, he tried to scrabble up the jagged rock ledge.

A hand clamped on his right wrist and, as he looked up, Lieutenant Commander Sykes hauled him bodily from the water, pulling him out with such effort that the two collapsed on the slick ledge. As Sykes regained his feet, Josh took long gasping breaths, and the pain in his shoulder throbbed into hideous life. He held the arm against his chest and looked up at Sykes.

"Thank you," he said. "Thank you." Though he knew getting out of the water was not the same as getting out alive.

Then Tori knelt beside him, her wet hair plastered to her face, eyes alight with fear and with something akin to fervor.

"You're all right," she told him. Only instead of reassurance, it sounded like a command. "Come on, get up. We have to get out of here."

But as Josh rose and glanced around, he saw that would be easier said than done. They were in the vast sub-chamber beneath the bowl—beneath the level of the grotto entirely. A broad section of the bowl had caved in, but not everyone had been fortunate enough to hit the water. In the illumination from the shafts of sunlight that came down from above, he could make out at least four bodies—sailors who had struck the rocky edges of the pool—and one tangled wreck of limbs half-buried in the pile of shattered black stone. Someone from the descent team, he figured, who had been hanging underneath the shelf before it gave way.

Alena Boudreau had survived, and stood talking quietly to Dr. Ridge, her geologist, a few feet away. Both were saturated with water, the woman's silver hair wet and stringy, making her suddenly look her age. Regardless of how well she'd maintained her body, this had to be hard on her.

Three sailors stood with Sykes right on the ledge, searching the water for signs of anyone else who had survived. But some of those who had landed in the subterranean pool had not surfaced. Josh knew without question that they would never surface. They had either been injured in the fall and drowned, or fallen prey to what swam in those waters.

"There!" one of the sailors shouted, pointing. "Did you see it?"

But Josh didn't, and no one else seemed to. At least, no one spoke of it. Tense moments passed with all of them holding their breath, but no streak of white surfaced in the pool or darted just below the surface.

"Kaufmann," one of the sailors said, the word either a curse or an indictment. "Fuck, Teddy, Kaufmann's dead."

"I know, man," another sailor replied. "A lot of guys are dead."

Josh steadied his breathing, forced himself to find control in the mire of his pain and fear. His sling remained around his neck, a sodden rag, and he worked it into place, every motion a fresh jolt. Then he stepped up beside Tori and followed her gaze upward.

"A second bowl," he said.

"What?"

But he didn't clarify. There was no need; she could see what he saw. They were down in a cave now. The upper bowl, the original chamber, had looked down into the mouth of the cave, which sloped inward to form what was, in essence, another bowl. At high tide, water would pour in through the cave mouth above them and the water level of the subterranean pool would rise. But the ledge where they had gathered, a slab of volcanic rock, put them thirty feet below the cave mouth. There would be no climbing back up.

Even if they did, he doubted they would be able to get through.

The shelf of the upper bowl had shattered and tons of black rock had crashed down like a landslide. Some of it had passed through the cave mouth and plunged into the water with and around them, but huge slabs and chunks had come to rest in the mouth of the cave, lodged there, blocking the rest from falling.

"We're cut off," Josh said.

"No," Tori argued. "Look, there are plenty of openings. Tons of light getting through. They can put ropes down and pull us up."

Sykes overheard. His boots scuffed the ledge as he turned to them. "No, they can't. Josh is right. All that rockfall is unstable. It could give way at any time. If they put someone through one of those holes, the whole thing could come down and crush us all. They'd never risk it. If they try, I'll order them not to. So will Captain Siebalt."

"Are you kidding me? They have to try!"

Sykes no longer had his radio, but two of his men had managed to get theirs working. Static and voices hissed. From above, someone tried to hail them. Sykes turned his back and went to take the radio.

Josh swayed on his feet, pain surging again. If Sykes was right, they were all dead. He turned to see Alena Boudreau and Ridge watching them and made his way over to them, Tori quickly following.

"Dr. Boudreau, this is your operation. Talk to him. Get on the radio and tell them we're down here," Josh said. "Your grandson isn't going to just leave you here."

A line of pain formed on her forehead at the thought of her grandson, but she shook her head. "I'm afraid none of that really matters, Agent Hart."

"How can you say it doesn't matter?" Tori snapped. "I'm not going to die down here."

Alena glanced at Ridge and took a deep breath, pressing a hand to her side. Josh wondered if she had broken some ribs or just bruised herself.

"Paul and I were just talking this through," she said, a terrible wisdom and apology in her eyes. "Even if they came for us without first trying to remove some of the rockslide, to do so safely would take hours. We can't afford that kind of time. The sun will keep shifting position and it won't be long before there's no direct sunlight down here at all. It may be that most of the creatures hibernate during the day, or that most are out in the deep water around the island, but I consider it sheer luck that we got onto this ledge alive."

"All the more reason—" Josh started.

Alena shot him a dark look that silenced him.

"It's worse," she said, gaze shifting between him and Tori. "In case you've forgotten, the tide is coming in. The water level in the pool is going to rise. And up above, when the tide is high enough, it's going to come pouring down on top of the tons of rock jammed into the cave mouth above us. That may bring the whole thing down, but even if it doesn't, the water is still going to pour into this chamber. We don't have until nightfall. If we stay here, we won't even make it to high tide. Either we'll drown, or they'll come for us."

Josh stared at her, feeling a connection with this woman, drawing on her strength. Despite the fate she had just described, she still did not seem beaten.

"You have an idea," he said.

Alena nodded, then turned to Dr. Ridge.

The geologist clicked on a Maglite he'd had clipped to his belt. The sailors all had them as well, though none had turned them on as yet.

Ridge turned and shone the thin but powerful beam into the darkness behind him. Four or five yards away, the ledge rose into a jagged slope, at the top of which was the yawning black void of a narrow tunnel.

"There's another way out," Ridge said. "Can't you feel the draft? The air's moving in that direction."

Now that he'd pointed it out, Josh could.

"Oh, my God," Tori whispered, and the hope in her voice was palpable.

"At high tide, that tunnel will flood," Sykes said from behind them.

They all turned to find that the lieutenant commander and his three surviving sailors had joined them, and overheard the last of the conversation.

Alena met Sykes's gaze with her own, unwavering.

"Then we'd better get started."

-79--

Thunder roused Gabe from his chair, but even as he got up, he tried slotting that sound into a different category. Not thunder at all. Three sequential booms like the whomp of a fireworks finale, the sound lingering in the air. Something had exploded.

The room they had locked him into had two windows, but from the one on the right all he could see was a curved, horizontal trail of smoke. He shuffled left, craning his neck, and saw burning wreckage in the distance, sinking slowly into the ocean. Gabe spent several seconds making sense of it, trying to tell himself they had towed some of the derelicts away from shore and detonated them to kill whatever sirens might be nesting inside. But even blackened and twisted, he knew that curve of hull. His face went slack as he watched the last of the *Antoinette* go down.

He sought within himself for the fury he thought he should feel, but found a curious alternative. Gabe Rio felt free. She had been his ship, more his home than the apartment he had shared with Maya. In all the ways that had mattered in the end, he had chosen the *Antoinette* over his own wife.

He hated the bastards for blowing her up, and he would miss her, yet Gabe found himself glad the ship was gone. If they had been kind enough to give him a bottle of whiskey or even a can of beer, he would have toasted the *Antoinette*'s destruction. That part of his life had been over ever since they had found the *Mariposa* adrift, but now there could be no going back. Not ever.

For long minutes he stood and watched the smoke curl into the air, losing track of time. His stomach growled, a deep down hunger that he had somehow failed to notice, and he wondered what kind of meal he could persuade his Coast Guard wardens to rustle up. His thoughts drifted a bit, and then his stomach growled again, and this time the hunger was enough to force him away from the window. There had to be at least one seaman on guard out in the corridor. If he banged on the door, they'd open up. Even a few crackers would be better than nothing.

Before Gabe even reached the door, he heard the lock click and it swung inward. He expected a sailor, or maybe Special Agent Turcotte, but it was Agent Voss who strode into the room. The broad-shouldered Mac stepped into the room beside her, crossed his arms, and stood next to the door—apparently just in case he should try to escape.

"So much for your case—" he started to say, but the look on Voss's face made him falter. The woman seemed on the verge of either screaming or puking, and he had no desire to witness either one. "What happened?"

Voss steadied herself, lips pressed tightly together as though desperate to control whatever words came out next.

"On the island," she said. "While you were searching for the guns, did you find any other caves that had water in them?"

Gabe frowned. "Water?"

"The water table under the island," she said, gaze fixed firmly on him. "Some of the caves are tunnels. Water runs underground. Did you see or hear water in any of the other caves?"

He hesitated. "I don't—"

"Think! It's a simple goddamn question."

Gabe stared at her, dreadful understanding seeping into his thoughts. He nodded. "One for sure. Probably others, but—"

"Which one?"

"Where we found the guns. I could hear running water, and the cave definitely went back farther. There were crevices, maybe going down into the bedrock. What happened? Is Tori—?"

"They were planting charges in the grotto. Every cave they can find is getting the same treatment. But one of the explosives in the lower part of the grotto triggered early. Seven casualties, all Navy. Miss Austin is still alive, and so is my partner. I intend for him to stay that way. They've found a side tunnel, but now they're under tons of rock and we've lost contact with them. We need to get down there and lend a hand, try to find them before the rising tide drowns them or the sirens realize they're there."

Gabe put his right hand over his mouth, ran his palm over the stubble on his chin. He and Tori had never been especially close, but they had survived the previous day and night together, and the news rocked him. He hated Josh—would never get past the man's deceit, just doing his job or not—but Tori . . . all she had wanted was to escape her old life, and to have a new one that would be hers alone. Dr. Boudreau had asked him to go, and he had refused. Tori had gone in his place.

He ran his hand over his eyes, pressed on the lids as though just waking up. And maybe he was. Gabe had used Miguel as an excuse for too long, had told himself he had given up life as one of the good guys so that he could take care of his little brother. But that had been convenient. He had never wanted to be involved with crime—with guns and drugs—but he had gone along with Viscaya not only on his brother's behalf, but his own. He liked the money, and he liked knowing the *Antoinette* was his ship.

He had blamed his infidelity on the cold distance between himself and Maya, but it was a distance that *he* had created. Miguel had come first, and then Viscaya had come first, but always and forever, the sea had come first. And for that sin, his brother and his wife had both betrayed him. But Gabe had not been blameless.

If he had done the right thing and agreed to help Dr. Boudreau in the first place, he would have been the one trapped underground with the sirens, not Tori. She didn't deserve that. Maybe he didn't, either, but if it came to a choice between the two of them, he knew which of them fate ought to have sacrificed.

Gabe dropped his hands to his sides and met Voss's stare with a single nod.

"Let's go. I'll show you where."

In the *Kodiak*'s ready room, David Boudreau could not manage to keep still. He paced to be moving, because when he stopped moving he felt suffocated by the temptation to surrender to grief. And if he surrendered, then Alena might as well be dead.

Might as well be? Hell, she might be dead already. What can you do for her?

A terrible question, but unavoidable. He paced the ready room and listened to the men in charge of the three branches of the operation conjecture about faulty munitions, the safety and possibility of excavations, and how much knockout gas they had on board the various Coast Guard and Navy ships combined, except all David heard was the ticking of the clock on the wall.

On a monitor screen, Captain Siebalt—still in the ready room over on the *Hillstrom* and joining them in video conference—started to debate the safety of digging out the caved-in grotto yet again, and David snapped.

"Enough!"

The three others in the room—Rouleau of the Coast Guard, Turcotte of the FBI, and his team biologist Sarah Ernst—turned to look at him in surprise. On the monitor, Siebalt did the same. David almost laughed at the surreality of it all.

"All of you just listen," he said. He knew they saw a young guy, clean cut and frayed with panic, and he wouldn't deny the impression. But with Alena off the board for the moment, this operation had fallen under his command.

"If we use enough gas to knock out all of the creatures— even if we had that much—we could kill any survivors down there. We do not have time to excavate. The afternoon is waning, and the tide is coming in. And, all due respect, Captain Siebalt, right now I don't give a fuck what set off the charge. Manufacturer's mistake or human error, what difference does it make? My grandmother is down there. She means more to me, and, frankly, to the Department of Defense, than you could imagine. None of that matters. We have to talk about reality here, and I mean this instant."

He turned to Dr. Ernst. "Sarah, from what you know about CMA-3, what are the odds that any of our people are still alive down there? Are the sirens fully conscious during the day? Can they hear things that are out of the water, or sense them, if they're not using their echolocation? What about in the water? Can they smell blood, or sense motion at a distance?"

Even as he spoke, Ernst slowly raised her hands. The woman looked sick, but he had no time for empathy.

"I'm sorry, David, but we just don't have anything concrete. It's all guesswork. Mr. Sykes radioed before they went underground, right? So at that point they were out of the water and had seen no sign of attack. We can extrapolate some hypotheses from that, and maybe when I examine the one you just brought over from the *Antoinette,* I'll have a better idea, but—"

David held up a hand. "I get it. And you're right. I shouldn't be wasting your time here. Go, see if you can learn anything from it that can help us. Don't worry about keeping it alive, but don't let it burn. We need answers."

Ernst nodded. "I'll see what I can do."

She departed quickly, not looking back, her focus already on the task ahead. Once she had closed the door behind her, David turned to the others.

"All right. We're not just going to wait for her. We go in after them."

"Now hang on," Rouleau began.

On the monitor, Captain Siebalt started to argue as well. "Dr. Boudreau, we've got to advise against it. Right now you're heading up this operation. But one of the people we're hoping to save is your grandmother, and questions of judgment—"

"I'm going," David said. All of his life he had been underestimated by people who judged his character and fortitude based on appearance alone. He had learned to show both in his eyes when they could not see past his youth.

"It's a question of protocol—" Turcotte began.

"Screw protocol. And that's the end of the discussion. We're wasting time. Agent Voss has Gabe Rio ready to go. I'm taking a team through the cave where Rio found the guns. If they're alive, and we can reach them, we'll get them out."

For a moment, the three men were silent.

Finally, it was Bud Rouleau, the Coast Guard man, who asked the question they must all have been thinking.

"And if *you* don't come out?"

David thought of his first glimpse of the sirens, but the image gave way to the look of pride his grandmother had worn on the day he received his doctorate—that gentle, knowing smile that she had always reserved for him, marking the kinship that ran between them, so much stronger than mere blood. She'd always had faith in him. Today, he would fulfill that faith.

"If we're not out of the ground by dusk, we'll all be dead," he said, striding toward the door. He opened it and paused. "At that point, detonate the whole damn island. Kill the bastards. That's why we're here."

—80——

What frightened Tori the most were the side tunnels, most of them too narrow for a person to fit through. Some were actually fissures, cleaved into the walls as though some giant axe blade had split the black, glassy rock. The darkness inside those clefts was absolute—a blackness unlike anything she had ever seen, like holes in the fabric of the world. From some of them she could hear a trickle of water, and in others a louder shushing ebb and flow. The tide was rising. Would water eventually come up through those holes and fissures, just as it would from the cave mouth they had left behind some long, tense minutes ago? She thought it would.

For now, though, there were only the sounds and, from some, the breath of steam—a hot mist that made the tunnel like a sauna. The volcano beneath them might be dormant—at least according to Dr. Ridge it was—but down in its heart, a furnace still burned.

The tunnel had widened as they moved deeper into it, enough so that they could walk two by two, although the craggy ceiling remained so low that they could only move in a crouch. Shuffling along, backs bent, had not slowed them at first, but Tori had felt them all slowing down as the discomfort of that hunched progress grew. Lieutenant Commander Sykes led the way with a Maglite, strobing the tunnel ahead, the barrel of his pistol pointed at every sharp edge and turn. Behind him ambled Alena and Dr. Ridge. Ridge had another flashlight, its powerful beam illuminating Sykes as much as it did any of the tunnel. He tried to insist that Alena allow him to help her, but the woman refused. She confessed to having cracked ribs, and she walked as gingerly as their need for speed would allow, one hand pressed to her side, but she never complained and never slowed.

Tough as nails, Tori thought, with deep admiration, as she and Josh followed behind the two scientists.

The other three sailors—Charlie, Mays, and Garbarino—brought up the rear, their own Maglite beams bouncing around Tori and Josh, illuminating bits of tunnel wall or ceiling for an instant before moving on. She took comfort in those lights, and in having those sailors behind her, and Sykes up front. It didn't make her safe—none of them were safe—but the illusion pleased her.

Josh stumbled and fell to his knees beside her, swearing in a low voice, and the three sailors came to a halt, shining their lights on him. In that brightness, the pain etched on his face was terrible to see. Small beads of sweat had formed on his forehead.

"You okay?" she asked.

His chuckle held a grim irony. "Not even close. Doc Dolan

gave me a couple of extra Vicodin for the road." Josh looked up, his smile a grimace. "I took them early, spoiling myself. Half an hour before the cave-in. They aren't doing shit."

Then a terrible thought hit him. Tori watched it reach his eyes. "Or maybe they are. I don't even want to think about that."

She understood. If the Vicodin were working and he was in this kind of pain, how much worse would it be when the drugs wore off?

Tori put a hand on his shoulder. Making love to him in her quarters on board the *Antoinette* seemed to have happened in another life, so distant now, but still the contact felt electric. Down here in the dark, with the promise of death all around them, that seemed far more important to her than the fact that he'd hidden his true identity from her.

"Come on. Up," she said, slipping a hand under his right arm and helping him to his feet.

Josh drew a sharp breath through his teeth.

"You gonna make it, Agent Hart?" asked one of the sailors. Mays, she thought, but their faces were hard to make out in the darkness behind their Maglite beams.

"So far, so good," Josh replied. Exhaling, he started walking again, and they began to catch up to Sykes, Alena, and Ridge.

"Poor baby," Tori said, softly so only he would hear.

Josh actually laughed, then grunted with pain. The laugh had hurt him, but she only felt a little sorry.

"You must be loving this," he replied.

"Trying to find a way out of a tunnel before something kills me? Not really."

"I meant seeing me in pain."

Without thinking, Tori settled in closer to him, let him put some of his weight on her. His legs were fine, but pain, shock, and blood loss were taking some of the fight out of him.

"It has its charms, I admit." But she couldn't keep up the facade, or the humor. "That's a lie. I never wanted you to be hurt."

"Never?"

Apparently, Josh hadn't lost his sense of humor, even if hers had deserted her. Maybe it was all that was keeping him going.

"Well, maybe for a while," she admitted. "But right now I just want to be able to stand up straight. And daylight would be nice."

"Yeah," Josh agreed. "It would."

They fell silent after that, moving together through the tunnel as it narrowed and then widened again, the beams from the sailors' flashlights bouncing all around them. More and more often, she heard Josh hiss through his teeth, trying to bite back his pain, and when the lights passed him, she could see the struggle on his face.

Tori realized that it might well be up to her to save his life, and the thought staggered her. Somehow the world had inverted. It felt like discovering an entirely new Tori . . . one that she had never known existed.

A powerful new sense of purpose filled her as she studied the crevices in the walls and the tunnel that Sykes, up ahead, led them all through. Survival had always seemed like a matter of luck or fate to her, but now she saw it differently. Survival, Tori realized at last, came from determination. It came not from hiding, but from acting.

They passed a crevice that slashed down through the tunnel wall and into the floor. From below she heard the ebb and flow of the tide—like the ocean breathing, in and out—but she felt sure something splashed down there as well. Something waiting.

"Mr. Sykes, we've got to pick up the pace," she said, calling forward to him. "The tunnel's not taking us any higher. If we don't find somewhere we can go up instead of just across, the water will be on us before we know it."

"I'm going as fast as I can," the lieutenant commander called back.

But Dr. Boudreau glanced over her shoulder at Tori, and then turned forward again, picking up her pace despite the way she clutched at her cracked ribs.

"No, you're not," Alena said. "She's right. You're matching my speed, taking it easy on me. And we can't afford that."

Sykes said nothing, but the pace did pick up.

"Thanks a lot," Josh complained.

But Tori knew he realized they had no choice, that someone had to say it.

"You're welcome."

-81--

Angie poured herself a mug of coffee and forced her shaking hands to be still. She wondered if Agent Plausky could see in her eyes or hear in her voice just how freaked out she was to be on board the *Hillstrom,* knowing one of them was out on the deck. It took an effort to keep her breathing even. At first, she hadn't even been able to do that. What were they thinking, trying to keep one of the monsters alive? They'd even brought it onto the ship, where there were people.

Her hand shook again and a bit of coffee spilled over the edge of the mug. She set the pot down and took a steadying breath. A chill spider-walked up her spine but she refused to let Plausky see it. Images crowded her mind of the night before, the things crawling up the hull, slithering over the railing . . . Sense memories exploded in her mind—the smell of cordite from gunshots, the sound of screams, the sickening noise of the sirens' teeth tearing at Dwyer's body . . .

Angie hated them even more than she feared them. To bring one on board, to keep it alive . . . what would they do, study it? Breed more? Use it as a weapon?

Hatred and fear were crowded out of her mind by panic. Her thoughts were out of control and she knew it, but she could not rein them in. Her mind would not settle down. Her pulse would not stop racing. She turned to Plausky and smiled, wondering if the grin looked crazy to him, if her eyes were too wide, if he could see that she was breaking into tiny, sharp pieces inside.

"You want another cup?" she asked.

Plausky sat at a small table, like in some tiny apartment kitchen. But this was no kitchen or galley. He had brought her to a small common room—maybe a kind of rec room—on the Navy ship, with chairs and a TV screen and a DVD player, and several game tables scattered around. A bookshelf against one wall was stacked with all kinds of board games and there were racks of DVDs.

The FBI agent looked up, coffee mug in his hand. He raised it in a little salute, like some 1950s husband in a TV ad. "Sure. A top-up would be great, thanks."

Her chest felt tight, her heart racing so fast that she would have done anything to make it slow down. Far away, muffled by walls and corridors, she could make out the sound of helicopters—maybe the fool that had brought that rusty container over from the *Antoinette* was making another run.

Angie tried to smile but only one corner of her mouth lifted, forming a weird, lopsided grimace. Plausky didn't seem to notice. Why would he? He was just a guy doing his job, waiting until he could hand her over into somebody else's custody so that she wouldn't be his problem anymore. Getting assigned to watch out for her was just luck of the draw.

Which made Plausky one unlucky son of a bitch.

She threw her coffee in his face. He shouted and raised his hands to try to keep the hot liquid from scalding him, and she took the opportunity to smash him in the temple with the metal coffeepot, hard enough that she heard something crack. The sound scared her—God, she didn't want to hurt him that badly—but even as he fell out of his chair, moaning in pain, she saw that his arms were still moving. His eyes were rolling back, but she saw no blood. He'd live. She hadn't killed him.

Before she slipped from the room into the corridor, Angie took his gun. She liked the weight in her hand. It gave her focus.

82

Voss had spent months trying to put together a case against Gabe Rio. Now she followed him through a tangle of tropical vegetation with no path or trail except what he had in his memory, and somehow they had become allies. Massive palm fronds rustled in the breeze above them. Gabe paused to look around and then spotted a place where a pair of trees leaned together like some grand archway. He seemed to recognize this as a landmark and adjusted course to go under the arch.

She didn't ask if he knew where he was going. Just talking to him fed an anger that she needed to extinguish if they were going to make it through the day. For the second time, she had to fight the temptation to give Josh up for dead, and battling that pessimistic whisper took all her strength. She didn't have the energy for spite. Besides, Gabe Rio had never been her real target. He was just a victim of Viscaya's schemes.

On the other hand, if he hadn't committed those crimes, she wouldn't ever have come here. *And Josh wouldn't be trapped down in the dark with those things.*

Voss picked up her pace. David Boudreau and Lieutenant Stone hurried along behind her with—how many sailors were there, three? Not enough, she felt sure. But how many would have been? They were either going to find Josh, David's grandmother, and the others, or they weren't. In the end, how many people went down into the island's womb didn't matter as much as how many came back up.

Sunlight came through the trees at enough of an angle to remind her that the afternoon wore on as the sun slid inexorably toward the western horizon. In several places they passed depressions in the ground where the vegetation grew even thicker and greener, and volcanic steam lay upon the ground like mist. Sweat beaded on her forehead and arms and the back of her neck, and trickled between her breasts and down the small of her back. Voss used the hem of her tank top to wipe her forehead and kept up her pace, slogging after Gabe.

The massive hill at the center of the island—it wasn't really big enough for her to think of it as a mountain—rose up in front of them, but there were smaller ridges and formations all around it. In between two of those, Gabe Rio stopped short, looking around to get his bearings.

"You better know where the fuck you're going," Voss said as she halted at his side. They had landed on the shore precisely where he had indicated, flying over the still-burning wreckage of the graveyard of derelict ships just offshore.

"We're fine," he replied. "But I'm going in the way we came out yesterday, so I'm trying to reverse course in my head. It's this way."

He started off again, cutting to the right at an angle that would take them around one of the lower hills. Over the eons since the volcano had erupted, local flora had grown wild all across those hills, but in places the black rock thrust up from the ground in jagged edges.

Voss could only follow, and because of that, she couldn't help hating Gabe a little. The thought brought her back to the argument she had had with Turcotte right before boarding the helicopter that had taken her out to the island. Despite the way he had abdicated all responsibility in the Viscaya case—abandoned any interest, regardless of how hard he had once fought to take the case away from her—he had been very unhappy with the idea of taking Gabe Rio away from the *Kodiak,* and out of his custody.

"You're treating him like a human being. Like he's part of the team, instead of the bastard who put us here!" Turcotte had shouted at her, his words hacked apart by the roar of the helicopter's rotors, out there on the deck of the Coast Guard ship.

The irony had sickened Voss. "What the fuck do you care? You gave up on this case! And if he's our shot at getting my partner and the others out of there alive, I'm taking it."

"And if I order you to stay here?" Turcotte had sneered.

The memory made Voss sniff in disgust. At that moment, though, she had laughed at him, told him if he wanted to pull rank as the agent in charge, he should be the first one on the chopper, heading out to save his man in the field. Turcotte hadn't even had the sense to be ashamed of himself, but it didn't matter. With Alena missing, David Boudreau held rank over them all, and he had approved bringing Gabe Rio along.

"Fine," Turcotte had said. "Go and die. I tried to stop you."

The words, like a slap in the face, would stay with her the rest of her life. However long that might be.

She rounded the bottom of the hill, ducked underneath low-hanging branches, and looked up to see that Gabe had come to a sudden halt. And then she saw why. Beyond him, the tangled brush thinned and opened into a natural clearing in front of a cave set into the steep hillside. A large rectangular plastic box sat just outside the cave, tilted on its side to reveal that it was empty. They had arrived.

"Looks like your people haven't found this one yet," Gabe said, glancing back at her.

Then David passed her, and she knew Gabe had not been speaking to her. David strode right up to the cave opening, ignoring the box. He paused to examine the entrance to the cave, then turned to Stone.

"Lieutenant, get on the radio and get someone over here immediately to set charges. I don't want to think about how many other caves they've missed."

Stone narrowed his eyes. "Don't jump to conclusions, Dr. Boudreau. The teams are being methodical, sweeping every square foot of the island. They didn't miss this cave. They just haven't gotten to it yet."

"They're going to run out of time."

"They'll do the job, Doctor," Stone insisted. "Drawing them away from their sweep patterns just to focus on this one cave—"

"No, no," David said, waving a hand. "I understand. Forget I said it."

He looked at Gabe, and Voss wondered if the young scientist would ask the guy to confirm that this was the cave where he had heard the water. How there could be any doubt, she had no idea. The plastic crate had obviously contained guns that had been consolidated into other containers or carried away. Now that she looked, she saw signs of footfalls and disturbance everywhere in the clearing, not to mention empty ammunition boxes just inside the mouth of the cave and splashes of blood on the rocks in one place.

But it turned out David had a different question.

"Are you coming in with us, Captain Rio, or are you staying topside?"

Gabe didn't hesitate. "I'm with you, Doctor. I owe Tori that."

Voss stared. She had seen the way Gabe had reacted to the news of Tori Austin's situation, so it had not surprised her when he had agreed to lead them to the cave. But she had not expected him to descend with them, to risk himself.

"I don't think that's a good idea," she said.

Gabe, David, and Stone all looked at her, so that Voss felt like she had to defend herself; her, the FBI agent, defending herself when Gabe Rio had smuggled drugs and guns.

"If things get ugly down there, I want to know I'm surrounded by people I can rely on," she said, staring at Gabe. He surprised her again by not turning away, instead keeping his gaze fixed firmly on hers.

"What do you think, Agent Voss, that I'm going to try to murder you all and escape?" he asked. "You've obviously got a file you put together on me. Do you see murder anywhere in there? And even if you really believed I was capable of something like that, where would I run? And what would I gain? Dr. Boudreau here gave me my free pass before we left the *Kodiak*. I'm not going to prison, lady. I'm out here for Tori. I'm no hero, but I'm not stupid, either. I know I've done things in my life I need to make up for."

David could have stepped in, then, and overruled her the way he had Turcotte. Even Lieutenant Stone could have offered an opinion. But both men waited to see what she would say, leaving it to her.

In reply, she unclipped the Maglite from her belt, shifted it to her left hand, and drew her gun. She glanced at David. "Fine, but he doesn't get a gun."

"Agreed," David replied.

Gabe's face went slack, but she did not think it was the lack of a weapon that had troubled him. With her objections removed, he had to face the prospect of descending into that cave without any protection but what Voss and the sailors could provide, and apparently that did not instill him with confidence.

Voss nodded her consent—though David did not need it—and started into the mouth of the cave, clicking her Maglite on. The flash beam wavered, but her gun hand did not.

"Hang on, Agent Voss," Stone said. He turned to one of the sailors. "Mr. Crowley, lead the way."

Wordlessly, the freckled Crowley hurried up to the cave, pulling out his own Maglite. He waited for Voss to step aside, and when she did so, he rushed through as though eager to explore the dark innards of the island. But she knew eagerness did not drive him. Duty did.

She didn't wait for the rest of them, following Crowley in, and this time Stone didn't try to call her back. She heard his voice, and those of David and the other sailors, as they entered behind her. They all carried small packs with water, some food rations, radios, and backup lights. Stone, Crowley, and the other two sailors had assault weapons in addition to their sidearms, while Voss and David carried only pistols. Manetti, a medic, had a med-kit so that he could provide emergency treatment, if needed, to the survivors of the grotto's collapse.

The cave went back thirty feet or more, diminishing in size until it jogged left and descended sharply. Flashlight beams played across the stone walls, black rock alternately reflecting the light and seeming to swallow it. Voss could hear trickling water and a kind of shushing noise of it moving far below, the ebb and flow of a current somewhere down there.

"Watch your step, Agent Voss," Crowley whispered.

She almost asked him why he wanted to keep his voice down, then felt stupid. Of course they should whisper. The sirens were probably in the lower tunnels, in the water, but they did not know enough about the creatures to truly predict their behavior. A chill went up her spine and she shone her flashlight beam at the ceiling above her, imagining one of the maggoty-white things stuck like a leech to the black rock, reaching for her, jaws wide.

But they were alone in here, at least for now.

With Crowley in the lead, they navigated through a narrow, low-ceilinged tunnel into an even narrower space that seemed more like a crevice or fissure. The slash in the volcanic rock went up vertically at least twenty feet until it became little more than a crack. Water dribbled down the walls, keeping them slick.

Voss aimed her Maglite down and saw that the crack went deeper as well.

"Have a look at this," she said, crouching, and the others followed suit.

"There's water down there," David said, shining his own light beside hers.

Gabe peered over his shoulder and Crowley had back-tracked to join them. The other sailors did not bother to look, shining their lights around, on guard for attack. The sight of them so vigilant gave Voss another chill, icy fingers dancing along her spine.

"Yeah," Voss said. "See anything else?"

They had been walking along a ridge inside the fissure, and perhaps twenty-five feet below, their lights shone on shimmering water. Though the slash in the rock was narrow, it provided access to the water below, and to the rising tide.

"No," David said, turning to her in alarm. "Did you?"

Voss stood up. "Not yet."

They went faster after that, and kept quiet.

83

Sarah Ernst had never been so terrified in her life, but she tried desperately not to show it. Her face felt warm, but that might have been the sun. Did she look flushed to those around her? Could they tell she had started breathing in short, quick breaths? Her lips felt dry and she ran her tongue out to moisten them, thinking, *Holy shit, this is real.*

When Alena Boudreau had recruited her for this job, it had seemed fascinating. There would be secrets laid bare for her that other biologists would sell their souls to learn. Yes, some of those secrets might end up being weaponized, but even as a professor, Sarah Ernst had taught her students about conditional ethics. Some things were wrong under any circumstances, but other decisions had to be weighted against the planet-wide political and cultural conditions in which they had to be made, and Dr. Ernst had faith in the U.S. government. Yes, corruption infected it, but the core, she believed, was still worthy of her trust and her service.

And so she served.

The work had been everything she had imagined. The samples Alena had sent back from Donika Cave alone would end up being the most remarkable things that she, as a biologist, had ever examined. Or they would have been, if not for today.

"Dr. Ernst?" Captain Siebalt said.

Again she wetted her lips. "Sorry. Just kind of bracing myself."

The captain smiled. "I don't blame you. I think we all are."

That made her feel a bit better and she allowed herself to take a look around. The chopper had set the rusty metal container down on the deck of the USS *Hillstrom*. She tried to count how many members of the Navy vessel's crew were gathered around the front of the container with weapons drawn and aimed at the doors, but lost track somewhere in the teens. A couple of dozen, at least.

Sarah had always hated guns. They did not make her feel any safer. She looked at the metal doors of the container and wondered about ricochets. Her palms felt clammy. The sailors had begun to take glances at her, obviously waiting for the word.

"Hopefully it's still unconscious," she said, and then— thinking herself too quiet—spoke louder. "If you have to shoot, try to wound it, and try to keep it in the dark. We don't want it exposed to sunlight."

With one last, deep breath, she glanced at Captain Siebalt and nodded.

"Open it," the captain commanded.

One of the sailors shouldered his weapon, strode purpose- fully to the front of the container, and swung up the heavy metal bar that latched the door. The man paused—she saw his back rise and fall as he took a breath—then hauled it quickly open, backpedaling out of the way.

Dozens of gun barrels rose and took aim.

Sarah held her breath, staring into the shadows of the con- tainer. Something rustled inside and she heard the ratcheting of weapons being cocked, but nobody fired. One of the sailors raised a fist, then opened it and gestured forward, and half a dozen men moved toward the open doorway.

"There's movement, Captain!" one of them called.

"But it's still in the body bag?" Siebalt replied.

"Yes, sir."

"Get it out of there, then, and fast."

Sarah nodded her head in agreement, though no one had bothered to ask her. As long as the thing posed no more threat than a weak twitch here and there, they needed to get it out of the container and into the room that had been set aside for her in the sick bay—no windows, no sunlight, metal and leather restraints. And the faster the better.

She watched as four more sailors slung their weapons over their shoulders and stepped into the container, and others stepped up to take their places, weapons trained on the black, shapeless lump on the floor. The four grabbed the body bag, wary but quick, hefted it off the ground with little visible effort, and hustled it out of the container. Sarah knew some light must still filter through the bag, and the creature—CMA-3, specimen one, as she now thought of it—began to twitch more vigorously. But the gas had not yet worn off enough for it to do more than that.

"Hurry," she called to them.

A path opened up among the sailors and two more raced through the opening carrying a long board between them—the kind of backboard that the medics would use if a member of the crew fell and broke his back or needed to be immobilized for some reason. They set it down and, as soon as the others had placed the body-bagged creature onto the backboard, began to strap the creature into place.

Sarah's fear began to give way to scientific curiosity and a kind of fevered elation that came over her only once in a very great while. No one in the modern world had ever studied one of these things up close. She would be the first to look at its cells under a microscope, the first to examine its physiology, the first to open one up and discover its organs and biological systems, what made it tick.

Her mind started racing ahead to the workspace she had been given and she realized that she needed a real camera array, some kind of setup rigged in there to properly record the procedure both on video and in still pictures.

She turned toward Captain Siebalt just as a figure darted through the ranks of the sailors, a black woman in oversized clothes, her hair tied back in a springy, overflowing ponytail. Angela Tyree, one of the survivors from the *Antoinette*—it had to be, given the lack of uniform. Sarah had known she was on board, ready to be transported to dry land, but she had never seen the woman before.

And Angie Tyree had a gun.

As the two sailors who had strapped it down moved around to lift the backboard, the woman took aim and pulled the trigger. She fired as she walked, once, twice, a third time. The two sailors jumped away, dropping the backboard, which struck the deck at an angle before falling flat.

The screech that came from the siren sounded nothing like music to Sarah. This was not a song, but a death cry. Angie fired twice more as the thing thrashed against the body bag and the backboard's restraints. It tore easily through the bag, letting in the sunlight, and Sarah Ernst watched in amazement as smoke started to rise from inside the bag. Flesh sizzled and crackled and popped and then tiny flames fanned to life and began to burn the openings in the bag.

It happened in seconds.

At least half of the weapons on the deck of the *Hillstrom* swung toward Angie Tyree. Tears streamed down the woman's face, glistening on her perfect dark skin. Her eyes were wide with panic and fear. Perhaps it was a reaction to the guns pointed at her, an instinctive thing, but Angie lifted her pistol in a shaking hand as though to defend herself with it.

"No!" Sarah shouted, seeing it coming.

But the gunfire drowned out her voice. Three quick shots, making Angie dance. Then the woman fell to the deck, her gun clattering a few feet away, blood pooling around her and streaming away in narrow rivulets as though eager to abandon ship.

"Oh, my God!" Sarah shouted. She might have repeated it—her mouth seemed still to be moving when she clapped a hand over it.

In horror, she turned away from the dying woman and saw the siren and the backboard rippling with flames. The body bag burned away, exposing more of its flesh. She watched as it blackened and crisped. A sailor ran over with a fire extinguisher, which put out the flames for a moment. But as soon as he stopped spraying the foam onto the corpse, it started to sizzle again and the fire came up from under its skin. Now they could only watch as it burnt away to cinder and ash and the Caribbean breeze across the deck swirled and eddied it away.

"We have to get another one," Sarah said, looking around numbly until her gaze found Captain Siebalt. "We need another."

But the captain did not reply, and she realized why. They

had already blown up the *Antoinette*. So if they were to capture another, they would have to go down into the sea to find one, and no one would risk that—at least, not today.

Whatever the Boudreaus faced in the caves under the island, there was now nothing that Sarah Ernst could do to aid them, no weakness in the creatures she could report, no data. No last-minute rescue. A feeling of helplessness engulfed her, and she turned away from the scene. Instead, she walked to the railing and looked out at the ocean.

For those on the island, and those below it, the handful of daylight hours must have been racing past. If Alena and David and Paul Ridge did not make it back, she would be the senior member of the team. But either way, if they survived or not, she knew she would resign upon her return.

Sarah no longer wanted to know things that other biologists did not. She would let someone else explore the world's secrets. Someone who, like her younger self, did not know better yet.

She broke down then, wiping at her tears and wondering if anyone watching her would see the way her shoulders shook as she cried. Wondering, but no longer caring.

As Angie lay on the deck, too tired even to blink, the sun burning her eyes, a figure loomed above her. Silhouetted against the sky, Agent Plausky looked down upon her with a terrible sadness etched on his face. He looked so sorry that it broke her heart.

He talked, but she could not make out the words. Her hearing seemed muffled, or maybe just numb, which would go along with the rest of her. Her body felt cold and though it ached in those places where she imagined the bullets had struck, she would not have described it as pain. Just a kind of emptiness, as if, in those places, she had already died.

Angie smiled at Plausky, though she could not be sure if her lips formed the smile properly. She hoped so. It made her glad to know that someone cared. Where she had hit him with the coffeepot, a red, swollen patch would soon turn a series of bruised colors, but he would be all right. Angie regretted having hurt him, but not very much. She had done what needed doing. She had overcome the fear that would otherwise have chased her into her grave; she had killed the monster.

Now she would sleep forever, but without nightmares. And that was all right.

She lifted a hand toward Plausky, wishing she could have formed the words to explain it all to him. And then she died.

-84--

Gabe Rio knew he ought to be more afraid. Perhaps he had just gone numb—maybe Miguel's death had done that—but he felt sure there must be something more to it. In a way, he was Orpheus, descending into the land of the dead, but the metaphor fell apart for him there, because he did not love Tori. He liked her all right, but she could never be his Eurydice. Once upon a time, Maya had been that important to him— she'd been his whole life—but he barely remembered being the man who had loved her that much.

And maybe that explained his numbness. Once upon a time, Gabe had been a man who loved the sea, and who would take any job as long as it put him aboard a ship. Maya had married that man, but over time, he had changed. Miguel had changed him. Viscaya had changed him. The discovery that Maya had not fallen in love with the young man he had been, but with the man she hoped to forge him into, had changed him. But that had been his life.

Yet all of that, the man he had been, Gabe had left behind when he stepped into this cave and began this descent. Maya, Miguel, Viscaya, the *Antoinette,* it was all the past now. When he emerged again, and finally left this island behind, that Gabe Rio would be gone and someone new would stand in his place. A second life waited for him, if he could survive to discover it.

His boot slipped on the ridge, snapping off a jagged bit of rock that skittered down into the dark crevice below. It must have plinked into the water, but he did not hear any splash. They had been down here for well over an hour, probably closer to two, and when he flashed his Maglite beam down into the gash below him, the water level had risen at least a dozen feet since they had begun moving through this fissure.

"I hate to bring this up," he whispered to David Boudreau, who walked in front of him, "especially since I have no idea how the tide works on the levels down here. But are you sure we're going the right way?"

David glanced back at him, stumbled a bit, then caught himself. The ridge they walked on consisted of vertical layers of rock, all of them jagged and uneven. Without shoes it would have been impossible to walk on, but the young Dr. Boudreau had problems even with his thick hiking boots. He might technically be the leader of the team, but how he justified carrying a gun but not giving Gabe one—even for self-defense—seemed a mystery.

"Lieutenant Stone has a compass," David said. "You know this, Mr. Rio. Why are you asking? The fissure is taking us a bit west of our goal—the rough location of the grotto—but it's got to open into some other cavern or tunnel eventually. Once it does, we'll have to risk making some noise to see if we can intersect with the cave-in survivors, and then—"

"What if we can't? I mean, why are you so sure that this fissure isn't a dead end? It could lead nowhere. Even if it puts us in another tunnel, there's no guarantee we'll be able to find any intersection between their location and ours."

David hesitated, flashed his Maglite in Gabe's face, and then continued. "It's a little late for questions like that, Gabe. We're taking our chances because we can't just abandon them down here."

Gabe blinked, pissed off about the light in his eyes, but they adjusted back to the relative darkness almost immediately. He shook his head.

"I bring it up, asshole, because the water's rising fast. We're at the point of no return now. If we don't find another way out up ahead, or run into them in the next few minutes, we're going to drown down here."

One of the sailors behind him cleared his throat. "You want to turn back, buddy, no one's stopping you."

"Exactly," David said, without turning.

Gabe felt his nostrils flare but wouldn't give in to anger. "I'm not turning back. I was just hoping you had more of a plan, or some reason to believe we'll find another way out other than you being such an optimist."

Neither of the two sailors behind Gabe spoke up this time, and neither did any of the people ahead of David—Crowley, Voss, and Lieutenant Stone. It seemed like they were all listening for his answer.

"My team's geologist, Paul Ridge, fell into that grotto with my grandmother," David said. "He wouldn't have gone into that tunnel unless he thought he could find a way out. They would have stayed down there and hoped we could dig them out in time."

"But Ridge is with them, not with us. You're just guessing," Gabe said.

"Yes."

Gabe nodded to himself. "All right. Good to know."

David glanced back to reply, but stumbled again. This time he went down, slamming his knee into the sharp rocks of the ridge. He swore and dropped the Maglite, which pinballed off the rocks before slipping down through the open crevice below. The light spun end over end and then splashed into the water. Gabe could see the beam's glow diminish as the Maglite sank into the darkness.

"Shit," David whispered.

The illumination from Gabe's own flashlight played shadows across the young scientist's face, exaggerating his haunted expression. Everyone else had frozen as well, waiting and listening, which Gabe thought a terrible idea. They needed to keep moving, and as fast as they could.

"Don't sweat it," he said. "We've been knocking stones loose the entire time we've been in here and it all slides down into—"

From the gash in the stone below them, he heard a second

splash. He twisted around, shone his light in the faces of the two sailors who trailed him.

"What was that? You guys drop something, too?"

They both shook their heads, their expressions grim.

"Come on," Voss called back to them, voice low. "Let's move, right now."

Crowley, in the lead, had already renewed his trek along the narrow ridge, left hand running over the smooth wall of the fissure, Maglite in his right. Voss and Stone followed. The instant David started forward again, Gabe hustled after him. He angled his flashlight ahead, trying to light David's path so the loss of his Maglite wouldn't end up slowing them all down.

All the while, he listened hard. Mostly what he heard were the scrapes of their soles against the ridge, the breathing of the men behind him, and his own heart thudding in his ears.

And then the singing began, soft but growing louder, echoing up through the open crevice below them. David faltered, but Gabe put out his free hand and shoved him forward.

"Fuck," one of the sailors breathed behind him.

Ahead, Voss shot a quick glance over her shoulder, looking past Stone and David, trying to see his face. "Gabe, is that—"

"What do *you* think?" he rasped. "Go, for Christ's sake. Go!"

Then they were running, stumbling, lights juddering wildly, flashing across walls and the fissure above them and the ridge below. Gabe felt flush, every nerve ending crackled, and as David stumbled again, he put his hands under the scientist's arms and hoisted him up like a marionette, forcing him forward. Up ahead there were curses and guns cocked.

"Lieutenant," Crowley called back to them, "we're going up."

A dozen steps later, Gabe saw what he meant, as the crevice narrowed and the ridge climbed, creating a path that took them up. Lights strobed ahead and Gabe saw what might have been a dead end.

The song rose in pitch and volume, beautiful and frantic, and now it echoed not just in the narrow space below but there in the fissure with them, bouncing off walls and corners in mad echoes that made finding the source impossible.

Behind him, one of the sailors tripped and fell. Gabe thought he heard bone crack and the sound unleashed a fear he had kept bottled up. He twisted around and flashed the Maglite and saw it was Manetti—the medic—who'd fallen. The man's face reddened with pain that built into a roar, even as the other sailor bent to help him.

A hand clamped on Gabe's wrist and he whipped around to see David hauling on him, nearly dragging him. Gabe surrendered to that grip and kept moving, and moments later he was at the top of the ridge. The darkness there had not been a dead end, but a turn in the tunnel, a place where the fissure ended, but a split in the stone led into a larger chamber—a void in the subterranean heart of the island.

They all stopped in that chamber—perhaps twelve feet wide and ten high—and stared back the way they'd come, waiting for Manetti and his companion to emerge. The song rose and multiplied into a harmony. More than one of the things had been lured by the splash of that Maglite, or the beam of light in the water—the presence of something down there with them that didn't belong.

Gunfire erupted back in the fissure, reports echoing, drowning out the sirens' song. And, amidst that cacophony, a man screamed.

"Damn it!" Lieutenant Stone snapped. He leveled his weapon and started back into the fissure, but David grabbed his arm to stop him. Stone looked like he might take a swing at the younger man.

"Listen!" David said.

They all did. At first there came no sounds at all—no cries of the wounded, no gunfire, no calls for help. But then the song began again, farther away, echoing.

"They're dead," Agent Voss said.

Stone glared at her a second, then relented.

"The light must have disturbed them. Or the splash, I don't know," David said. "But the singing, I think it really is some kind of echolocation, like bats. They have eyes, but they must use that also. If we were still back in the fissure, they would know we were there."

The song continued.

Gabe felt ice trickle down his back. "So that, right now? That sound is them hunting for us?"

"And maybe talking to each other. There's too much we still don't know."

Gabe stared at him. He might be young and even a bit clumsy, but all of a sudden Dr. David Boudreau seemed far more valuable, and formidable.

"We know all we need to know," Voss said, "which is that we can't go back that way."

Nobody bothered to argue. Especially when the lone song was joined by another. Crowley led the way into the new tunnel, taking point again, with David following.

Gabe looked at Voss and Stone. "I'll cover the flank," he said, showing them his empty hands, "but not without a gun."

"I've got it," Stone said, gesturing with the barrel of his assault rifle. "Go ahead."

But Voss didn't move. She stared at Gabe a long moment, then sighed. "Fuck it," she said, handing him her pistol and then drawing a second from a holster at the small of her back.

"Thanks," Gabe said, meaning it.

Voss shot him a hard look. "I hope you can aim."

Then she vanished into the tunnel, and Gabe followed, the pistol in one hand and the Maglite in the other.

-85--

Alena kept pace with Sykes and Paul Ridge, with the rest of the group following behind. All her life she had been active, and as she had aged she had done everything in her power to preserve herself. It had pleased her to defy the years, and often enough she had indulged that defiance in dalliances with younger men—sometimes much younger. Now she cared nothing for her appearance. All that mattered was the thousands of hours she had spent in the gym or the pool, the hundreds of hiking trips, the years of exploration in rough terrain.

In the dark, with the weight of the island pressing around her, Alena forged ahead, silently challenging the rest of the team to keep up with her. She worried about Agent Hart and the woman, Tori. The FBI man had slowed considerably—and who could blame him with a bullet wound in his shoulder—but with the tide rising and the daylight aboveground by now beginning to dim, at some point they might have to move faster. She feared what might happen to him then. If she could, she wanted to see every single one of them get out of this. But if that proved impossible, she would settle for as many as possible.

She didn't want to die.

The fear would have engulfed her if she let it. Instead, she forced it down and back, so that it sat in a tight little ball at the base of her skull. She had lived a long and fascinating life, but she planned to continue doing so, and the years she'd already had would be no consolation to her if she died now, down here in the dark.

She waved the Maglite beam ahead of her, narrowing her gaze.

"Paul?"

Sykes looked at her, but Alena ignored him, stepping aside for Ridge to pass. All three of them trained lights on the tunnel ahead, where it split into two forks: a gentle left and a hard right. Upon quick perusal, it seemed the left fork narrowed but sloped upward, while the right widened and led down. Tumbles of black stone shards indicated that the right-hand tunnel might not be entirely stable.

We're essentially inside a volcano, she chided herself. *Nothing is stable.*

"Which way?" she asked.

Ridge and Sykes both shone their lights first to the left and then the right. Sykes started off to the right a few feet while Ridge went left.

"Why are we even talking?" Tori asked. "Left is up, and up means out."

Ridge glanced back at her. "It might not be that simple."

Tori sighed, but her focus remained on Agent Hart. Alena kept her Maglite beam aimed at the ground so as not to shine it in anyone's eyes, but the illumination gave her enough light to see the sweat on Josh Hart's brow and the way he propped himself against the tunnel wall, as though the smooth black stone was the only thing keeping him standing. Tori caught Alena looking, and a wordless communication passed between them. If Josh had to sit down, he probably wouldn't be getting back up.

Alena glanced at the three sailors who brought up the rear—Mays, Garbarino, and Charlie. If they had to carry Josh, it would slow things down even more. Every second of indecision now could end up being costly.

"Paul, check out the left tunnel. Let's find out if it really does lead up and out," she said.

Ridge nodded grimly, aimed his Maglite, and stepped into the tunnel.

"Mr. Deaver," Lieutenant Commander Sykes called. "Go with Dr. Ridge. Cover him."

"Yes, sir!" Charlie snapped off a salute, and Alena realized she had just learned his last name.

Ridge vanished into the tunnel with Charlie close on his tail, the barrel of his assault rifle tipped toward the ceiling. Mays and Garbarino shuffled up closer, just behind Tori and Josh, and Alena thought they were all holding their breath.

"Do you hear that?" Tori whispered.

Alena frowned and stared at the tunnel where Ridge and Charlie had gone, thinking she referred to their progress, but she didn't hear anything.

"What is that?" Mays asked.

Sykes turned toward the right-hand path and started down it again, just a few steps, and then at last Alena heard the sound that had distracted them. Somewhere off in the tunnels—impossible to know how far with all of the echoes and twists and turns—a siren song had begun.

"I guess we're not going that way," Josh said, sliding up the wall to stand straight, a determined look in his eyes.

They all looked to the dark opening where Ridge and

Charlie had gone. Just as they did, another sound interrupted the siren song down to their right—a ripple of distant, muffled gunfire.

Alena froze, staring, aiming her flashlight beam at Sykes and beyond, down along that tunnel. Immediately, she knew David had come for her, and he wouldn't be alone.

"What the hell?" Tori asked.

"My grandson," Alena replied, heartbreaking love doing combat with fury and frustration inside her. "Goddamn fool."

"He's brought a whole team down here?" Sykes asked.

Alena turned to him, irony twisting in her. "He loves me."

But she could see that Sykes understood that the stakes had changed. The gunfire and the unnerving, hideous song of those monsters meant David and his team were either retreating by now or rushing this way. It also meant there must be no exit ahead, unless they wanted to fight their way past the sirens to get there.

Alena hurried to the entrance of the tunnel Ridge had entered. Someone would have to run the other way and try to lead David back here with whoever he'd brought with him, and then, if this truly offered a way out . . . but it had to. There was no other way.

"How are you doing up there, Paul?" she called.

"Good! Maybe great!" Ridge shouted back down to her. "It keeps going up, and there's light! It won't be an easy—"

Alena had just started into the tunnel, light picking out the easiest footholds on the rough slope, thinking that the climb would be rough on Josh, when Ridge cried out. Charlie Deaver swore loudly, and then she heard what sounded like a splash.

Panic seized her. "Paul? Damn it, Paul!"

Behind her, questions and curses merged into one stunned reaction—sailors' voices merging with Tori's frantic query. Alena did not stop to think; she steadied herself with her free hand and scrambled up the slope.

Ahead, someone began to scream.

"Paul!" she shouted, and far ahead and above her she saw the glimmer of daylight that had so excited Ridge. Silhouetted in that light, Charlie Deaver knelt on the ground, and only now did she hear the sailor's shouts.

"Dr. Ridge!" Charlie called. "Take my hand. Grab my fucking hand!"

Alena shone her Maglite on the scene and saw what had happened. The tunnel floor vanished a few feet from her, some past tremor having split the stone there. Focused on the daylight ahead, Ridge had gone one step too far before he had seen the drop, and slid into the crevice, and into bubbling, foaming seawater ten feet below.

"Jesus, Alena, help me!" Ridge cried.

Her flashlight beam struck his face and he closed his eyes but did not stop scrabbling for purchase, trying to climb back up. Charlie dropped flat on his stomach, arms thrust into the crevice. He had Ridge by the wrists and strained, cursing madly, trying to haul him back up.

Paul Ridge had tears in his eyes. No matter how hard Charlie pulled, he seemed to keep slipping. Alena couldn't breathe. She knew—knew—even before she flashed her beam lower and the light picked out the sickly pearl-white hand wrapped around Ridge's ankle, suckers tugging at flesh as Charlie attempted to haul Ridge out of the hole.

Something broke the surface of the water below Ridge, and she expected to see those black eyes, the glistening white scar-tissue face. Instead what coiled out from the dark water was the thing's tail. It wrapped around Ridge's leg, curling up as far as his groin.

"Charlie, let go," Alena whispered.

"Fuck that!" the sailor said. "Take my gun. Shoot the damn thing!"

Her flashlight picked out his weapon, there on the black rock. He'd set it aside so he could use both hands to grab for Ridge—a brave and foolish thing to do. But maybe he was right, maybe she could do it. She picked up the assault rifle, stepped to the edge, aimed just over Ridge's back at the thing in the water.

Sykes came up behind her, then put a strong hand on her hip and moved her aside. He took aim and pulled the trigger, squeezing off two careful shots. One of them hit the siren's tail and its head surfaced, mouth opening to reveal rows of needle teeth, screaming.

It burst from the water, reached up with both hands and sank talons into Ridge's back, and peeled him off the rock wall with sheer strength and its own weight. Screaming, Ridge did not let go of Charlie's wrists, instead dragging him over the lip and down into the crevice with him. Both men plunged into the water.

In the glow of Alena's flashlight beam, they struggled and died, blood foaming up in the roiling water.

"Deaver!" Sykes shouted, and Alena heard his voice crack, just once, before it became a roar. "Goddammit, Deaver!"

Sykes clicked over to automatic and pulled the trigger, bullets punching into the water and into flesh as well. Alena knew some of the shots would hit Ridge and Deaver, but she didn't try to stop Sykes. To her, it was a mercy if the bullets killed them.

One of the sirens bobbed to the surface, dead.

Sykes lowered his weapon.

But then, one by one, three pale faces pushed up from the dark water, one of them painted with human blood. They opened their mouths, teeth gleaming, and screeched that inhuman melody.

Sykes fired again but they submerged the moment his gun barrel twitched, and there would be no telling if he hit them.

Alena grabbed his arm. "Stop. We've got to run."

"Screw that, they'll only come after us," he said, shaking her off.

"Let them. At least you'll get a clear shot. But the tide's rising. If water floods through here, we're in their element."

Sykes fired again into the pit. "This is their element! It's their home!"

"And right now only a handful of them know we're here, or we'd be dead already," Alena snapped. "We don't know how they communicate, but the others will find out. We've got to go!" She grabbed the barrel of the gun, so that he twisted to meet her gaze. "Now!" she snapped.

With one last look into the water, Sykes nodded and together they scrambled down the slope and back to the fork. Tori and Josh had already started along the right-hand tunnel. Mays and Garbarino waited for orders.

"Move!" Sykes barked.

Alena could see the questions in the sailors' eyes. They'd heard the siren song and gunfire from up ahead as well. Weren't they running toward the same thing they were running away from? And maybe they were, but Alena told herself there might still be a way out up ahead, a branching tunnel or a cave mouth. If not, at least they would all be together—she and David would be together, one last time—and they would have all the guns in one place. As long as they were still breathing and moving, there was hope.

From the tunnel she and Sykes had just vacated, the song rose again. The sirens were coming after them.

"Watch our flank!" Lieutenant Commander Sykes told his men. "Kill anything that moves in behind you!"

"Yes, sir!" Garbarino and Mays snapped.

Then Sykes nodded to Alena and they were running along that right-hand tunnel, wider but sloping downward three or four feet. The water level couldn't have been more than six feet beneath them. By now it had already flooded into the tunnel they'd originally entered, hours ago in the grotto. Soon it would rush through these damp, dripping channels, and then it would be over. But until then . . .

"Run!" she shouted to Tori and Josh, who were ahead of them.

Her own heartbeat pounded loud in her ears and her breath came in ragged gasps, and it didn't seem to matter anymore what shape she was in. Fear aged her, made her feel slow and vulnerable. As she gained on Tori and Josh, she saw that the FBI agent had quickened his pace but only to a staggering jog, and she knew he would never get out of there alive.

For the first time, Alena Boudreau knew that they were going to die down there.

86

Voss saw daylight.

"Lieutenant!" Crowley called from up ahead.

"I see it!" Stone shouted. "Go!"

The tunnel had widened but the ceiling had dropped by several feet, so even Voss—the shortest of them—had to crouch to run. Crowley hustled, moving ahead so fast that Voss could barely keep up.

"It's got to be a vent or something," David Boudreau said behind her.

"I'll take it, whatever it is," Voss replied, ducking quickly to avoid bashing her temple against an outcropping. "Watch your head."

Gabe Rio and Lieutenant Stone came last, with Stone flashing his Maglite over his shoulder every few steps. Their faces spoke of desperation, and Voss found herself unable to draw a distinction between them. A criminal and an officer, they were both men trying to stay alive, and willing to fight to keep others alive as well. A part of her—a little voice in the back of her mind—tried to remind her that hunting Gabe Rio had led her to this place, but she ignored it. Who they were up in the sunlight didn't mean a damn thing down here in the dark.

The song pursued them as well—the insidious banshee wail of the sirens—but instead of a scream it seemed a whisper, and came only in small snatches of melody. The things were back there, following them in the tunnel, but they scuttled along, keeping out of the reach of flashlights and bullets, and Voss felt sure they were waiting for an opening.

"Here!" Crowley called. "Be careful!"

Voss blinked as she emerged into sunlight. Crowley grabbed her arm and pulled her aside and as her eyes adjusted she saw why. The rest of them followed, spilling out onto a wide ledge, and Voss felt her heart sink.

They were in an open volcanic vent, not unlike what the grotto might have been before time had worn one of its walls away. Half a dozen tunnels opened into the chamber—a thirty-foot-wide shaft that went up at an eighty-five-degree angle to the surface. The sight of the sky should have lifted her spirits—the daylight shone down into the shaft all the way to the ledge where they stood, and the creatures could not follow them out without burning—but the sky had darkened and the angle of the dimming light revealed just how close they were to dusk, and how long they had been down there, under the ground.

The ledge that ran around the shaft alternated in width, as much as four feet in some places but barely an inch in others. The water had risen to just three feet below the ledge.

"Get away from the tunnel!" Stone snapped.

Voss moved, skirting the shaft on the ledge, and turned just in time to glimpse something pale and white dart back into the deeper shadows of the tunnel from which they had just emerged.

The sirens had been following closer than they'd thought.

"Beautiful," Gabe said, looking around at the various fissures and caves that formed tunnels leading away from the shaft. "Which way do we go?"

Voss twisted around to stare at him. "Are you kidding?" She pointed to the water, where in addition to the tide rising, the reach of the daylight streaming down from above moved toward them with every passing moment. "The sun's going down. We'll be in the dark again, and then nothing will stop them."

As if in punctuation, Stone fired a couple of rounds back into the tunnel they had just escaped.

"We go up!" Voss snapped, shuffling along the ledge toward the front of the shaft, where the wall canted slightly, so the climb would be less sheer. Her throat tightened and her mouth had gone completely dry. Her heart thudded in her chest as she realized this was their only possible exit, their last chance.

The siren song grew louder, echoing off the walls of the shaft in an eerie, ghostly cry. Something splashed, and when she glanced over she saw two of the sirens slithering from the water in the places the sun had already abandoned. Something white breached the water, rolled, then submerged again.

"Look at that fissure in the back," Crowley said, right behind her.

"Son of a bitch," Gabe whispered.

In the fissure opposite their position, where there was no ledge at all, several of the things lay motionless, black eyes watching, unblinking, waiting. One of them uncoiled its lower body as lazily as a snake in the desert sun.

"Climb," David said, nearly drowned out by the maddening, growing song. "Just climb."

Gunshots echoed up through the shaft.

Voss spun and saw a flash of white emerging from yet another tunnel, but this one was still washed in sunlight. She blinked in amazement as she saw it was not white, but silver— Alena Boudreau's hair. Lieutenant Commander Sykes followed her out onto the ledge, both of them looking around in a panic only to come up short, expressions stunned, when they saw Voss and David and the others.

Then Tori Austin emerged.

Voss held her breath, not daring to hope, until Tori reached back into the tunnel and helped a staggering figure out onto the ledge. He looked pale and weak, but her partner was alive.

"Josh!" she shouted.

He looked up. Their eyes met. Without another word, they nodded to each other across the sun-splashed water, with the night and the tide and the devils moving in, and both started moving.

Two sailors practically spilled out onto the ledge, firing into the tunnel behind them. One of the sirens lunged out after them and it began to smoke and then burn. Screaming, it kept going, rolled off the ledge and into the cooling water with a hiss of steam that rose as it plunged into the dark.

"Climb!" Voss shouted.

And they were all in motion, reaching for handholds, racing the encroaching dark.

87

If the shaft had been straight, a sheer ninety-degree angle, Josh wouldn't have had a chance. He knew it, and from the look in her eyes, Tori knew it, too. The Vicodin had long since worn off. Instead of feeling as though he swam inside a fishbowl, looking out at the world, he felt like Caesar, a dozen knives stabbing him from every angle. But no matter how bad his pain might be, Josh had no intention of surrendering to it.

He climbed.

Sling tossed aside, unabashedly shouting and cursing God and Miguel Rio, he launched himself up the ragged rocky wall of the shaft as fast as he could manage. The pain blinded him for seconds at a time, during which he had to pause, take deep breaths, and then reach up again for a new handhold. A bullet had made the wound, but now it felt like someone had thrust a knife into it and begun to twist, hacking at muscle and scraping bone. Sweat poured down his face.

But he climbed, only somewhat aware of the others around him, of the siren song and the diminishing reach of the sun.

"Come on, Josh. Faster," Tori urged. She reached down and got a grip under his right arm, trying to pull.

"I'm going as fast as I can," he said through pain-gritted teeth.

But he did manage to find more speed, to drag himself higher, fresh rivulets of blood pouring from his shoulder down his chest, trickling down his side, soaking into his shirt. He imagined it dripping into the water far below, driving the creatures into a frenzy, like throwing chum in the water to stir up sharks.

I'm not fucking chum, he thought.

But his left hand felt numb. He held on to a rocky outcropping and could not feel his fingers for a moment. Alarmed, he pulled the hand away from the wall and then started to slip. Josh laid himself out flat, his right foot maintaining its hold even as he scrabbled for a better grip with his left and with both hands. His numb left hand couldn't grasp properly and he knew he would fall.

Tori and Voss, just above her, called out his name.

A strong hand pressed against his back, shoving him against the stone.

"Just hang on," a voice said. "Wait there for a second." And as he waited, the owner of that voice moved sideways on the wall below him, breathing hard with the effort, and then came up on his left side. Another hand grabbed him under the left arm, and Josh managed to turn his face to see who had come to his aid.

Gabe Rio.

"You've gotta be kidding me," Josh said.

Gabe didn't even blink, his face washed in the dimming daylight that streamed down from above. The former captain just grimaced, settling himself more securely against the shaft wall, and got a better grip on Josh.

"We go in tandem," Gabe said. "First me, then you. I'll go up a few feet, then help you after, and keep you steady, then climb up after you. Tori'll watch you on that side. But we've gotta move our asses."

Josh stared. Seconds ago he'd been cursing this man's dead brother. Gabe had been guilty of multiple crimes, and Josh had come along and ruined his life. Now, without hesitation, the man came to his aid. He had no words to thank Gabe, or to express his doubt or surprise. He doubted anything he said would be welcome, or sufficient.

"Let's go," Josh said.

They climbed just as Gabe had described, but it felt excruciatingly slow. Sykes and three of the other sailors were scrambling high above them, having covered nearly twenty feet already. To Josh's right, Alena and her grandson had their reunion on the rock wall but there were no tearful hugs. The two Boudreaus exchanged a few words and then they were climbing, breathing hard and focused entirely on where their feet and hands could find purchase. One of the sailors, a lieutenant, had a harder time than the others and kept about even with Voss, who had slowed down so as not to get too far ahead of Josh.

"What happened to Dr. Ridge?" Voss asked.

Josh swallowed hard, remembering the screams. "Wrong turn."

He didn't mean it as a joke, and Voss didn't take it as one. They were past the point of humor. Long past.

For minutes that seemed an eternity, he climbed, Gabe gripping his armpit and pulling upward on muscles that burned with strain. His clothes were tacky with blood and stuck to his skin and the flesh around his wound tugged with every movement of his arm, but still he climbed, unwilling to consider the alternative.

"Jesus," said the lieutenant, above him and to the right.

Josh risked a glance up at him, noticing how fast the light was fading, and saw that the sailor was staring back down the shaft. When next he rested, with Gabe scrabbling up a few more feet, Josh looked over his shoulder.

The ledge where they had come into the shaft had been submerged. Now that the tunnels were flooding, water pouring in from all sides, the tide had begun to rise even faster. But it was no longer the tide that made his muscles clench and his heart race.

The tide could only rise so far, but even as the tide rose, the light receded. They were on the eastern wall of the shaft, climbing in the last vestiges of sunlight that peeked in over the rim above. A clear line separated day from night in that shaft, and it moved up toward them as fast as they could climb, perhaps faster.

And just behind that demarcation, like runners at the starting line, the sirens clung to the walls of the volcanic shaft, creeping upward along with the encroaching darkness, just out of the sun's range. If some of them were sluggish during the day, they had certainly woken now. In a single glimpse, even with his eyes not adjusted to the balance of light and dark, he could make out fifteen or more of them, and others were climbing the western wall of the shaft, where the sun had long since surrendered its hold.

"Oh, my God," he whispered.

His numb fingers missed a hold. He scraped them raw grabbing for another, slammed his shoulder against the wall and screamed at the impact. His voice sounded a little like a shriek, and even something like the cry of the sirens that echoed all around them.

"Careful!" Voss shouted.

Tori shot her a hard look. "We're being careful! He's fine!"

If he could have managed it, Josh would have laughed. He was far from fine.

"Just keep going," he rasped, breathing hard. Even his eyes hurt. His whole body felt heavier and he knew that blood loss and trauma were taking their toll. He would be lucky to hang on, never mind climb.

Yet with Gabe's help, he kept going.

Tori didn't know why she stayed with him. She wanted to just climb. Sykes and Mays, and another sailor she didn't know, were moving fast, maybe twelve or fifteen feet from the top. Garbarino and another sailor had moved over to try to help speed the Boudreaus along, but they were making decent time.

She should climb. She should leave Josh behind. He had said as much himself at least half a dozen times back in the tunnel and she knew he would not blame her now. And maybe that was why she couldn't do it.

It wasn't love. No matter what she'd been through, or how many foolish things she had done in her life for the sake of unworthy men, she wasn't stupid enough to believe that. But she had made a connection with him, gone to a place inside herself that she had never found before, and it had made her see herself in a new way. And the woman she now saw in herself would never abandon this man, or perhaps any man, just to save herself.

So close to death, and yet it made her feel alive.

Voss hated her. She wanted to peel Tori right off the wall and toss her down into the water like feeding time at the zoo.

Over the years they had been partners, Josh had become her best friend. How was it possible that he could get tangled up with this woman, a suspect, in the middle of a case? How was it possible that he could feel something for her, could sleep with her, endangering his career and the squad and their partnership? Could Voss have misjudged him so completely, or was there just something about Tori Austin?

Voss hated her, but she admired her, too. Six feet away, Tori mirrored her terror back to her. An invisible link tethered them together, two women striving to survive. Two women who couldn't conceive of letting this one man die. Voss had been hardened by her career choice and the things she had seen, but what had forged that steel in Tori Austin?

Jealousy didn't suit Voss. She despised it in herself. She loved Josh but had never been in love with him, would never have jeopardized their partnership by pursuing something sexual—something complicated—with him. But they had developed an intimacy that she had never felt with anyone, and intimacy wasn't easy for her.

Now this woman they ought to be putting in jail had gotten a piece of that, and Voss hated her for it.

But she wanted her to live.

"Come on, Tori!" she snapped. "Don't let him slow down. We're racing the goddamn sun."

And they were. Both women looked down and saw the line between light and darkness sliding up at them, chasing them toward the surface and the sky, and they climbed faster.

Alena's chest burned. It felt tight and her breath came too fast and she focused on the muscles in her arms, waiting for pain that would be a telltale sign of a heart attack. But that pain didn't come. The fist in her chest was the grip of fear, as all of her illusions about her life were stripped away. Her work was important—more important, maybe, than she had ever realized—but she thought of her daughter, and the time they could have spent together. Time squandered in favor of adventure and discovery. Alena loved those things—they meant the world to her—but not as much as her family meant.

Her fingers searched for a crevice, found it, plunged in, and she boosted herself a few more feet before reaching for higher toeholds. The shaft angled downward at about eighty percent here, and the climb was getting easier. Faster. Above her, Lieutenant Commander Sykes and one of his men were nearly at the top, the sun limning them in golden halos, like gods coming down from Olympus. Nearer, but still a few feet higher than she was, Garbarino and a sailor she didn't know scrabbled side to side in search of better grips, moving like spider-men, then pausing to check her progress.

The song of the sirens echoed off the walls, and it had become maddening. She wanted to scream back, and so she did, opening her lips and crying out at them in wordless fury.

"Alena," David said.

She turned to look at him. So handsome, her grandson. Only a few feet away, he climbed at her side, and now he focused on her, locking eyes.

"We're almost there. Keep going."

"Keep going," she repeated. "Don't tell me, kid. I'm in better shape than you'll ever be."

As he plastered himself to the shaft wall and slid his knee up, boot probing, he actually managed to smile at her, though fear and desperation glittered in his eyes. David hauled himself up a few more feet and Alena redoubled her efforts, keeping pace with him. She glanced down and caught her breath.

The darkness had come within six or seven feet of Josh, Tori, and Gabe. Lieutenant Stone and Voss were only a few feet higher. The sirens clung like leeches to the wall, black eyes gleaming like the volcanic rock. They had fifteen feet or so to reach the rim, and Alena didn't think they were going to make it.

She reached up, not paying enough attention, and her fingers slipped off a tiny outcropping of rock. She slid, scraping her right cheek on the wall and banging her chest, bruising ribs, but she managed to catch herself.

David put out a hand to steady her, shifting his weight, and his foothold gave way, crumbling beneath him. His eyes went wide and he tried to grab hold of the wall, but his fingers scraped downward. Without a hand or foothold on the right side, and with his weight tilted that direction, he began to fall.

Alena screamed his name. Eyes wide, she watched as he pressed himself against the shaft wall, dragging bloody fingers down the black stone. One foot caught and his knee buckled and he nearly tipped backward but he shook it free and somehow managed to slow his descent and finally stop.

Not soon enough.

Half in darkness now, he looked up at her, his face still in sunlight. Instead of fear, his eyes were full of a terrible sadness and a kind of confusion, as if he did not know how he had come to be there.

Alena started to descend, half climbing and half sliding after him.

"Doctor, no!" Garbarino shouted. "Get out of the way!"

The sharpness of the command forced her to look up. Garbarino clung to the wall with one hand even as he used the other to grasp the strap of his assault rifle and swing it around from where it had dangled against his back. One-handed, he took aim. Beside him, the other sailor did the same, fumbling with the gun, foot slipping, getting a new toehold, barely hanging on.

"You'll hit David!" Alena screamed at him.

Others were shouting as well, voices merging with the screeching song of the sirens, echoing around the shaft.

Garbarino ignored her, focused on David. "Head down!" he shouted.

Alena twisted again in time to see David press himself hard against the wall, even as he tried to climb with torn and bloody fingers. Garbarino fired, bullets tearing into the darkness, clipping stone outcroppings and ricocheting. Two of the sirens were ripped away from the wall by bullets and tumbled into the darkness, sickly, fishbelly-white bodies uncoiling as they fell.

But Garbarino and the other sailor couldn't hit the ones coming up beneath David without shooting him as well, and as Alena watched, her grandson began to scream. Panic made him tear his gaze from hers, but she could not look away as the things swarmed over him. One of them, overzealous, scaled his body like a ladder but climbed too high, into the sunlight, where it smoldered and ignited and screamed. Its serpentine lower body twisting, it shoved off from the wall and plunged into the water below, the splash dousing its fire and its cries.

"Damn it!" Garbarino shouted.

From the corner of her eye, Alena caught his movement. He tried to scramble to one side, searching for a better angle, a cleaner shot, and he lost his grip. As he fell, panic seized him and he pulled the trigger, but the bullets chipped at the stone walls with little effect and then Garbarino screamed the rest of the way, following the siren into the water, from which he would never surface.

"Alena!" David shrieked, voice ragged as they tore at him. "Go!"

But Stone and Voss had been in motion all along, and now they opened fire, shooting the sirens that were attacking him. One by one, the creatures peeled off the wall and fluttered into the abyss.

"Climb, David!" Alena shouted.

Somehow, he did. She could see the agony etched into his features and she wondered what his legs must look like after the sirens' jaws had been at work, and the suckers on their hands had scoured the flesh. But he climbed.

Voss shot at the things that were still coming up as Stone edged over beside David to speed him along.

"Climb, damn it!" David shouted up at her.

That got Alena moving.

"We're out!" Lieutenant Commander Sykes called from above. "Move it!"

And then Alena felt a hand grip her wrist and looked up to see Voss and Mays reaching for her. They hauled her over the rim, onto a thick mat of vegetation, trees sparse overhead. She climbed to her feet and glanced at the horizon, where the sun slid rapidly into the water. Its light reached only a few feet into the cave they had just escaped, and the leech-white creatures stirred at the edges of the dark, ready to erupt in pursuit the moment the last sliver of the sun vanished in the west.

The high, keening melody diminished, and then she heard Sykes barking into a radio and the roar of helicopter rotors not far off.

Gabe, Tori, and Josh crawled out of the cave shaft. Voss and the nameless sailor lifted the sweating, glassy-eyed Josh to his feet, even as Alena went to help Stone haul David out onto the ground.

"Are you all right?" she asked.

It was a foolish question. The legs of his trousers were soaked with blood and his hands were scraped raw. He swayed, barely able to remain sitting up.

"Not yet," he murmured. "Get us out of here."

"Which way?" Tori said, shouting to be heard, all of them casting frantic looks into the shaft.

Sykes raised a hand and pointed down the hill—for they were on the mountainside now. "There! West toward the sun, stay in the light as long as you can, but run for the beach! The chopper's coming down there!"

As Stone bent to lift David in a fireman's carry, Alena looked down into the shaft and saw those pale, hideous faces with their black eyes staring back. But they were not the only things out of place. Spaced all around the shaft's rim there were small gray rectangles—explosive charges that had been set sometime in the past few hours. A radio signal would set them all off at once, and the idea woke her up. She stared at the sirens and hatred filled her. It gave her back some strength, but she knew it wouldn't last.

Then they were all running, Josh staggering, and Tori grabbed her wrist as she went by. Alena careened through the trees with her, branches whipping at her face, and as she caught a fresh glimpse of the horizon, the sun going down, shadows gathering all around them in the trees and brush, a single thought filled her mind.

Detonate. Push the goddamn button. Burn them all.

On the bridge of the USS *Hillstrom,* Ed Turcotte watched the sun slide into the Caribbean with a horrid fascination. His every muscle taut, he glanced back and forth between Captain Siebalt and the communications officer. A terrible weight bore down on every man and woman there as the last of the golden daylight faded.

"Sir?" the communications officer said, glancing at the captain. "Mr. Keck's awaiting the detonation order."

Siebalt glared at him, and Turcotte knew that look. *Don't tell me my business,* it said. He had given the look enough times himself.

Every cave and vent the sweep teams could find out on the island had been mined with charges as the afternoon wore on, even as others explored tunnels and tried radio and phone signals to get some update on the people they had lost below and those who had gone down after them. All of the ships had moved in closer to the island after the *Antoinette* had been scuttled—but not too close, the captains far too wary of sharing the freighter's fate. The choppers had evacuated all personnel just before dusk, but now kept doing flyovers, searching for some sign of the Boudreaus, Voss, and Hart, and the others who were inside the warren of tunnels in the island's womb.

Bud Rouleau, the *Kodiak*'s captain, had kept his Coast Guard ships close, but he deferred to Siebalt, just as Turcotte had to. In the wake of the clusterfuck on the *Kodiak*'s deck, with the Tyree woman's death and the destruction of the creature they'd retrieved from the *Antoinette*—their one test subject—the civilian chopper had been grounded. Nobody would be allowed to leave the area until someone took control of this mess, and right now the person in control was either dead, or they were about to kill her.

Siebalt took a deep breath, glanced at the sliver of the sun still visible out on the ocean, the horizon striated with color, and turned as though to give the order.

"Don't!" Turcotte snapped.

Captain Siebalt shot him a dark look. "Dr. Boudreau left us with an order—"

"Yeah, *David* Boudreau. He's a kid, for Christ's sake. You can't detonate with all of those people still unaccounted for! We both have people still out there."

"We did," Siebalt said, his gray eyes hard. "In a minute, it will be full-on dark. Anyone left in those tunnels is dead. And anyone on the island *will* be. My orders are to blow the place and kill as many as we can."

"You won't get them all now anyway," Turcotte snapped.

Siebalt turned away, looking to the communications officer. The whole bridge was silent. "We'll start cleanup at dawn. For now, we follow our orders. Lieutenant Chang, the order is given. Detonate."

"Yes, sir," the communications officer replied. He tapped a key on his console. "The order is given—"

But Lieutenant Chang didn't finish. He raised a hand to the earpiece of his headset and turned in his seat. "Captain, message coming through from Chopper Three. They're out. Lieutenant Commander Sykes is radioing for evac."

Turcotte whispered the first grateful prayer he'd said in years.

-89--

Tori ran so fast she could barely keep her legs beneath her, and somehow Josh kept pace. His face had gone pale as the moon and he held his arm tight to his body as they careened down the hill together. Gravity seemed to give him the momentum and speed he needed, but how he kept his feet under him she had no idea. Voss dodged around trees and crashed through vegetation to Tori's left. Up ahead, Alena Boudreau navigated with remarkable grace, alongside the lieutenant she'd heard called Stone, who carried David over one shoulder, sometimes running and sometimes staggering under the burden. Lieutenant Commander Sykes and the other surviving sailors—Mays and Crowley—ran a dozen yards ahead of them.

In the shadows of the trees and the thick tangles of brush, night had already fallen. A sliver of sunlight remained on the horizon ahead, but it could not reach those dark places. The last golden light of day splashed the island in broad swathes, and Tori aimed for those, darting from light into shadow and then into twilight again. Her face burned like it was on fire—blood rushing through her, flushing her skin—but from the back of her neck and all down her back, Tori felt cold. That was the chill of vulnerability, the icy weight of the creatures' *attention*.

For they were there, in the shadows already. She caught a glimpse of sickly white as she sprinted from one splash of light to another, moving from a small slash of black rock, a narrow cave in the face of the hill. Only one of them, and only that cave, but there had to be others beginning to emerge.

No one screamed to run. They were long past such urgings, and fleeing for their lives now. Her breath came in gasps and gulps and her arms pumped at her sides. Branches whipped at her face and she brushed them aside, her focus alternating between Josh—whose every step brought a grunt of pain—and the horizon, where the sun seemed to melt into the darkness of the ocean, her skin prickling with awareness of the hunger that exuded from the island. And all along their path, the maddening song of the sirens began to rise from a whisper to a wail.

At the bottom of the hill, they hit a clearing of rock and scrub and Tori searched frantically for any sign of a cave, but saw none. From here she could see, through sparser trees ahead, the white sand of the beach and the indigo gleam and white foam of the water beyond. The sun only peeked over the edge of the world now, and she knew that, close as they were, they would never make it. The song rose, and she could picture the creatures in her mind, climbing out of their watery caves or slithering up onto shore.

They had seconds. A minute or two at most.

Josh faltered and nearly went sprawling. She reached out to grab his hand, but Voss beat her to it, pulling hard on Josh's wrist.

"*Run,* goddammit!"

Tori didn't know if the woman meant her or Josh, but she put on speed. Voss hauled Josh along beside her, shouting at him not to fall, to put one foot in front of the other.

Lieutenant Stone stumbled, and he and David Boudreau went sprawling. David cried out in pain at the impact on his bloody legs, but then Mays and Crowley were there, hoisting him up again. This time Crowley carried him, with Stone and Mays on either side, ready to take over if necessary. They weren't going to leave anyone behind.

Alena kept pace with the sailors who were trying so hard to save her grandson's life.

Left arm pinned to his side, Josh careened toward a ridge of black rock. He managed to plant his foot on it and spring forward. Tori felt sure he would trip and fall, but still he crashed forward.

Watching him, Tori stepped on a stone, twisted her ankle, threw out her arms for balance and tried to get her feet under her again, only to catch the toe of her boot on a root. She fell hard, rolling over twice, a third time, slamming her back against a ridge of stone.

In shadow.

To her right, the darkness had grown thick. The singsong voice of the sirens had taken on an almost taunting air and as she rolled to her knees and started to rise, she saw them in the trees—three of the creatures moving low to the ground, in the brush, out of the twilight. They slid toward her, too fast.

In the same moment, she realized the little light around her had become moonlight. The last of the sun had vanished into the ocean. Up at the top of the hill, the sirens would be swarming out of the volcanic shaft. They were close enough to hear the roar of the chopper's rotors, out on the beach, maybe fifty yards away, but she would die here in the night's shadows.

But Tori didn't give up. She pistoned her legs, leaping to her feet, and turned to run.

"Get down!" Josh snapped.

Tori had no time to think. She dropped to her knees again just as Josh and Rachael Voss strode toward her with the righteous purpose that came with authority, guns raised. They had only pistols, not the Navy's assault weapons, but they fired again and again, and the bullets tore the sirens apart.

It was all Josh had. He dropped the gun, swaying on his feet, and nearly fell. He would have, if Tori and Voss hadn't been there to prop him up, and then they were nearly dragging him through fifty feet of sparse trees toward the beach.

Alena Boudreau went past them, headed the wrong way.

"What are you doing?" Voss shouted.

"Not leaving his gun behind!" Alena replied, snatching up Josh's gun and then racing to keep up with them.

Then the hillside they had just descended came alive with white, undulating flesh—the sirens that had nearly taken them underground, at last giving chase. Alena and Voss fired in motion. Tori shouldered as much of Josh's weight as she could, but Voss held him up as well, still managing to shoot at the things churning down the hill behind them.

"Let's go!" Sykes called from up ahead, as if they were dragging their feet and not one hundred eighty pounds of bleeding FBI agent.

Then they burst out of the trees and onto soft sand that gave way beneath Tori's boots, making it hard to run and even harder to drag Josh. Stone and Crowley had run ahead to the chopper, which waited on the beach with its door open. She saw Agent Nadeau leap out, beckoning and shouting, though his voice could not be heard over the chopper and the sirens. He helped them load David onto the helicopter.

Sykes and Mays and Gabe Rio had waited for them, and now all three of them raised guns to cover their race for the chopper. Tori saw something rise from the water and looked into the waves. They were there as well, emerging from the darkness of the deep water, rushing through the surf, mouths opening to reveal those needle teeth, faces split by rictus grins—as if the things could smile.

And they sang.

Mays fell under the onslaught from the water in seconds. He tried to shoot, tried to tear the creatures off, but arms and tentacle-like bodies wrapped around him, and the sailor went down amidst the teeth and the screaming melody of the sirens.

Gabe spun, took aim, and tore up the water and the sirens slithering from it in a hail of bullets. White flesh and splashes of dark ichor spattered the waves. Mays was already dead, but Gabe killed as many as he could and kept the line back.

Sykes and Crowley, who came back from the chopper to help, took aim at the creatures surging from the undergrowth and opened fire. Tori did not even turn to look. Her eyes were on the helicopter, on the open door, and she barely even saw the three men with their assault rifles now, two Navy heroes and one gun smuggler who seemed to have forgotten who he'd once been. And she realized that she had forgotten as well. The past didn't matter anymore, only tomorrow. Only the next sunrise.

Nadeau rushed to meet them, and helped Tori and Voss half-drag and half-carry Josh the last dozen feet, and then they were scrambling into the back of the chopper. Nadeau and Voss slid Josh away from the door, their focus on their fellow agent, and that left Tori alone to reach for Alena's hand, helping the woman in beside her. She went immediately to David and began to investigate his wounds, shouting for a med-kit.

Gabe and Crowley jumped onto the helicopter, but Sykes shouted something none of them could hear over the roar and kept firing into the dozens of creatures even as the chopper began to lift off. Only then did the lieutenant commander throw himself into the back of the helicopter. The gunfire ceased for a second or two, and then he and Crowley were both hanging out the door, firing again as they rose into the air.

Several of the leeches clung to the undercarriage and one crawled up the door on the other side of the chopper, but as they picked up speed and roared away from the shore, out over the dark water, they peeled away and tumbled into the sea.

Tori heard a voice, shouting, and looked up to see the pilot barking something into his headset, radioing the *Hillstrom* with the news. The first explosion came three seconds later, punching the air and rocking the chopper, propelling them toward the small cluster of ships a mile or two offshore. In the space of several heartbeats, hundreds of charges blew, spewing black stone and dust and chunks of earth into the air, lighting up the sky, and setting fire to the trees.

They were out of the caves. They'd have nowhere to go when the sun rose except into the water, and tomorrow morning, the extermination would begin. Those who weren't crushed in collapsed caves or burned by the flames or the sun would have to be killed, and that would take time. Eventually, Alena's people would destroy them all. Tori found comfort in that, and in the knowledge that when they finally killed the last of the creatures, she would be far, far from here.

She turned to look at Josh and saw that he had fallen unconscious at last, passed out in Rachael Voss's lap. His partner stroked his hair, her own clothes stained with Josh's blood, and Tori knew she was alone.

But alone didn't scare her anymore.

-epilogue--

Gabe sat in the dark, in a chair he had never used when he and Maya had shared this apartment. Its plush burgundy fabric gathered dust in the far corner of the living room, near the windows, where Maya had intended to use it for reading or for extra seating when they had company. A floor lamp arced from behind and the windows would have provided light during the day; it really was the perfect reading chair, though she had only rarely used it for that. As for company, they'd had very little over the past couple of years.

The window looked out at the lights of Miami. Even with the air-conditioning up too high, the way Maya liked it, the view of the sparkling city warmed him. He relished it, knowing that tonight would be the last he ever spent in Miami. The window also looked down on the street that ran by the front of the apartment building, and he could see the dark sedan parked across the road, and even the orange flicker of a burning cigarette inside. Agent Nadeau smoked. His partner, McIlveen—Mac, they called him—gave him shit about it: a constant stream of banter that Gabe would not miss.

He wanted quiet now.

Outside the apartment door there came the jangle of keys, followed by the scrape of one seeking the lock. With a click, the door swung inward and Maya entered, silhouetted in the light from the corridor, which made the red highlights in her hair glow. Just watching her move, the shape and gentle, familiar curve of her, Gabe felt his heart break all over again. His breath caught in his throat and he wondered if it had been a mistake coming here.

Maya dropped her keys on the little table under the mirror beside the door and set down her purse as she flicked on the light.

As she turned, Gabe breathed her name.

She jumped, and might have cried out if she hadn't brought a hand up to her mouth to silence herself. The gesture broke him a little more inside, for she had always done the same while making love, embarrassed by the noise her body wanted to make.

"Gabriel. What are you doing here?" she asked, not approaching, eyes full of questions.

He wondered if she could see the broken pieces of him in his smile. "So, you missed me then?"

Maya exhaled, walking over to the sofa but not sitting. Instead, she stood behind it as though using it as some kind of shield, tracing her fingers along the sofa's back.

"You blame me for being surprised? Last time we talked, you made your feelings pretty clear," Maya said, fresh hurt and the old frustrations coming together in her tone. "Now I find you sitting in the dark, and . . . seriously, what the hell are you doing here? Something you left behind that you can't live without?" Bitterness had crept into her voice.

"Miguel's dead."

The words startled her, like someone had slammed a door. And Gabe thought maybe that was near enough to the truth. Maya paled and stared at him, her breath coming a bit quicker. Her makeup was just so, her hair perfect, her hoop earrings the perfect accent for her face. Denim hugged her legs and ribbed cotton clung to her breasts and flat belly, all propped up on expensive heels. All in all, Maya Rio had the air of a woman confident in herself, the sort of woman who would draw stares she would pretend never to see.

But her husband knew the girl she had been, and now he watched part of that fragile girl shattering.

"You're awful," Maya said. "That's not even funny, Gabe. What a terrible thing to say."

Gabe only looked at her and she stared back, her denial crumbling.

"No, no. Come on, Gabe. Please don't . . . No."

At last he rose from Maya's reading chair, the only time he would ever sit in it, and he went around the sofa and took her in his arms. Despite all that had passed between them, bitterness and bad blood and recriminations, she did not protest as he embraced her. For long minutes he held her, the night ticking away outside but time at a standstill for Gabe and Maya Rio. For a brief moment, they were husband and wife again.

"How . . . how did it happen?" she asked, her head still resting on his shoulder. "I thought you were still at sea."

Gabe tried to reply, but the words wouldn't come. They had not given him much time. How could he speak the things he had come here to say? He had never been eloquent. But perhaps truth would succeed where eloquence might fail him.

"Maya," he said, holding her out at arm's length, finding her gaze with his own, making sure they connected. He fought the anger and bitterness that churned like bile in the back of his throat and twisted his gut in knots.

"What?" she urged. "What aren't you telling me, Gabe?"

He took a deep breath and released her, leaning back against the sofa. Best to give her space now.

"I know about you and Miguel."

Before his eyes, Maya started to fall apart. She didn't even try to deny it. Strange sounds came from her throat, little choking gasps, and then—hands shaking—she began to cry. The tears fell without sobs or even words, at least at first. Several times she tried to speak but emotion overcame her and she could only wave her hands about, angry with herself.

"Gabe," she said at last.

And then it occurred to her, as he had known it would, and a wave of fear and suspicion spread across her features. One fluttering hand covered her mouth again and she took a step away from him.

"No," he said. "I didn't kill him, Maya." Gabe glanced at the floor a moment. "I won't say I didn't think about it. I hated both of you, and I wanted to hurt you both, badly. But Miguel saved my life, *chica*. He died to give me a chance to live, and that bought me time to think. I don't have a lot of words for the things I feel. Never have. But I know that we drifted really far from each other, and that was at least as much my fault as it was yours. You didn't just betray me, you betrayed us. But you're not the only one. I can't put it all on you."

He took a breath, and then a risk. He held out his hand for hers.

"My brother . . ." he said, emotion welling up inside him, studying Maya's eyes, searching for the girl he'd first fallen in love with. "Miguel is gone, but we're still here."

"After everything . . ." she began.

"I know."

"We can't just—"

"I *know*."

They stared at each other, and in her eyes Gabe saw fury and shame and regret that mirrored his own. Tentatively, she reached out and took his hand, and they stood like that for a few seconds, still far apart but connected by that uncertain connection.

"Miguel's really . . . he's really dead?"

Gabe nodded.

"I'm so sorry."

Then she stepped gingerly forward and slipped her arms around him, careful—as though afraid he might break.

"What happened?"

Gabe took a deep breath and once more released her. He turned and walked to the window, wondered how long it would be before Nadeau and Mac ran out of patience. No one had seen Gabe coming into the building, and they could not afford to have anyone see him leaving, either.

"You might want to sit down," he said.

Maya searched his eyes for some clue to what might be coming, what other dreadful news he might have brought with him, but she did as he suggested, perching on the edge of the sofa.

"You're going to have a lot of questions about what I'm about to say," he explained, "but I'm not going to be able to answer them. What I tell you now is all I'm allowed to tell you, do you understand?"

"Allowed? Allowed by—"

"Maya," Gabe interrupted, "it's all I'm allowed to say. Do you understand that?"

Wiping at her tears, she nodded.

"When I walk out of here, I won't be coming back," he said, his heart heavy. "Not to the apartment, and not to Miami. As far as the world will know, the *Antoinette* sank with all hands on board."

"Christ," Maya whispered.

Gabe swallowed hard, the words difficult for him. "Miguel's dead. And you'll be told that I'm dead, too. If you talk about me coming here, and this conversation, doctors will say you imagined it, that grief made you see things you wished to see. The government will confirm my death. And it will be like I really am dead. I'll be just as gone, and just as impossible to find again.

"I'm vanishing tonight, *chica*," Gabe went on, his heart turning gentle, knowing how her mind must be awhirl. "And I hope you'll come with me."

Maya's mouth hung open in a little O and then she looked around the room, as though the answers could be found there. She leaned back, sinking deeper into the sofa.

"Where?" she asked.

"I can't tell you. But I won't lie to you; it won't be anything like Miami. Someplace they don't speak English, a fishing village," he said, and sat beside her on the sofa so she could see his eyes up close and maybe see the truth. "I can't give up the sea, Maya. Not ever. But I won't be wandering far again. I'll have a fishing boat, and I'll be up before sunrise, but I'll come home every night for dinner."

She scoffed, half-turning from him in doubt.

Gabe took her hand. "I mean it."

Maya shook her head, gaze shifting around before at last meeting his. "Do you really think you could live like that?"

"I could if you could."

Her lower lip trembled. "It's all I ever wanted. You know that. But after everything . . ."

"I know," he said, squeezing her hand. He reached up and brushed her hair away from her eyes.

Defiant, she stared at him. "You really think we can forgive each other?"

"Truth? I don't know," he confessed. "But after the mistakes I've made, and all I've lost, and everything that's gone on between us, I've got a chance to start over, and it kills me to think of doing that without you."

Long seconds ticked by. Maya's breaths came evenly, the way they did when she slept. Her gaze grew distant, lost in contemplation. Then she looked up at Gabe and gave him a quick nod.

For so long—all the way back to the day he had taken the job at Viscaya to help Miguel—Gabe had felt like a passenger in his own life. He could captain a ship, but his own fate had seemed out of his hands. But that Gabe Rio, the one who never faulted himself but seethed at the betrayals of those he loved, who could never have conceived of giving or receiving forgiveness . . . that man was dead, lost with the *Antoinette*. Captain Rio had gone down with his ship.

Gabe stood, and Maya rose with him, still holding his hand.

"Come on," he said. "They're waiting. We won't have much time."

"Sure we will," Maya replied, releasing his hand and hurrying to pack some things. She glanced back over her shoulder at him. "Sure we will."

WASHINGTON, D.C.

Alena came awake with a start, drawing a sharp breath and jerking a bit in the chair. She woke to a painful stiffness in her back and a headache that started above her right eye and spiked in deep. The sun was too bright, and she raised her head and turned away, settling down again where she had fallen asleep the night before—at David's desk, in his office.

Memory returned, unwelcome. Then, much as she wished it, sleep refused to claim her again.

The doorbell chimed, its echo lingering too long.

"Son of a bitch," she rasped.

Sitting up, she slid her hands across the desk and knocked last night's whiskey glass onto the floor. It shattered on the wood, a few ounces of amber liquid dappling the boards, beading up like mercury.

Had the doorbell already rung once? Was that what had woken her?

Alena rose, pushing back the chair, and cast a baleful glance at the broken glass, as though it had leaped from the desk to its splintered doom purely to vex her. Unsteady on her feet, she paused in the open office door, surprised to find that she gripped something in her left hand. Even as she glanced down, fingers opening, she remembered clutching the thing last night, tapping the desk with it, idly passing it from hand to hand, contemplating it. As if it were some sacred talisman, she had fallen asleep with it tight in her grasp.

Now she stared at the object in her open palm—a shard of glassy, volcanic rock only slightly bigger than a marble.

The doorbell rang again.

"Goddammit!" Alena cried, and hurled the rock shard back into the room, where it struck one of the ocean charts David had pinned to the wall and fell harmlessly to the floor.

All of the charts and news clippings were still on the wall, all of the maps still spread on the table, all of the rock samples and photographs still arrayed on the shelves with her grandson's books and journals.

Alena left them behind, hurrying down the stairs now that she had come fully awake. She ran both hands through her silver hair, unruly from sleep, and smoothed the front of the charcoal-black top she'd been wearing the night before.

When she unlocked the door and pulled it open, she found General Henry Wagner standing out on the sidewalk of M Street, his face drawn into the sorrowful grimace of a penitent child.

"Alena," he said.

She put a hand to her head, massaging her right temple. "Hank," she said. "Come in. I need an entire bottle of Excedrin."

Leaving him on the threshold, she turned and strode into the kitchen. Her eyes itched and her head felt like someone had lodged an axe in her skull and just now decided to work it back and forth, trying to free it.

The general must have closed the front door and followed, because by the time she retrieved the Excedrin from a cabinet, filled a glass of water, and tossed back four of the pills, the man was standing in the kitchen half a dozen feet away from her.

Hank Wagner stood six and a half feet tall and had the build of a washed-up football star. Fifty-two or -three, he had done nothing to remedy his thinning blond hair or the failing eyesight that required thick glasses on gold wire rims. Sometimes dour, always intense, the general had always struck her as a good man who believed he had found his calling. If she would not have called him a friend, that detracted not at all from the respect she felt for him.

In the eleven years since he had taken the place of the general who had run her division before him, Hank Wagner had never once showed up at her front door. In fact, now that she considered it, he had never been to her residence.

"Alena, I can't tell you how sorry I am," he said.

She considered putting on a pot of coffee, but realized that would be an invitation for him to stay long enough to drink it.

"Thank you, General."

If it insulted him that she would remain so formal, Hank Wagner didn't show it.

"How are you?"

Alena attempted a wry smile, expecting it to come off tragic and sad, but knowing even as the expression contorted her face that she had only managed brittle and bitter.

"My daughter, Marie—David's mother—has severed all ties with me."

The big man shrank a little. "I'm sorry. That's awful."

That smile again, no better than before. "Apparently she needs to blame me. I forged him, you see, from the time he was a little boy. His passion for science and discovery was my fault."

"Alena—"

"No," she said, and now, somehow, she felt herself relax. Maybe the Excedrin taking effect. "It's all right. I'll take the credit, and the blame. If my work inspired him, I think of it as a gift. And when my own enthusiasm flagged—it does sometimes, you know. I'm not as young as I used to be.

When I faltered, he'd give the gift right back with fresh insight and inspiration."

The moment dragged long enough to become awkward. Wagner seemed at a loss, as though trying to figure out how to frame his next thought.

"You didn't come here to ask how I'm faring," Alena said.

The general slid his hands into his pockets. "Not exactly."

"You've got a case. Let me guess, the skeletons at Mount Kazbek?"

Wagner nodded, then gave a small shrug. "I've got to send someone. Sarah Ernst resigned yesterday, Ridge is dead, and without you and David . . . well, I need to rebuild, and I was hoping you could offer me some guidance. You know every-one in this field. Any suggestions?"

Alena rubbed her eyes. Her headache had begun to recede nicely, but the whiskey from the night before had still left her feeling like her skull was stuffed with cotton.

"There's a little bakery up the street with excellent coffee," she said. "Would you take a walk up there, pick me up a cin-namon Danish and a massive cup of the hazelnut blend, and whatever you want?"

Confused, the general shrugged again. "Of course. And then—"

"While you're gone I'll shower and change, and throw a bag together."

Wagner held up both hands. "Wait a minute, Alena, I'm not asking you to do this. Honestly, I assumed . . . well, I just figured this would be it for you."

Alena Boudreau narrowed her eyes. "Eleven years, and you don't know me at all, Hank. My daughter won't speak to me anymore, but David would be horrified if I let that stop me. Our goals have always been clear—keep searching, keep dis-covering, keep drawing back the curtains to get at the world's mysteries."

The general smiled. "David thought this case was a waste of time."

"No," she said. "He just had other things on his mind. And when I get back from Mount Kazbek, we're going to talk about those things. If there are three of these habitats out there, you and I both know there could be more. The sooner we find them, the sooner we can destroy them, and we'll save a lot of lives."

"All that in exchange for coffee and a Danish?"

Alena chuckled. "Actually, you'd better make it two coffees and throw in a chocolate cruller. It'll save me having to make David breakfast."

"It's a deal," Wagner said. "As long as you're sure he won't mind."

"Mind? He loves chocolate crullers."

"That's not what I meant. Is he going to be all right with you going away?"

Now Alena rolled her eyes. "Please. He'll be thrilled to be rid of me. I've been hovering over him constantly. He says it's very 'un-Alena' of me. Besides, the nurse who comes in to look after him is very cute. I'm sure I'm cramping his style."

It was Wagner's turn to chuckle.

Promising a swift return, he left for the bakery, and Alena let her smile fade. Everything she'd said had been the truth, but it did nothing to lighten her heart. Marie blamed her for what had happened to David, but no more than Alena blamed herself.

She climbed the stairs, but did not go to her own room. Instead, she continued up to the third floor and looked in on David, relieved to find that he was still sleeping. He needed his rest, and the painkillers helped. Though the doctors seemed confident he would walk again, the damage to his legs—the left in particular—had been substantial.

She started to pull his door closed, but then thought better of it. He seemed to be sleeping peacefully now, but his dreams had been worse than ever. If he woke from a nightmare, she wanted to be there.

When the general returned, she would rouse David and fill him in on her trip to Mount Kazbek. And then she would repeat the promise she had made to him every day since they had returned home, that when he was better, they would start over.

They would chase the nightmares together.

ST. CROIX

The Hotel Caravelle on the island of St. Croix boasted a popular restaurant called Rum Runners. With an awning that stretched across an outdoor patio, expanding the dining area, Rum Runners looked much like a thousand other waterfront restaurants in a thousand other places. But the view made all the difference.

Tori sat under an umbrella on the patio drinking iced tea and gazing out at the sailboats anchored just offshore, bobbing in the gentle swell of the Caribbean. A handful of clouds drifted across the sky, tinting it white, which only served to enhance the rich, bright blue of the water. Rum Runners came just to the edge of the island, separated from the water only by a couple of palm trees and a seawall of gray granite foundation stones. A narrow channel—barely wide enough to act as a boat slip—ran alongside the restaurant, and parallel to that a dock made of what appeared to be freshly cut wood. And then nothing but the Caribbean—a vision of paradise as far as the eye could see.

But Tori knew that out there in the open sea, closer to this heaven than anyone would ever imagine, there also existed a little slice of hell.

"Sorry to keep you waiting."

The words erased the momentary chill that had come over her. She turned, already smiling, and saw Josh standing by her table, awaiting an invitation to sit. He still wore a sling—the wound from Miguel Rio's bullet would take time to heal—but after a couple of days' rest and proper food, he looked strong and his color had returned, his bruises mostly faded.

Josh would be just fine, and Tori found herself relieved.

"Rachael's not coming?"

Josh smiled uncertainly. "Oh, she's here."

He nodded toward the dock. Tori glanced over at the two FBI agents who had driven her to the restaurant—and who would accompany her on the next leg of her journey as well—and watched as Special Agent Rachael Voss strode along the gleaming wooden dock to join them. The three of them would watch and wait.

"Do they really think I'm going to make a run for it?" Tori asked. "Why would I want to do that? Where would I go?"

The waitress came over and hovered by Josh—a beautiful woman with a heart-shaped face and a Creole accent.

"What can I get you, sir?" she asked.

"Nothing, thanks. I can't stay."

The waitress arched an eyebrow but Josh paid her no attention. He seemed to have said it as much for Tori's benefit as for hers.

"Let me know if you change your mind," the woman said and hurried away.

Tori tried not to think about the irony.

"So how much trouble are you in?" she asked.

"I'll be all right," Josh replied. He nodded toward Voss and the others waiting on the dock. "That's why they're over there watching us, actually. So if us meeting like this comes up at all, it's on record as having been part of the case, and under supervision."

"It was actually pretty cool of Rachael to go along with it," Tori said, picking up her iced tea. "She's the boss, right? Of your unit or squad or whatever?"

Josh nodded. "And cool of your babysitters over there to cooperate. So, have you decided where they're taking you? I know it isn't the life you chose, but it's a pretty unique opportunity to get to start your life all over again, even after—"

Tori smiled at his loss for words. After she had already been declared dead once, already started over? After she had taken part in crimes that could have landed her in prison for years? She took a sip of iced tea.

"I hear Oregon is beautiful and quiet," she said. "Somewhere on the coast, I think. In high school I worked in this café, and I've always loved books, so I'm thinking of a little bookstore café. Someplace people would come and sit for hours."

"Someplace peaceful," Josh said.

And a warmth spread through her. He understood. She sipped her iced tea again, and over the rim of the glass their eyes met.

"Have you decided on a new name?" he asked, his voice tight with uncertainty.

"Yeah. I have."

And that was all. Nobody had put a price on her head, but this new life she was getting was much like witness protection. For the second time, she would be declared dead and would become a new person, with a new name.

Josh gave her a sheepish grin. If she didn't want to tell him her new name, that spoke volumes.

"Listen, there are some things I want to say. Some things I should have said—"

"Please, don't." She smiled to take the sting out of it. "We've said what needs saying, I think. I only wanted to see you to tell you good-bye, and that I'll miss you."

Josh dropped his gaze and gave a slow shake of his head. "I wish things had been different."

Tori laughed. He looked up, maybe a little hurt, until he saw the real mirth that must have been in her expression.

"Which part?" she asked. "Getting beaten up and shot, or running for our lives?"

The absurdity of it touched him then, and he chuckled softly. A silence fell between them and several long seconds ticked by. Tori wondered if Josh filled those seconds with the same thoughts that she did, memories of the days they had spent flirting in the galley on board the *Antoinette* and the few precious hours they had passed making love in her quarters. She thought perhaps he did.

In all of the ways that mattered, when she parted company with him here, she would be leaving Tori Austin behind as well. By the end of the day, she would have a new identity, a new name, and Josh Hart would be the only person in the world who had ever really known a woman named Tori Austin, and who cared that she had been erased from the world.

"You know," he said, "you could get a new name and a new life right here in St. Croix."

Tori gave a small sigh and rose from her chair. Nothing more could come of the conversation. "Somehow, I don't think Rachael would like that. She wants you all to herself."

Josh stood as well. "I already told you, we're partners. It isn't like that between us."

Tori glanced over at the dock, saw the way Voss stood tensed, watching them, and turned back to Josh. She reached up and touched his face, fighting the bittersweet feelings that welled inside her. Holding her breath, she slid her hand behind his neck and pulled him down for a kiss—to hell with what her FBI handlers might put in their report. Her lips brushed his and she breathed in his breath.

"If you don't think it's like that between you," Tori whispered in his ear, "you're just not paying attention."

She withdrew from him, chuckled at the confusion etched on his face, and then touched his arm. "Sit a minute, Josh. Finish my iced tea. It's probably better all around for me to leave first."

"Okay," he said, but he didn't sit. "Take care of yourself."

"You, too. Maybe work on not getting shot in the future. Try not to die."

That earned her a grin. "Not dying," he said. "Pretty much my whole plan."

Tori nodded. "Mine, too."

And she left him standing there, drinking the rest of her iced tea, and headed off to begin again. She only hoped that this time she would get it right.